# BALANCE
## - OF -
# TRADE

# BALANCE

# -OF-

# TRADE

A Liaden Universe® Novel

by

## Sharon Lee

&

## Steve Miller

Meisha Merlin Publishing, Inc.
Atlanta, GA

Balance of Trade Copyright © 2004 by Sharon Lee & Steve Miller [Portions of this novel were first published in Absolute Magnitude, issue 11 (Summer 1999), as the novella "Balance of Trade," by Sharon Lee and Steve Miller]

**Balance of Trade**

Published by Meisha Merlin Publishing, Inc.
PO Box 7
Decatur, GA  30031

Editing by Stephen Pagel
Copyediting and Proofreading by Teddi Stransky
Interior layout by Lynn Swetz
Cover art by Donato Giancola
Cover design by Kevin Murphy

ISBN:  Hard Cover      1-59222-019-3

Printed in the United States of America

# Table of Contents

# Introduction

One of the hazards of being a writer is generating too many ideas. The unused ones tend to pile up in drifts in the corners, which makes for an untidy house.

Back before we'd written *Plan B*, we had an idea for a story—a scene, really—a good, meaty scene. The trouble was, none of the characters on-roll were willing to take it on and make it their own.

The idea languished, and every so often we'd dust it off and put it on offer, but nobody stepped forward to claim it. In the meantime, the scene had gotten larger, more complex, and had developed some interesting resonances—enough to move a certain Master Trader to take an option on the project, contingent upon locating an appropriate lead.

About then we got a request for a Liaden Universe® story from *Absolute Magnitude* editor Warren Lapine, and, well, there was the Master Trader's interest, and…this kid. We'd never seen him before, but Jethri—his name was Jethri—said he could do the job. He *liked* the scene.

So, we let him take it for a spin; the resulting novella, "Balance of Trade," was published in *Absolute Magnitude*. And we figured that was that.

But while we felt we were done with Jethri, he wasn't done with us. When Stephe Pagel at Meisha Merlin asked, "what are you doing next?" Jethri jumped up and said, "Me!"

And here he is, having earned it. We hope you enjoy his adventures.

Sharon Lee and Steve Miller
September 2003
Unity, Maine

# BALANCE
## -OF-
# TRADE

## Liaden Currency

12 dex to a tor

12 tor to a kais

12 kais (144 tor) to a cantra

One cantra = to 35,000 Terran bits

## Standard Year

8 Standard Days in One Standard Week

32 Standard Days in One Standard Month

384 Standard Days in One Standard Year

## Liaden Year

96 Standard Days in One Relumma

12 Standard Months in One Standard Year

One Relumma = to Eight 12-day weeks

Four Relumma = One Standard Year

# Cast of Characters

## *Gobelyn's Market*
### out of New Carpathia

Arin Gobelyn, Iza's deceased spouse, Jethri's father
Cris Gobelyn, first mate, Iza's eldest child
Dyk Gobelyn, cook
Grig Tomas, back-up everything, Arin's cousin
Iza Gobelyn, captain-owner
Jethri Gobelyn
Khatelane Gobelyn, pilot
Mel Gobelyn
Paitor Gobelyn, trader, Iza's brother
Seeli Gobelyn, admin, Iza's second child
Zam Gobelyn

## *Elthoria*
### out of Solcintra

Kor Ith yo'Lanna, captain
Norn ven'Deelin, master trader
Pen Rel sig'Kethra, arms master
Gar Sad per'Etla, cargo master
Gaenor tel'Dorbit, first mate
Ray Jon tel'Ondor, protocol master
Vil Tor, ship's librarian
Kilara pin'Ebit, technician
Rantel ver'Borith, technician

## Tarnia's Clanhouse

Stafeli Maarilex, Delm Tarnia
Ren Lar Maarilex, Master of the Vine
Pet Ric Maarilex, his son
Pen Dir, a cousin, off at school
Mcicha Maarilex, a daughter of the house
Miandra Maarilex, a daughter of the house
Flinx, a cat
Mr. pel'Saba, the butler
Mrs. tor'Beli, the cook
Anecha, a driver
Graem, Ren Lar's second in the cellars
Sun Eli pen'Jerad, tailor
Zer Min pel'Oban, dancing master

There are secrets in all families—
—George Farquhar, 1678-1707

# Day 29
## Standard Year 1118

## *Gobelyn's Market*
## Opposite Shift

"DOWN ALL THAT long, weary shift, they kept after Byl," Khat's voice was low and eerie in the dimness of the common room. The knuckles of Jethri's left hand ached with the grip he had on his cup while his right thumb and forefinger whirled ellipses on the endlessly cool surface of his lucky fractin. Beside him, he could hear Dyk breathing, fast and harsh.

"Once—twice—three times!—he broke for the outring, his ship, and his mates. Three times, the Liadens turned him back, pushing him toward the center core, where no space-going man has right nor reason to be.

"They pushed him, those Liadens, moving through the night-levels as swift and sure as if it were bright world-day. Byl ran, as fast as long legs and terror could speed him, but they were always ahead of him, the canny Liadens. They were always ahead—'round every corner, past every turning in the hall."

Mel, on Jethri's left, moaned softly. Jethri bit his lip.

"But then!" Khat's voice glittered in the gloom. "Then, all at once, the luck changed. Or, say, the gods of spacers smiled. He reached a corridor that was empty, turned a corner where no Liaden crouched, gun aiming for his heart. He paused then, ears craned to the rear, but heard no stealthy movement, nor boot heels sounding quick along the steel floor.

"He ran then, light of heart and all but laughing, and the way stood clear before him, from downring admin all the way to the outring, where his ship was berthed; where his mates, and his love, lay awaiting his return.

"He came to the bay door—Bay Eight, that was where. Came to the bay door, used his card and slipped through as soon as the gap was wide enough to fit him. Grinning, he pushed off in the lighter grav, taking long bounds toward Dock Three. He took the curve like he'd grown wings, singing now, so glad to be near, so glad to be home…

"That was when he saw the crowd, and the flashing lights that meant ring cops—and the others, that meant worse.

"He shouted and ran, waving his arms as if it all made a difference. Which it didn't. Those lifelines had been cut good hours ago, while he had been harried, hounded and kept away— and there was eight zipped bags laid out neat on the dockside, which was all that was left of his mates and his love."

Silence. Jethri's jaw was so tight he thought teeth might shatter. Mel gasped and Dyk groaned.

"So," said Khat, her voice shockingly matter-of-fact. "Now you see what comes to someone who cheats a Liaden on cargo."

"Except," Jethri managed, his voice breathless with tension, though he knew far better than what had been told— Khat on a story was *that* good. "Excepting, they'd never done it that way—the Liadens. Might be they'd've rigged something with the docking fees—more like, they'd've set the word around, so five ports later Byl finds himself at a stand—full cans and no buyers, see? But they wouldn't kill for cargo— that's not how their Balancing works."

"So speaks the senior 'prentice!" Dyk intoned, pitching his voice so deep it rumbled inside the steel walls like a bad encounter with a grabber-hook.

"C'mon, Jeth," Mel put in. "You was scared, too!"

"Khat tells a good story," he muttered, and Dyk produced a laugh.

"She does that—and who's to say she's wrong? Sure, you been studying the tapes, but Khat's been studying portside news since before you was allowed inside ship's core!"

"Not that long," Khat protested mildly, over the rustle and scrape that was her moving along the bench 'til she had her hand on the controls. Light flooded the cubby, showing four startlingly similar faces: broad across the cheekbones and square about the jaw. Khat's eyes, and Jethri's, were brown; Dyk and Mel had blue—hers paler than his. All four favored the spacer buzz, which left their scant hair looking like dark velvet caps snugged close 'gainst their skulls. Mel was nearest to Jethri in age—nineteen Standards to his seventeen. Khat and Dyk were born close enough to argue minutes when questions of elder's precedence rose—twenty Standard Years, both, and holding adult shares.

Their surname was Gobelyn. Their ship was *Gobelyn's Market*, out of New Carpathia, which homeworld none of them had ever seen nor missed.

"Yah, well maybe Jethri could tell us a story," said Dyk, on the approach to mischief, "since he knows so many."

Jethri felt his ears heat, and looked down into his cup. Koka, it had been—meant to warm his way to slumber. It was cold, now, and Khat's story was enough to keep a body awake through half his sleep-shift.

Even if he did know better.

"Let him be, Dyk," Khat said, surprisingly. "Jethri's doing good with his study—Uncle's pleased. Says it shows well, us having a Liaden speaker 'mong us."

Dyk started to laugh, caught something in her face and shrugged instead. Jethri wisely did not mention that his "Liaden speaking" was barely more than pidgin.

Instead, he drank off the dregs of his cold koka, managing without much of a shudder, then got himself up and across the room, right hand still fingering the ancient tile in search of comfort. He put the cup in the washer, and nodded to his cousins before he left to find his bunk.

"Good shift," he murmured.

"Good shift, Jethri," Khat said warmly. "Wide dreaming."

"Sleep tight, kid," Dyk added and Mel fluttered her fingers, smiling. "Be good, Jeth."

He slipped out of the cubby and paused, weighing the likelihood of sleep against the lure of a history search on the fate of Byl—and the length of Uncle Paitor's lecture, if he was found reading through his sleep shift again.

That was the clincher, his uncle being a man who warmed to a scolding. Sighing, Jethri turned to the right. Behind him, in the cubby, he heard Dyk say, "So tell us a scary one, Khat; now that the kid's away."

HAVING FOUND SLEEP late, it was only natural that Jethri overslept the bell, meaning hard biscuit and the dregs of the pot for breakfast. Chewing, he flipped through the duty roster and discovered himself on Stinks.

"Mud!" he muttered, gulping bitter coffee. It wasn't that he begrudged his cousins their own round of duty—which they had, right enough; he wasn't callin' slackers—just, he wished that he might progress somewhat above the messy labor and make-work that fell his lot all too often. He had his studies, which was work, of its kind; emergency drill with Cris; and engine lore with Khat. 'Course, him being youngest, with none on the ladder 'neath him—that did go into the equation. *Some*body had to do the scutwork, and if not juniormost, then who?

Cramming the last of the biscuit into his mouth, he scanned down to dinner duty—and nearly cussed again. Dyk was on cook, which meant the meal would be something tasty, complicated and needful of mucho cleanup. Jethri himself being on clean up.

"That kind of shift," he consoled himself, pouring the dregs of the dregs into the chute and setting the cup into the washer. "Next shift can only be better."

Being as they were coming into Ynsolt'i Port next shift, barring the unexpected, that at least was a given. Which

realization did lighten his mood a fraction, so he was able to
bring up a thin, tuneless whistle to stand him company on
his way down to the utility lockers.

HE WORKED HIS way up from quarters, stripping the sweet-
sheets off sleeping pallets, rolling up the limp, sweat-flavored
mats and stuffing them into the portable recycler. Zam, Seeli,
and Grig were on Opposite; the doors to their quarters sealed,
blue privacy lights lit. Jethri left new sheets rolled up and
strapped outside their doors and moved on, not in any particular scramble, but not dallying, either. He had it from
experience that doing Stinks consumed considerably less time
than was contained inside a duty-shift. Even doing Stinks
thoroughly and well—which he had better or the captain'd
be down his throat with her spacesuit on—he'd have shift
left at the end of his work. He was allowed to use leftover
duty time for study. What had to be measured with a fine
rule was how much time he could claim before either Uncle
Paitor or the captain called slacker and pulled him down to
the core on discipline.

Stinks being a duty short on brain work, the brain kept
itself busy. Mostly, Jethri used the time to review his latest
studies, or daydream about the future, when he would be a
trader in his own right, free to cut deals and commit the ship,
without having to submit everything to Uncle Paitor, and getting his numbers second-guessed and his research questioned.

Today, the brain having started on a grump, it continued,
embroidering on the theme of scutwork. Replacing the sheets
in his own cubby, he tried to interject some happy-think into
what was threatening to become a major mood, and found
himself on the losing side of an argument with himself.

He was juniormost, no disputing that—youngest of Captain Iza Gobelyn's three children—unintended, and scheduled
for abort until his father's golden tongue changed her mind.

Despite unwelcome beginnings, though, he was of value
to the ship. Uncle Paitor was teaching him the trade, and had

even said that Jethri's researches into the Liaden markets had
the potential to be profitable for the ship. Well, Uncle Paitor
had even backed a major buy Jethri had suggested, last port,
and if that didn't show a growing faith in the juniormost's
skill, then nothing did.

*That's all right*, the half of himself determined to set into
a mood countered. *Uncle Paitor might allow you value to the ship,
but can you say the same for your mother?*

Which was hardly a fair question. Of course, he couldn't
say the same for his mother, who had put him into Seeli's
care as a babe and hadn't much use for him as a kid. When
his father died—and only owning the truth—captain'd had
a lot of changes to go through, one of them being she'd lost
the lover and listening post she'd had since her second voyage out of her homeship, *Grenadine*. She'd taken three days
of wild-time to try to recover some balance—come back
drunk and black and blue, proclaiming herself cured. But
after that, any stock Jethri'd held with his mother had vanished along with everything that had anything to do with
his father, from photocubes to study certificates to his and
Jethri's joint collection of antique fractins. It was almost as
if she blamed him for Arin's death, which was plain sense-
less, though Seeli did her best to explain that the human
heart wasn't notoriously sensible.

Quarters finished, and in a fair way to seeing that mood
set in plate steel, Jethri went down to Ops.

The door whined in its track when it opened and Jethri
winced, sending a quick glance inside to see if his entrance
had disturbed anybody at their calcs.

Khat was sitting at the big board, the captain shadowing
her from second. Cris, on data, glanced over his shoulder and
gave Jethri a quick jerk of the chin. Khat didn't turn, but she
did look up and smile into the screen for him. The captain
never stirred.

Dragging the recycler to the wall, he moored it, then went
back to the door, fingering the greaser pen from his kit belt.

He pulled open the panel and switched the automatic off. Kneeling, he carefully penned a beaded line of grease along the outer track. The door whined again—slightly softer—when he pushed it open, and he applied a second row of grease beads to the inner track.

He tucked the pen away and stood, pushing the door back and forth until it ran silent in its tracks, nodded, and switched on the automatics again.

That minor chore taken care of, he moved along the stations, backmost first, working quick and quiet, replacing the used sweet-sheets with new, strapping fresh sheets to the board at each occupied station.

"Thanks, Jeth," Cris said in his slow, easy voice. "'preciate the door, too. I should've got it myself, three shifts back."

Thanks from Cris was coin worth having. Jethri ducked his head, feeling his ears heat.

"Welcome," he murmured, putting the new mat down at second and reaching for the strap.

The captain stood. "You can replace that," she said, her cool brown eyes barely grazing Jethri before she turned to Khat. "Keep course, Pilot."

"Aye, Cap'n."

She nodded, crossed the room in two long strides and was gone, the door opening silently before her. Jethri bit his lip, spun the chair and stripped off the used sheet. Glancing up, he saw his cousins pass a glance between the two of them, but didn't catch its meaning, being short of the code. He smoothed the new mat into place, stowed the old one with all the rest, unmoored the recycler and left.

Neither Khat nor Cris looked 'round to see him go.

STINKS WAS A play in two parts. Between them, Jethri took a break for a mug of 'mite, which was thick and yellow and smelled like yeast—and if anyone beyond a spacer born and bred could stomach the stuff, the fact had yet to be noted.

One mug of 'mite delivered a cargo can load of vita-
mins and power nutrients. In the old days, when star travel
was a new and risky undertaking, crews had lived on 'mite
and not much else, launch to planetfall. Nowadays, when
space was safe and a ship the size of *Gobelyn's Market* carried enough foodstuffs to supply a body's needed nutrients
without sacrificing taste and variety, 'mite lingered on as a
comfort drink, and emergency ration.

Jethri dunked a couple whole grain crackers in his mug,
chomped and swallowed them, then drank off what was
left. Thus fortified, he ambled down to the utility lockers, signed the camera out, slotted the empties and a tray
of new filters into the sled and headed out to the
bounceway.

OPS RAN *MARKET'S* grav in a helix, which was standard for a
ship of its size and age. Smaller vessels ran whole-ship
light, or even no-grav, and weight work was a part of every
crew member's daily duty roster. *Market* was big enough to
generate the necessary power for a field. Admin core was
damn' near one gee, as was Ops itself. Sleeping quarters
was lighter; you slept strapped in and anchored your possessions to the wall. The outer edges of the ship, where the
cans hooked in, that was lighter still—as near to no grav as
mattered. On the outermost edge of E Deck, there was
the bounceway, a rectangular space marked out for rec,
where crew might swoop, fly, bounce off the walls, play
free-fall tag, and—just coincidentally—sharpen their reaction times and grav-free moves.

It being a rec area, there were air vents. It being the largest
open atmosphere section on the ship, it also had the highest
amount of ship air to sample for pollen, spores, loose dust,
and other contaminants. Jethri's job was to open each vent,
use the camera to record the visual patterns, change the camera to super and flash for spectrographic details, remove the
used filter, install a fresh, and reseal the vent. That record

would go right to command for analysis as soon as he plugged the camera into the charge socket.

Not quite as mindless as replacing sweet-sheets, but not particularly demanding of the thought processes, either.

Mooring the sled, he slid the camera into the right pocket of his utility vest, a new filter and an envelope into the left, squinted thoughtfully at the position of the toppest vent— and kicked off.

Strictly speaking, he *could* have gone straight-line, door to vent. In the unlikely circumstance that there'd been hurry involved, he would, he told himself, curling for the rebound off the far wall, have chosen the high leap. As it was, hands extended and body straight, he hit the corner opposite the vent, somersaulted, arcing downward, hit the third wall with his feet, rising again, slowing, slowing—until he was floating, gentle and easy, next to the target vent.

Bracing himself, he slid the door open, used the camera, then unsnapped the soiled filter, slipped it into the envelope and snapped in the replacement. Making sure his pockets were sealed, he treated himself to a cross-room dive, shot back up to the opposite corner, dove again, twisted in mid-dive, bounced off the end wall, pinwheeled off the ceiling, hit the floor on his hand, flipped and came upright next to the sled.

Grinning like a certified fool, he unsealed his pocket, slotted the used filter, took out a clean one, turned and jumped for the next vent.

IT MIGHT'VE BEEN an hour later and him at the trickiest bit of his day. The filter for the aromatics locker was special—a double-locking, odor-blocking bit of business, badly set over the door, flush to the angle with the ceiling. Aromatics was light, but by no means as light as the bounceway, so it was necessary for anyone needing to measure and change the filter to use their third hand to chin themselves on the high snatch-rod, knees jammed at right angles to the ceiling, while simultaneously using their first and second hands to do the actual work.

Normal two-handers were known to lament the lack of that crucial third appendage with language appropriate to the case. Indeed, one of Jethri's fondest memories was of long, easy-speaking Cris, bent double against the ceiling, hanging over the vent in question, swearing, constantly and conversationally, for the entire twenty minutes the job required, never once repeating a cuss word. It had been a virtuoso performance to which Jethri secretly aspired.

Unfortunately, experience had taught him that he could either hang and cuss, or hang and work. So it was that he wrestled in silence, teeth drilling into lower lip, forcing himself to go slow and easy, and make no false moves, because it would be a serious thing if an aromatics spill contaminated the ship's common air.

He had just seated and locked the clean inner filter, when the hall echoed with a titanic *clang*, which meant that the cage had cycled onto his level.

Jethri closed his eyes and clenched into the corner, forcing himself to wait until the wall had stopped reverberating.

"It's settled," the captain's voice echoed in the wake of the larger noise.

"*Might* be settled." That was Uncle Paitor, his voice a rumble, growing slightly fainter as the two of them walked outward, toward the cans. "I'm not convinced we've got the best trade for the ship in this, Iza. I'm thinking we might be underselling something—"

"We've got space issues, which aren't leaving us," the captain interrupted. "This one's Captain's Call, brother. It's settled."

"Space issues, yeah," Paitor said, a whole lot more argumentative than he usually was when he was talkin' to the captain, and like he thought things weren't settled at all. "There's space issues. In what case, sister o'mine, you'd best remember those couple o'seal-packs of extra you been carrying in your personal bin for damn' near ten Standards. You been carrying extra a long time, and some of what's there ought to get shared out so choices can be made—"

"No business of yours—none of it, Paitor."

"You's the one called kin just now. But I'm a trader, and what you got's still worth something to somebody. You make this trade and that stuff ought to be gone, too!"

"We'll chart that course when we got fuel for it. You done?"

Paitor answered that, but Jethri only caught the low sound of his voice, no words.

Cautiously, he unclenched, reached for the second filter and began to ease back the locks, forcing himself to attend to the work at hand, rather than wonder what sort of trade might be Captain's Call...

LATER, IN THE galley, Dyk was in a creative frenzy.

Jethri, who knew his man, had arrived well before his scheduled time, and already there were piles of used bowls, cruets, mixers, forks, tongs, spoons and spice syringes littering every possible surface and the floor. It was nothing short of awesome. Shaking his head, he pulled on his gloves and started in on first clean up.

"Hey, Jeth! Unship that big flat pan for me, willya?"

Sighing, Jethri abandoned the dirties, climbed up on the counter and pulled open the toppest cabinet, where the equipment that was used least was stowed. Setting his feet careful among the welter of used tools, he reached for the requested pan.

The door to the galley banged open, Jethri turned his head and clutched the edge of the cabinet, keeping himself very still.

Iza Gobelyn stood in the doorway, her face so tight the lines around her mouth stood in stark relief. Dyk, lost in his dream of cookery, oblivious to clear danger, smiled over his shoulder at her, the while beating something in a bowl with a power spoon.

"Good shift, Captain!" he called merrily. "Have we got a surprise ordered in for you tonight!"

"No," said Iza.

That got through.

Dyk blinked. "Ma'am?"

"I said, *no*," the captain repeated, her voice crackling with static. "We'll want a quick meal, no surprises."

The spoon went quiet. Dyk put the bowl aside, real careful, and turned to face her. "Captain, I've got a meal planned and on course."

"Jettison," she said, flat and cold. "Quick meal, Dyk. Now."

There was a moment—a long moment, when Jethri thought Dyk would argue the point, but in the end, he just nodded.

"Yes'm," he said, real quiet, and turned away toward the cabinet.

The captain left, the door swinging shut behind her.

Jethri let out the breath he hadn't known he'd been holding, slid the flat pan back into its grips, closed the door, and carefully got himself down to the floor, where he started back in collecting dirties.

He was loading the washer when it came to him that Dyk was 'way too quiet, and he looked up.

His cousin was staring down at the bowl, kinda swirling the contents with the power spoon turned off. Jethri moved a couple steps closer, until Dyk looked at him.

"What was you making?" Jethri asked.

"A cake," Dyk said, and Jethri could believe it was tears he saw in the blue eyes. "I—" he cleared his throat and shook his head, pushing the bowl away. "It was a stupid idea, I guess. I'll get the quick meal together and then help you with clean up, right?"

Dyk wasn't a prize as a partner in clean up, and Jethri was about to decline the favor. And a cake—why would he have been after making a cake, just coming into port? *Another one of those everybody-knows-but-me things,* Jethri thought, frowning at his larger cousin.

Something about the set of his shoulders, or even the tears, Dyk not being one to often cry, counseled him to think better of refusing the offered aid. He nodded, trying to remake his frown into something approaching agreeable.

"Sure," he said. "Be glad of the help."

# Day 32
# Standard Year 1118

## *Gobelyn's Market*
## Jethri's Quarters

JETHRI WAS BEHIND closed door—which he didn't usually do on his off-shift—because the volume on the recorder
was iffy at best, and besides, there were a couple of the cousins who weren't all that happy to hear Liaden words, even if
they were spoken on archive, by a relative.

"If you trade with Liadens, trade careful, and for the gods'
love don't come sideways of honor."

One upside of having the door closed was an unimpeded view of the gift Dyk had given him two ports back,
to much guffawing at the entrance hatch. The Unofficial
Up-To-Date Combine Com-Code Chart issued by Trundee's
Tool and Tow. Besides the codes, most of which hadn't
changed in the dozen or so years Jethri had been aware of
them, there was a constantly changing view, in simulated
3D, of the self-declared "Best Saltwater Bathing Beach in
the Galaxy."

Jethri had—on several occasions, truth told—tried to count
the different views offered by the chart. Dyk had helpfully
showed him how to change the pace, or even stop on a particular image. Jethri discovered, by plain accident, that you
could "tune out" the images of people without bathing suits—
or the ones with bathing suits, for that matter, and also how to
close up on the people and the sand, blocking out the long,
unsettling sweep of sky.

His eye was caught now by a series that intrigued him. A couple, hand in hand, moved across several images, walking along the sandscape by the roiling, splashing waves, each wearing a suit (if something covering only a very small part of the anatomy could really be called a suit!). Both suits had decorations on them, shapes very much like his lucky fractin. The woman's suit was basically white, with the fractins arrayed in several fetching patterns, but they were blue, with the lettering in yellow. Her partner's suit was blue, the fractins white and the lettering black, which was like no fractin he'd ever seen—not that he thought he'd seen them all.

The distraction of the woman's shape and beauty, and the way she moved, made it hard for him to pay attention to the old tape. He sighed, so loud he might have been heard in the companionway if anyone was there to listen.

He had work to do. They were set to put in at a Liaden port right soon, and now was time to study, not indulge high-oxy dreams of walking hand-held with a lady 'way too pretty to notice a ship-kid...

Teeth chewing lower lip, he punched the button on the recorder, backing up to the last sentence he remembered hearing.

This set of notes was old: recorded by Great-Grand-Captain Larance Gobelyn more than forty Standard years ago, dubbed to ship's library twenty Standards later from the original deteriorating tape. Jethri fiddled with the feed on the audio board, but only succeeded in lowering the old man's voice. Sighing, he upped the gain again, squinting in protest of the scratchy, uneven sound.

"Liaden honor is—active. Insult—any insult—is punished. Immediately. An individual's name is his most important possession and—"

"Jethri?" Uncle Paitor's voice broke across Cap'n Larance's recitation. Jethri sighed and thumbed 'pause'.

"Yessir," he said, turning his head toward the intercom grid set in the wall.

"Come on down to the trade room, will you? We need to talk over a couple things."

Jethri slipped the remote out of his ear. As senior trader, Paitor was specifically in charge of the senior apprentice trader's time and education.

"Yessir," Jethri repeated. Two quick fingertaps marked his place in the old notes file. He left at a brisk walk, his thoughts half on honor, and only slightly less than half on the image of the woman on the poster.

HIS UNCLE NODDED him into a chair and eased back in his. They were coming in on Ynsolt'i and next hour Paitor Gobelyn would have time for nothing but the feed from the port trade center. Now, his screen was dark, the desk-top barren. Paitor cleared his throat.

"Got a couple things," he said, folding his hands over his belt buckle. "On-Port roster: Dyk an' me'll be escorting the payload to the central trade hall and seeing it safe with the highest bidder. Khat's data, Grig's eatables, Mel's on tech, Cris'll stay ship-side. You…"

Paitor paused and Jethri gripped his hands together tight on his lap, willing his face into a trader's expression of courteous disinterest. They had textile on board—half a dozen bolts of cellosilk that Cris had taken on two stops back, with Ynsolt'i very much in his mind. Was it possible, Jethri wondered, that Uncle Paitor was going to allow…

"Yourself—you'll be handling the silk lot. I expect to see a kais out of the lot. If I was you, I'd call on Honored Sir bin'Flora first."

Jethri remembered to breathe. "Yes, sir. Thank you." He gripped his hands together so hard they hurt. His own trade. His own, very first, solo trade with no Senior standing by, ready to take over if the thing looked like going awry.

His uncle waved a hand. "Time you were selling small stuff on your own. Now." He leaned forward abruptly, folded his arms on the desk and looked at Jethri seriously. "You know we got a lot riding on this trip."

Indeed they did—more than a quarter of the *Market's* speculation capital was tied up in eighteen Terran pounds of *vya*, a spice most commonly sold in five gram lots. Jethri's research had revealed that *vya* was the active ingredient in *fa'vya*, a Liaden drink ship's library classified as a potent aphrodisiac. Ynsolt'i was a Liaden port and the spice should bring a substantial profit to the ship. Not, Jethri reminded himself, that profit was ever guaranteed.

"We do well with the spice here," Paitor was saying, "and the captain's going to take us across to Kinaveral, do that refit we'd been banking for *now*, rather than two Standards from now."

*This* was the news that might have had Dyk baking a cake. Jethri sat up straighter, rubbing the palms of his hands down the rough fabric of his work pants.

"Refit'll keep us world-bound 'bout a Standard, near's we can figure. Captain wants that engine upgrade bad and tradeside's gonna need two more cargo pods to balance the expense." He grinned suddenly. "Three, if I can get 'em."

Jethri smiled politely, thinking that his uncle didn't look as pleased with that as he might have and wondering what the down-side of the trade was.

"While refit's doing, we figured—the captain and me—that it'd be optimum to re-structure crew. So, we've signed you as senior 'prentice with *Gold Digger*."

It was said so smoothly that Jethri didn't quite catch the sense of it.

"*Gold Digger?*" he repeated blankly, that much having gotten through, by reason of him and Mac Gold having traded blows on last sighting—more to Jethri's discomfort than Mac's. He hadn't exactly told anyone on the *Market* the full details of the incident, *Gold Digger's* crew being cousins of his mother, and his mother making a point more'n once about how she'd nearly ended up being part of that ship instead of this.

Jethri came forward in his chair, hearing the rest of it play back inside the whorlings of his ears.

"You signed me onto *Gold Digger*?" he demanded. "For how long?"

His voice echoed into the hall, he'd asked that loud, but he didn't apologize.

Paitor raised a hand. "Ease down, boy. One loop through the mines. Time they're back in port, you'll be twenty—full adult and able to find your own berth." He nodded. "You make yourself useful like you and me both know you can and you'll come off *Digger* a full trader with experience under your belt—"

"Three *Standards*?" Jethri's voice broke, but for once he didn't cringe in shame. He was too busy thinking about a converted ore ship smaller than the *Market*, its purely male crew crammed all six into a common sleeping room, and the trade nothing more than foodstuffs and ore, ore and mining tools, oxy tanks and ore...

"*Ore*," he said, staring at his uncle. "Not even rough gem. Industrial ore." He took a breath, knowing his dismay showed and not caring about that, either. "Uncle Paitor, I've been studying. If there's something else I—"

Paitor showed him palm again. "Nothing to do with your studying. You been doing real good. I'll tell you—better than the captain supposed you would. Little more interested in the Liaden side of things than I thought reasonable, there at first, but you always took after Arin, anyhow. No harm in learning the lingo, and I will say the Liadens seem to take positive note of you." He shook his head. "Course, you don't have your full growth yet, which puts you nearer their level."

Liadens were a short, slight people, measured against Terran averages. Jethri wasn't as short as a Liaden, but he was, he thought bitterly, a damn sight shorter than Mac Gold.

"What it is," Paitor said slowly. "We're out of room. It's hard for us, too, Jethri. If we were a bigger ship, we'd keep you on. But you're youngest, none of the others're inclined to change berth, and, well—Ship's Option. Captain's cleared it. Ben Gold states himself willing to have you." He leaned back, looking stern. "And ore needs study, too, 'prentice. Nothing's as simple as it looks."

*Thrown off*, thought Jethri. *I'm being thrown off of my ship.* He thought that he could have borne it better, if he was simply being cast out to make his own way. But the arranged berth on *Gold Digger* added an edge of fury to his disbelief. He opened his mouth to protest further and was forestalled by a *ping!* from Paitor's terminal.

The senior trader snapped forward in his chair, flipping the switch that accepted the first of the trade feeds from Ynsolt'i Port. He glanced over at Jethri.

"You get me a kais for that silk, now. If the spice sells good for us, I'll OK that Combine key you been wanting. You'll have earned it."

That was dismissal. Jethri stood. "Yessir," he said, calm as a dry mouth would let him, and left the trade room.

# Day 33
## Standard Year 1118

## Ynsolt'i Port
## Textile Hall

"PREMIUM GRADE, HONORED sir," Jethri murmured, keeping his eyes modestly lowered, as befit a young person in discourse with a person of lineage and honor.

Honored Sir bin'Flora moved his shoulders and flipped an edge of the fabric up, frowning at the underweave. Jethri ground his teeth against an impulse to add more in praise of the hand-loomed Gindoree cellosilk.

*Don't oversell!* he could hear Uncle Paitor snap from memory. *The Trader is in control of the trade.*

"Eight tor for the six-bolt," the buyer stated, tossing the sample cloth back across the spindle. Jethri sighed gently and spread his hands.

"The honored buyer is, of course, distrustful of goods offered by one so many years his inferior in wisdom. I assure you that I am instructed by an elder of my ship, who bade me accept not a breath less than two kais."

"Two?" The Liaden's shoulders moved again—not a shrug, but expressive of some emotion. Amusement, Jethri thought. Or anger.

"Your elder mis-instructs you, young sir. Perhaps it is a testing." The buyer tipped his head slightly to one side, as if considering. "I will offer an additional pair of tor," he said at last, accent rounding the edges of the trade-tongue, "in kindness of a student's diligence."

*Wrong,* Jethri thought. Not to say that Honored bin'Flora wasn't the heart of kindness, which he very likely was, on his off days. A trade was something else again.

Respectful, Jethri bowed, and, respectful, brought his eyes to the buyer's face. "Sir, I value your generosity. However, the distance between ten tor and two kais is so vast that I feel certain my elder would counsel me to forgo the trade. Perhaps you had not noticed—" he caught himself on the edge of insult and smoothly changed course—"the light is poor, just here…"

Pulling the bolt forward, he again showed the fineness of the cloth, the precious irregularities of weave, which proved it hand woven, spoke rapturously of the pure crimson dye.

The buyer moved his hand. "Enough. One kais. A last offer."

*Gotcha,* thought Jethri, making a serious effort to keep his face neutral. One kais, just like Uncle Paitor had wanted. In retrospect, it had been an easy sell.

Too easy? he wondered then, looking down at the Liaden's smooth face and disinterested brown eyes. Was there, just maybe, additional profit to be made here?

*Trade is study,* Uncle Paitor said from memory. *Study the goods, and study the market. And after you prepare as much as you can, there's still nothing says that a ship didn't land yesterday with three holds full of something you're carrying as a luxury sell.*

Nor was there any law, thought Jethri, against Honored Buyer bin'Flora being critically short on crimson cellosilk this Port-day. He took a cautious breath and made his decision.

"Of course," he told the buyer, gathering the sample bolt gently into his arms, "I am desolate not to have closed trade in this instance. A kais… It is generous, respected sir, but—alas. My elder will be distressed—he had instructed me most carefully to offer the lot first to yourself and to make every accommodation… But a single kais, when his word was two? I do not…" He fancied he caught a gleam along the edge of the Liaden's bland face, a flicker in the depths of the careful eyes, and bit his lip, hoping he wasn't about to blow the whole deal.

"I don't suppose," he said, voice edging disastrously toward a squeak, "—my elder spoke of you so highly...I don't suppose you might go a kais-six?"

"Ah." Honored Sir bin'Flora's shoulders rippled and this time Jethri was sure the gesture expressed amusement. "One kais, six tor it is." He bowed and Jethri did, clumsily, because of the bolt he still cradled.

"Done," he said.

"Very good," returned the buyer. "Set the bolt down, young sir. You are quite correct regarding that crimson. Remarkably pure. If your elder instructed you to hold at anything less than four kais, he was testing you in good earnest."

Jethri stared, then, with an effort, he straightened his face, trying to make it as bland and ungiving as the buyer's.

He needn't have bothered. The Liaden had pulled a pouch from his belt and was intent on counting out coins. He placed them on the trade table and stepped back, sweeping the sample bolt up as he did.

"Delivery may be made to our warehouse within the twelve-hour." He bowed, fluid and unstrained, despite the bolt.

"Be you well, young sir. Fair trading, safe lift."

Jethri gave his best bow, which was nowhere near as pretty as the buyer's. "Thank you, respected sir. Fair trading, fair profit."

"Indeed," said the buyer and was gone.

BY RIGHTS, HE should have walked a straight line from Textile Hall to the *Market* and put himself at the disposal of the captain.

Say he was disinclined just yet to talk with Captain Iza Gobelyn, coincidentally his mother, on the subject of his upcoming change of berth. Or say he was coming off his first true solo trade and wanted time to turn the thing over in his mind. Which he was doing, merebeer to hand at the Zeroground Pub, on the corner of the bar he'd staked as his own.

He fingered his fractin, a slow whirling motion—that had been his thinking pattern for most of his life. No matter the captain had told him time and time that he was too old for such fidgets and foolishness. On board ship, some habits were worse than others, and the fractin was let to pass.

As to thinking, he had a lot to do.

He palmed the smooth ivory square, took a sip of the tangy local brew.

Buyer bin'Flora, now—that wanted chewing on. Liadens were fiercely competitive, and, in his experience, tight-fisted of data. Jethri had lately formed the theory that this reluctance to offer information was not what a Terran would call spitefulness, but *courtesy*. It would be—an *insult*, if his reading of the tapes was right, to assume that another person was ignorant of any particular something.

Which theory made Honored Sir bin'Flora's extemporaneous lecture on the appropriate price of crimson cellosilk—interesting.

Jethri sipped his beer, considering whether or not he'd been insulted. This was a delicate question, since it was also OK, as far as his own observations and the crewtapes went, for an elder to instruct a junior. He had another sip of beer, frowning absently at the plain ship-board above the bar. Strictly no-key, that board, listing ship name, departure, arrival, and short on finer info. Jethri sighed. If the *vya* did good, he'd one day soon be able to get a direct line to the trade nets, just by slipping his key into a high-info terminal. 'Course, by then, he'd be shipping on *Digger*, and no use for a Combine key at all...

"'nother brew, kid?" The bartender's voice penetrated his abstraction. He set the glass down, seeing with surprise that it was nearly empty. He fingered a Terran bit out of his public pocket and put it on the bar.

"Merebeer, please."

"Coming up," she said, skating the coin from the bar to her palm. Her pale blue eyes moved to the next customer and she grinned.

"Hey, Sirge! Ain't seen you for a Port-year."

The dark-haired man in modest trading clothes leaned his elbows on the counter and smiled. "That long?" He shook his head, smile going toward a grin. "I lose track of time, when there's business to be done."

She laughed. "What'll it be?"

"Franses Ale?" he asked, wistfully.

"Coming up," she said and he grinned and put five-bit in her hand.

"The extra's for you—a reward for saving my life."

The barkeeper laughed again and moved off down-bar, collecting orders and coins as she went. Jethri finished the last of his beer. When he put the glass down, he found the barkeeper's friend—Sirge—looking at him quizzically.

"Don't mean to pry into what's none of my business, but I noticed you looking at the board, there, a bit distracted. Wouldn't be you had business with *Stork?*"

Jethri blinked, then smiled and shook his head. "I was thinking of—something else," he said, with cautious truth. "Didn't really see the board at all."

"Man with business on his mind," said Sirge good-naturedly. "Well, just thought I'd ask. Misery loves company, my mam used to say—Thanks, Nance." This last as the barkeeper set a tall glass filled with dark liquid before him.

"No trouble," she assured him and put Jethri's schooner down. "Merebeer, Trader."

"Thank you," he murmured, wondering if she was making fun of him or really thought him old enough to be a full trader. He raised the mug and shot a look at the ship-board. *Stork* was there, right enough, showing departed on an amended flight plan.

"Damnedest thing," said the man next to him, ruefully. "Can't blame them for lifting when they got rush cargo and a bonus at the far end, but I sure could wish they waited lift a quarter-hour longer."

Jethri felt a stir of morbid curiosity. "They didn't—leave you, did they, sir?"

The man laughed. "Gods, no, none of that! I've got a berth promised on Ringfelder's *Halcyon*, end of next Port-week. No, this was a matter of buy-in—had half the paperwork filled out, happened to look up at the board there in the Trade Bar and they're already lifting." He took a healthy swallow of his ale.

"Sent a message to my lodgings, of course, but I wasn't at the lodgings, I was out making paper, like we'd agreed." He sighed. "Well, no use crying over spilled wine, eh?" He extended a thin, calloused hand. "Sirge Milton, trader at leisure, damn the luck."

He shook the offered hand. "Jethri Gobelyn, off *Gobelyn's Market*."

"Pleasure. *Market*'s a solid ship—Arin still senior trader?"

Jethri blinked. The routes being as they were, there were still some who had missed news of Arin Gobelyn's death. This man didn't seem quite old enough to have been one of his father's contemporaries, but...

"Paitor's senior," he told Sirge Milton steadily. "Arin died ten Standards back."

"Sorry to hear that," the man said seriously. "I was just a 'prentice, but he impressed me real favorable." He took a drink of ale, eyes wandering back to the ship-board. "Damn," he said, not quite under his breath, then laughed a little and looked at Jethri. "Let this be a lesson to you—*stay liquid*. Think I'd know *that* by now." Another laugh.

Jethri had a sip of beer. "But," he said, though it was none of his business, "what happened?"

For a moment, he thought the other wouldn't answer. He drank ale, frowning at the board, then seemed to collect himself and flashed Jethri a quick grin.

"Couple things. First, I was approached for a closed buy-in on—futures." He shrugged. "You understand I can't be specific. But the guarantee was four-on-one and—well, the

lodgings was paid 'til I shipped and I had plenty on my tab at
the Trade Bar, so I sunk all my serious cash into the future."

Jethri frowned. A four-on-one return on speculation? It
was possible—the crewtapes told of astonishing fortunes made
Port-side, now and then—but not likely. To invest all liquid
assets into such a venture—

Sirge Milton held up a hand. "Now, I know you're thinking exactly what I thought when the thing was put to me—
four-on-one's 'way outta line. But the gig turns on a  Liaden
Master Trader's say-so, and I figured that was good enough
for me." He finished his ale and put the glass down, waving
at the barkeeper.

"Short of it is, I'm cash-poor til tomorrow midday, when
the pay-off's guaranteed. And this morning I came across as
sweet a deal as you'd care to see—and I know just who'll want
it, to my profit. A kais holds the lot—and me with three ten-
bits in pocket. *Stork* was going to front the cash, and earn half
the profit, fair enough. But the rush-money and the bonus was
brighter." He shook his head. "So, Jethri Gobelyn, you can
learn from my mistake—and I'm hopeful I'll do the same."

"Four-on-one," Jethri said, mind a-buzz with the circumstance, so he forgot he was just a 'prentice, talking to a full
trader. "Do you have a paper with the guarantee spelled out?"

"I got better than that," Sirge Milton said. "I got his card."
He turned his head, smiling at the bartender. "Thanks, Nance."

"No problem," she returned. "You got a Liaden's card?
Really? Can I see?"

The man looked uneasy. "It's not the kind of thing you
flash around."

"Aw, c'mon, Sirge—I never seen one."

Jethri could appreciate her curiosity:  he was half agog,
himself. A Liaden's card was as good as his name, and a
Liaden's name, according to great-grand-captain Larance, was
his dearest possession.

"Well," Sirge said. He glanced around, but the other patrons
seemed well-involved in their own various businesses. "OK."

He reached into his pouch, pulled out an out-of-date Combine trading key—the SY 1118 color was red, according to the chart on the back of Jethri's door; blue-and-white was last year's short-term color—along with a short handful of coins and a cargo head socket wrench. Finally, with a satisfied grunt, he fingered out a flat, creamy rectangle.

He held up it face up between the three of them, his hands cupping it like was a rare stone that he didn't want nobody else to see.

"Ooh," Nance said. "What's it say?"

Jethri frowned at the lettering. It was a more ornate form of the Liaden alphabet he had laboriously taught himself off the library files, but not at all unreadable.

"Norn ven'Deelin," he said, hoping he had the pronunciation of the name right. "Master of Trade."

"Right you are," said Sirge, nodding. "You'll go far, I'm sure, friend Jethri! And this here—" he rubbed his thumb over the graphic of a rabbit silhouetted against a full moon— "is the sign for his Clan. Ixin."

"Oh," Nance said again, then turned to answer a hail from up-bar. Sirge slipped the card away and Jethri took another sip of beer, mind racing. A four-on-one return, guaranteed by a Master Trader? It *was* possible. Jethri had seen the rabbit-and-moon sign on a land-barge that very day. And Sirge Milton was going to collect tomorrow midday. Jethri thought he was beginning to see a way to buy into a bit of profit, himself.

"I have a kais to lend," he said, setting the schooner aside.

Sirge Milton shook his head. "Nah—I appreciate it, Jethri, but I don't take loans. Bad business."

Which, Jethri acknowledged, was exactly what his uncle would say. He nodded, hoping his face didn't show how excited he felt.

"I understand. But you have collateral. How 'bout if I buy *Stork's* share of your Port-deal, payoff tomorrow mid-day, after you collect from Master ven'Deelin?"

"Not the way I like to do business," Sirge said slowly.

Jethri took a careful breath. "We can write an agreement," he said.

The other brightened. "We can, can't we? Make it all legal and binding. Sure, why not?" He took a swallow of ale and grinned. "Got paper?"

"NO, MA'AM," JETHRI said, some hours later, and as respectfully as he could, while giving his mother glare-for-glare. "I'm in no way trying to captain this ship. I just want to know if the final papers are signed with *Digger*." His jaw muscles felt tight and he tried to relax them—to make his face trading-bland. "I think the ship owes me that information. At least that."

"Think we can do better for you," his mother the captain surmised, her mouth a straight, hard line of displeasure. "All right, boy. No, the final papers aren't signed. We'll catch up with *Digger* 'tween here and Kinaveral and do the legal then." She tipped her head, sarcastically civil. "That OK by you?"

Jethri held onto his temper, barely. His mother's mood was never happy, dirt-side. He wondered, briefly, how she was going to survive a whole year world-bound, while the *Market* was rebuilt.

"I don't want to ship on *Digger*," he said, keeping his voice just factual. He sighed. "Please, ma'am—there's got to be another ship willing to take me."

She stared at him until he heard his heart thudding in his ears. Then she sighed in her turn, and spun the chair so she faced the screens, showing him profile.

"You want another ship," she said, and she didn't sound mad, anymore. "You find it."

# Day 34
# Standard Year 1118

## Ynsolt'i Port
## Zeroground Pub

"NO CALLS FOR Jethri Gobelyn? No message from Sirge Milton?"

The barkeeper on-shift today at the Zeroground Pub was maybe a Standard Jethri's elder. He was also twelve inches taller and out massed him by a factor of two. He shook his head, setting the six titanium rings in his left ear to chiming, and sighed, none too patient. "Kid, I told you. No calls. No message. No package. No Milton. No *nothing*, kid. Got it?"

Jethri swallowed, hard, the fractin hot against his palm. "Got it."

"Great," said the barkeep. "You wanna beer or you wanna clear out so a paying customer can have a stool?"

"Merebeer, please," he said, slipping a bit across the counter. The keeper swept up the coin, went up-bar, drew a glass, and slid it down the polished surface with a will. Jethri put out a hand—the mug smacked into his palm, stinging. Carefully, he eased away from the not-exactly-overcrowded counter and took his drink to the back.

He was on the approach to trouble. Dodging his senior, sliding off-ship without the captain's aye—approaching trouble, right enough, but not quite established in orbit. Khat was inventive—he trusted her to cover him for another hour, by which time he had better be on-ship, cash in hand and looking to show Uncle Paitor the whole.

And Sirge Milton was late.

A man, Jethri reasoned, slipping into a booth and setting his beer down, might well be late for a meeting. A man might even, with good reason, be an hour late for that same meeting. But a man could call the place named and leave a message for the one who was set to meet him.

Which Sirge Milton hadn't done, nor sent a courier with a package containing Jethri's payout, neither.

So, something must've come up. Business. Sirge Milton seemed a busy man. Jethri opened his pouch and pulled out the agreement they'd written yesterday, sitting at this very back booth, with Nance the bartender as witness.

Carefully, he smoothed the paper, read over the guarantee of payment. Two kais was a higher buy-out than he had asked for, but Sirge had insisted, saying the profit would cover it, not to mention his 'expectations.' There was even a paragraph about being paid in the event that Sirge's sure buyer was out of cash, citing the debt owed Sirge Milton, Trader, by Norn ven'Deelin, Master of Trade, as security.

It had all seemed clear enough yesterday afternoon, but Jethri thought now that he should have asked Sirge to take him around to his supplier, or at least listed the name and location of the supplier on the paper.

He had a sip of beer, but it tasted flat and he pushed the glass away. The door to the bar slid open, admitting a noisy gaggle of Terrans. Jethri looked up, eagerly, but Sirge was not among them. Sighing, he frowned down at the paper, trying to figure out a next move that didn't put him on the receiving end of one of his uncle's furious scolds.

*Norn ven'Deelin, Master of Trade...* The name looked odd, written out in Terran, approximating spelling across two alphabets that didn't precisely match, edge-on-edge. Norn ven'Deelin, who had given his card—his *name*—into Sirge Milton's keeping. Jethri blinked. Norn ven'Deelin, he thought, would very likely know how to get in touch with a person he held in such high esteem. With luck, he'd be inclined to share that information with a polite-talking 'prentice.

If he wasn't inclined...Jethri folded his paper away and got out of the booth, leaving the beer behind. No use borrowing trouble, he told himself.

IT WAS LATE, but still day-Port, when he found the right office. At least, he thought, pausing across the street and staring at that damned bunny silhouetted against the big yellow moon, he hoped it was the right office. He was tired from walking miles in gravity, hot, gritty—but worse than any of that, he was scared. Norn ven'Deelin's office—if this *was* at last his office—was well into the Liaden side of Port.

Not that there was properly a *Terran* side, Ynsolt'i being a Liaden world. But there were portions where Terrans were tolerated as a necessary evil attending galactic trade, and where a body caught the notion that maybe Terrans were cut some extra length of line, in regard to what might be seen as insult.

Standing across from the door, which might, after all, be the right one, Jethri did consider turning around, trudging back to the *Market* and taking the licks he'd traded for.

Except he'd *traded for* profit to the ship, and he was going to collect it. That, at least, he would show his senior and his captain, though he had long since stopped thinking that profit would buy him pardon.

Jethri sighed. There was dust all over his good trading clothes. He brushed himself off as well as he could, and looked across the street. It came to him that the rabbit on Clan Ixin's sign wasn't so much howling at that moon, as laughing its fool head off.

Thinking so, he crossed the street, wiped his boots on the mat, slid his fractin manfully out of his palm and into his public pocket, and pushed the door open.

The office behind the door was airy and bright, and Jethri was abruptly glad that he had dressed in trading clothes, dusty as they now were. This place was high-class—a body could smell profit in the subtly fragrant air, see it in the floor covering and the real wooden chairs.

The man sitting behind the carved center console was as elegant as the room: crisp-cut yellow hair, bland and beardless Liaden face, a vest embroidered with the moon-and-rabbit worn over a salt-white silken shirt. He looked up from his work screen as the door opened, eyebrows lifting in what Jethri had no trouble reading as astonishment.

"Good-day to you, young sir." The man's voice was soft, his Trade only lightly tinged with accent.

"Good-day, honored sir." Jethri moved forward slowly, taking care to keep his hands in sight. Three steps from the console, he stopped and bowed, as low as he could manage without falling on his head.

"Jethri Gobelyn, apprentice trader, *Gobelyn's Market*." He straightened and met the bland blue eyes squarely. "I am come to call upon the Honored Norn ven'Deelin."

"Ah." The man folded his hands neatly upon the console. "I regret it is necessary that you acquaint me more nearly with your business, Jethri Gobelyn."

Jethri bowed again, not so deep this time, and waited 'til he was upright to begin the telling.

"I am in search of a man—a Terran," he added, half-amazed to hear no quaver in his voice—"named Sirge Milton, who owes me a sum of money. It was in my mind that the Honored ven'Deelin might be willing to put me in touch with this man."

The Liaden frowned. "Forgive me, Jethri Gobelyn, but how came such a notion into your mind?"

Jethri took a breath. "Sirge Milton had the Honored ven'Deelin's card in pledge of—"

The Liaden held up a hand, and Jethri gulped to a stop, feeling a little gone around the knees.

"Hold." A Terran would have smiled to show there was no threat. Liadens didn't smile, at least, not at Terrans, but this one exerted himself to incline his head an inch.

"If you please," he said. "I must ask if you are certain that it was the Honored ven'Deelin's own card."

"I—the name was plainly written, sir. I read it myself. And the sigil was the same, the very moon-and-rabbit you yourself wear."

"I regret." The Liaden stood, bowed and beckoned, all in one fluid movement. "This falls beyond my area of authority. If you please, young sir, follow me." The blue eyes met his, as if the Liaden had somehow heard his dismay at being thus directed deeper into alien territory. "House courtesy, Jethri Gobelyn. You receive no danger here."

Which made it plain enough, to Jethri's mind, that refusing to follow would be an insult. He swallowed, his breath going short on him, the *Market* suddenly seeming very far away.

The yellow haired Liaden was waiting, his smooth, pretty face uncommunicative. Jethri bowed slightly and walked forward as calmly as trembling knees allowed. The Liaden led him down a short hallway, past two closed rooms, and bowed him across the threshold of the third, open.

"Be at ease," the Liaden said from the threshold. "I will apprise the master trader of your errand." He hesitated, then extended a hand, palm up. "It is well, Jethri Gobelyn. The House is vigilant on your behalf." He was gone on that, the door sliding silently closed behind him.

This room was smaller than the antechamber, though slightly bigger than the *Market's* common room, the shelves set at heights he had to believe handy for Liadens. Jethri stood for a couple minutes, eyes closed, doing cube roots in his head until his heartbeat slowed down and the panic had eased back to a vague feeling of sickness in his gut.

Opening his eyes, he went over to the shelves on the right, half-trained eye running over the bric-a-brac, wondering if that was really a piece of Sofleg porcelain and, if so, what it was doing set naked out on a shelf, as if it were a common pottery bowl.

The door whispered behind him, and he spun to face a Liaden woman dressed in dark trousers and a garnet colored shirt. Her hair was short and gray, her eyebrows straight and black. She stepped energetically into the center of the room as the door slid closed behind her, and bowed with precision, right palm flat against her chest.

"Norn ven'Deelin," she stated in a clear, level voice. "Clan Ixin."

Jethri felt the blood go to ice in his veins.

Before him, Norn ven'Deelin straightened and slanted a bright black glance into his face. "You discover me a dismay," she observed, in heavily accented Terran. "Say why, do."

He managed to breathe, managed to bow. "Honored Ma'am, I—I've just learned the depth of my own folly."

"So young, yet made so wise!" She brought her hands together in a gentle clap, the amethyst ring on her right hand throwing light off its facets like purple lightning. "Speak on, young Jethri. I would drink of your wisdom."

He bit his lip. "Ma'am, the—person—I came here to find—told me Norn ven'Deelin was—was male."

"Ah. But Liaden names are difficult, I am learning, for those of Terran Code. Possible it is that your friend achieved honest error, occasioned by null-acquaintance with myself."

"I'm certain that's the case, Honored," Jethri said carefully, trying to feel his way toward a path that would win him free, with no insult to the trader, and extricate Sirge Milton from a junior's hopeless muddle.

"I—my friend—did know the person I mistakenly believed yourself to be well enough to have lent money on a portweek investment. The—error—is all my own. Likely there is another Norn ven'Deelin in Port, and I foolishly—"

A tiny hand rose, palm out, to stop him. "Be assured, Jethri Gobelyn. Of Norn ven'Deelin there is one. This one."

He had, Jethri thought, been afraid of that. Hastily, he tried to shuffle possibilities. Had Sirge Milton dealt with a go-between authorized to hand over his employer's card? Had—

"My assistant," said Norn ven'Deelin, "discloses to me a tale of wondering obfusion. I am understanding that you are in possession of one of my cards?"

Her assistant, Jethri thought, with a sudden sharpening of his wits on the matter at hand, had told her no such thing. She was trying to throw him off-balance, and startle him into revealing a weakness. She was, in fact, *trading*. Jethri ground his teeth and made his face smooth.

"No, ma'am," he said respectfully. "What happened was that I met a man in Port who needed loan of a kais to hold a deal. He said he had lent his liquid to—to Norn ven'Deelin, master trader. Of Clan Ixin. He said he was to collect tomorrow—today, midday, that would be—a guaranteed return of four-on-one. My— my payout contingent on his payout." He stopped and did not bite his lip, though he wanted to.

There was a short silence, then, "Four-on-one. That is a very large profit, young Jethri."

He ducked his head. "Yes, ma'am. I thought that. But he had the—the card of the—man—who had guaranteed the return. I read the name myself. And the clan sign—just like the one on your door and—other places on Port.." His voice squeaked out. He cleared his throat and continued.

"I knew he had to be on a straight course—at least on this deal—if it was backed by a Liaden's card."

"Hah." She plucked something flat and rectangular from her sleeve and held it out. "Honor me with your opinion of this."

He took the card, looked down and knew just how stupid he'd been.

"So wondrously expressive a face," commented Norn ven'Deelin. "Was this not the card you were shown, in earnest of fair dealing?"

He shook his head, remembered that the gesture had no analog among Liadens and cleared his throat again.

"No, ma'am," he said as steady as he could. "The rabbit-and-moon are exactly the same. The name—the same style, the same spacing, the same spelling. The stock was white, with black ink, not tan with brown ink. I didn't touch it, but I'd guess it was low-rag. This card is high-rag content…"

His fingers found a pattern on the obverse. He flipped the card over and sighed at the selfsame rabbit-and-moon, embossed into the card stock, then looked back to her bland, patient face.

"I beg your pardon, ma'am."

"So." She reached out and twitched the card from his fingers, sliding it absently back into her sleeve. "You do me a service, young Jethri. From my assistant I hear the name of this person who has, yet does not have, my card in so piquant a fashion. Sirge Milton. This is a correctness? I do not wish to err."

The ice was back in Jethri's veins. Well he knew that Khat's stories of blood vengeance were just that—fright tales to spice an otherwise boring hour. Still and all, it wasn't done, to put another Terran in the way of Liaden Balance. He gulped and bowed.

"Ma'am, I—please. The whole matter is—is *my* error. I am the most junior of traders. Likely I misunderstood a senior and have annoyed yourself and your household without cause. I—"

She held up a hand, stepped forward and laid it on his sleeve.

"Peace, child. I do nothing fatal to your *galandaria*—your countryman. No pellet in his ear. No nitrogen replacing good air in an emergency tank. Eh?" Almost, it seemed to Jethri that she smiled.

"Such tales. We of the clans listen in Port bars—and discover ourselves monsters." She patted his arm, lightly. "But no. Unless he adopts a mode most stupid, fear not of his life." She stepped back, her hand falling from his sleeve.

"Your own actions reside in correctness. Very much is this matter mine of solving. A junior trader could do no other, than bring such at once before me.

"Now, I ask, most humbly, that you accept Ixin's protection in conveyance to your ship. It is come night-Port while we speak, and your kin will be distressful for your safety. Myself and yourself, we speak additionally, after solving."

She bowed again, hand over heart, and Jethri did his best to copy the thing with his legs shaking fit to tip him over. When he looked up the door was closing behind her. It opened again immediately and the yellow-haired assistant stepped inside with a bow of his own.

"Jethri Gobelyn," he said in his soft Trade, "please follow me. A car will take you to your ship."

"She said she wouldn't kill him," Jethri said hoarsely. The captain, his mother, shook her head and Uncle Paitor sighed.

"There's worse things than killing, son," he said, and that made Jethri want to scrunch into his chair and bawl, like he had ten Standards fewer and stood about as tall as he felt.

What he did do, was take another swallow of coffee and meet Paitor's eyes straight. "I'm sorry, sir."

"You've got cause," his uncle acknowledged.

"Double-ups on dock," the captain said, looking at them both. "Nobody works alone. We don't want trouble. We stay close and quiet and we lift as soon as we can without making it look like a rush."

Paitor nodded. "Agreed."

Jethri stirred, fingers tight 'round the coffee mug. "Ma'am, she—Master Trader ven'Deelin said she wanted to talk to me, after she—settled—things. I wouldn't want to insult her."

"None of us wants to insult her," his mother said, with more patience than he'd expected. "However, a Master Trader is well aware that a trade ship must trade. She can't expect us to hang around while our cargo loses value. If she wants to talk to you, boy, she'll find you."

"No insult," Paitor added, "for a 'prentice to bow to the authority of his seniors. Liadens understand chain of command real well." The captain laughed, short and sharp, then stood up.

"Go to bed, Jethri—you're out on your feet. Be on dock second shift—" she slid a glance to Paitor. "Dyk?"

His uncle nodded.

"You'll partner with Dyk. We're onloading seed, ship's basics, trade tools. Barge's due Port-noon. Stick *close*, understand me?"

"Yes, ma'am." Wobbling, Jethri got to his feet, nodded to his seniors, put the mug into the wash-up and turned toward the door.

"Jethri."

He turned back, thinking his uncle's face looked—sad.

"I wanted to let you know," Paitor said. "The spice did real well for us."

Jethri took a deep breath. "Good," he said and his voice didn't shake at all. "That's good."

# Day 35
# Standard Year 1118

## *Gobelyn's Market*
## Dockside

"OK," SAID DYK, easing the forks on the hand-lift back. "Got it." He toggled the impeller fan and nodded over his shoulder. "Let's go, kid. Guard my back."

Jethri managed a weak grin. Dyk was inclined to treat the double-up and Paitor's even-voiced explanation of disquiet on the docks as a seam-splitting joke. He guided the hand-lift to the edge of the barge, stopped, theatrically craned both ways, flashed a thumbs-up over his shoulder to Jethri, who was lagging behind, and dashed out onto the *Market's* dock. Sighing, Jethri walked slowly in his wake.

"Hey, kid, hold it a sec." The voice was low and not entirely unfamiliar. Jethri spun.

Sirge Milton was leaning against a cargo crate, hand in the pocket of his jacket and nothing like a smile on his face.

"Real smart," he said, "setting a Liaden on me."

Jethri shook his head, caught somewhere between relief and dismay.

"You don't understand," he said, walking forward. "The card's a fake."

The man against the crate tipped his head. "Is it, now."

"Yeah, it is. I've seen the real one, and it's nothing like the one you've got."

"So what?"

"So," Jethri said patiently, stopping and showing empty hands in the old gesture of goodwill, "whoever gave you the card wasn't Norn ven'Deelin. He was somebody who *said* he was Norn ven'Deelin and he used the card and her—the honor of her name—to cheat you."

Sirge Milton leaned, silent, against the cargo bail.

Jethri sighed sharply. "Look, Sirge, this is serious stuff. The master trader has to protect her name. She's not after you—she's after whoever gave you that card and told you he was her. All you have to do—"

Sirge Milton shook his head, sorrowful, or so it seemed to Jethri. "Kid," he said, "you still don't get it, do you?" He brought his hand out of the pocket and leveled the gun, matter-of-factly, at Jethri's stomach. "I know the card's bogus, kid. I know who made it—and so does your precious master trader. She got the scrivener last night. She'd've had me this morning, but I know the back way outta the 'ground."

The gun was high-gee plastic, snub-nosed and black. Jethri stared at it and then looked back at the man's face.

*Trade*, he thought, curiously calm. *Trade for your life.*

Sirge Milton grinned. "You traded another Terran to a Liaden. That's stupid, Jethri. Stupid people don't live long."

"You're right," he said, calmly, watching Sirge's face and not the gun at all. "And it'd be real stupid for you to kill me. Norn ven'Deelin said I'd done her a service. If you kill me, she's not going to have any choice but to serve you the same. You don't want to corner her."

"Jeth?" Dyk's voice echoed in from the dock. "Hey! Jethri!"

"I'll be out in a second!" he yelled, never breaking eye contact with the gunman. "Give me the gun," he said, reasonably. "I'll go with you to the master trader and you can make it right."

"'Make it right'," Sirge sneered and there was a sharp snap as he thumbed the gun's safety off.

"I urge you most strongly to heed the young trader's excellent advice, Sirge Milton," a calm voice commented in accentless Trade. "The master trader is arrived and balance may go forth immediately."

Master ven'Deelin's yellow-haired assistant walked into the edge of Jethri's field of vision. He stood lightly on the balls of his feet, as if he expected to have to run. There was a gun, holstered, on his belt.

Sirge Milton hesitated, staring at this new adversary.

"Sirge, it's not worth killing for," Jethri said, desperately.

But Sirge had forgotten about him. He was looking at Master ven'Deelin's assistant. "Think I'm gonna be some Liaden's slave until I worked off what she claims for debt?" He demanded. "Liaden Port? You think I got any chance of a fair hearing?"

"The portmaster—" the Liaden began, but Sirge cut him off with a wave, looked down at the gun and brought it around.

"No!" Jethri jumped forward, meaning to grab the gun, but something solid slammed into his right side, knocking him to the barge's deck. There was a *crack* of sound, very soft, and Jethri rolled to his feet—

Sirge Milton was crumbled face down on the cold decking, the gun in his hand. The back of his head was gone. Jethri took a step forward, found his arm grabbed and turned around to look down into the grave blue eyes of Master ven'Deelin's assistant.

"Come," the Liaden said, and his voice was not—quite— steady. "The master trader must be informed."

THE YELLOW-HAIRED assistant came to an end of his spate of Liaden and inclined his head.

"So it is done." Norn ven'Deelin said in Trade. "Advise the portmaster and hold yourself at her word."

"Master Trader." The man swept a bow so low his forehead touched his knees, straightened effortlessly and left the *Market's* common room with nothing like a backward look.

Norn ven'Deelin turned to Jethri, sitting shaken between his mother and Uncle Paitor.

"I am regretful," she said in her bad Terran, "that solving achieved this form. My intention, as I said to you, was not thus. Terrans—" She glanced around, at Paitor and the captain, at Dyk and Khat and Mel. "Forgive me. I mean to say that Terrans are of a mode most surprising. It was my error, to be think this solving would end not in dyings." She showed her palms. "The counterfeit-maker and the, ahh—*distributor*—are of a mind, both, to achieve more seemly Balance."

"Counterfeiter?" asked Paitor and Norn ven'Deelin inclined her head.

"Indeed. Certain cards were copied—not well, as I find—and distributed to traders of dishonor. These would then use the—the—*melant'i*—you would say, the *worth* of the card to run just such a shadow-deal as young Jethri fell against." She sat back, mouth straight. "The game is closed, this Port, and information of pertinence has been sent to the Guild of Traders Liaden." She inclined her head, black eyes very bright. "Do me the honor, Trader Gobelyn, of informing likewise the association of Traders Terran. If there is doubt of credentials at a Liaden port, there is no shame for any trader to inquire of the Guild."

Paitor blinked, then nodded, serious-like. "Master Trader, I will so inform Terratrade."

"It is well, then," she said, moving a hand in a graceful gesture of sweeping away—or, maybe, of clearing the deck. "We come now to young Jethri and how best I might Balance his service to myself."

The captain shot a glance at Paitor, who climbed to his feet and bowed, low and careful. "We are grateful for your condescension, Master Trader. Please allow us to put paid, in mutual respect and harmony, to any matter that may lie between us—"

"Yes, yes," she waved a hand. "In circumstance far otherwise, this would be the path of wisdom, all honor to you, Trader

Gobelyn. But you and I, we are disallowed the comfort of old wisdom. We are honored, reverse-ward, to build new wisdom." She looked up at him, black eyes shining.

"See you, this young trader illuminates error of staggering immensity. To my hand he delivers one priceless gem of data: Terrans are using Liaden honor to cheat other Terrans." She leaned forward, catching their eyes one by one. "Liaden honor," she repeated; "to cheat other Terrans."

She lay her hand on her chest. "I am a master trader. My—my *duty* is to the increase of the trade. Trade cannot increase, where honor is commodity."

"But what does this," Dyk demanded, irrepressible, "have to do with Jethri?"

The black eyes pinned him. "A question of piercing excellence. Jethri has shown me this—that the actions of Liadens no longer influence the lives only of Liadens. Reverse-ward by logic follows for the actions of Terrans. So, for the trade to increase, wherein lies the proper interest of trader and master trader, information cross-cultural must increase." She inclined her head.

"Trader, I suggest we write contract between us, with the future of Jethri Gobelyn in our minds."

Uncle Paitor blinked. "You want to—forgive me. I think you're trying to say that you want to take Jethri as an apprentice."

Another slight bow of the head. "Precisely so. Allow me, please, to praise him to you as a promising young trader, strongly enmeshed in honor."

"But I did everything wrong!" Jethri burst out, seeing Sirge Milton laying there, dead of his own choice, and the stupid waste of it...

"Regrettably, I must disagree," Master ven'Deelin said softly. "It is true that death untimely transpired. This was not your error. Pen Rel informs to me your eloquence in beseeching Trader Milton to the path of Balance. This was not error. To solicit solving from she who is most able to solve—that is only correctness." She showed both of her hands, palms up. "I honor you for your actions, Jethri Gobelyn, and wonder if you will bind yourself as my apprentice."

He wanted it. In that one, searing moment, he knew he had never wanted anything in his life so much. He looked to his mother.

"I found my ship, Captain," he said.

# Day 42
# Standard Year 1118

## *Gobelyn's Market*
## Departing

WHEN IT WAS all counted and compressed, his personal possessions fit inside two crew-bags. He slung the larger across his back, secured by a strap across his chest, snapped at shoulder and hip. Hefting the smaller, he took one more look around the room—a plain metal closet it was, now, with the cot slid away and the desk folded into the wall. He'd tried to give the com chart back, but Dyk insisted that it would fit inside the bag with a little pushing, and so it had.

There was nothing left to show the place had been his particular private quarters for more than half his lifetime. Looking at it, the space could be anything, really: a supply closet; a specialty cargo can...

Jethri shook his head, trying to recapture the burning joy he'd felt, signing his line on the 'prentice contract, finding himself instead, and appallingly, on the near side of bawling his eyes out.

*It's not like you're wanted here,* he told himself, savagely. *You were on the good-riddance roster, no matter what.*

Still, it hurt, staring around at what had once been his space, feeling his personals no considerable weight across his back.

He swallowed, forcing the tears back down into his chest. Damned if he would cry. Damned if he would.

Which was well. And also well to remember that value wasn't necessarily heavy. In fact, it might be that the most valuable thing he carried away from the ship weighed no more than an ounce—Uncle Paitor had come through with the Combine key, springing for the ten-year without a blink— a measure of how good the *vya* had done. Khat had donated a true-silver long-chain, and now it hung round his neck, with key in place.

He'd been afraid, nearly, that Khat would kiss him right then, when she put the key on the chain and dropped it 'round his neck, then stood close and reached out to tuck the key sudden-like down his day-shirt.

"Promise me you'll wear this and remember us!" she said, and hugged him, as unexpected as the potential kiss, and missed as greatly as soon as she released him.

And so he had promised, and could feel the key becoming familiar and comfortable as he got himself together.

Then there was his ship-share, which had come to a tidy sum, with a tithe atop that, that he hadn't expected, and which Seeli'd claimed was his piece of the divvy-up from his father's shares.

"Payable in cash," Seeli had said, further, not exactly looking at him. "On departure from the ship. Since you're going off to trade for another ship, this counts. Those of us who stay, the ship carries our shares in General Fund."

He'd also taken receipt of one long, assaying, straight-eyed glance from the captain with the words said, in front of Dyk before they signed those papers—

"You chose your ship, you got your inheritance, you think you know what you want. So I witness you, Jethri son of Arin, a free hand." She'd shook his hand, then, like he was somebody, and turned away like he was forgot.

So, now, here he stood, on the edge of an adventure, kit and cash in hand. A goodly sum of cash, for a Terran juniormost; an adequate kit, for the same. 'mong Liadens, who knew where he stood?—though soon enough he'd find out.

He felt his private pocket, making sure he had coin and notes and his fractin, then patted his public pocket, making sure of the short-change stowed there.

The ship clock chimed, echoing off the metal walls. Jethri took one more look around the bare cubby. Right. Time to get on with it.

As SOON AS the door slid closed behind him he remembered the last thing Paitor had said, leaning over to tap his finger against the nameplate set in the door.

"You pull that on the way out, y'hear? Rule is, when crew moves on, they take their nameplate so there ain't any confusion 'case of a crash." He nodded, maybe a little wise with the Smooth, and clapped Jethri on the shoulder. "That's yours as much as anything on this ship ever was."

Right.

Jethri slid the duffle off his shoulder, opened the door, and pulled the wrench-set off his belt. The nameplate showed through a blast resistant window set into the body of the door, with the access hatch on the inside. One-handed, he quickly undid the eight inset-togs probably last touched by his father, second hand held ready to catch the hatch when it fell.

Except, even with the togs loose the cover didn't fall right out, so he sighed and reached for his side-blade, and unsnapped it from the holster.

*Who'd have thought this would be so tough?*

He could see that asking for help getting his nameplate out of the door wouldn't play too well with his cousins—and wasn't it just like Mister Murphy to be sure and make an easy task hard, when he was needing to be on time...If Paitor and Grig hadn't kept him up clear through mid-Opposite—

The captain had made it plain that she'd look dimly on any celebration of Jethri's new status—which was bad form when any crew left a ship but 'specially bad when a child of the ship went for a new berth. Strictly speaking, they should've called 'round to the other ships on port, and had a party, if not a full-blown shivary. In time, the news would spread through the free-ships—and news it was, too. But, no; it was like the captain was embarrassed that her son was 'prenticed to a Liaden master trader; which, as far as Jethri could find, was a first-time-ever event.

So, everyone was nice to him, 'cept the captain, and there wasn't any party, so he'd taken his time going through his belongings and packing up, finding so much of what he had was left over from being a kid; so much was stuff he didn't need, or even want. And, o'course, there was the stuff that he *did* want that he hadn't had since his father died. The fractin collection, of which his lucky tile was the last link; the pictures of Arin; the trade journal they'd been working on together—Seeli'd let on, without exactly coming out and saying so, that the captain had spaced it all years ago, so it wasn't no sense feeling like he'd just been stripped of what was his.

But, still, he wished he had those things to pack.

All that being so, he was in something of a mood when the tap came on his door, just after Opposite shift rang in. And he'd been surprised right out of that mood to find Grig and Paitor on the other side; asking permission to enter.

Lanky Grig—back-up navigator, back-up pilot, back-up cook, back-up trader, and in-system engineer—folded himself up on the edge of the bunk/acceleration couch while Jethri and Paitor took the magna-tracked swivel stools.

Once they were situated, Paitor pulled a green cloth bag from his pocket, and Grig brought three stainless drinking cups from his pouch. Jethri sat, his fractin snug in his hand, and wondered what was up.

"Jethri," Paitor began, then stopped as if he'd forgot what he was going to say for a second. He took a look at the bag on his knee, then untied the silver cord with its pendant tag from around the top, and handed the cord off to Jethri, who slid it into his public pocket, along with the fractin.

Paitor slipped the bag down, revealing a blue bottle, sealed with gold foil.

"The time has come, ol' son," Grig said quietly. "You're a free hand now—time for you to have a drink with your peers."

Paitor smiled like he only half wanted to, and lifted the bottle in two hands, like it was treasure.

"If I may do the honors here," he said, holding the bottle out so Jethri could read the label. "This here's Genuine Smooth Blusharie. Been with us since the day you was born. Arin picked it up, see? Since the captain drinks a meaner line than this, bottle was just gathering dust in the locker, and we figured we'd better make use of it before someone who don't really 'preciate it drinks it by mistake."

He smiled again, more like he meant it this time, and twisted the seal. There was a crackle as it gave way, and sharp *pop* a moment later, as the cork come out. Grig held the cups out, carefully, one after the other, and Paitor filled each with gem-colored liquid.

When they were each holding a cup and the bottle was recorked and stowed next to Grig on the bunk, Paitor cleared his throat.

"Now, Jethri," he said, talking slow, "I know you heard a lot of advice from me over your years and you probably got right tired of it—" Grig snorted a laugh and Jethri nodded in rueful agreement, holding his cup carefully— "but there's just a little bit more you got to hear. First is this: Don't never gulp Blusharie, whether it's smooth or whether it's not. If it *ain't* smooth, gulping it will knock you off your pins so hard you'll think you had a code red collision. If it *is* smooth, you'll be wasting one of the rare joys of this life and didn't deserve to have it."

Paitor lifted his cup and Grig, his. Jethri lifted his, looking from one lifelong familiar face to another, seeing nothing but a concentration on the moment.

"To Jethri Gobelyn, free hand!"

"Long may he trade!" Grig added, and he and Paitor clinked their cups together, Jethri joining them a second late. He looked into the amber depths of the liquid, and sipped himself a tiny sip.

It all but took his breath, that sip, leaving a smooth tartness on his tongue and a tingling at the back of his throat. Fiery and mellow at once—

He noticed that he was being watched, and had a second sip, smiling.

"It's not like ale or beer at all!"

Grig laughed, low and comfortable. "No, not at all."

"So there, Jethri, that's some advice for you, and a secret, of a kind," said Paitor, sipping at his own cup. "There's traders all over the Combine who got no idea where to get this or why they'd want to. But you find yourself someone who fancies himself a knowing drinker, and you can get yourself a customer for life."

Jethri nodded, remembering the silver cord on his pocket, with the name of the vintage and the cellar stamped on the seal.

"'Course, there's more to life than Smooth Blusharie, too," Paitor said after another gentle sip. "So, what we got to tell you, is—there's things you gotta know."

His latest sip of Smooth Blusharie heavy on his tongue, Jethri looked up into Paitor's face, noting that it had changed again, from sadly serious to trading-bland, and sat up straight on his stool.

"All families have their secrets," Paitor said slowly. "This ship and this family're no different'n most. Thing is, sometimes not all secrets get shared around so good, and some things that should've been kept so secret they're forgot get talked about too much." He took a short sip from his cup. "One of the things that might've been kept secret but wasn't, was how you wasn't expected."

Jethri looked down into his cup, biting his lip, and figured this was a good time to have another sip.

"Now," Paitor went on, still talking slow and deliberate. "What likely *was* kept  secret was what Arin and Iza were doing together in the first place, seein' as some would call—and did call—them a mismatch from ignition to flare out."

What was this?  Seeli, his source of all information about his parents, had never hinted that there'd been any trouble between Iza and Arin.  All the trouble had come later, with Jethri.

"What it was, see, Jethri," his uncle was saying, "is that the Gobelyn side goes back a long way in the Combine. Gobelyns was founding members of the Combine—and part of the trade teams before that. An' even before the trade teams, Gobelyns was ship folk."

Jethri frowned. "That's no secret, Uncle. The tapes…"

Grig snorted, and had a sip of the Smooth. His face was hooded; closed, like he was misdirecting a buyer around a defect. Paitor looked across to him.

"Your turn now?" he asked, real quiet.

Grig shook his head. "No, sir—and I'm damned if that ain't another secret been kept! But, no. Go on."

After a minute, Paitor nodded, and sipped and leaned over to gently shake the bottle.

"That's fine, then," he murmured. "A glass to talk on and a glass to clear it."

"We'll do it," Grig said, nodding, too, with his face still a study in grim. "Really."

"Right. We will." Paitor took a hard breath. "So, Jethri, the way it was—Arin come along about the time the Gobelyns was set to call precedence at a shipowner meeting. Timing was bad, you might say, it being right near the time when the internal power-shift went from ship-base to world-base. The Combine had got so big, it owned pieces of planets, big and small, not to mention controlling shares in a good many Grounder corps, and its interest shifted from securing the trade-lanes to protecting its investments. Which meant that the ships and shipowners who'd founded the Combine and built it strong wasn't in charge no more.

"So, anyway, they'd called an owners' meeting there on Caratunk, and the Gobelyns had the backin' they needed. That's when Arin showed up with the word that the owners' meeting had been downgraded from rule-making to advisory, by a twenty-seven to three commissioner vote. Now understand, Arin come from trade background too, but he'd started real young gettin' formal educated.

Spent years on-planet—went to college planet-side, went to University, took history courses, took pilot courses, took trading and economics—and so when that vote came up, he was one of the three commissioners on the losing end."

Jethri blinked, cup half-way to his lips, Smooth Blusharie forgotten in blank astonishment.

"My father was a *commissioner*?"

Grig laughed, short and sharp.

"Not once he got out to Caratunk he wasn't," Paitor answered, sparing a quick glare for the lanky man on the bunk. "Left his vote card right there on the table, grabbed up his money, his collections, and his co-pilot, and quit on the spot. Figured the best way to help the owners an' preserve the routes was to be out with us. And so he did that."

"Finish your sip, boy," Grig instructed, taking one of his own. Jethri followed suit. He'd met a commissioner once, when he was young—

"Right," said Paitor, "you might remember the ship was busy once. Lots of folks comin' by when we was in port, lots of talk, presents for the youngers...Even though Arin wasn't a commissioner no more, him knowing how the systems worked, Combine and planet-side—the owners, they come to him for advice, for planning out how to maybe not rely so heavy on Combine contacts and Combine contracts."

"But it stopped. After...the accident." Jethri could vaguely remember a day when they were in port and Arin got called away—as he so often did—and then the ship was locked down, and his mother screamed and—

"It was a bad time. Thought we'd lose your mother too. Blamed herself for lettin' him go, like there was some way she could have stopped him.

"But see, your dad, he was from old stock, too. Not ship-folk; not 'til later. They was kinda roamers—archaeologists, philosophers, librarians... Had strange ideas, some of 'em. Figured us Terrans had been around a longer time than we got the history for, that Terra—what they call the homeworld—is maybe the third or fourth Terra we've called home in sequence. Some other—"

"Paitor..." Grig's voice was low and warning. Jethri froze on his stool; he'd never heard long, easy-going Grig so much as sharp, never mind out-'n-out menacing.

"Your turn then," Paitor said, after a pause. He lifted his cup.

"My turn," Grig said, and sighed. He leaned forward on the bunk, looking hard into Jethri's face.

"You know I was your father's co-pilot. We were cousins, yeah, but more than that in someways, 'cause we had the same mentor when we was growing up, and we both got involved in what Paitor calls useless politicking and we thought was more than that. A lot more than that. Now thing is, your mam, and her-side of the cousins, like the Golds—they're Loopers. Know what that is?"

Jethri nodded. "I know what it is. But I don't like to hear the captain—"

Grig held up a hand, fingers wagging in the hand-talk equivalent of "pipe down."

"Tell me what it is before you get riled."

*My last night on ship and I draw a history quiz,* Jethri thought, irritated. He had a sip of Smooth to take the edge off his temper, and looked back to Grig.

"Loopers is backwards. Don't want to come out to the bigger ports, only want to deal with smaller planets, and places where they don't have to deal with regs or with..."

Grig flicked a couple fingers—"stop," that was.

"Part right and part wrong. See, Loopers comes from an article in the Combine charter which was writ awhile back and got pretty popular—probably have five copies of it in the records on-board here if you know where to look. The idea came from the fact that most ship-folk believe in following a loop of travel—pretty often it's a closed loop. And some Looper families, they've been on ship for a hundred Standards, maybe, and everybody onboard knows that month seventeen of the trip means they're putting into so-and-so port to pick up fresh 'runion concentrate.

"Fact is, 'way back when this was all first worked out, the idea was that *every* route would be a Loop, with some Loops intersecting others, for transshipping and such.

"Now, I think you know, and I think I know, and I think Paitor knows, that's nonsense. This closed system stuff only works so long—and as long—as the economy of most of the ports in the Loop're expanding. Everybody does their bit, nobody introduces no major changes—then your Loop's stable and everybody profits. Now, though, just speaking of changes, we got Liadens, who got no interest in *our* expanding system—they got their own systems and routes to care about. Then you got some of the planets putting their own ships into the mix without knowing history, nor caring. So now you got instability and running a Loop ain't such a good notion no more. You got the trading families losing out to the planets, and the Combine—well, buying up all them shares and corporations cost money, which means we pay more taxes and fees, not less. 'Cause the Combine, see, it can't let the ships go altogether, though we're getting troublesome; it needs to keep a certain control, exercise a certain authority, and bleed us 'til we—"

Next to Jethri, Paitor coughed. Grig jerked to halt and rubbed a hand over his head.

"Right," he said. "Sorry." He sipped, and sighed lightly.

"So, where was I? Trade theory, eh? Say f'rinstance that you, Jethri Ship-Owner, want to live off the smaller ports and set yourself up a pretty good Loop. Sooner or later the good business is going to shift, and your Loop'll be worth less to the ship. You end up like *Gold Digger*, runnin' stones from place to place and maybe something odd on the side to make weight.

"What Arin saw was that the contract runs was the money runs. You go hub-to-hub, you don't ship empty; if conditions change—you can adapt; you ain't tied to the Loop.

"Arin had a good eye for basic contracts, and the ones he fixed up for the *Market* are just now needing adjustment. That's why this is a great time for the overhaul—your mam's on course, there. And you—you're in a spot to be big news. 'prentice trader on a Liaden ship? Studying under a *master trader*? You not only got a shot to own a ship, boy. Unless I read her wrong, that master trader is seeing you as—kind of like a commissioner 'tween Liaden interests and Terran."

Jethri blinked. "I don't—"

Grig glanced at Paitor, then back to Jethri.

"Let it go then," he said. "Learn your lessons, do good—for yourself and for your name." He moved a hand, apologetic-like. "There's one more thing, and then we can finish up this nice stuff and let you get some sleep." He took a breath, nodded to himself.

"*There are secrets in all families.* That's a phrase. You meet someone else who believes, who knows, they'll get that phrase to you. You don't know nothing but there's a secret, and that's all you have to know, now. But put that in your backbrain—*there are secrets in all families.* It might serve you; it might not. Course you're charting, who knows?"

Jethri was frowning in earnest now, his thought process just a little slow with the Smooth.

"But—what does it mean? What happens if somebody—"

Grig held up his hand. "You'll know what'll happen if it ever does. What it means…It means that there's some stuff, here and there around the galaxy left over from the time of the Old War—the big war, like Khat tells about in stories. It means that your lucky fractin, there, that's not a game piece, no matter how many rules for playing with 'em we all seen—it's a Fractional Mosaic Memory Module—and nobody exactly knows what they're for." He looked at Paitor. "Though Arin thought he had an idea."

Paitor grunted. "Arin had ideas. Nothin' truer said."

Grig ran his hand over his head and produced a grin. "Paitor ain't a believer," he said to Jethri, and sat back, looking thoughtful.

"Listen," he said, "'cause I'll tell you this once, and it might sound like ol' Grig, he's gone a little space-wise. But just listen, and remember—be aware, that's all. Paitor don't want to hear this again—didn't want to hear it the first time, I'm bettin'—but him and me—we agreed you need a place to work from; information that Iza don't want you to have." He paused.

"These fractins, now—they're Old Tech. Really Old Tech. Way we figured it, they was Old Tech when the big war started. And the thing is—we can't duplicate them."

Jethri stared, and it did occur to him that maybe Grig had started his drinking before the Blusharie. The big war—the Old War—well, there'd been one, that much was sure; most of the Befores you'd come up with, they was pieces from the war—or from what folks called the war, but could've been some other event. Jethri'd read arguments for and against had there been or had there not been a war, as part of history studies. And the idea of a tech that old that couldn't be duplicated today...

"What kind of tech?" he asked Grig. "And why can't we copy it?"

"Good questions, both, and I'd be a happier man if I had an answer for either. What I can tell you is—if that fractin of yours is one of the real ones—one of the old ones—it's got a tiny bit of timonium in there. You can find that from the out-side because of the neutrinos—and all the real ones ever scanned had its own bit of timonium. Something else you find is that there's structure inside—they ain't just poured plas-tic or something. Try to do a close scan, though, maybe get a looksee at the shape of that structure, and what happens? *Zap!* Fried fractin. The timonium picks up the energy and gives off a couple million neutrinos and some beta and gamma rays—and there's nothing left but slagged clay. Try to peel it? You can't; same deal."

Jethri took of sip of his dwindling drink, trying to get his mind around the idea that there was tech hundreds of Standards old that couldn't be cracked and duplicated.

"As I say," Grig said, soft-like, "Paitor ain't a believer. What him, and Iza and a whole lot of other folks who're perfectly sane, like maybe I'm not on the subject, nor Arin neither— what they think is that the Old War wasn't nearly as big as others of us believe. They don't believe that war was fought with fractins, and about fractins. Arin thought that; and he had studies—records of archeological digs, old docs—to back him. He could map out where fractins was found, where the big caches were, show how they related to other Before caches—and when the finds started to favor the counterfeits over the real thing." He sighed.

"So, see, this just ain't our family secret. Some of the earlier studies—they went missing. Stolen. Arin said some people got worried about what would happen if Loopers and ship owners got interested in Befores as more than a sometime high-profit oddity. If they started looking for Old Tech, and figured out how to make 'em work.

"Arin didn't necessarily think we should make these fractins work—but he thought we should know what they did—and how. In case of need. Then, he got an analysis—"

Grig sipped, and sat for a long couple heartbeats, staring down into his cup.

"You know what half-life is, right?" He asked, looking up. Jethri rolled his eyes, and Paitor laughed. Grig sighed.

"Right. Given the half-life of that timonium, Arin figured them for about eighteen hundred Standards old. Won't be long—say ten Standards, for some of the earlier ones; maybe a hundred for the latest ones—before the timonium's too weak to power—whatever it powers. Might be they'll just go inert, and anybody's who's interested can just take one, or five, or five hundred apart and take a peek inside.

"Arin, now. Arin figured fractins was maybe memory— warship, library, and computer, all rolled into one, including guidance and plans. That's what Arin thought. And it's what he wanted you to know. Iza and the Golds and all them other sane folks, they think they don't need to know. They

say, only a fool borrows trouble, when there's so much around
that's free.  Me?  I think you ought to know what your father
thought, and I think you ought to keep your eyes and your
mind open.  I don't know that you particularly need to talk
to any Liadens about it—but you'll make that call, if and
when you have to."

He looked deep into his cup, lifted it and drained what
was left.

"That it?"  Paitor asked, quietly

Grig nodded.  "It'll do."

"Right you are, then."  He held out a hand; Grig passed
him the bottle, and he refilled the cups, one by one.

He stood, and Grig did, and after a moment, Jethri did.
All three raised their cups high.

"To your success, your honor, and your duty, Free Hand!"
his kin said, loud enough to set the walls to thrumming.  And
Jethri squared his shoulders, and blinked back the sudden
tears—and they talked of easier things until the cups were
empty again.


"Mud," Jethri muttered, as his blade scraped across the
hatch.  Lower lip caught between his teeth, he had another
go with the wrench-set, and was at last rewarded with an
odd fluttering hiss, that sent him skipping back a startled
half-step.

*Pressure differential*, he thought, laughing at himself.

The sound of squeezing air faded and the cover plate
popped away when he probed it with the blade point.

Stuffed into the cavity was some paper, likely to stop the
plate from rattling the way Khat's did whenever they were
accelerating, and he pulled it out, ready to crumple and toss
it—and checked, frowning down at the paper itself.

Yellow and gritty—it was printout from the comm-
printer the captain didn't use any more. She'd always called
it Arin's printer, like she didn't want anything to do with it,
anyway, 'cause she didn't like to deal with nothing ciphered.

Curiously, he separated the edges and opened the paper. There was his birth date, a series of random letters and numbers that likely weren't random at all if you knew what you was looking at and—

...WILDETOAD WILDETOAD WILDETOAD like an emergency beacon might send out.

*WildeToad?* Jethri knew his ship histories, but he would've known this one, anyway, being as Khat told a perfect hair-raiser about *Toad's* last ride. *WildeToad* had gone missing years ago, and none of the mainline Wildes had been seen since. Story was, they'd gone to ground, which didn't make no sense, them having been spacers since before there was space, as the sayin' went.

Jethri squinted at the paper.

*Mismatch, there's a mismatch, going down*
WILDETOAD WILDETOAD WILDETOAD
*We're breaking clay. Check frequency*
WILDETOAD WILDETOAD WILDETOAD
*Thirty hours. Warn away Euphoria*
WILDETOAD WILDETOAD WILDETOAD
*Racks bare, breaking clay*
WILDETOAD WILDETOAD WILDETOAD
*Lake bed ahead. We're arming. Stay out.*
*L.O.S. TRANSMISSION ENDS*

*Lake bed,* he thought. And, *gone to ground.* Spacer humor, maybe; it had that feel. And it got him in the stomach, that he held in his hand the last record of a dying ship. Why had his father used such a thing to shim the plate in his door? Bad luck... He swallowed, read the page again, frowning after nonsense phrases.

Breaking clay? Racks bare? This was no common ship-send, he thought, the grainy yellow paper crackling against his fingers. Arin's printer. The message had come into Arin's printer. Coded, then—but—

A chime sounded, the four notes of "visitor aboard." Jethri jumped, cussed, and jammed the paper and the nameplate into his duffle, resealed the hatch as quick as he could, and took off down the hall at a run.

IT WAS A small group at the main lock: Khat, Iza, and Uncle Paitor to witness his farewell. Master ven'Deelin's assistant, Pen Rel, stood more at his ease than seemed likely for a man alone on a stranger ship, his smooth, pretty face empty of anything like joy, irritation, or boredom. His eyes showed alert, though, and it was him who caught Jethri first, and bowed, very slightly.

"Apprentice. The master trader assigns me your escort."

Jethri paused and bowed, also slightly—that being the best he could manage with the bag slung across his back.

"Sir. The master trader does me too much honor," he said.

The blue eyes flickered—very likely Pen Rel agreed—but give the man his due, neither smirk nor smile crossed his face, either of which he had every right to display, according to Jethri's counting.

Instead, he turned his attention to Iza Gobelyn and bowed again—deep, this time, displaying all proper respect to the captain-owner.

"The master trader sends felicitations, Captain. She bids me say that she has herself placed a child of her body into the care of others, for training, knowing the necessity at the core of her trader's heart. A mother's heart, however, is both more foolish and more wise. She therefore offers, mother to mother, route-list and codes. Messages sent by this method will reach Jethri Gobelyn immediately. Its frequent use is encouraged."

Another bow—this one no more than a heavy tip of the head—a flourish, and there was a data card between the first and second fingers of his extended hand.

Iza Gobelyn's mouth pursed up, as if she'd tasted something sour. She didn't quite place her hands behind her back—not quite that. But she did shake her head, side-to-side, once, decisive-like.

Jethri felt himself draw breath, hard. Not that he had expected his mother would have wanted to keep in touch with him when he was gone, like she'd never bothered to do when he was a member of her crew. It was just—the rudeness, when Master ven'Deelin… He blinked, and sent a short glance straight to Khat, who caught it, read it, and stepped forward, smooth and soft-footed.

Gently, she slipped the card from between Pen Rel's fingers, and bowed, deeper than he had done, thereby showing respect for the master trader's emissary.

"Please convey to the master trader our appreciation of her kindness and her forethought," she said, which deepened the frown on Iza's face, and put some color back into Paitor's.

For his part, Jethri felt his chest ease a little—*catastrophe averted,* he thought, which should have been the truth of it, except that Master ven'Deelin's aide stood there for a heartbeat too long, his head cocked a mite to one side, waiting…

…and then waiting no longer, but bowing in general farewell, while his eyes pegged Jethri and one hand moved in an unmistakable sweep: *Let's go, kid.*

Swallowing, Jethri went, following the Liaden down the ramp.

"'bye Jethri," he heard Khat whisper as he went past her. "We'll miss you."

Her hand touched his shoulder fleetingly, and under his shirt the key clung a bit, then *Gobelyn's Market* clanged as the portals closed behind him.

AT THE END of the *Market's* dock, Pen Rel turned left, walking light, despite the gravity. Jethri plodded along half a step behind, and pretty soon worked up a sweat, to which the Port dust clung with a will.

Traffic increased as they went on, and he stretched his legs to keep his short guide in sight. Finally, the man paused, and waited while Jethri came up beside him.

"Jethri Gobelyn." If he noticed Jethri's advanced state of dishevelment, he betrayed it by not the flicker of an eyelash. Instead, he blandly inclined his bright head.

"Shortly, we will be rising to *Elthoria*. Is there aught on port that you require? Now is the time to acquire any such items, for we are scheduled to break orbit within the quarter-spin."

Breathless, Jethri shook his head, caught himself, and cleared his throat.

"I am grateful, but there is no need." He lifted the smaller bag somewhat. "Everything that I require is in these bags."

Golden eyebrows rose, but he merely moved a languid hand, directing Jethri's attention down the busy thoroughfare.

"Alas, I am not so fortunate and must fulfill several errands before we board. Do you continue along this way until you find Ixin's sign. Present yourself to the barge crew, and hold yourself at the pilot's word. I will join you ere it is time to lift."

So saying, he stepped off the curb into the thronging traffic, vanishing, to Jethri's eye, into the fast-moving crowd.

*Mud!* he thought, his heart picking up its rhythm, then, "Mud!" aloud as a hard elbow landed on his ribs with more force than was strictly necessary to make the point, while a sharp voice let out with a liquid string of Liaden, the tone of which unmistakably conveyed that this was no place for ox-brained Terrans to be napping.

Getting a tighter grip on his carry-bag, Jethri shrugged the backpack into an easier position and set off, slow, his head swiveling from one side to the next, like a clean 'bot on the lookout for lint, craning at the signs and sigils posted along both sides of the way.

It didn't do much to calm the crazy rhythm of his heart to note that *all* the signs hereabouts were in Liaden, with never a

Terran letter to be found; or that everyone he passed was short, golden-skinned, quick—Liaden.

Now that it was too late, he wondered if Master ven'Deelin's aide was having a joke on him. Or, worse, if this was some sort of Liaden test, the which of, failing, lost him his berth and grounded him. There was the horror, right there. *Grounded.* He was a spacer. All ports were strange; all crews other than his own, strangers. Teeth drilling into his bottom lip, Jethri lengthened his stride, heedless now of both elbows and rude shouts, eyes scanning the profusion of signage for the one that promised him clean space; refuge from weight, dirt, and smelly air.

At last, he caught it—half-a-block distant and across the wide street. Jethri pulled up a spurt of speed, forced his dust-covered, leaden body into a run and lumbered off the curb.

Horns, hoots and hollers marked his course across that street. He heeded none of it. The moon-and-rabbit was his goal and everything he had eye or thought for. By the time the autodoor gave way before him, he was mud-slicked, gasping and none-too-steady on his feet.

What he also was, was safe.

Half-sobbing, he brought his eyes up and had a second to revise that opinion. The three roustabouts facing him might be short, but they stood tall, hands on the utility knives thrust through wide leather belts, shirts and faces showing dust and the stains of working on the docks.

Jethri gulped and ducked his head. "Your pardon, gentles," he gasped in what he hoped they'd recognize for Liaden. "I am here for Master ven'Deelin."

The lead roustabout raised her eyebrows. "ven'Deelin?" she repeated, doubt palpable in her tone.

"If you please," Jethri said, trying to breathe deeply and make his words more than half-understandable gasps. "I am Jethri Gobelyn, the—the new apprentice trader."

She blinked, her face crumpling for an instant before she got herself in hand. The emotion she didn't show might have been anything, but Jethri had the strong impression that she would have laughed out loud, if politeness had allowed it.

The man at her right shoulder, who showed more gray than brown in his hair, turned his head and called out something light and fluid, while the man at her left shoulder stood forward, pulling his blade from its nestle in the belt and thoughtfully working the catch. Jethri swallowed and bent, very carefully, to put his carry-bag down.

Twice as careful, he straightened, showing empty palms to the three of them. This time, the woman did smile, pale as starlight, and put out a hand to shove her mate in the arm.

"It belongs to the master trader," she said in pidgin. "Will you be the one to rob her of sport?"

"Not I," said the man. But he didn't put the knife away, nor even turn his head at the clatter of boot heels or the sudden advent of a second Liaden woman, this one wearing the tough leather jacket of a pilot.

She came level with the boss roustabout and stopped, a crease between her eyebrows.

"Are we now a home for the indigent?" she snapped, and apparently to the room at large.

Jethri exerted himself, bowing as low as his shaking legs would allow.

"Pilot. If you please. I am Jethri Gobelyn, apprenticed to Master Trader Norn ven'Deelin. I arrive at the word of her aide, Pen Rel, who bade me hold myself at your word."

"Ah. Pen Rel." The pilot's face altered, and Jethri again had the distinct feeling that, had she been Terran, she would have been enjoying a fine laugh at his expense. "That would be Arms Master sig'Kethra, an individual to whom it would be wise to show the utmost respect." She moved a graceful hand, showing him the apparently blank wall to his left.

"You may place your luggage in the bay; it will be well cared for. After that, you may make yourself seemly, so that you do not shame Master sig'Kethra before the ven'Deelin." She looked over her shoulder at the third roustabout. "Show him."

"Pilot." He jerked his head at Jethri. "Attend, boy."

Seen close, the blank wall was indented with a series of unmarked squares. The roustabout held up an index finger, and lightly touched three in sequence. The wall parted along an all-but invisible seam, showing a holding space beyond, piled high with parcels and pallets. Jethri took a step forward, found his sleeve caught and froze, watching the wall slide shut again a bare inch beyond his nose.

When there was nothing left to indicate that the wall was anything other than a wall, the roustabout loosed Jethri's sleeve and jerked his chin at the indentations.

"You, now."

He had a good head for patterns—always had. It was the work of a moment to touch his index finger to the proper three indentations in order. The wall slid aside and this time he was not prevented from going forward into the holding bay and stacking his bags with the rest.

The door stayed open until he stepped back to the side of the roustabout, who jerked his head to the left and guided him to the 'fresher, where he was left to clean himself up as best he might, so Master ven'Deelin wouldn't take any second thoughts about the contract she'd made.

SOME WHILE LATER Jethri sat alone in the hallway next to the pilot's office, face washed, clothes brushed, and nursing a disposable cupful of a hot, strong, and vilely sweet beverage his guide had insisted was "tea."

At least it was cool in the hallway, and it was a bennie just to be done with walking about in grav, and carrying all his mortal possessions, too. Sighing, he sipped gingerly at the nasty stuff in the cup and tried to order himself.

It was clear that his spoken Liaden wasn't as close to tolerable as he had thought. He didn't fool himself that dock-pidgin and Trade was going to go far at the trading tables Norn ven'Deelin sat down to. Language lessons were needful, then; and a brush-up on the protocols of cargo. His math was solid—Seeli and Cris had seen to that. He could do OK here. Better than he'd have done on an ore ship running a dying Loop...

That thought brought him back to now and here. Damn straight Norn ven'Deelin didn't run no Loop.

He leaned back in the chair, considering what sorts of cargo might come to a ship bearing a master trader. Gems, he figured, and rare spice; textile like Cris would weep over; artworks... He considered that, frowning.

Art was a chancy venture, given differing planetary taboos and ground-hugger religions. Even a master trader might chart a careful course, there. Khat told a story—a true one, he thought—regarding the tradeship *Sweet Louise*, which had taken aboard an illustrated paper book of great age. The pictures had been pretty, the pages hand-sewn into a real leather cover set with flawed, gaudy stones. The words were in no language that any of *Louise's* crew could read, but the price had been right; and the trader had a line on a collector of uniquities two planets down on the trade-hop. Everything should have been top-drawer, excepting that the powers of religion on the planet between the collector and the book declared that item "blasphemous," meaning the port police had it off ship in seconds and burned it right there on the dock. *Louise* lost the investment, the price, the fine— and the right to trade on that port, which was no loss, as far as Jethri could see...

A light step at the top of the hall pulled him out of his thoughts; a glance and he was on his feet, bowing as low as he could without endangering the tea.

"Arms Master sig'Kethra."

The man checked, neither surprise on his face, nor parcels in his hands, and inclined his head. "Apprentice Trader. Well met. A moment, if you please, while I consult with the pilot."

He moved past, walking into the pilot's office with nary a ring, like he had every right to the place, which, Jethri thought, he very well might. The door slid shut behind him and Jethri resumed his seat, reconciled to another longish wait while business was discussed between pilot and arms master.

Say that Pen Rel was a man of few words. Or that the pilot was eager for flight. In either case, they were both coming out the door before Jethri had time to start another line of thought.

"We lift, Jethri Gobelyn," Pen Rel said. "Soon we will be home."

And that, at least, Jethri thought, rising with alacrity, was a proper spacer's sentiment. Enough of this slogging about in the dust—it was time and past time to return to the light, clean corridors of a ship.

# Day 42
## Standard Year 1118

## *Elthoria*
## Arriving

"IS THE WHOLE ship heavy, then?" he asked Pen Rel's back.

The Liaden glanced over his shoulder, then stopped and turned right around in the center of the ridiculously wide hallway, something that might actually have been puzzlement shadowing the edges of his face.

"Is the gravity worrisome, Jethri Gobelyn? I did note that you disliked the port, but I had assumed an aversion to…the noise, perhaps—or the dirt. I regret that it had not occurred to me that the ship of your kin might have run weightless."

Jethri shook his head. "Not weightless," he panted. "Just—light. The core—admin, you know—was near enough to heavy, but the rest of the ship ran light, and the rim was lightest of all." He drew a deep breath, caught by the sudden and awful realization that no one knew what the normal grav of the Liaden homeworld was. It could be that Ynsolt'i normal was light to them, and if the ship got heavier, the further in they—

Pen Rel moved his hand like he was smoothing wrinkles out of the air. "Peace, Jethri Gobelyn. Most of *Elthoria* runs at constant gravity. The areas that do not are unlikely to be of concern to one of your station. You will suffer no more than you do at this moment."

Jethri gaped at him. "Runs *constant*," he repeated, and shook his head. "How big is this ship?"

The Liaden moved his shoulders. "It is large enough. Doubt not that the master trader will provide a map—and require you to memorize it, as well."

Where he came from, holding the map of the ship and the location of bolt holes, grabs and emergency suits in your head was only commonsense. He shrugged, no where near as fluid as his companion. "Well sure she will. No problem with that."

"I am pleased to hear you say so," Pen Rel said, and turned about-face, moving briskly out down the hall. "Let us not keep the master trader waiting."

In fact, she kept them waiting, which Jethri could only see as a boon, for he used the time to catch his breath and surreptitiously stretch his sore muscles, so he wasn't blowing like a grampus when they were finally let in to see her.

Her office wasn't as big as admin entire—not quite. Nor was her workspace quite as wide as his private quarters on the *Market*. Screens were set above the desk, which was itself a confusion of lading slips, catalogs and the ephemera of trade—that much was familiar, so much so that he felt the tears rising to his eyes.

The master trader, she was familiar, too, with her gray hair and her snapping black eyes.

"So," she said, rising from her chair and coming forward. "It is well." She inclined her head and spoke to Pen Rel—a rapid burst of Liaden, smooth and musical. The arms master made brief reply, swept a bow to her honor, treated Jethri to a heavy tip of the head, and was gone, the door snapping behind him like a hungry mouth.

Black eyes surveyed him blandly. Belatedly, Jethri remembered his manners and bowed, low. "Master ven'Deelin. I report for duty, with joy."

"Hah." She tipped her head slightly to the right. "Well said, if briefly. Tell me, Jethri Gobelyn, how much will it distress you to find that your first duty is dry study?"

He shrugged, meeting her gaze for gaze. "Uncle Pai—Trader Gobelyn taught me that trade was study, ma'am. I wouldn't expect it otherwise."

"A man of excellent sense, Trader Gobelyn. My admiration of him knows no limit. Tell me, then, oh wise apprentice, what will you expect to study firstly? Say what is in your heart—I would know whether I must set you to gemstones, or precious metals, or fine vintage."

Had she been Terran, Jethri would have considered that she was teasing him. Liadens—none of his studies had led him to believe that Liadens held humor high. Honor was the thing, with Liadens. Honor and the exact balancing of any wrong.

"Well, ma'am," he said, careful as he was able. "I'm thinking that the first thing I'll be needing is language. I can read Liaden, but I'm slow—and my speaking is, I discover, nothing much better than poor."

"An honest scholar," Master ven'Deelin said after a moment, "and of something disheartened." She reached out and patted his sleeve. "Repine not, Jethri Gobelyn. That you read our language at all is to be noted. That you have made some attempt to capture the tongue as it is spoken must be shown for heroic." She paused.

"Understand me, it is not that we of the clans seek to hide our customs from those traders of variant ilk. Rather, we have not overindulged in future thinking, whereby it would have been immediately understood that steps of education must be taken." She moved her shoulders in that weird not-shrug, conveying something beyond Jethri's ken.

"Very nearly, the masters of trade have walked aside from their duty. Very nearly. You and I—we will repair this oversight of the masters and rescue honor for all. Eh?" She brought her palms together sharply.

"But, yes, firstly you must speak to be understood. You will be given tapes, and a tutor. You will be given the opportunity to Balance these gifts the ship bestows. There is one a-ship who wishes to possess the Terran tongue. Understand that her case is much as yours—she reads, but there is a lack of proficiency in the spoken form. She, you will tutor, as you are tutored. You understand me?"

So, he had something of worth that he could trade for his lessons and his keep. It was little enough, and no question the ship bore the heavier burden, but it cheered him to find that he would be put to use.

Smiling, he nodded; caught himself with a sharp sigh and bowed. "I understand you, ma'am. Yes."

"Hah." Her eyes gleamed. "It will be difficult, but the need is plain. Therefore, the difficult will be accomplished." She clapped her hands once more. "You will be a trader to behold, Jethri Gobelyn!"

He felt his ears warm, and bowed again. "Thank you, ma'am."

She tipped her head. "The tutor will attend likewise to the matter of bows. Continue in your present mode and you will be called to answer honor before ever we arrive at gemstones."

Jethri blinked. He had just assumed that, the deeper the bow the better, and that, as juniormost everywhere he walked, he could hardly go wrong bowing as low as he could without doing structural damage.

"I...hope that I haven't given offense, ma'am," he stammered, in Terran.

She waved a tiny hand, the big purple ring glittering. "Worry not," she answered, in her version of the same tongue. "You are fortunate in your happenstances. We of *Elthoria* are of a mode most kind hearted. To children and to Terrans, we forgive all. Others," she folded her hands together solemnly; "are less kindly than we."

Oh. He swallowed, thinking of Honored Buyer bin'Flora, and others of his uncle's contacts, on the Liaden side of the trade.

"There are those," Master ven'Deelin said softly, switching to Trade, "for whom the trade is all. There are others for whom...the worth of themselves is all. Are these things not likewise true of Terrans?"

Another flash of memory, then, of certain other traders known to him, and he nodded, though reluctantly. "Yes, ma'am. I'm afraid they are."

"No fear, Jethri Gobelyn. A man armored and proficient with his weapons need have no fear." A small hesitation, then—"But perhaps it is that you are wise in this. A man without weapons—it is best that he walk wary."

"Yes, ma'am," he said again, his voice sounding breathless in his own ears.

If Master ven'Deelin noted anything amiss, she didn't say so. Instead, she waved him over to her desk, where she pressed the promised ship's map upon him, pointing out the location of his quarters and of the ship's library, where he would find his study tapes and his tutor awaiting him at some hour that slid past his ear in an arpeggio of Liaden.

"I—" he began, but Master ven'Deelin had thought of that, too. From the riot of papers atop her desk, she produced a timepiece, and a schedule, printed out in Liaden characters.

"So, enough." She clapped her hands and made shooing motions toward the door. "This shift is your own. Next shift, you are wanted at your station. Myself, yourself, we will speak again together before the trade goes forward on Tilene. In the meanwhile, it is your duty to learn, quickly and well. The ship accepts only excellence."

Dismissed, clutching the papers and the watch untidily to his chest, he bowed, not without a certain feeling of danger, but Master ven'Deelin had turned back to her desk, her attention already on the minutiae of trade.

In the hall outside her office, he went down on a knee and took a few moments to order his paperwork, slap the watch 'round his wrist, and glance through the schedule. Running his finger down the table, being careful with the Liaden words, and checking his timepiece frequently, he established that the shift which was "his own" had just commenced. More searching in the schedule produced the information that "nuncheon" was on buffet in the galley.

Squinting at the map, he found that the galley was on the short route to his quarters, at which point his stomach commented rather pointedly that his breakfast of 'mite and crackers was used up and more.

One last squint at the map, and he was on his way.

THERE WERE MAYBE a dozen people in the galley when he swung in. They all stopped talking and turned to look at him, smooth Liaden faces blank of anything like a smile or any honest curiosity. Just...silence. And stares. Jethri swallowed, thinking that even a titter, or a "Look at the Terran!" might be welcome.

Nothing like it forthcoming, he walked over to the cool-table where various foods were laid out, and spent some while looking over the offerings, hoping for something familiar, while all the time he felt the eyes boring bland, silent holes into his back.

It got to him, finally, all that quiet, and the sense of them staring at him, so that he snatched up a plate holding something that looked enticingly like a pan-paste handwich and bolted for the door, map and schedule clutched under one arm.

His dash was two steps old when a dark-haired woman swung into his path, one hand held, palm out, and aiming for his chest.

He skidded to a halt, all but losing the papers, the handwich dancing dangerously on its plate, and stood there staring like a stupid Grounder, wondering what piece of politeness he had, all unknowing, shattered, and whether word had gotten out to the crew that they were more forgiving than most.

The woman before him said something, the sounds sliding past his ear, *almost* sounding like... He blinked and leaned slightly forward.

"Say again," he murmured. "Slowly."

She inclined her head, and said again, slowly, in Terran so thickly accented he could barely make out the words, though he was craning with all his ears: "Tea will be wanting you."

"Tea," he repeated, and smiled, from unadorned relief. "Thank you. Where is the tea?"

"Bottle," she said, waving a quick hand toward a second table, set at right angles to the first, lined with what looked to be single serving vacuum bottles. "Cold. Be for to drinking with works."

"I see. Thank you…" He frowned at the badge stitched onto her shirt…"First Officer Gaenor tel'Dorbit."

Eyebrows rose above velvet brown eyes, and she tipped her head, face noncommittal.

"Apprentice Terran, you?" She asked, and put her hand against her chest. "Terran student, I."

He nodded and smiled again. "I'm Master ven'Deelin's apprentice. I'll be helping you with your Terran. Here…" He fumbled the schedule out from beneath his arm and held it out, gripped precariously between two fingers, while the handwich jigged on its plate. "What's your shift? I've got—"

She slipped the paper from between his fingers, gave it a quick, all-encompassing glance, and ran a slim fingertip under a certain hour, showing him.

"Hour, this," she said, and waved briefly around the galley. "Here we meet."

"Right." He nodded again.

Gaenor tel'Dorbit inclined her head and left him, angling off to the left, where a table for three showed one empty chair and a half-eaten meal; the other two occupants considering him with silent blandness.

Jethri grabbed a tea bottle from the table and all but ran from the room.

Using the map, he found his assigned quarters handily, and stood for a long couple minutes, staring at his name, painted in Liaden letters on the door, before sliding his finger into the scanner.

The scan tingled, the door opened and he was through, staring at a cabin maybe three times the size of his quarters on the *Market*. The floor was covered in springy blue carpet, in the center of which sat his bags. The bed and desk were folded away, and he couldn't have said if it was the strangeness of it, or the sameness of it, but all at once he was crying in good earnest, the tears running fast and dripping off his chin.

Carefully, he put the handwich and the bottle on the floor next to his bags, then sat himself down next to them, taking care to put schedule and map well out of harm's way. That done, he folded up, head on knees, and bawled.

# Day 60
# Standard Year 1118

## *Gobelyn's Market*
## Approaching Kinaveral

KINAVERAL HUNG MIDDLING big in the central screen. Khat had filed her approach with Central, done her system checks and finally leaned back in the pilot's chair, exhaling with a will.

Cris looked up from the mate's board with a half-grin and a nod. "Two to six, Central will argue the path."

Khat laughed. "I look a fool, do I, coz? Of *course* Central will argue the path. I once had a fast-look at a Lane Controller's manual. First page, Lesson One, writ out in letters as high as my hand was, 'Always Dispute the Filed Approach'."

Cris' smile widened to a grin. "First lesson, you say? There was pages after that?"

"Some few," Khat allowed, straight-faced; "some few. Mind, the next six after was blank, so the student could practice writing out the rule."

"Well, it being so large and important a rule..." Cris began, before the intercom bell cut him short.

He spun back to his board and slapped the toggle. "Mate."

"First Mate," Iza Gobelyn's voice came out of the speaker, gritty with more than 'com buzz. "I'm looking for the approach stats."

"Captain," Cris said, even-voiced. "We're on the wait for Central's aye."

There was a short, sizzling pause.

"As soon as we're cleared, I'll have those stats," Iza snapped.

"Yes, Captain," Cris murmured, but he might just as easily said nothing; Iza had already signed off.

Cris sighed, sharp and exasperated. Khat echoed him, softer.

"I thought she'd lighten, once Jeth was gone," she said.

Cris shook his head, staring down at his board.

"It ain't Jethri being gone so much as Arin," he muttered. "She's gotten harder, every Standard since he died."

Khat thought about that, staring at Kinaveral, hanging in the center screen. "There's a lot more years ahead, and Arin in none of them," she said, eventually.

Cris didn't answer that—or, say, he answered by not answering, which was Cris' way.

Instead, he said, "I got a reply on that franchise job. They want me to stop by their office, dirtside, take the test. If that's a go, it'll mean a temp berth for the next ten months, Standard."

Khat nodded, her eyes still on Kinaveral. "Paitor figures to pick up some training or consulting at Terratrade," she said. "Me, I'll file with Central as a freewing."

"Sensible. The rest sticking to dirt?"

She laughed. "Now, how likely is that? Might take a few port cycles til they get tired of breathing dust, but you know they'll be looking for space work, too."

"Huh," Cris said, fiddling with a setting on his board. "Iza?"

Khat shrugged. "Way I heard it, she was staying dirtside, with the *Market*." She held up a hand. "Paitor did try to talk her out of it. Pointed out that Seeli's able. Iza wasn't having any. She's the captain, the job's hers, and by all the ghosts of space, she'll do it."

"Huh," Cris said again—and seemed on the edge of saying something more when the comm screen came live with Central's request that *Gobelyn's Market* amend her filed approach.

# Day 63
# Standard Year 1118

## *Elthoria*

*ELTHORIA* KEPT A twenty-eight hour "day," divided into
four shifts, two on, two off, which made for a slightly longer
work day than the *Market's* twenty-four hour, two-shift cycle.
Jethri, who had been used to reading and studying well into his
off-shift, scarcely noticed the additional hours.

His work now—that was different. No more Stinks. If
*Elthoria* had Stinks, which Jethri took leave to doubt, it was
nothing mentioned to him by his new acquaintances, though
they were careful to show him as much of the ship as an apprentice trader might need to know. His new status meant no
more assisting in the galley, a duty he might've missed, if there'd
been any time for it, which there wasn't, his time being entirely and systematically crammed full with lessons, study and
more lessons.

Some things were routine, and it eased him somehow to
find that *Elthoria* kept emergency protocols—in which he was
relentlessly trained by no lesser person than Arms Master
sig'Kethra. Over the course of three shifts, he was drilled in
the location and operation of the lifeboats, shown the various
boltholes, emergency hatches and hand-grabs. He was also
measured for a suit, it being discovered to the chagrin of the
supply master that none of those on draw would fit.

Other things, they weren't so routine—more of that, which
is what he'd figured to find. For instance, he had a trade locker
all to himself, which was scrupulously the same size as his

stateroom, it being the policy on *Elthoria* that traders should
have as much room to work in as they had to sleep in. He
wished he'd thought to convert some of his cash to something
useful out of the *Market*—but he hadn't had much time to cry
about that missed opportunity, either.

First thing on shift, right after breakfast, he sat with the
tutor-tapes in the ship's library, brushing up on his written and
spoken Liaden. Then, he met with Protocol Officer Ray Jon
tel'Ondor, which was more language lessons, putting dry learning into practical use. Master tel'Ondor was also of an ambition to teach Jethri his bows, though he made no secret of the
fact that Jethri was the least apt pupil he had encountered in
long years of tutoring arrogant young traders in protocol.

After Master tel'Ondor, there was exercise—a mandated
ship's hour every day at the weights and the treadmills, then a
shower, a meal, and more reading, this on the subjects of trade
guild rules and custom regs. After that, there was the Terran-
tutoring with Gaenor tel'Dorbit. The first mate being of a
restless habit, that meant more exercise, as they walked the
long hallways of *Elthoria*. Despite the extra walking, Jethri
quickly came to look forward to this part of his duty-day.
Gaenor was younger than Master ven'Deelin and Pen Rel, and
she smiled nicely from time to time in her lessons, which Jethri
particularly liked.

Gaenor's idea of being tutored was to just start talking—
about the events of the previous shift, her family's home in a
dirt-based city called Chonselta, the latest book she was reading, or the ship's itinerary. Jethri's responsibility was to stop
her when she misspoke, and say the words over in the right
order and pronunciation. So it was that he became informed
of ship's policy, gossip and ports o'call, as well as the names
of certain flowers which Gaenor particularly missed from home.

The first mate having access to just about every portion of
the ship, Jethri also found himself informed of various lockers
and pod connections, and was introduced to each of the ship's
company as they were encountered during the ramble. Some

of the crew seemed not so pleased to see him, some seemed...puzzled. Most seemed not to care much, one way or the other. All were grave and polite, like they oughta be, Jethri thought, with the first mate looking on. Still, he thought that these catch-as-can introductions at the mate's side...helped. Helped him put names and faces and responsibilities together. Helped them to see he really was part of the crew, pulling his weight, just like they were.

One person who seemed outright happy to welcome him was Vil Tor, ship's librarian. As it happened that Vil Tor also had an ambition to add Terran to his speakables, Gaenor and Jethri had taken to including the library as a regular stop. This time out, though, they'd found the door locked, lights out. Gaenor sighed, slim shoulders dropping for a moment, then turned and started back down the hall, swinging out with a will.

"This our ship, *Elthoria*," Gaenor said, as they hit the end of the hall and swept left, toward Hydroponics; "will be in-putting to Spacestation Kailipso..."

"Putting in," Jethri panted. "*Elthoria* will be putting in to Kailipso Station."

"Hah." Gaenor flicked a glance his way; *she* wasn't even breathing hard. "*Elthoria*," she repeated, slowing her pace by a fraction, "will be putting in to Spacestation Kailipso—bah!— *Kailipso Station*—putting in to Kailipso Station within three ship days. There is a—a..." She stopped entirely and turned to face Jethri, holding two hands up, palm out, signifying she had not the necessary Terran words to hand.

"It is to have a meeting of the masters, on subjects interested in the masters..."

The immediate phrase that came to mind was "jaw-fest," which Jethri thought might not be the sort of Terran Master ven'Deelin wanted Gaenor to be learning. He frowned after the polite and after a moment was able to offer, "a symposium."

"Sim-po-zium," Gaenor said, her mouth pinching up like the word tasted bad. "So, there is a *sim-po-zium* upon Kailipso.

The ven'Deelin attends—the ven'Deelin *will attend*. The crew will be at leave." She moved her shoulders, not quite a Terran shrug, but not quite admiring of Kailipso Station, all the same.

"Don't like Kailipso much?" he ventured, and Gaenor's mouth pinched again before she turned and recommenced marching down the hall.

"It is cold," she said to the empty corridor, and then began to tell him of the latest developments in the novel she was reading. He had to catch up, hoping that she put his delay down to his being somewhat less fit, and not his taking a moment to admire her walk.

# Day 65
# Standard Year 1118

## Kinaveral

BEFORE THEY CLEARED a freewing to fly, Kinaveral
Central wanted to be assured that the candidate could find her
way through a form or six. That done, there were the sims to
fly, then a chat with the stable boss, at the end of which a time
was named on the morrow when the candidate was to return
and actually lift one of Central's precious ships—and an observer—for the final and most telling part of the test.

In between now and then, Khat knew, they'd be checking
her number and her ship, and verifying her personals. She'd
hoped to have the test lift today, but, there, the stable boss
needed to know if the applicant freewing tended toward sober
in the morning.

No problem for the applicant on that approach, Khat
thought, walking down the dusty, noisy main street. Not
to say that a brew would be unwelcome at the moment.
Make that a brew and a handwich, she amended, as her
stomach filed notice that the 'mite and crackers she'd fed
it for breakfast were long past gone.

Up ahead, she spied the flashing green triangle which
was the sign of an eat-and-drinkery, and stretched her legs,
grimacing at the protest of overworked muscles. *That'll
teach you to stint your weight exercise,* she scolded herself, and
turned into the cool, comfortably dim doorway.

A lightscape over the counter showed a old style fin-
ship down on a flat plain, mountains marking the horizon.

Beneath, a tag box spelled out the name of the joint: *Ship 'n Shore*.

There was a scattering of folk at the tables—spacers, mostly—and plenty of room at the counter. It being only herself, Khat swung up onto a stool 'neath the tag box and waved at the barkeep.

"Dark brew and a handwich for a woman in need!"

The keeper grinned, drew the beer and sat it on the counter by her hand. "There's the easy part," he said. "What's your fondness for food? We got local cheese and vegs on fresh bake bread; potmeat on the same; 'mite paste and pickles; side o' fish—"

Khat leveled a finger. "Local cheese without the vegs?"

"We can do it," he promised.

"That's a deal, then. Bring her on."

"Be a sec. Let me know how you find the beer." He moved down counter, still grinning, and Khat picked up the mug.

The beer was cold, which was how she liked it. Bitter, too, and thick. She'd brought the mug down to half-full by the time her handwich arrived, two generous halves sharing a plastic plate with a fistful of saltpretzel.

"Brew's good," Khat said. "I'll want another just like it in not too long."

The keeper smiled, pleased, and put a couple disposable napkins next to the plate. "Just give a yell when you're ready," he said.

She nodded and picked up one of the halves. The unmistakable smell of fresh-baked bread hit her nose and her stomach started clamoring. For the next while, she concentrated on settling that issue. The bread was whole grain, brown and nutty; the cheese butter smooth and unexpectedly spicy. Khat finished the first half and the brew, waved the empty mug at the barkeep and started in on the second round.

Couple times, folk from the tables came up to the counter for refills. A crew of three came in from the street and staked out stools at the end of the row. Khat paid none of them particular notice, except to register that they were spacers, and nobody she knew.

At last, the final saltpretzel was gone. Khat pushed the plate away with a regretful sigh and reached for her mug. A couple more sips, settle her bill and then back to the lodgings, she thought, with a sinking in her well-full stomach. Wasn't nothing wrong with the lodgings, mind, except that they was full-grav lodgings, and dirtside, and subject to the rules of the lodge-owner. But still, *Market's* crew had a section to themselves, inside which each had their own cubby, with cot and desk and entertainment bar. No complaints.

Excepting that Captain Iza was nothing but complaints—well, she hated dirt, always had; and didn't have much of a fondness for worldsiders. Without the routine of her ship, she stood at sevens and eights and spent 'way too much of her time down to the yards, doubtless making life a hell for the crew boss assigned to *Market's* refit.

Zam had suggested the captain might file as freewing with Central, for which insubordination he had his head handed to him. Seeli'd come by no gentler treatment when she spoke to her mother, and Dyk declined even to try. Paitor had his own quarters at Terratrade, and when the temp slot went solid on Cris their second day a-ground, he all but ran to the space field.

Which left them a mixed bag—and bad tempered, too, held uneasy by Iza's moods.

And the year was barely begun.

Khat sighed again, and finished off her brew. She put the mug down and waved at the keeper for the bill. He, up-counter with the crew of three, held up two fingers—*be there in a few.* She nodded, shifted on the stool…

"Hey, Khati," an unwelcome voice came from too near at hand.

"Shit," Khat muttered beneath her breath and spun the stool around to face Mac Gold.

He hadn't changed much since the last time she'd seen him—some taller, maybe, and a little broader in the shoulders. Khat nodded, curt.

"Mac."

He grinned, and ran a hand over his head. His hair was pale yellow; buzzed, it was nearly invisible, which his eyelashes were. Behind those invisible lashes, his eyes were a deep and unlikely blue, the rest of his face square and bony. A well enough looking boy, taken all together. If he hadn't also happened to've been Mac Gold.

"Good to see you," he said, now, deliberately aiming those unlikely eyes at her chest. "Buy you a brew?"

She shook her head, teeth gritting. "Just on my way. Next time, maybe."

"Right," he said, but he didn't move, other than to cock his head. "Listen, while we're face to face—square with me?"

She shrugged. "Maybe."

"I'm just wondering—what happened to Jethri? I mean, what *really* happened to Jethri?"

"He's 'prenticed to the trader of a big ship," she said. "Cap'n Iza must've told your dad so."

"She did," Mac agreed, "and I'm sharing no secrets when I tell you my dad was some pissed about the whole business. I mean, here's Iza asking us to make room for your extra, and m'dad willing to accommodate, and what happens but then she says, no, the boy ain't coming after all. He's gone someplace else." Mac shook his head and held up a hand, thumb and forefinger a whisper apart.

"Dad was *this close* to calling breach."

Khat sighed. "Breach of what? The legal wasn't writ."

"Still, there'd be the verbal—"

"Deals fall through every day," Khat interrupted and caught sight of the barkeep out of the corner of her eye. She turned on the stool and smiled at him.

Behind her, Mac, raised his voice conspicuously—

"Rumor is, Khat, that Paitor sold the boy to Liadens!"

That drew starts and stares from those close enough to hear; some turned carefully away but others lifted eyebrows and raised their heads to watch.

Deliberately, Khat turned, away from the barkeep and back to Mac Gold. Deliberately, she drew a deep breath, and glared straight into those blue eyes.

"The *boy* holds a Combine key. He's as legal as you or me. He's a 'prentice trader—signed his own papers. Jethri ain't no *boy.*"

"Well, rumor is that Liadens paid for this upgrade the *Market's* gettin'."

Khat laughed and rolled her eyes.

"Least now Mr. Rumor's got it right. Jethri sold a load of cellosilk back at Ynsolt'i, and on top of that, Paitor bought some special risk merchandise Jethri'd pointed out—an' didn't *that* turn into high-count coin in the private hall—just like Jethri said it would! So, sure, Liadens bought this upgrade all right—cans, nodes, and engines."

"But someone got shot, they say, and next thing—"

Khat sighed, loud and exasperated.

"Look, Jethri was ready to trade, Mac, and captain told him if he wanted something more than pushing gravel from here to there, he'd have to find his own ship. Can't fault him for that call. So he found himself a better berth, 'prenticed to nothing less than a master trader, and for a good-bye, he buys us new drives and a full upgrade."

She paused, hearing a slight thump of glass behind her and raised her hand, fingers wriggling *just sec.*

"Jethri's got him a berth, Mac. Papers're signed proper and legal. *His* business—not mine, not yours. That other stuff Mr. Rumor been tellin' you—nobody got shot but some fool who decided it was easier to die than clear an honest debt. Not your problem." She tipped her head, like she was considering that, and asked, sweetly, "Or is it?"

Mac's eyes tightened and his face reddened.

"It sure is my problem if the word gets out Jethri'd rather crew with a bunch of Liadens than come with an honest ship like—"

"You better watch your mouth, Mac Gold," Khat snapped. "Lest somebody here figures you was gonna say something about how *Gold Digger's* honest and Jethri's ship ain't. Not the kind of thing you'd be wanting to discuss with a Liaden, now, is it?"

Mac blinked, and swallowed hard. Point won, Khat turned back to the bartender, raised her eyes briefly and expressively at the ceiling, and smiled.

"What's the damage?"

He smiled back. "Two bit."

"Done." She slid four across the counter and dropped to her feet, leg muscles sending up a shout for their team leader. She ignored them. The walk back to the lodgings would work the kinks out. Or cripple her for life.

"So, Khat—" Mac said from beside her.

"So, Mac," she overrode, and turned sharp, feeling a dangerous tingle along the brawlin' nerves when he went back a step. She kept going, and he kept backin', until she got the throttle on it and stopped.

Mac's pretty blue eyes was showing some red, and his face was damp. Khat gave one more hard glare, before she nodded, kinda half-civil.

"See you 'round port," she said, and forced her aching legs to swing out, carrying her down the room and out in the dusty day.

# Day 66
# Standard Year 1118

## Kailipso Station
## At Leave

"COME, COME, YOUNG Jethri, tarry not!" Pen Rel's voice was brisk, as he waved Jethri ahead of him into the entry tube. "All the wonders of Kailipso Station await your discovery! Surely, your enthusiasm and spirit of adventure are aroused!"

Had it been Dyk behind him in the chute, Jethri would have counted both his legs yanked proper, and been alert for second stage mischief. He thought Pen Rel too dignified for Dyk's sort of rough-'n-tumble; he was less sure of his tendencies on the leg-pulling side of things.

Jethri felt the odd twitter of the grav field where it intersected the station's own grav-well; though flat and level to the eyes the deck felt as if it fell away into the chute. Maybe Pen Rel was watching for a bobble, but such boundaries were learned by shipcrew at the knees of their mates and family.

The airflow, that was a surprise—definitely a positive, cool flow *toward* the ship—No, Jethri discovered, after a moment's study; the tube itself had a circulation system, and he could see the filters set flush to the walls. He gave a quiet sigh of relief for this homey precaution—all long-spacers did their most to keep station, port, or planet air *out* in favor of proper controlled and cleaned ship air.

Curiosity satisfied, Jethri stepped forward—and then stepped back, his hand going up, fingers shaping the hand-talk for "hold."

Two Liadens were coming up the slanted ramp at a pace that made Jethri's chest ache in sympathy. One—by far the pudgiest Liaden Jethri had seen so far—was carrying a full duffle; his slimmer companion clutched what looked to be a general business comp to his chest. They were in earnest conversation, heads turned aside and eyes only for each other.

"What is—" Pen Rel began, but by then the duo was on the flat and heading full throttle out, never realizing that they was anything but alone.

"'ware the deck!" Jethri snapped.

It had the desired effect, whether either of them had understood the Terran words. Both slammed to a graceless halt. The man with the comp raised it a fraction, as if to ward Jethri away.

Pen Rel stepped forward, claiming attention with a flicker of a hand, and a slight inclination of the head.

"Ah, Storemaster," he murmured, and Jethri thought he heard a bare thread of...disapproval in the bland, dry voice. "You are somewhat before time, I believe."

The man with the comp bowed. "Arms Master. I am instructed to supply crew with specialty baking experience, and I have here such a one. It remains to be found that he can operate *Elthoria's* ovens and bread vats. So we arrive, for a testing."

Pen Rel looked to the second man.

"Have you shipboard experience?"

The pudgy guy bowed lower than Jethri would have thought possible with the duffle over his shoulder, and straightened to show a wide eyed, slightly damp face. "Three voyages, Honored. The Storemaster has my files..."

"Very good." Pen Rel was back with the Storemaster. "Next time, you will come at the mate's appointed hour, eh? This time, you have interfered in ship's business."

The applicant cook's round eyes got rounder; the Storemaster pursed his mouth up. Both bowed themselves out of the way, even sparing brief nods for the unexpected Terran in their midst.

"So," Pen Rel said, catching Jethri's eye. He moved a hand toward the ramp. "After you, young Jethri."

AT THE BOTTOM of the chute was the inevitable uniformed station ape, card-reader to hand.

Jethri handed over his shiny new shipcard. The inspector took it, glanced at it—and paused, eyes lifting to his face.

"*Elthoria* signs Terran crew," she stated—or maybe she was asking. Jethri ducked his head, wondering if she expected an answer and what, exactly, would be seen as discourteous behavior in a Terran, here on an all-Liaden station. That he was an anomaly was clear from the pair they'd surprised coming on-ship. *But, then,* he said to himself, *you expected you were going to be an oddity. Best get used to it.*

"Must the ship clear its roster with the station?" Pen Rel asked from behind him, in Trade. "Do you find the card questionable?"

The inspector's mouth tightened. She swiped the card sharply through the reader, displaying bit of temper, or so Jethri thought, and stood holding it in her hand until the unit beeped and the tiny screen flashed blue.

"Verified and valid," she said, and held the card out, still something pettish.

Jethri grabbed it and slid it away into his belt. "Thank you, Inspector," he said politely.

She ignored him, holding out a hand to Pen Rel.

Bland-faced, he put his card in her palm, and watched as she swiped it and handed it back. The unit beeped and the screen flashed.

"Verified and valid," she said, and stepped back, obviously expecting them to go on about their business.

Pen Rel stayed where he was, waiting, bland and patient, until she looked up.

"A point of information," he said, still sticking with Trade. "*Elthoria* does not hold her crew lightly."

It was said mild enough, but the inspector froze, her face losing a little of that rich golden color. Jethri counted to five before she bent in a bow and murmured, "Of course, Arms Master. No disrespect to *Elthoria* or to her crew was intended."

"That is well, then," Pen Rel said, mildness itself. He moved a hand in a easy forward motion. "Young sir, the delights of the station are before you."

As hints went, it wasn't near subtle, but apparently Pen Rel was still making his point, because the inspector looked up into his face and inclined her head.

"Young trader, may you enjoy a profitable and pleasurable stay on Kailipso Station."

Right. He inclined his head in turn, murmured his very best, all-Liaden, "My thanks," and quick-stepped down the dock toward the bay door.

On the other side of the door, he pulled up. Pen Rel stepped through, and Jethri fell in beside him. The Liaden checked.

"Forgive me, Jethri," he said. "What do you do?"

Jethri blinked. "I thought I was partnered with you."

"Ah." Pen Rel tipped his head to a side. "Understand that I find your companionship all that is delightful. However, I have errands on the day which are…of no concern to one of your station. The master trader's word was that you be put at liberty to enjoy those things which Kailipso offers." He moved a hand in the all-too-familiar shooing gesture.

"So, enjoy. You are wanted back on board at seventh hour. I need not remind you to comport yourself so as to bring honor to your ship. And now," he swept a slight, loose-limbed half-bow; "I leave you to your pleasure, while I pursue my duties."

And he turned and walked off, just like that, leaving the juniormost and most idiot of his crew standing staring after, jaw hanging at half-mast.

Pen Rel had gone half the length of the corridor and turned right down a side way before Jethri shook himself into order and started walking, trying to accommodate himself to the fact that he was alone and at liberty on a Liaden owned and operated spacestation, where the official staff had already demonstrated a tendency to consider him a general issue nuisance. He shook his head, not liking the notion near so well as he should have done.

He did get to thinking, as he walked, that Master ven'Deelin surely knew what Kailipso was—just as surely as Pen Rel did. And certainly neither of those canny old hands was likely to turn him loose in halls where he might find active danger.

He hoped.

An overhead sign at the junction of halls where Pen Rel had vanished offered him routes, straight on to Main Concourse, right hall to Station Administration, and left hall to Mercantile Station. Working on the theory that there would be information booths in the Main Concourse, Jethri went straight on.

INFOBOOTHS WERE THE least of the wonders offered by the Main Concourse and its affiliated sections. He explored Market Square first, finding it not a trading center, as he had expected, but a retail shop zone offering goods at exorbitant mark-ups.

Nonetheless, he browsed, comparing prices shop to shop, and against his best guess of trade-side cost. Some of the items offered for sale were, by his admittedly unscientific calculation, marked up as much as six hundred percent over trade. He took a bit of a shock, for he saw in one window a timepiece identical to the one Norn ven'Deelin had casually given him—and found its price at three kais. 'Course, a master trader wasn't going to ever pay shop-price, but—He glanced down and took a second to make sure the slap strap was secure around his wrist.

Kailipso being a station, there were special considerations. Stations were dependent on outside supply; if one *needed* what was here it was very much a seller's market.

That got him to wondering just how much this particular station *was* dependent on outside supply, so he hunted up another booth and got directions to Education Square. Of course, it was opposite the Market, which meant a long walk back the way he'd come and through the Concourse, but he didn't grudge it. Station lived a thought lighter than *Elthoria*, so he fairly skipped along.

Education was almost useless. The tapes offered for rent were every one narrated in Liaden. He was about to give up when his eye snagged on a half-sized shop, sort of crammed in sideways to the hall, in a space between a utility bay and a recycling chamber.

The small opening spilled yellow light out into the hall-way, and a table was sitting almost into the common area, holding the fabulous luxury of six bound books. Behind them was a hand-written sign, stating that all sales were final, cash only.

Jethri moved forward, picked up the topmost book with reverence, and carefully thumbed the pages.

Paper rustled, and a subtle smell wafted up. He allowed the book to fall open in his hands and found the Liaden words almost absurdly easy to read as he was at once captivated by an account of one Shan el'Thrassin, who was engaged in a matter of honor with a set of folk who seemed something less than honorable.

"May I assist you, young sir?" The voice was soft, male, slightly hesitant in Trade. Jethri started, ears warming, closing the book with a snap.

"I apologize," he said. "I was looking for information about the history, economics and structure of the station. I am look-ing to fill some hours while visiting…. This…" Carefully, he bent and placed the volume he had been reading back in its place on the table. He experienced a genuine pang as the book left his hand.

"…I cannot possibly afford this. If I have offended by using it without pay…"

The man moved a hand, slowly, formally. "Books are meant to be read, young sir. You honor them—and me—with your interest. However, you intrigue me, for is not the entire square full with sight and sound recordings of the awesome past and glorious  present of our station?"

Jethri ducked his head. "Sir, it is. However—while I read the written form, my tongue and ear run far behind my eyes."

"Hah." The man's eyes gleamed. "You are, in fact, a scholar. It is nothing less than my duty to assist you. Come. I believe I have just what you are wanting."

As it happened, he did: A thin paper book simply entitled *Guide To Kailipso Station.*

"It is slight, but well enough to satisfy the first level of questions and engage the mind upon the second level," the shopkeeper said easily. "It will, I think, serve you well. Though used, it is new enough that the information is reasonably dependable. "

"I thank you," Jethri said. "However, again, I fear that my coins may be too few." And of the wrong sort, he thought suddenly, with a sinking feeling in his stomach. He was wearing his trading coat, but what he had in his public pocket was Terran bits and his fractin. He'd clean forgotten to stop at ship's bank to pull money out of his account in proper tor and kais...

The man looked up at him. "Do you know, young sir, I believe we are in Balance. It is seldom enough that one sees a Terran. It is rarer to see a Terran unaccompanied and unhurried. To meet and have converse with a Terran who reads Liaden—even the gods must own themselves privileged in such an encounter." He smiled, slight and gentle.

"Have the book, child. Your need is greater than mine."

Jethri bit his lip. "Sir, I thank you, but—I request an elder's advice. How should a young and inexperienced person such as myself Balance so generous a gift from a stranger?"

For a moment, he thought he'd gone well beyond bounds, though by all he knew there ought to be no offense given in asking for a clue to proper behavior. But the man before him was so still—

The shopkeeper bowed, lightly, right hand over belt-buckle. "There is," he said, straightening to his full, diminutive height, "a...protocol for such things. The proper Balance for the receipt of a gift freely given is to use it wisely and with honor, so that the giver is neither shamed nor regretful of his generosity."

Oh. Feeling an idiot, Jethri bowed, low enough to convey his thanks. He hoped. "I am grateful for the information, sir. My thanks."

The man waved a dismissive hand. "Surely, it is the duty of elder to instruct the young." Once again, he smiled his slight smile. "Enjoy your holiday, child."

"Thank you, sir," Jethri murmured, and bowed again, figuring that it was better to err on the side of too many than not enough, and moved out of the shop, trying not to let his eyes wander to those shelves full of treasure.

HE FOUND A vacant bench in the main square and quickly became absorbed in the guidebook. From it, he learned that Kailipso Station had come into being as a way station for cargo and for galactic travelers. Unfortunately, it very shortly became a refugee camp for those who managed to escape the catastrophic climatic upsets of a colony world called Daethiria. While many of the homeless colonists returned to the established Liaden worlds from which they had emigrated, a not inconsiderable number chose to remain on Kailipso Station rather than return to the conditions which had forced them away in the first place.

Kailipso Admin, realizing that it would need to expand quarters to support increased population, got clever—or desperate—or both—and went wooing the big Liaden Guilds, like the Traders and the Pilots, and got them to go in for sector offices on Kailipso.

Where most ports and stations would automate scut-work, Kailipso used people wherever possible, since they had people—and they not only got by, but they thrived.

So, Kailipso expanded, and soon enough became a destination all its own. Like any other station, it was vulnerable to attack, and dependent on imports for luxury items and planet-bred food.  If it had to be, though, it was self-suffi-cient.  On-station yeast vats produced enough boring, wholesome nutrition to feed Kailipso's denizens.  Off-sta-tion, there were farm pods—fish, fruits and vegetables—which made for tastier eating in sufficient quantities to keep those same denizens in luxury if they could so afford.

Kailipso also offered recreation.  There was a power-sled track, swimming facilities, climbing walls to challenge a num-ber of skill levels, and more than two dozen arenas for sports Jethri had never heard of.

The guide book also provided a list of unsafe zones, ac-companied by a cutaway station map with each danger out-lined in bright green.  Most were construction sites, and a few out-ring halls that dead-ended into what looked to be emergency chutes, marked out as *Danger: Low Gravity Zones.*

He likewise learned from the guide book that the Kailipso Trade Bar was in the Mercantile Zone, and that it was open to all with a valid license of trade or a tradeship crew card.  There, at least, he could directly debit his ac-count on ship, and get himself some walking-around money.  A brew and a looksee at the ship-board wouldn't be amiss, either.

So thinking, he came to his feet and slipped the book away into a leg-pocket.  He took a second to stretch, luxu-riating in the lower grav, then headed off at a mild lope, bound for the Mercantile Zone.

HE RAN HIS card through the reader; the screen flashed blue, and the door to the Trade Bar swung open before him.

*Valid and verified,* he thought, grinning, and then remem-bered to put on his trading face—polite, non-committal, and supposedly unreadable; it wasn't much, set against your usual Liaden's ungiving mask.  Still, grinning out loud in a place crammed with folks who just didn't couldn't be polite.  And polite was all he had.

What hit him first were the similarities to the Terran Trade
Bars he'd been in with Uncle Paitor or Cris or Dyk. The high-
info screens were set well up on one wall, showing list after
list: ships in dock; traders on duty; goods at offer, stationside;
goods at offer, dockside; goods sought. The exchange rates
were missing, which made him blink until he realized that
everybody on this station was buying in cantra and kais.

The milling of bodies seemingly at random around the
various stations—that was familiar too—and even the
sound—lots of voices, talking at once, maybe a little louder
than needful.

But then the differences—damn near everybody was shorter
than him, dressed in bright colors, and soft leather boots. Jewelry gleamed on ears, hands, throats. Not a few wore a weapon,
holstered, on their belts. For the most, they walked flat, like
born mud-grubbers, and not like honest spacers at all. And
the slightly too loud voices were saying things in a quick,
liquid language which his ear couldn't begin to sort.

He found himself a corner where two booths abutted,
and settled back out of the general press to study the
screens. Stationside goods at offer tended toward art stuffs
and information—reasonable. The longest list by far,
though, was for indenture—folks looking to buy their way
off-station, maybe all the way back to Liad, by selling out
years of their lives. By Jethri's count, there were forty-
eight contracts offered, from sixteen years to thirty-four,
from general labor to fine craftsperson.

"Well, what do we find ourselves here?" a woman's voice
asked, too close and too loud, her Trade almost unintelligible.
"I do believe it's a Terran, Vil Jon."

Jethri moved, but she was blocking his exit, and the man
moving up at her hail was going to box him in proper.

"A Terran?" the man—Vil Jon—repeated. "Now what
would a Terran be doing in the Trade Bar?" He looked up into
Jethri's face, eyes hard and blue. "Well, Terran? Who let you
in here?"

Jethri met his eyes, trying with everything in him to keep his face smooth, polite and non-committal.

"The door let me in, sir. My ship card was accepted by the reader."

"It has a card," the woman said, as if the man hadn't heard. "Now, what ship in dock keeps tame Terrans."

The man glanced over his shoulder at the boards. "There's *Intovish*, from Vanthachal. They keep some odd customs, local." He looked back at Jethri. "What ship, Terran?"

He considered it. After all, his ship was no secret. On Terran ground, asking for someone's ship was a common courtesy. From these two, though, it seemed a threat—or a challenge in a game he had no hope of understanding.

"*Elthoria*," he said, soft and polite as he knew how. "Sir."

"*Elthoria?*" The woman exchanged a long glance with her mate, who moved his shoulders, pensive-like.

"Could be it's bound for Solcintra Zoo," he said.

"Could be it's gotten hold of a card it shouldn't have," the woman returned, sharply. She held out her hand. "Come, Terran. Let us see your ship card."

And that, Jethri thought, was that. He was threatened, cornered and outnumbered, but he was damned if he was going to meekly hand his card over to this pair of port hustlers.

"No, ma'am," he said, and jumped forward.

The grav was light—he jumped a fair distance, knocking the woman aside as gentle as he could, out of reach before the man thought to try and grab him.

Having once jumped, Jethri stayed in motion, moving quick through the crowded room. He met a few startled glances, but took care not to jostle anybody, and very soon gained the door. It was, he thought, time to get back to his ship.

THEY KNEW THE station better than him—of course they did. They turned him back, hall by hall, crowding him toward the Concourse, cutting him off from the docks and his ship.

In desperation, he went down three floors, hit the hall beyond the lift doors running and had broken for the outer ring before he heard them behind him, calling "Terran, Terran! You cannot elude us, Terran!"

That might be so, Jethri thought, laboring hard now, light grav or not. He had a plan in his mind, though, and if this was the hall as he remembered it from the guide book's map of danger zones...

He flashed past a blue sign, the Liaden letters going by too fast for his eye to catch, but he recognized the symbol from the map, and began to think that this might work.

The hall took a hard left, like he remembered it from the map, and there was the emergency tunnel at end of it, gaping black and cold.

"Terran!" The woman's voice was suddenly shrill. "Wait! We will not hurt you!"

*Right*, Jethri thought, the tunnel one long stride away. He hit it running, felt the twist inside his ear that meant he had gone from one gravitational state to another —

He jumped.

Somewhere behind him, a woman screamed. Jethri fell, slow-motion, saw a safety pole, slapped it and changed trajectory, shooting under the lip of the floor above, anchoring himself with a foot hooked 'neath a beam.

The woman was talking in Liaden now, still shrill and way too loud. The man answered sharply, and then shouted out, in pidgin, "Terran! Where are you?"

Like he was going to answer. Jethri concentrated on breathing slow and quiet.

They didn't wait all that long; he heard the sound of their footsteps, walking fast, then the sound of the lift doors working.

After that, he didn't hear anything else.

He made himself sit there for a full twenty-eighth by the Liaden timepiece on his wrist, then eased out of hiding. A quick kick against the side of the chute sent him angling upward. He caught the edge of the floor as he shot past and did a back flip into the tunnel. He snatched a ring, righted himself, and skated for the hall.

A Liaden man in a black leather jacket was leaning against the wall opposite the tunnel.

Jethri froze.

The Liaden nodded easily, almost Terran-like.

"Well done," he said, and it was ground-based Terran he was talking, but Terran all the same. "I commend you upon a well-thought-out and competently executed maneuver."

"Thanks." Jethri said, thinking he could scramble, go over the edge again, make for the next level up, or down...

The Liaden held up a hand, palm out. "Acquit me of any intent to harm you. Indeed, it is concern for your welfare which finds me here, in a cold hallway at the far edge of nowhere, when I am promised to dinner with friends."

Jethri sighed. "You see I'm fine. Go to dinner."

The Liaden outright *laughed*, and straightened away from the wall.

"Oh, excellent! To the point, I agree." He waved down the hall vaguely, as if he could see through walls, and so could Jethri "Come, be a little gracious. I hear you are from *Elthoria*, over on Dock Six, is that so?"

Jethri nodded, warily. "Yes."

"Delightful. As it happens, I treasure an acquaintance with Norn ven'Deelin which has too long languished unrenewed. Allow me to escort you to your ship."

Jethri stood, feeling the glare building and not even trying to stop it. The man in the jacket *tsk'd*.

"Come now. Even a lad of your obvious resource will find it difficult to outrun a Scout on this station. At least allow me to know that *Elthoria* is on Dock Six. Also—forgive me for introducing a painful subject—I must point out that your late companions will no doubt have called in an anonymous accident report. If you wish to avoid awkward questions from the Watch, you would be well-advised to put yourself in my hands."

Maybe it was the Terran. Maybe it was the laugh, or the man's easy and factual way. Whatever, Jethri allowed that he trusted this one as much as he hadn't trusted the pair who had been chasing him. Further down the hall, a lift chimed—and that decided it.

"OK," he agreed, and the man smiled.

"Not a moment too soon," He said, and stepped around the edge of the wall he'd been leaning against.

"This way, young sir. Quickly."

HIS GUIDE SET a brisk pace through the service corridors, his footsteps no more than whispers.

Jethri, walking considerably more noisy behind him, had time to appreciate that he was at this man's mercy; and the likelihood that his murdered body could lie in one of the numerous, dark repair bays they passed for days before anyone thought to look…

"Do not sell your master trader short, young sir," the man ahead of him said. "I can understand that you might be having second thoughts about myself—a stranger and a Scout, together! Who knows what such a fellow might do! But never doubt Norn ven'Deelin."

Apparently it wasn't just his face that was found too readable, Jethri thought sourly, but his footsteps, too. Still, he forced himself to chew over what the man had said, and produced a question.

"What's a Scout?"

Two steps ahead, the Liaden turned to face him, continuing to walk backward, which he seemed to find just as simple as going face-first, and put his hand, palm flat, against his chest.

"I am a Scout, child. In particular: Scout Captain Jan Rek ter'Astin, presently assigned to the outpost contained in this space station."

Jethri considered him. "You're a soldier, then?"

Scout Captain ter'Astin laughed again, and turned face forward without breaking stride.

"No, innocent, I am not a soldier. The Scouts are… are—an exploratory corps. And to hear some, we are more trouble than we are worth, constant meddlers that we are—Ah, here is our lift! After you, young sir."

It looked an ordinary enough lift, Jethri thought, as the door slid away. And what choice did he have, anyway? He was certainly lost, and had no guide but this man who laughed like a Terran and walked as loose and light as a spacer.

He stepped into the lift, the Scout came after, punched a quick series of buttons, and relaxed bonelessly against the wall.

"I don't wish to be forward," he said, slipping his hands into the pockets of his jacket. "But I wonder if you have a name."

"Jethri Gobelyn."

"Ah, is it so? Are you kin to Arin Gobelyn?"

Jethri turned and stared, shock no doubt plain on his face, for the Scout brought his right hand out of his pocket and raised it in his small gesture of peace.

"Forgive me if I have offended. I am not expert in the matter of Terran naming customs, I fear."

Jethri shook his head. "I'm Arin Gobelyn's son," he said, trying to shake away the shock, as he stared into the Scout's easy, unreadable face. "My mother never told me he had any Liaden…connections."

"Nor should she have done so. My acquaintance with Arin Gobelyn was unfortunately curtailed by his death."

Jethri blinked. "You were at the explosion?"

"Alas, no. Or at least, not immediately. I was one of the Port rescue team sent to clean up after the explosion. We arrived to find that an impromptu rescue effort was already underway. The Terran ship crews, they reacted well and with purpose. Your father—he was as a giant. He went back into that building twice, and brought out injured persons. Was it three or five that he carried or guided out? The years blur the memory, I fear. The third time, however…" He moved his shoulders. "The third time, he handed his rescue off to the medics, and paused, perhaps to recruit his strength. Behind him, the building collapsed as the inner roof beams gave way sequentially—throwing out debris and smoke with enormous energy.

"When the dust cleared, I was down, your father was down—everyone in a two-square radius was down. After I had recovered my wits, I crawled over to your father. The wreckage was afire, of course, and I believe I had some foolish notion of trying to drag him further from the flames. As it happens, there was no need. A blade of wood as long as I am had pierced him. We had nothing to repair such a wound, and in any case it was too late. I doubt he knew that he had been killed." Another ripple of black-clad shoulders.

"So, I only knew him as a man of courage and good heart, who spent his life so that others might live." The Scout inclined his head, suddenly and entirely Liaden.

"You are fortunate in your kin, Jethri Gobelyn."

Jethri swallowed around the hard spot in his throat. He'd only known that his father had died when the warehouse had collapsed. The rest of this…

"Thank you," he said, huskily. "I hadn't known the—the story of my father's death."

"Ah. Then I am pleased to be of service."

The lift chimed, and the Scout straightened, hands coming out of his pockets. He waved Jethri forward.

"Come, this will be our stop."

"Our stop" looked like nothing more than a plain metal square with a door at one end. Jethri stepped out of the lift, and to one side.

The Scout strolled past, very much at his leisure, put his palm against the door and walked through.

Jethri followed—and found himself on Dock Six, practically at the foot of *Elthoria's* ramp. Despite it all, he grinned, then remembered and bowed to the Scout.

"Thank you. I think I can make it from here."

"Doubtless you can," the Scout said agreeably. "But recall my ambition to renew my acquaintance with Norn ven'Deelin." He moved forward with his loose, easy stride that was much quicker than it looked. Jethri stretched his legs and caught up with him just as he turned toward the ramp…startling the young replacement doc-checker into a flabbergasted, "Wait, you!"

The Scout barely turned his head. "Official Scout business," he said briskly and went up the ramp at a spanking pace, Jethri panting at his heels.

At the top, a shadow shifted. Jethri looked up and saw Pen Rel coming quickly down toward them—and just as suddenly braking, eyebrows raised high.

"Scout. To what do we owe the honor?"

"Merely a desire to share a glass and a few moments with the master trader," the Scout said, slowing slightly, but still moving steadily up the ramp. "Surely an old friend may ask so much?"

Jethri sent a glance up into Pen Rel's face, which showed watchful, and somewhat, maybe, even—annoyed.

"The master trader has just returned from the trade meeting—" he began.

"Then she will need a glass and a few moments of inconsequential chat even more," the Scout interrupted. "Besides, I wish to speak with her about her apprentice."

Pen Rel's glance found Jethri's face. "Her tardy apprentice."

"Just so," said the Scout. "You anticipate my topic."

He reached Pen Rel and paused at what Jethri knew to be comfortable talking distance for Liadens. It was a space that felt a little too wide to him, but, then, he'd come up on a ship half the size and less of *Elthoria*.

"Come, Arms Master, be gracious."

"Gracious," Pen Rel repeated, but he turned and led the way into the ship.

If Master ven'Deelin felt any dismay in welcoming Scout Captain Jan Rek ter'Astin onto her ship, she kept it to herself. She saw him comfortably seated, and poured three glasses of wine with her own hands—one for the guest, one for herself, and one for Jethri.

She sat in the chair opposite the Scout; perforce, Jethri sank into the remaining, least comfortable, chair, which sat to the master trader's right.

The Scout sipped his wine. Master ven'Deelin did the same, Jethri following suit. The red was sharp on the tongue, then melted into sweetness.

"I commend you," the Scout said to the master trader, and in Terran, which Jethri thought had to be an insult, "on your choice of apprentice."

Master ven'Deelin inclined her head. "Happy I am that you find him worthy," she replied, in her accented Terran.

The Scout smiled. "Of course you are," he murmured. "I wonder, though, do you value the child?" He raised his hand. "Understand me, I find him a likely fellow, and quick of thought and action. But those are attributes which Scouts are taught to admire. Perhaps for a trader ?"

"I value Jethri high," Master ven'Deelin said composedly.

"Ah. Then I wonder why you put him in harm's way?"

Master ven'Deelin's face didn't change, but Jethri was abruptly in receipt of the clear notion that she was paying attention on all channels.

"Explain," she said, briefly.

"Certainly," the Scout returned, and without even taking a hard breath launched the story of Jethri's foray into the Trade Bar, and all the events which followed from it. Master ven'Deelin sat silent until the end, then looked to Jethri.

"Jethri Gobelyn."

He sat up straighter, prepared to take his licks, for the whole mess had been his own fault, start to finish, and—

"Your lessons expand. Next on-shift, you will embrace *menfri'at*. Pen Rel will instruct you as to time."

What in cold space was *menfri'at*, Jethri wondered, even as he inclined his head. "Yes, Master Trader."

"Self-defense," the Scout said, as if Jethri had asked his question out loud, "including how to make calm judgments in…difficult situations." Jethri looked at him, and the Scout smiled. "For truly, child, if you had not run—or run only so far as one of the tables—there would have been no need to leap off into a gravity-free zone which is sometimes not quite so gravity free as one might wish."

Jethri looked at him, mouth dry. "The book said—"

"No doubt. However, the facts are that the station does sometimes provide gravity to those portions marked 'free fall'."

Jethri felt sick, the wine sitting uneasily on his stomach.

"Also," the Scout continued, "a book is—of necessity—somewhat behind the times in other matters; and I doubt that yours attempted more than a modest discussion of station culture. Certainly, a book could tell you little of which ships might be in from the outer dependencies, with crews likely to be looking for hijinks."

And that, Jethri admitted, stomach still unsettled, was true. Just like he'd know better than to head down Gamblers Row on any Terran port he could name after a rock-buster crew came in, he ought to know—

But the ship names meant nothing to him, here, and though some—perhaps twenty percent—had showed Combine trade codes along with Liaden, he didn't yet have those Liaden codes memorized. Jethri swallowed. He shouldn't have been let loose on station without a partner, he thought. That was fact. He was a danger to himself and his ship until he learned not to be stupid.

The Scout was talking with Master ven'Deelin. "I see, too, that Ixin, or at least *Elthoria*, may need to be brought to fuller awareness of the, let us call them…climate changes…recently wrought here. Indeed, these changes are closely related to my own sudden stationing."

Norn ven'Deelin's face changed subtly, and the Scout made a small, nearly familiar motion with his hand. Jethri leaned forward, the roiling in his gut forgotten—hand-talk! It wouldn't be the same as he knew, o'course, but maybe he could catch—

"So," the master trader murmured, "it is not a mere accident of happiness that you are on-station just as my apprentice becomes beset by—persons of loutishness?"

"It is not," the Scout replied. "The politics of this sector have altered of late. The flow of commerce, and even the flow of science and information has been shifting. You may wish—forgive me for meddling where I have no right!—but perhaps you may wish to issue ship's armbands to those who walk abroad unaccompanied."

The Scout's fingers moved, casually, augmenting his spoken words. Jethri tried to block his voice out and concentrate on the patterns that were *almost* the patterns he knew. He thought for a second that he'd caught the gist of it—and the Scout turned up the speed.

Defeated for the moment, Jethri sat back, and tried another sip of his wine.

"For I am certain," the Scout was saying out loud, "that there were enough of those present with Ixin's interest at heart that they would not have permitted a bullying. As it is, you may wish to ask your most excellent arms master to—"

Master ven'Deelin's hand flashed a quick series of signs as she murmured, "Ah. I have been so much enjoying your visit that I of my duty am neglectful. This is what you wish to say?"

The Scout laughed. The master trader—perhaps she smiled, a little, before turning her attention to Jethri and using her chin to point at the door.

"Of your goodness, young Jethri. Scout ter'Astin and I have another topic of discourse between us, which absolutely I refuse to undertake in Terran."

"Yes, ma'am." He stood and bowed, made clumsy by reason of the still-full wine glass. "Good shift, ma'am. Scout—I thank you."

"No, child," the Scout said, sipping his wine. "It is I who thank you, for enlivening what has otherwise been a perfectly tedious duty cycle." He moved a hand, echoing Master ven'Deelin. "Go, have your meal, rest. Learn well and bring honor to your ship."

"Yessir," Jethri gasped, and made his escape.

# Day 67
# Standard Year 1118

## *Elthoria*
## Protocol Lessons

"YES!" RAY JON tel'Ondor cried, bouncing 'round Jethri like a powerball on overload.

"*Precisely* would a shambling, overgrown barbarian from the cold edge of space bow in acknowledgment of a debt truly owed!" Bouncing, he came briefly to rest a few inches from Jethri's face.

Frozen in the bow, Jethri could see the little man's boots as he jigged from foot to foot, in time to a manic rhythm only he could hear. Jethri forced himself to breathe quietly, to ignore both the crick in his back and the itch of his scalp, where the hair was growing out untidily.

"Well played, young Jethri! A skillful portrayal, indeed! Allow me to predict for you a brilliant career in the theater!" The boot heels clicked together, and Master tel'Ondor was momentarily, and entirely, still.

"Now," he said, in the mode of teacher to student, "do it correctly."

Having no ambition to hear Master tel'Ondor on the foolishness of allowing one's emotions rule—a subject upon which he was eloquent—Jethri neither sighed, nor cussed, nor wrinkled his nose. Instead, he straightened, slowly and with, he hoped, grace, and stood for a moment, arms down at his sides, composing himself.

It was not, as he had hoped, the new boots which had been waiting for him in his quarters—five pairs to choose from!—that were the problem with his bows this shift, nor was it that the silky blue shirt bound him, or that the equally new and surprising trader's jacket limited his range of motion. Though he was very much aware all of his new finery, he was in no way hampered. The problem had been and was, as he understood Master tel'Ondor on the matter, that Jethri Gobelyn had ore for brains.

Don't doubt that his lessons with Master tel'Ondor had taught him a lot. For instance, learning how to speak Liaden wasn't anywhere like learning how to speak a new dialect of Ground Terran, or dock-pidgin or Trade. Spoken Liaden was divided into two kinds—High and Low—and then divided again, into *modes*, all of which meant something near and dear and different to Liaden hearts. Improper use of mode was asking for a share in a fistfight, if nothing worse. That was if Master tel'Ondor let him live, which by this time in the proceedings, Jethri wasn't so sure he would.

Truth told, and thanking the tapes, not to mention Vil Tor and Gaenor, he did have a yeoman's grip on the more work-a-day modes in the High Tongue—enough, Master tel'Ondor allowed, that educated people would understand him to be literate, though tragically afflicted with an impediment to the tongue.

No, it was the *bows* that were making him into a danger to himself and his teacher. Dozens of bows, of varying depths, each delivered at its own particular speed, with its own particular gesture of hand—or lack—held for its own particular count…

"Forgive me, young Jethri," Master tel'Ondor said, delicately. "Have I time to drink a cup of tea before your next performance?"

His one triumph was his ability to remain trader-faced, no matter the provocation. Carefully, he inclined his head, bending his neck so far, but no further, straightening without haste and only then making his reply.

"Your pardon, Master. I was absorbed by thought."

"At this moment, thought is extraneous," Master tel'Ondor told him. "The honorable to whom you find yourself in debt stands before you. Show proper respect, else they become bored—or discover that they are in receipt of an insult. Perhaps you do intend an insult; if so, you must chart your own course. The ven'Deelin did not bid me instruct you in matters of the duel."

"Yes, Master." Jethri took a deep breath, began the count in his head, moved the right arm—*so*—on the same beat extending the left leg—*so*—and bent from the waist, forehead on an interception course with the left knee.

At the count of fourteen, he stopped moving, holding the pose for six beats, then reversed the count, coming slowly to his full height, right hand and left leg withdrawing to their more usual positions—and he was at rest.

"So." Before him, Master tel'Ondor stood solemn and still, his head canted to one side. "An improvement." He held up a hand, as if to forestall the grin Jethri kept prisoned behind straight lips. "Understand me—an *improvement* only. Those who had not had the felicity of observing your former attempts might yet consider that they had been made the object of mockery."

Jethri allowed himself an extremely soft and heartfelt sigh. It wasn't that he doubted the tutor's evaluation of his performance—he *felt* like he was hinged with rusty metal when he bowed. According to Gaenor, they were due to raise Tilene within the ship-week, where, according to no body less than Norn ven'Deelin, he would be expected to assist at the trade booth.

"Forgive me, Master, for my ineptitude," he said now to Master tel'Ondor. "I wish to succeed in my studies."

"So you do," the master replied. "And so I do—and so, too, does the ven'Deelin. It is, however, possible to wish so ardently for success that the wish cripples the performance. It is my belief, Jethri Gobelyn, that your very desire to do well limits you to mediocrity." He began to move around Jethri, not his usual manic bounce, but a sedate stroll, as if he were a trader and Jethri a particularly interesting odd lot.

For his part, Jethri stood with patience, his stomach recovered from yesterday's adventures and the off-hour meal he'd wolfed in the cafeteria under the view of an entire shift he was barely known to.

Master tel'Ondor had completed his tour.

"You are large," he murmured, hands folded before him, "but not so large as to hamper ease of movement. Indeed, you possess a certain unaffected grace which is pleasing in a young person. Understand me, I do not counsel you to be *easy*, but I do ask that you allow your natural attributes to aid you. Respect, duty, honor—all arise effortlessly from one's *melant'i*. You know yourself to be a man who *does not* give inadvertent insult—ideally, your bow—and all your dealings—will convey this. I would say to you that the strength of your *melant'i* is more important in any bow than whether you have counted precisely to fourteen, or only to thirteen."

He tipped his head. "Do you understand me, Jethri Gobelyn?"

He considered it. *Melant'i* he had down for a philosophy of hierarchy—a sort of constant tally of where you stood in the chain of command in every and any given situation. It was close enough to a plain spacer's "ship state" to be workable, and that was how he worked it. Given the current situation, where he was a student, trying hard to do—to do honor to his teacher...

*Think*, he snarled at himself.

OK, so. He was junior in rank to his teacher, and respectful of his learning, while being more than a little shy of his tongue. At the same time, though, a student ought to be respectful of himself, and of his ability to learn. He wasn't an idiot, though that was hard to bear in mind. Hadn't Master ven'Deelin herself signed him on as 'prentice trader, knowing—which she had to—the work it would mean, and trusting him to be the equal of it?

So thinking, he nodded, felt the nod become a bow—a light bow, all but buoyant; with the easy move of the left hand that signaled understanding.

Still buoyant, he straightened, and surprised a look of sheer astonishment in his tutor's face.

"Yes, precisely so," Master tel'Ondor said, softly, and himself bowed, acknowledging a student's triumph.

Jethri bit his lip to keep the grin inside and forced his face into the increasingly familiar bland look of a trader on active business.

"Jethri Gobelyn, I propose that we break for tea. When we meet here again, I believe we should concern ourselves with those modes and bows most likely to be met on the trade floor at Tilene."

It was too much; the grin peeped out; he covered with another soft, buoyant bow, slightly deeper and augmented by the hand-sign for gratitude. "Yes, Master. Thank you."

"Bah. Return here in one twenty-eight, and we shall see what you may do then." The master turned his back as he was wont to do in dismissal.

Grinning, Jethri all but skipped out of the classroom. Still buoyant, he made the turn into the main hallway— and walked into a mob scene.

He might have thought himself on some port street, just previous to a rumble, but there were faces in the crowd he recognized, and it was *Elthoria's* increasingly familiar walls giving back echoes of excited voices and, yes—laughter.

At the forefront, then, there was Pen Rel, and Gaenor, and Vil Tor—all talking at once and all sporting a state of small or extra-large dishevelment. There was a bruise high up on Gaenor's fragile, pointy face, and her lips looked swollen, like maybe she'd caught a smack. More than one of the crew members at her back were bloody, but of good cheer, and when Gaenor spotted Jethri she cried out, "Company halt!"

It took a bit, but they mostly settled down and got quiet. When there was more or less silence, Gaenor bowed—Jethri read it as the special bow made between comrades—and spoke through an unabashed grin.

"The First Mate reports to Jethri Gobelyn, crewman formerly at risk, that the Trade Bar of Kailipso will be pleased to cordially entertain him whenever he is in port. I also report that a house speciality has been named in your honor—which is to say, it is called *Trader's Leap,* and is mixed of 'retto and kynak and klah. On behalf of the ship, I have tasted of this confection and have found it to be...an amazement. There are other matters, too, of which you should be advised, so, please, come with us, and we will tell you of our visitation and correction."

Visitation and correction? Jethri stared at the bunch of them—even *Vil Tor* rumpled and his shirt torn and dirty.

"You didn't bust up the bar?"

Gaenor laughed, and Pen Rel, too. Then Gaenor stepped forward to catch his hand in hers, and pull him with her down the hall.

"Come, honored crewmate, we will tell you what truly transpired before it all becomes rumor and myth. In trade, you will then tell us of your training and skill, for already there are a dozen on station who have attempted to duplicate your leap and have earned for their efforts broken arms and legs."

She tugged his hand, and he let her pull him along, as the mob moved as one creature down the hall toward the cafeteria.

"But," Jethri said, finding Vil Tor at his side, "I thought Balance required craft and cunning and care—"

The librarian laughed, and caught his free hand. "Ah, my friend, we need to teach you more of *melant'i*! What you describe would be seemly, were we dealing with persons of worth. However, when one deals with louts—"

At that there was great laughter, and the mob swept on.

# Day 80
# Standard Year 1118

# Kinaveral

IT WAS MIDDAY on the port by the time Khat cleared the paperwork and took receipt of her pay. By her own reckoning, it was nearer to sleep-shift, which activity she intended to indulge in, soon as she raised the lodgings.

Her step did break as she passed by the *Ship'n Shore*, but the prospect of ten hours or more of sleep was more compelling than a brew and a bite, so she moved on, and caught a tram at the meeting of the cross streets.

She was in a light doze when her stop was called; got her feet under her and bumbled down the steps to the street, where she stood for far too long, eyes narrowed against the glare, trying to sort out where, exactly, she was, with specific relation to her cubby and her cot. Eventually, she located the right building, mooched on in at quarter-speed, swiped her key through the scanner and took the lift to the eighth floor.

The Gobelyn Family Unit was, thanking all the ghosts of space, quiet and dim. Khat charted a none-too-steady course across the main room to her cubby, stripping off her clothes as she went. She stuffed the wad of them into the chute, pushed aside the drape and fell into her cot, pulling the blanket up and over her head.

It occurred to her that she ought to hit the shower; her being at least as ripe as her clothes, but she was asleep almost as soon as she'd thought it.

"ALL CREW ON deck!"

There are those things that command a body's attention, no matter how deep asleep it is. Khat jerked awake with a curse, flung the blanket aside and jumped for the common room, stark naked and reeking as she was.

Seeli stood in the center of the room, hands on hips and looking none too pleased. Apparently Khat was the sole crew the all-hands had roused.

"Are you the only one here?" Seeli snapped, which wasn't her usual way. Seeli snapping was Seeli upset, so Khat made allowance and answered civil.

"I'm guessing. Place was empty when I come in—" she looked across the room at the clock. "Two hours ago."

Her cousin vented an exasperated sigh.

"It's our shift, then," she muttered, and then appeared to see Khat's condition for the first time. "Just down from the free-wing job?"

"Two hours ago," Khat said. "They had me running solo. Sleep is high on the list of needfuls, followed by a shower and food."

Seeli nodded. "I'm sorry. If there was anybody else to hand—but it's you an' me, an' it's gotta be now." She pointed to the 'fresher. "Rinse an' get decent. I'll fix you a cup o'mite and some coffee. You can drink it on the way."

Khat stared. "What's gone wrong?"

Seeli was already moving toward the galley, and answered over her shoulder. "Iza got in a cuffing match with the yard boss, and the port cops have her under key."

"Shit," Khat said, and sprinted for the 'fresher.

Seeli'd gone down to the yard, to talk with the boss and smooth over what she could, which left Khat to bail Iza out.

IT WAS A cross-port ride on the tram, by which time the 'mite and the caffeine were working, and she walked into the cop shop more or less awake, if none too easy in the stomach.

"Business?" The bored woman behind the info counter asked.

"Come to pay a fine and provide escort," Khat said, respectfully. She wasn't over-fond of port police—what spacer was?—but saw no reason to pay an extra duty for her attitude. The ghosts of space bear witness, Iza had likely scored enough of that for the crew at large, if they'd interrupted her in a cuffing match.

"Name?" the cop asked.

"Iza Gobelyn. Brought in this afternoon from the yards."

The cop looked down at her screen, grunted, and jerked her head to the right.

"Down the end of the hall. If you step lively, you can get her out before the next hour's holding fee kicks in."

"Thank you," Khat said, and made haste down the hall, there to stand before another counter just like the one at the front door, and repeat her information to an equally bored man.

"Kin?" he asked, peering at her over the edge of his screen.

"Yessir. Cousin. Khatelane Gobelyn."

"Hmph." He poked at some keys, frowned down at the screen, poked again. Khat made herself stand quiet and not shout at him to hurry it along, and all the while the big clock behind the counter showed the time speeding toward the hour-change.

"Gobelyn," the cop muttered, head bobbing as he bent over the screen. "Here we are: public display of hostility, striking a citizen, striking a port employee, striking a law enforcement officer, swearing at a law enforcement officer, Level Two arrest, plus transportation, booking, three hours' lodging, usage fees, tax and duty, leaving us with a total due of eight hundred ninety-seven bits." He looked up. "We also accept trade goods, or refined gold. There is a surcharge for using either of those options."

Sure there was. Khat blinked. Eight *hundred*—

"Duty?" she asked.

The cop nodded, bored. "You're offworld. All transactions between planetaries and extra-planetaries are subject to duty."

"Oh." She slipped a hand into her private pocket, brought out her personal card, and swiped it through the scanner on the front of the counter. There was a moment of silence, then the cop's screen beeped and initiated a noisy printout.

"Your receipt will be done in a moment," he said. "After you have it, please go down the hall to the first room on your left. Your cousin will be brought to you there."

"Thanks," Khat muttered. She took the printout when it was done with a curt nod went to wait for Iza to be brought up.

"LEVEL TWO ARREST" involved sedation—the construction of the drug, duration of affect, known adverse reactions, and chemical antidotes were all listed at the bottom of the two-page receipt. Khat scowled. The drug lasted plus-or-minus four hours. Iza had been arrested three-point-five hours ago. There wasn't enough credit left on her card to rent a car to take them 'cross port, and the prospect of woman-handling a half-unconscious Iza onto the tram was…daunting, not to dance too lightly on it.

She'd barely started to worry when the door to the waiting room opened, admitting a port cop in full uniform, a thin woman in bloodstained overalls and spectacularly bruised face walking, docile, at her side.

"Khatelane Gobelyn?" The cop asked.

"That's me." Khat stepped forward, staring into Iza's face. Iza stared back, blue eyes tranquil and empty.

"She's good for about another forty minutes," the cop said. "If I was you, I'd have her locked down in thirty. No sense running too close to the edge."

"Right," Khat said, and then gave the cop a nod, trying for cordial. "Thank you."

"Huh." The cop shook her head. "You keep her outta trouble, space-based. You copy that? She put Chad Perkin in the hospital when he tried to get the restraints on her—broken kneecap, broken nose, cracked ribs. You hurt a cop on this port once, and you're a good citizen ever after, because there ain't no maybes the second time."

Khat swallowed. "I don't—"

"Understand?" The cop hit her in the chest with an ungentle forefinger. "If your buddy here gets into another fistfight and the cops are called on it, she ain't likely to survive the experience. That plain enough for you, space-based?"

"Yes," Khat breathed, staring into the broad, hard face. "That's plain."

"Good. Now get her outta here and tied down before the stuff wears out."

"Yes," Khat said again. She reached out and took Iza's hand, pulling her quick time down the hall.

THE TRAM WAS within two blocks of the lodgings and the time elapsed from the cop shop was rising onto forty-two minutes, when Khat felt Iza shift on the seat beside her. The shifting intensified, accompanied by soft growls and swear words. Khat bit her lip, in a sweat for the tram to *hurry*—

"'scuse me." A hand landed, lightly, on Khat's shoulder. She looked up into the face of an older Grounder woman.

"'scuse me," the woman said again, her eyes mostly on Iza. "Your friend just fresh from the cop shop?"

"Yes."

"You take my advice—get her off this tram an' *down*. That drug they use has a kick on the exit side. M'brother threw seven fits when it wore offa him—took all us girls to hold him down, and my uncle, too."

"Damn dirtsider," Iza muttered beside her. "Trying to cheat me. Short my ship, will he…"

Khat grabbed her arm, leaned over and yanked the cord. The tram slowed and she leapt to her feet, dragging Iza with her.

"Thank you," she said to the Grounder woman, and then thought to ask it—"What happened to your brother?"

The woman shrugged, eyes sliding away. "He was born to trouble, that one. Cop broke his neck not a year later—resisting arrest, they said."

The tram stopped, the side door slid open. "Mud sucker!" Iza yelled, and Khat jumped for the pavement. Perforce, Iza followed; she staggered, swearing, and Khat spun, twisting her free hand in Iza's collar, using momentum and sheer, naked astonishment to pitch the older woman off the main walk and into a gap between two buildings.

"Cheat! Filth!" shouted Iza. Khat hooked a foot around her ankle, putting her face down into the mud, set a knee into the small of her back, and pulled both arms back into a lock.

Iza bucked and twisted and swore and shouted—to not much effect, though there were a few bad seconds when Khat thought she was going to lose the arm-lock.

After half an hour or an eternity, the thrashing stopped, then the swearing did, and all Iza's muscles went limp. Cautiously, Khat let the lock down, and eased her knee off. Iza lay, face down, in the mud. Khat turned her over, checked her breathing and her pulse, then, stifling a few curses herself, she got Iza into a back carry and staggered off toward the lodgings.

The lodgings were in sight when Seeli showed up on Khat's left. Wordlessly, she helped ease Iza down, and then the two of them got her distributed between them and walked her the rest of the way. Seeli swiped her key through the scan and they maneuvered Iza into the lift, then through the common room and into her own quarters, where they dropped her, muddy and bloody as she was, atop her cot.

"How bad at the yard?" Khat asked Seeli as they moved toward the galley.

"Bad enough," Seeli said after more hesitation than Khat liked to hear. She sighed, and opened the coldbox. "Brew?"

"Nothing less. And some cheese, if there's any." She closed her eyes, feeling the electric quiver of adrenaline-edged exhaustion in her knees and arms.

"Brew," Seeli said, and Khat heard a solid, welcome thump on the table before her. She opened her eyes just as a block of spicy local cheese and a knife landed next to the bottle.

Sighing, she had a mouthful of brew, then sliced about a third of the cheese.

Seeli sat down across, cradling her brew between her two hands, and looking about as grim as she got.

"How bad," Khat asked between bites of cheese, "is bad enough?"

Seeli sighed. "The yard wants an extra bond posted. They want a guarantee that Iza will be kept from their premises. They want the name and contact code for somebody—*not* Iza—who is empowered to speak for the ship. That person will be allowed in the offices of the yard no more than once per port-week, at pre-scheduled times. Monthly inspection of progress stays in force, so long as the inspector ain't Iza Gobelyn. Any further disturbance, and the yard will invoke breach and impound the *Market*."

Khat had another piece of cheese and a swallow of brew.

"That's bad enough," she allowed, and pointed at the cheese. "Eat."

"Later," Seeli said, and made a production out of sipping her beer.

Khat sighed. "Understand, there was a couple bad minutes when the drug went over, but I gathered that Iza had reason to believe the yard was cheatin' us."

"There might be some of that. Problem is, Iza going off the dial put us into the disadvantage with regard to amicable discovery. I've got a call in to Paitor. Crew meeting here, tomorrow port-night."

"What about Cris?"

Seeli shrugged, and stared hard down into her brew. "I beamed a precis and a plea for a recommend to his ship. Could be we'll have his answer by meeting." She looked up, face hard, which was Seeli when she'd taken a decision, no different from her ma. "We gotta settle this, Khat. Iza goes off the dial again, we could lose the *Market*. It's that near the edge."

"I hear it," Khat said, and finished her brew. "I'm for sleep, coz. Central's got me on for a hop to the station tomorrow middle day. I'll be down in plenty of time for the meeting." She stood and stretched. "Best thing would be for Iza to take a temp berth—you know she's always crazy on the ground."

"I know," Seeli said, too soft. "Sleep sound, cousin. 'preciated the assist, today."

Khat nodded and headed for the door. Before she got there, she checked and looked over her shoulder.

"Almost forgot—eight hundred ninety seven paid out from my personal account."

Seeli closed her eyes briefly. "I'll authorize the transfer from Ship's General,"

"'preciate it," Khat said, and left, on a course for sleep.

# Day 81
# Standard Year 1118

## Kinaveral

IT WAS A grim-faced lot of Gobelyns gathered in the lodging's common room when Khat finally got there, dusty, hungry and all too out of patience with stationer attitude and port red tape, both.

"Sorry," she said to Seeli, who was sitting circle-master with Grig at her left hand and Paitor at her right. "They told me about the lift. Nobody thought to mention there'd be three hours of paperwork waitin' for me on station, and a matching three portside, when I got back down."

It was notable that Dyk, sitting between Mel and Zam, didn't bother to assure her that she looked fine in red tape. Seeli only nodded and pointed at the empty chair between Mel and Paitor, which seat Khat took with a fair amount of trepidation. Seeli'd called Full Circle on Iza. This was not going to be fun.

No sooner had she sat then Paitor got his feet under him and come to his full standing height. "Captain," he said, loud enough to be heard down the hall and into the next lodgings over. "Your crew wants a Word."

Khat felt some of the tightness in her gut ease. They were going to do the reasonable—well, o'course they was, she told herself, with Seeli settin' it up. So, a Word, first, with Ship's Judgement held in reserve, in case Iza wasn't inclined to meet reasonable with reasonable. Whether she'd be so inclined, Khat couldn't have said—and by the look on Seeli's face, she didn't know which way Iza was likely to jump, either.

"Iza Gobelyn," Paitor said, stern and loud. "Your crew's waitin'."

For what seemed like a long time, nothing happened. Khat realized she was holding her breath, and took note of the fact that the palms of her hands were damp.

Away down the room, something stirred, and there was Iza, long and lean and tough and walking with something less than her usual swagger.

She stopped walking just behind Grig's chair and raised her face, catching Paitor's eyes on hers.

"Well, brother?" she snapped, and Khat winced, her voice was that sharp.

"Just a Word with you, Captain," Paitor answered, smooth and calm as you please. "On a matter of ship's safety."

Say what you would about Iza Gobelyn, she was all of that, and canny, too. Another two heartbeats, she stood behind Grig, her eyes flicking 'round the Circle, touching each of their faces in turn, letting each of them see her—their mother, their cousin, their captain, who had kept them out of trouble and bailed them out of trouble; who'd kept ship and crew together for all of Khat's lifetime—and before.

When they'd all had a good look at her, and her at them, that's when she slid between Grig and Seeli and walked forward to stand in the center of the Circle, and hold her hands out, palms up and showing empty.

"I'm listenin'," she said, and let her hands fall to her sides.

Paitor sat down again, and folded his arms over his chest, face shut, eyes alert. Next to him, Seeli straightened.

"There's concern," she said, her voice firm and clear. "The yard boss ain't happy with the captain's behavior. He's gone so far as to state he'll invoke breach and impound the *Market*, in the case that Iza Gobelyn's seen on his deck again."

Iza turned lazily on her heel until she faced Seeli, which gave Khat the side of her face.

"They was shortin' us on the shielding, Admin."

"Yes, Captain, I don't doubt they was, having seen it with my own eyes. Fact remains, the yard boss has the legal on his side. He's filed a paper with the local cops, stating that one Iza Gobelyn approaches his yard at her peril. If she's found on or around, the *Market's* forfeit."

Iza glared; Khat could see it in the thrust of a shoulder.

"That's legal, is it?"

"It is," Seeli said. "And if it weren't, we'd still be outta luck, being as the cops ain't sworn to aid us."

Iza's shoulder twitched.

"On account," said Grig, his voice as hard as Khat had ever heard it, "you pitched the cop you swung on into light duty til his knee and his ribs and his nose all heal, and the cops here-port don't care to look out for them who break their mates."

"Worse," Khat said, leaning forward in her chair as Iza swung 'round to face her. "There's active malice involved. Woman on the bus told me. Comes to that, cop down the shop told me. You hurt a cop on this port, you stay outta trouble forevermore, because the day you come against another cop is the day you stop breathing."

Iza stared at her, eyes hooded, then gave her a nod. "'preciate the bail-out, cousin."

"It was expensive enough," Khat told her.

"Looks like getting more expensive before it gets less," Iza answered and turned back to face Seeli.

"Lay it out, Admin."

"All right, Captain," Seeli's voice was cool as the skin of a cargo can. "What I'm seeing is this—I'll take oversight of the upgrades and repairs. Grig, here, he's my expert on shielding, and he's already found us a second opinion, like the contract says we can have. We'll keep close watch and we won't let them get away with nothin', but we won't take no risks, neither, nor put the ship at peril."

"Fine work for you and yours, Admin. What about the captain?"

"The captain," Seeli said firmly, "should find herself a long-berth, get off Kinaveral until we're ready to go, and stay outta trouble."

In the center of the Circle, Iza laughed. "By this age in my life, you think I'd be expert in that." She turned, rotating lazily on her heel, and looked at them, one by one.

"Anybody else have a Word? Or does Admin speak for all of you?"

"In the case, Admin's on it," Mel said, while Dyk muttered, "No other Words, Captain," and Zam just shrugged his shoulders.

"And you're all staying dirtside, as I hear it, to give Admin a hand?"

"I'm signed as cook on a private yacht," Dyk said. "Lift in two days, back in 'leven month."

"Me an' Mel're for a miner," Zam said, looking down at his boots. "Signed the papers today. Lift tomorrow. Back, like Dyk, in 'leven, and trusting our ship'll be here for us."

"Cris is already on long-haul," Khat said, since it was her turn. It've been easier to talk to her boots, like Zam, but pilots were bolder than that—Khat Gobelyn was bolder than that—and she met her captain's eyes, level. "Me, I'm all fixed as a freewing, based on-port. There's some longer lifts comin', they tell me, but most of what's on offer is shuttle work and short hops. Don't fly every day, can file 'unavailable' at decent notice, so Seeli'll have an extra hand, when she needs one."

Iza nodded, solemn-like, and looked over to Paitor.

"I'm on-port, doing some little chores for Terratrade," he said, not uncrossing his arms. "Seeli needs me, she calls, I come."

"Just like you always done, eh, brother?"

His mouth thinned some, but the rest of his face stayed bland. "That's right, Captain."

Iza turned again, past Seeli, and showed her back to Khat, full face to Grig.

"You're staying on-dirt to back up Admin, is that so, Grig Tomas?"

"That's so, Captain."

"Then you'll see the jettison list attended to proper. That would be an order, which I know you can take," she said, provoking-like, 'cept it didn't make no sense, as far as Khat had ever seen, to provoke Grig. He just went all soft and agreeable on you, an' took his revenge when you needed it least.

Except not this time.

"Beggin' the captain's pardon, but there's some things on that jettison list belong to absent crew."

"Absent crew." Khat didn't need to see Iza's face; the tone of voice was enough. She drew a careful breath and indulged in a spot of wishful telepathy, trying to send Grig a message not to whip Iza into a rage—not now, when she'd been so reasonable...

"You'll be referring to Arin's son?" Iza was asking Grig.

There was a short pause, before he answered, voice neutral, "That's right, Captain."

"Spit of his father, ain't he, Grig?"

And what was this? Khat thought. Iza sounded almost conversational.

"Jethri's a good-lookin' boy. Smart, too. Done you proud, Iza."

"Ain't done me proud. Nothing to do with me, *as* you know it. Arin's boy, clear through—wouldn't you say so, Grig?" She shifted of a sudden, leaning forward hard, like she was going to grab him by the shoulders and haul him up to face her.

"Done's done, Iza. Arin's gone, and Jethri, too. Send the boy his things, and call it square."

"It'd be what's right, Iza," Paitor put in, calm, while the rest of them sat mum and stupid.

She spun to glare at him, shoulders stiff. "You think so, do you, brother? Fine, then. Send Arin's boy his things. So long as they're finally gone from my ship, I don't care where they are—destroyed or on Liad makes the same difference to me."

"That's settled then," said Seeli, shockingly matter-of-fact. "What ain't settled is what you'll do, Captain."

"Didn't think I had a choice," Iza said, turning back, and showing Seeli empty hands. "I'll go down to the hire-hall tomorrow and find myself a berth."

"I'll come with you," Khat heard her own voice say, and looked up to catch Iza's glance coming at her over one bony shoulder.

"Thanks, cousin," she said, with no shortin' the irony.

"No trouble," Khat answered, forcing herself to sound calm. "I'm not flying tomorrow and I know a couple of the sign-ons at the hall."

"Then we're square, captain and crew," Seeli said. Paitor nodded and got back on his feet.

"The crew talked, the captain heard. The ship's in harmony."

There was an uneasy sort of silence, then, like nobody knew exactly what to do, now the agreement was made and the right phrases spoke. When it had gone on long enough for Khat to start feeling it in her gut, she stood up and stretched, hands reaching for the ceiling.

"Let's all have us some brew and a snack," she said. "And say our good-byes and be-wells. We're going to be scattered across the star lanes this next while. Let's part on terms."

Dyk laughed and bounced to his feet in a sudden return to normal behavior. "Maybe I should ship out more often!"

"Maybe you should," Mel said cordially, standing up. Zam laughed. Across the circle, Seeli was up, Grig beside her, lanky and limpid like always, watching as Paitor held a hand out to Iza.

"Buy you a brew, sister?" he asked, and after a moment Iza put her hand in his.

"A brew'd be welcome, brother."

# Day 106
# Standard Year 1118

## Tilene Trade Theater

TAN SIM PEN'AKLA, adopted of Clan Rinork, left the Tilene Star Bar in a wine-induced glow of good fellowship for all beings, everywhere.

That the glow was wine-induced, Tan Sim well knew, having entered the establishment in question some hours previous with the specific intent of imbibing wine sufficient to ease the sting of the latest slight delivered by his foster kin. Since he had not cut his teeth yesterday, he was also well-aware that the wine on draw at the Star Bar was of a more virulent vintage than he was accustomed to drink, and that he had thereby made an appointment on the morrow with the very devil of a hangover.

That, however, was in the future. For the present, restored to good humor and only slightly unsteady on his feet, he sauntered, whistling unmelodically, down the supply hallway which was a shortcut to the main trading theater.

It would not do to be late to the second round of trading. Of course, his beloved foster brother Bar Jan would smell the wine; and wouldn't it just grate along his fine-drawn, High House sensibilities to be unable to send his drunkard junior away. But he dared not do that, Tan Sim thought waggishly. Oh, no, Bar Jan dared not send him away and hold the booth on his own while their mutual mother was gone a-calling. A *melant'i*-blind idiot Bar Jan might be, but he knew well enough that Tan Sim was the superior trader, in his cups or sober.

Would that he did not.

But, there, that line of thought ventured too close to the quadrant he wished to avoid. Resolutely, Tan Sim turned his consideration to the franchise Alt Lyr had for sale. A well enough venture—or so it seemed on the surface. He had set word about, before his visit to the wine shop, and he would be wanting to do more research before mentioning the matter to his mother, but...

He checked, whistle dying on his lips, eyes rapt upon a performance the like of which he had not beheld since— well, since he had first come to Rinork, and spent so many hours before the mirror, shining his bows for High House display.

Alas, the person bowing so earnestly and with such...interesting...results in the wide space in the hall meant to accommodate a service jitney, had no mirror. Style was also sadly absent, though there was, Tan Sim allowed, after observing for a few heartbeats, a certain vivacity in delivery that was not...entirely...displeasing.

At just that point, the person in the shadows executed a bow with a vivacity sufficient to set him staggering and Tan Sim felt it was time to take a hand.

"Here then!" he called out in the mode spoken between comrades, which would surely have set Bar Jan to ranting. "There's no sense breaking your head over a bow, you know."

The figure in the shadows turned to face him, light falling on a face pale, angular and wholly un-Liaden. There was an unfinished appearance about the jaw and shoulders which said *halfling* to Tan Sim, though he had to look up to meet the chocolate brown eyes. Despite he was indisputably Terran, he was dressed in well-tailored trading clothes, made very much in the Liaden style, down to the fine leather boots which encased his feet and the short blue jacket that proclaimed him an apprentice in trade.

In fact, he was a riddle.

Tan Sim delighted in riddles.

Delighted, he swept a bow of introduction to the startled youth.

"Tan Sim pen'Akla Clan Rinork."

The boy hesitated infinitesimally, then bowed in return, with somewhat less verve, and stated, laboriously, and very nearly in the mode of introduction:

"Jethri Gobelyn, apprentice trader aboard *Elthoria*."

Ixin's lead tradeship, forsooth. Tan Sim allowed his interest to be piqued. The ven'Deelin was canny and devious—even when held against other masters of trade, a lot known for their devious ways. Indeed, he had long admired her from afar—necessary, as Ixin and Rinork did not meet—and studied her guild files closely, so that he might, perhaps, upon one far distant day, aspire to even one-twelfth of her trading acumen.

And this lad here, this *Terran* lad, was the ven'Deelin's apprentice? He filed that away, for sober thought on the far side of the hangover, and moved a hand, softly, offering aid.

"I see you in the throes of just such a task as I myself have undertaken in the past. Wretched, aren't they? Who would suppose that one race could *need* so many bows?"

The angular face wavered as the lips bent in a quickly suppressed smile—and, aye, that, too, struck an uneasy memory. Tan Sim felt a spurt of sympathy and deliberately let his own smile show.

Some of the starch went out of the thin shoulders, and the boy—Jeth Ree, was it?—inclined his head.

"Indeed," he stammered, almost in the mode between equals—which was an impertinence, thought Tan Sim, but what else was the lad to do? "It is...difficult...to bear so much in mind. I have been tutored, but I fear that I am not fully...cognizant..."

"Hah." Tan Sim held up his hand. "I understand. You have been given a set number and form, eh? And you wish to shame neither your teacher nor your trader." He smiled again, gently. "Nor take delivery of a scold."

Jeth Ree fairly grinned—a dazzling display, too soon vanished.

"Well," said Tan Sim, "you won't find me a scolding fellow. I have only admiration for one who is so devoted to his duty that he uses his break-time to hone his skill. Such diligence…" He left the sentence for a moment as he recalled again that Ixin and Rinork did *not* meet. The proper course for himself, as one of Rinork, then, was to turn his back on this boy and—

And what did he care for some long-ago, cold quarrel? Depend upon it, he thought, sadly unfilial, the whole brangle, whatever it was, could be squarely lain at Rinork's feet. Here before him stood an apprentice trader in need of the guidance of a trader. His *melant'i*—and Guild rule, if it came to that—was plain.

He showed Jeth Ree another smile, and was pleased to gain one in return.

"Well, then, let us see what we might manage between us," he said, settling comfortably against the friendly wall. "Show me your repertoire."

This, the boy was willing enough to do, and Tan Sim spent the next while leaning, tipsy, against the wall, observing a series of common mercantile bows. Happily, the task was not more than his befogged faculties could accommodate, nor Jeth Ree any less apt than the larger number of new 'prentices Tan Sim had now and then had occasion to observe. The lad had apparently been driven to this lonely practice site in a fit of stage fright. Which Tan Sim quite understood. So.

"You are well-enough," he said, when the boy had straightened from his last endeavor, "for an apprentice newly come to the floor. It speaks well that you wish to bring only honor to your master, but you must not allow your sensibilities to overset your good sense." He inclined his head. "You will do exceedingly, Jeth Ree Gobelyn."

The boy stood a moment, as if struck, then bowed once more; this very precise, indeed. "I am in your debt, Tan Sim pen'Akla."

*And wouldn't* that *be a grand thing to bring to the table?* Tan Sim thought in sudden horror. *"Mother, I have the advantage of ven'Deelin's Terran apprentice in a matter of Balance."* Gods.

He moved a hand, smoothing the debt away. "Honor me by forgetting the incident, as I have done."

Jeth Ree looked doubtful—then proved himself a lad of sense and worthy to be the ven'Deelin's apprentice, by inclining his head.

"Thank you," he said, in what Tan Sim knew to be Terran, that being another of his clandestine studies.

"You are welcome," he replied in the same tongue, somewhat more slowly than he would have liked. The boy did not burst into derisive laughter, or even smile overmuch, which gave him hope for a successful outcome of study.

"If you please," Jeth Ree said abruptly. "How shall I bow to you, if we meet again on the floor? Since we are known to each other…"

Tan Sim pushed away from his wall. How, indeed, should the lad acknowledge him, should they meet? Almost, he laughed aloud at the unlikelihood of such an event.

Still, it was a reasonable question and deserved a fitting reply. He took a moment to be sure his feet were well under him, then swept the bow he'd practiced in his own ironic honor as a youth—*most honored child of the house.* He watched as the boy reproduced it, several times, and inclined his head, satisfied.

"Twill do. And now I must depart, amiable companion though you have been. My brother requires my assistance at our booth. Fare thee well, Jeth Ree Gobelyn."

He bowed, jauntily, the beginning of a headache teasing in back of his eyes, straightened to receive the boy's farewell, and walked away down the hall, whistling.

JETHRI'S TIMING WAS fortunate; he returned to Ixin's trade booth just as the floor opened for the second shift. Master ven'Deelin inclined her head, which he hoped meant she was impressed with his promptness, and reached beneath the counter.

"Our Tilene agent took delivery of this message for you, young Jethri. You may have a moment to read it. There was also a crate—that has been moved to your trade-bin on ship."

Heart thumping heavy, he slipped a folded sheet of paper from between her fingers. He did remember his bow, and to give a soft, "My thanks, Master Trader." Courtesy satisfied, he took himself to the back corner of the booth, hunkered down on his heels beside the hanging rugs and strings of spice, and unfolded the crackling thin paper.

> To Jethri Gobelyn, in the care of Norn ven'Deelin Clan Ixin
> From Khatelane Gobelyn, Pilot on Duty, Gobelyn's Market
> Transmit Standard Day 75, SY 1118
>
> Hey, Jeth.
> Don't let the POD fool you—I'm doing administrative while Seeli catches up some stuff with the yard. It's looking like a long process; actually a near complete refit. I don't know if they told you. A Standard dirtside, minimum. Iza said she'd be staying with the ship, but—before you hear it from some Looper you run into, what it was, she had a disagreement with the local gendos and got herself a couple levels of arrested. Wasn't what you'd call pretty, or quiet, and even made some of the portside print papers. Point is, she's not stir-stuck here like she might be if we hadn't been around but off on the longest run she could fit inside the schedule. Seeli's acting as agent-on-the-spot, with Grig to keep her company. I'm on willfly with the Port, and running part-time back-up for the two of them. Cris has a gig with a franchise ship—and the rest of us found some little thing to do off-dirt, so we'll be a scattered crew for the next while. I'll try to keep in touch, Jethri, but—no promises, you know? Be sure I'll zap you the news when the Market lifts out of here. I'm sending

*this in front of Elthoria's published route; if they keep schedule it'll only be a bit old when you get it.*

*I'm also sending along a size B shipping crate; Iza says you're to have it.*

*The rest of the circumstance is that I had a chance to look over the duty roster for the past few Standards and noticed that you was default on Stinks. Thing is, Stinks carries a pay premium that somehow didn't make it to your account. It's kind of a joke on a per-shift, but I totted up the last five Standards' worth and figured in the interest, and it came out to a nice round number. We all figured you was saving up to buy a ship, Jeth, but who thought you'd finance it out of Stinks?*

*Paitor's running jobs for Terratrade, and I didn't know how to make the transfer, so that cash is in the crate with the other stuff.*

*Anyhow, I know you're in the middle of the biggest adventure ever, learning all you can from Master ven'Deelin, so I won't keep you any longer. Think about us sometime; we think about you often.*

*With love,*
*Khat*

He refolded the paper along its creases, and slid it away into the inner pocket of his jacket, in spite of which he didn't immediately rise to his duty. Instead, he stayed where he was, sitting low on his heels, head bent while he blinked the sudden fog of tears away.

Wasn't no cause for crying, he told himself. The ghosts of space witness, Khat's news was slim enough—hardly news at all, really. It was given that his cousins would reach for quick-jobs and temp berths—none of them had been born with mud on their feet. Likewise, he could have foretold that the detail work would fall to Seeli, and that Grig would stand her second. The captain...that was bad news, but almost expectable the way she tended to get a bit wild anytime she was planet-side. Probably there was more to it—and come to think of it, it seemed like there was more to a bunch of stuff than he'd realized.

Still, nothing to cry about in any of that, not with him having the biggest adventure ever.

He cleared his throat, raised his head and stood, pausing for a moment to be sure his face was properly ordered; then moved to his station at Master ven'Deelin's elbow.

HIS JOB THIS shift, as it had been last, was to stand next to and two steps behind Master ven'Deelin, where he could look and listen and soak up her style of trade and converse. More of that last was available to him than he would've thought, for the customers kept to the trading mode, and after one blank-faced stare at himself, would follow Master ven'Deelin into a more deliberate way of talking, which mostwise fell intelligible on his ear.

He had it as a working theory that a Liaden-born apprentice might likewise stand in need of practice in the trading mode, as it might not have been one they'd necessarily been taught in their growing-up years. With all those modes available between High and Low, surely no one but a lifelong student could be proficient in them all?

Whatever the reason, the customers treated him respectful—treated *Master ven'Deelin* respectful—and he was learning so much his head was in a fair way to exploding.

"That is well, then," Master ven'Deelin told the present customer—a black-haired man with a diamond drop in his left ear, wearing a jacket so heavy with embroidery that Jethri had to remind himself not to squint in protest. "We shall deliver no later than the third hour of Day Port, two days hence."

"Precisely so, Master Trader," the customer said, his voice quick and light. He held out a counter and a trade-card. Master ven'Deelin received both gravely and slotted them on the wires strung overhead—third one in, for "two day delivery."

"I am hosting a dinner party tomorrow evening, in the Little Hall," she murmured, as she finished with the card and token. "You would honor me by attending."

"Master Trader." The customer bowed, low. "The honor would be mine."

"That is well, then." She inclined her head and the customer moved off, giving up his place to the next in line, a boxy-built lady whose look-out was textile.

"Ah." Master ven'Deelin inclined her head. "This, my apprentice, will assist you. Textile is his specialty." She moved her hand, discovering Jethri to the lady, who gave no sign of either pleasure or dismay at being turned over to himself.

Jethri's feelings were all a-spin, though he did his best to maintain a bland and polite expression. He did take a deep breath, to center himself, which might have been too long, since the Master Trader murmured.

"Young Jethri?"

"Yes, Master," he said, and was mortified to hear his voice wobble.

Knees knocking, he stepped up the counter and bowed to the customer.

"Ma'am," he said, painfully slow, and deliberate. "How may I be honored to assist you?"

It were the handlooms the lady was after, which was good news of its kind. Jethri moved up-counter to where the bolts were stowed and pulled down the book. He looked over his shoulder, then, just to be aware how closely Master ven'Deelin was shadowing his work.

To his horror, she was about no such thing, but stood deep in conversation with another customer at the counter; all of her attention on that transaction and none whatsoever on him...

"Forgive me," murmured boxy-built lady. "I regret that my time is limited."

"Certainly, ma'am," Jethri murmured, opening the book on the counter in front of her. "As you can see, we have many fine weavings to choose from..."

For a lady short of time, she showed no disposition to rush her decision. She had him pull this bolt and that, then this again, and that other. With each, he steadied a little, found the words coming more smoothly, remembered the trick— taught by Uncle Paitor—of flipping the end over the top of the bolt, so that he could speak of the underweave and the irregularities born of hand looming.

In the end, the lady bought nothing, though she thanked him for the gifts of his time and expertise.

Jethri, shirt damp with exertion, racked the book and ordered the samples, then stepped back to Norn ven'Deelin's side.

Through the course of the shift, he heard her invite no fewer than two dozen traders and merchants to her dinner party. Three more times, she gave him to customers desirous of textile; twice, he scored chip and card, which he triumphantly threaded on the wires he found near the bolts.

And at last, the bell sounded, signaling the end of daytrading. Norn ven'Deelin reached up and turned off the booth light. Jethri closed his eyes and sagged against the bolt rack, head pounding. It was over. He had lived. He had, just maybe, not done anything irrevocably stupid. Now, they would go back to the ship, get out of the dirt, and the noise.

"So," Norn ven'Deelin said brightly, and he heard her clap her palms gently together. "Do me the honor of bearing me company on a stroll, Jethri Gobelyn. We shall amaze Tilene-port!"

He opened his eyes and looked at her, meeting bright black eyes. There was something in the way she stood, or maybe in the set of her face, that conveyed itself as a challenge. Jethri ground his teeth, straightened out of his lean and squared his shoulders, despite the holler put up by his back muscles.

"Yes, ma'am," he said, and bowed obedience to the Master Trader's word.

THE WALK WAS leisurely, and they stopped often to acknowledge the bows of Master ven'Deelin's numerous acquaintances, who every one stared at him like he was the four-headed calf from Venturis. Jethri sighed behind his mask of bland politeness. You'd think he'd be used to the stares by now, but someway every new one scraped a little deeper, hurt a little more.

Otherwise, the stroll was a better idea than he'd thought. Tilene's gravity was a hair less than ship's grav, which he'd at last gotten used to. And the simple act of putting one foot in front of the other seemed enough to ease the ache in his head, and smooth the kinks out of his spine.

Master ven'Deelin paused to receive a particularly low bow, augmented by the hand-sign for "greatest esteem" from a red-haired woman in upscale trading clothes.

"Bendara Tiazan," Master ven'Deelin inclined her head. "Allow me to be delighted to see you! You must dine with me upon the morrow."

The redhead straightened. Her eyes showed a little stretch, but give her credit, Jethri thought sourly, she didn't stare at him—her whole attention was on Norn ven'Deelin. "I am honored, Master Trader," she said, in the mode of junior to senior.

Again, Master ven'Deelin inclined her head. "Until to-morrow, Bendara Tiazan."

"Until tomorrow, Master Trader," the redhead murmured, and bowed herself out of the way.

Master ven'Deelin continued her stately progress, Jethri keeping pace, just behind her left elbow.

"So, Jethri Gobelyn," she murmured as they passed out of the red-haired trader's hearing. "What do you deduce from our guest list so far?"

He blinked, thinking back over those she had pressed to dine with her tomorrow.

"Ma'am, I scarcely know who these traders are," he said carefully. "But I wonder at the number of them. It seems less like a dinner and more like a—" he groped for the proper word. After a moment, he decided that it wasn't in his Liaden reper-toire and substituted a ship-term, "shivary."

"Hah." She glanced at him, black eyes gleaming. "You will perhaps find our poor entertainment to be a disappointment. I make no doubt that there will be dancing until dawn, nor no more than two or three visits from the proctors, bearing requests for silence."

He grappled the laugh back down deep into his chest and inclined his head solemnly. "Of course not, ma'am."

"Ah, Jethri Gobelyn, where is your address?" she said surprisingly. "A silver-tongue would grasp this opportunity to assure me that nothing I or mine might do could ever disappoint."

Jethri paused, looking down into her black eyes, which showed him nothing but tiny twin reflections of his own serious face. Was she pulling his leg? Or had he just failed a test? He licked his lips.

"I suppose," he said, slowly, "that I must not be a silver-tongue, ma'am."

Her face did not change, but she did put out a hand to pat him, lightly, on the arm. "That you are not, child. That you are not."

They moved on, Jethri trying to work out how to ask if being a silver-tongue was a good thing—and if it was how to go about learning the skill—without sounding a total fool. Meanwhile, Master ven'Deelin took the bows of three more traders of varying ranks, as Jethri read their clothing, and invited each to dine with her upon the morrow. If she kept at her current pace, he thought, they'd have to empty the trade theater itself to accommodate the crowd.

They strolled further down the flowered promenade. There were fewer people about now, and Master ven'Deelin picked up the pace a bit, so Jethri needed to stretch his legs to keep up. Ahead, the walkway split into three, the center portion rising into an arch, the others going off at angles to the right and left. Somewhere nearby was the sound of water running, enormous amounts of water, it must be, from the racket it was making, and the air was starting to feel unpleasantly soggy.

Jethri frowned, maybe lagging a little from his appointed spot at Master ven'Deelin's elbow, trying to bear down on the feeling that he was breathing *water*, which was by no means a good thing…

From the left hand path came voices, followed quickly by three top-drawer traders: A woman, star blond and narrow in the face, flanked by two young men—one as fair and as narrow as she and the other taller, with hair of a darker gold, his face somewhat rounder, and his eyes a trifle a-squint, as if he had a headache.

With a start, Jethri recognized his friend of the utility corridor, who had been so patient and understanding in the matter of bows. His first notion was to break into a fool-wide grin and rush forward to grab the man by the shoulders in a proper spacer greeting—which would never do, naturally, besides being one of the three top ways, if Arms Master sig'Kethra was to be believed, to take delivery of a knife between the ribs.

Still, if it would be rude to give way to the full scope of his feelings, he could at least give Tan Sim pen'Akla the honor of a proper bow.

Jethri placed himself before the threesome, and paused, awaiting their attention. The woman saw him first, her pale narrow brows plunging into a frown, but he cared not for her. He looked over her shoulder, made eye contact with Tan Sim and swept the bow of greeting the other had shown him, supplemented with the gesture that meant "joy."

He quickly realized he should have gone with his initial notion.

The fair, narrow young man shouted something beyond Jethri's current lexicon, his hand slapping at his belt, which gesture he understood all too nicely. He fell back a step, looking for a leap-to, when Tan Sim jumped instead, knocking the other's hand aside, with a sharp, "Have done! Will you harm the ven'Deelin's own apprentice?"

"You!" The other shouted. "You saw how he bowed to you! If you had the least bit of proper feeling—"

Oh. Jethri felt his stomach sink to the soles of his boots. He *had* botched it. Badly.

Stepping forward, he bowed again—this a simple bow of contrition.

"Please forgive me if my bow offended," he said, speaking in the mode of junior to senior, which *had* to be right, no matter which of the three chose to hear him. "Master Tan Sim himself is aware that I am…less conversant with bows than I would be. My only thought was to honor one who had given me kindness and fellowship. I regret that my error has caused distress."

"It speaks Liaden, of a fashion." The woman said, apparently to her sons, Jethri thought, but meaning for him to hear and take damage from it.

"He speaks Liaden right well for one new come to it," Tan Sim returned, heatedly. "And shows an adult's melant'i, as well. I taught him that bow myself—which he does not tell you, preferring to take all blame to himself."

"Speak soft to my mother, half-clan!" The pale young man jerked and spun, palm rising, his intent plain. Jethri jumped forward, arm up, intercepted the man's slap at the wrist, and grabbed hold just tight enough to get the message across.

"Here now!" he said in Terran, sounding remarkably like Cris, to his own ears. "None of that."

"Unhand me!" shouted the man, trying, unsuccessfully, to pull his wrist free, and "Call the proctors!"

"No need for proctors, young chel'Gaibin," Master ven'Deelin's voice was shockingly cool in that heated moment. "Jethri, of your goodness, return to Lord chel'Gaibin the use of his arm."

"Yes, ma'am," he said, and did as she asked, though he stayed close, in the event the lordship took it into his head to swing out at Tan Sim again.

He needn't have worried; all eyes were on Master ven'Deelin, who stood calm and unworried, her hands tucked in her belt, considering the other trader.

"Norn ven'Deelin," the woman said at last, and it didn't sound respectful at all.

The master trader inclined her head. "Infreya chel'Gaibin. It has been some years since we last spoke. I trust I find you well."

"You find me insulted and assaulted, *Master Trader*. I will have Balance for the harm done."

Master ven'Deelin tipped her head. "Harm? Has the heir's sleeve been crushed?"

Infreya chel'Gaibin glared. "You may put the assault of an unregulated Terran upon a registered guildsman no higher than amusing, if it pleases you. I assure you that the guild and the port will take a far different view."

"And yet," Master ven'Deelin murmured. "Jethri is hardly unregulated. He stands as my apprentice—"

"Oh, very good!" chel'Gaibin interrupted. "A 'prentice lays hands upon a trader while the master stands by and smiles!"

"—and my son," Master ven'Deelin finished calmly. Jethri bit his lip, hard, and concentrated on keeping his face empty of emotion. He darted a quick look at Tan Sim, but found that young man standing at his ease, watching the proceedings with interest but no apparent dismay.

"Your son!" Apparently Trader chel'Gaibin wasn't convinced, for which Jethri blamed her not at all.

Master ven'Deelin swept a languid hand in the general direction of Tan Sim. "As much mine as that one is yours." She tipped an eyebrow. "But come, you wished satisfaction for insult and assault. We may settle that between us now, you and I."

Trader chel'Gaibin licked her lips and though she seemed to Jethri a woman unlikely to back down in a tight spot, there was something to the cast of her shoulders that strongly suggested she was looking for a way out of this one.

Behind her, Tan Sim shifted, drawing all eyes to himself. "Mother, surely there is no insult here? Jeth Ree bowed as I had taught him, and when he saw one who was to him a stranger threaten one with whom he has had honorable dealings, he acted to nullify the threat—and most gently, too!"

"Gently!" spat the other man. Tan Sim turned wondering eyes his way.

"Never tell me he bruised you, brother! A mere halfling? Surely—"

"This must be the Terran, Mother!" Lord chel'Gaibin interrupted excitedly, turning his back on his brother. "Recall that it was a Terran off of *Elthoria* who began the brawl at Kailipso—"

"Enough," the woman snapped. She stood silent for a moment, staring, none-too-pleasantly, at Tan Sim. Jethri felt his chest tighten in sympathy: Exactly did Iza Gobelyn stare just before she cut loose of mayhem and brought a body to wishing he'd been born to another ship, if at all.

Composing her face, she turned back to Master ven'Deelin and inclined her head, grudging-like.

"Very well. My son speaks eloquently in defense of yours, Master Trader. We are to see nothing more than halfling high spirits—and a misunderstanding of custom."

"It would seem indeed to be the case," Master ven'Deelin said calmly; "and no cause for experienced traders such as ourselves to be calling for Balance. Well we know what halflings are." Her eyes moved to Tan Sim, and she inclined her head gently. "Young pen'Akla."

Tan Sim's eyes widened and he bowed low with graceful haste. "Master ven'Deelin."

"Enough!" Tan Sim's mother snapped again. She turned her glare on the master trader and gave a bare dip of the head. "Master Trader. Good evening." She didn't wait for a return bow—maybe, Jethri thought, because she knew she didn't rate one. Turning, she gathered her boys by eye, and stalked off.

When they were alone, Jethri turned and bowed, very low and very careful—and held it, eyes pointing at the toes of his boots.

Above him, him heard Master ven'Deelin sigh.

"In all truth, young Jethri, you have a knack. How came you by chel'Gaibin's Folly?"

Bent double, he blinked. "Ma'am?"

"Stand up, child," she interrupted and, when he had, said, "Tan Sim pen'Akla. How came you to his attention?"

Jethri cleared his throat. "I was—practicing my bows in the service corridor and he came upon me. He was most k-kind and helpful, ma'am, and when I said that I was in his debt, he declared no such thing. So then I thought to ask how I should bow to him, if we were to meet again, and he showed me thus—"

He performed the thing—and heard Master ven'Deelin sigh once more.

"Yes, of course. Well he might yearn to receive such a bow—" She moved a hand, eloquent of exasperation.

"Young things. All is anguish and high drama." She turned her head; a moment later Jethri heard it too—voices approaching down the right hand way.

"Come along, young Jethri. Our evening has just become full."

Obediently, he took his place at her elbow, and they moved on. But for themselves, the promenade was empty and Jethri cleared his throat.

"Please, ma'am. I am not really—really your son."

"Indeed you are; did you not hear me say it? Surely, a momentous occasion for us both. We return now to our ship to discuss the matter in more detail. Until then, I ask that you repose in silence. I have thoughts to think."

Jethri bit his lip. "Yes ma'am," he whispered.

# Day 106
## Standard Year 1118

## *Elthoria*

"YOU KNOW TOO little of our customs." Master ven'Deelin folded her hands on her desk and considered him out of her sharp black eyes. "Indeed, how could it be otherwise? Similarly, you are ignorant of the—histories that may lie between clans and the children of clans. The child of a Terran trade vessel has no need to know these things. And I—foolishly, I thought we might separate trade from clan. Pah! Trade and culture are twined more deeply than I had wished to understand. And now we are together caught in the nets of culture, and a child of ven'Deelin may *not* be a fool."

Jethri shifted miserably in the chair across from her. "Ma'am, I'm not a child of ven'Deelin—"

She held up a hand, and he swallowed the rest of his protest.

"Peace. The tale unfolds. Listen, and cultivate patience. They are two skills which serve every trader well."

"Yes, ma'am," he said, folding his hands tightly on his knee and pressing his lips together.

After a moment, she lowered her hand and continued.

"A child of ven'Deelin must need know both history and custom. We commence your education now, with excerpts of both."

"First, custom. It is Law that each member of each clan shall marry as the clan instructs, to produce children for the clan and also to seal and cement what alliances the clan may require in order to prosper. I have myself been contracted twice; once in order that the clan should have my heir to re- place me as Ixin's master of trade, in due time. Again, to seal the peace between Ixin and Aragon; the child of that contract of course went to Aragon. So it is with most of us; some may be required to marry but once, some several times. Some few unfortunates discover themselves to be the perfect halves of a wizard's match—but those matings need not concern us here.

"Here, we discuss contract marriage and the fact that Infreya chel'Gaibin—a dutiful daughter of Clan Rinork—did some twenty-five Standards gone marry as her delm instructed, the fruit of that union being Bar Jen chel'Gaibin, her heir.

"Six Standards later, she married again, somewhat behind the fact as it is said and counted, into Clan Quiptic—a House of the lower mid-tier." Once more she held up her hand, though Jethri hadn't made a sound.

"I know that this will seem odd to you, Rinork being, as it is, so very High, but there were reasons beyond the fact that she was already pregnant by the time the thing was arranged, and by none other than Quiptic Himself. A very young delm he was, and not by any means stupid. But Infreya was a beauty in her youth and his mother had died before tutoring him suf- ficiently in all the faces that treachery might wear.

"In any case, the child—young Tan Sim—went to Quiptic, and Quiptic's mines went to Rinork, in settlement of the con- tract fees." She paused, eyes closed, then shifted sharply in her chair, as if annoyed with herself, and continued.

"The loss of the mines was very close to a mortal blow in itself, but as I said, the young delm was no fool. With the leverage he gained from his alliance with Rinork, he thought to win certain short term—but decisive!—advantages in sev- eral trades. Very nearly, he brought Quiptic about. In the end, alas, it was a quirk of the Exchange which pushed the blade home. The clan was dissolved; the young delm hung himself. Infreya petitioned Rinork and received permission to adopt Tan Sim pen'Akla, who might well have one day been Quiptic Himself, as a child of the clan alone." She moved her shoulders.

"So, that tale. You may consider it located *here*, if your stories need locations. The other story you need to hear takes place at a tavern in far Solcintra Port, where one For Don chel'Gaibin cheated a certain young trader at a game of cards. The trader, understanding that the play had been underhanded, called his lordship to answer her on the field of honor." She sighed. "Young things. All is anguish and high drama. I doubt it ever occurred to her to call the games master and ask that he set the thing right, though she thought it many a time, after. No, it must be a duel. For Don, who was a fool besides being many years the trader's senior, accepted the challenge and chose pistols at twenty-four paces. They met at the appointed place, at dawn, their seconds in train. The duel itself was over in a matter of moments. The young trader had killed her man." She looked at Jethri, and there was nothing that he could read on her smooth, golden face.

"Depend upon it, Ixin was displeased. As was Rinork, of course. How they roared for Balance, though the witnesses to a soul swore it was fairly done and For Don the favorite for the victor—as the tavern wager book clearly showed! Well, you have seen how it is with Rinork and Balance. In any wise, nothing was owed and the price was met. Ixin sent me on the long route, to learn, as she would have it, common sense. By the time I returned to Liad, there were new scandals to occupy the gossips, and Rinork and Ixin had agreed not to meet. This evening was the first time we have done so, in more than three dozen Standards." She inclined her head, possibly ironic.

"All hail to you, young Jethri."

Jethri blinked, trying to picture a young Norn ven'Deelin, alone with her pistol in the dawn, facing down a man older and more skilled than she...

"Oh, aye," Master ven'Deelin said, as if reading his mind— though more likely, Jethri thought, it had been his unguarded face—"I was a sad rogue in my youth. But there—a mother has no secrets from her son."

Right. Jethri frowned at her. "If you please, Master Trader, how am I now your son?"

"Because I had told Rinork so, child—else their Balance would have been worth your life. An 'unregulated Terran,' 'prenticed to ven'Deelin or no, is nothing to give a Rinork pause in a rage." She moved a hand, showing him the litter of papers on her desk.

"When I and your true-kin wrote contract, it was with the best interest of the trade in our minds. I contracted to teach you the art, as well as a certain understanding of matters Liaden—this to improve and facilitate the trade, which is the duty of a master trader. Nowhere was it intended that you should take your death of this, Jethri Gobelyn. Forgive me, but, should you die, there will be damage dealt to more than those who value you for yourself. Pray bear this in mind the next time you befriend strangers in back hallways."

Jethri felt his ears heat. This whole mess was his fault, right enough…

"Have you other questions?" Norn ven'Deelin's voice cut through the thought.

Other questions? Only dozens. He shook his head helplessly, and chose one at random.

"Why did she—did Trader chel'Gaibin adopt Tan Sim? I mean, if the only reason her clan—"

"Rinork," said Master ven'Deelin.

He nodded impatiently. "Rinork—if the only reason Rinork started the kid in the first place was to trap Quiptic and steal his mines, then why did she care what happened to him?"

There was a small pause, during which Master ven'Deelin took some care about arranging the way her fingers nested against each other as she folded her hands together.

"An excellent question, young Jethri. I have often wondered the same. Perhaps it was merely self-preservation; if the child were left to be absorbed by whatever clan might take him, questions would possibly arise regarding the contract which had produced him, and whether certain parties could have been said to be acting in good faith.

"Or, perhaps, she could not bear to see one of her blood— even half-blooded—slide away into obscurity. They have a great deal of self-worth, Rinork." She moved her shoulders. "In the end, why does not matter. The boy was brought into the house of his mother and has been given an education and a place in the clan's business. I find him to be a young trader of note, in his talents far superior to the honorable chel'Gaibin heir." As careful as she had been in their folding, she unfolded her hands all at once, and put them palm-flat against the desk.

"It is late and tomorrow we trade early and shivary to meet the dawn, eh? As my fostered son, you will stand at my side and be made known to all. You will wear this—" She extended a hand; something gleamed silver between her fingers. Jethri leaned forward and took the small token: The Clan Ixin moon-and-rabbit, cast in—he weighed the thing thoughtfully in his hand—platinum, with a punch pin welded to the back.

"You will honor me by wearing that at all times," Norn ven'Deelin said, pushing herself to her feet, "so that all will know you for one of Ixin.

"In keeping with your new status, your course of study will be accelerated and broadened." Suddenly, amazingly, she *smiled*.

"We will make a Liaden from you yet, young Jethri."

# Day 107
# Standard Year 1118

## *Elthoria* and Tilene

HE HIT THE bunk with half his sleep-shift behind him, closed his eyes, touched sleep—and dropped it as the wake-up chime dinned.

"Mud," he muttered, pushing himself upright and blinking blearily at the clock across the room. It displayed a time more than an hour in advance of his usual wake-up.

"Mud, dirt, dust and pollen!" he expanded, and swung his feet over the edge, meaning to go over and slap the buzzer off, then get himself another hour's snooze.

He was halfway across the cabin on this mission when his eye caught the amber glow over his inbox. Frowning, bleary and bad-tempered, he changed course, and scooped a short handful of ship's flimsies out of the bin.

The top sheet was his amended schedule for the day, by which he saw he was presently in danger of being late for a "security meeting" with Pen Rel. He'd been late for a meeting with Pen Rel once, and had no ambition to repeat the experience. That being the case, he did turnabout and headed for the 'fresher, sorting pages as he went.

The second flimsy was from Cargo Master Gar Sad per'Etla, informing him that a crate had arrived and been placed in his personal bin. He nodded; that would be Khat's B crate. He'd need to check that out soon, if he could pry five personal minutes between lessons and trade.

The third flimsy was from Norn ven'Deelin and that one stopped him cold.

*Greetings to you, my son. I trust that the new day finds you in health and high spirits. Pray bestow the gift of your presence upon me immediately you conclude your business with Arms Master sig'Kethra. We shall break our fast together and tell over the anticipated joys of the day.*

Jethri rubbed his head. She was taking this mother-and-son thing serious, he thought and then sighed. After all, it was a matter of keeping her word. In a sense—no, he thought, mouth suddenly dry—in *fact* she had given him her name. And she'd expect him to set the same value on that priceless commodity as she did herself.

"Mud," he whispered. "Oh, mud and dust, Jethri Gobelyn, what've you got yourself into?"

"As you have no doubt learned from your study of our route, we remain at Tilene for five more days. At the end of that time, we shall set course for Modrid, and thence the inner worlds, which, as you will readily perceive, is a change of schedule."

Jethri stifled a yawn and sipped his morning tea. There was caffeine present in the beverage, true enough, but he found himself wishing after a cup of true coffee—aye, and maybe a mug o'mite too.

"You are disinterested," the master trader said softly, "and yet it is solely for the benefit of yourself that we alter our itinerary."

Soft it was said, yet it hit the ear hard. Jethri put his cup down, and looked at her.

"You do not approve?" she asked, face bland.

He took a breath, wishing he felt more awake. "Ma'am, it's only that I wonder why the ship's route needs to be changed on my account."

"An excellent question." She spread jam on her roll and took a bite. Jethri looked down at his plate, picked up a roll and tore it in half, releasing the scent of warm, fresh bread.

"It is understood that a son of ven'Deelin will need training which is not available to those of one ship, on a trade tour of the far outworlds. Thus, we plot a course nearer to the centers of civilization, where you may receive those things which you lack. You will, also, I hope, benefit by observing a different style of trade than that which is practiced along the edge." She picked up her teacup.

Roll forgotten in his hand, Jethri sat, thinking back on names and honor and Balance, and on his deficiencies as so far discovered. He cleared his throat.

"Ma'am," he said slowly, feeling his way around phrasing that she might find disrespectful of her honor. "I've been thinking and it—I don't think that I would be a—an exemplary son. Not," he amended quickly, as her eyebrows lifted quizzically, "that I wouldn't do my best, but—I wouldn't want to dishonor you, ma'am."

"Ah." She put her cup down and inclined her head. "Your concern speaks well of you. However, I know that it is not possible for you to dishonor me. I know you for a person of melant'i, whose every instinct is honorable. I repose the utmost confidence in you, my child, and I am at peace, knowing that you hold my name in your hands."

Jethri's stomach dropped, even as his eyes filled with tears. "Ma'am…"

She held up a hand. "Another way, then. Say that the dice have been cast—there is a similar saying in Terran, is there not? So. We play the game through."

Except that her good name was nothing like a game, Jethri thought—and he knew so little.

"Yes, ma'am," he said, trying not to sound as miserable as he felt.

"Good. Now, while we are in the mode of change—you will find your duty cycle has likewise changed. You will spend tomorrow and the following four days assisting Cargo Master per'Etla with the pods. It is mete that you have an understanding of the intricacies of the cargo master's art."

As it happened, he had a pretty good understanding of the cargo master's art, the *Market* not exactly shipping a cargo master.  He remembered sitting next to his father, staring in fascination while Arin worked out the logistics of mass and spin.  Come to that, neither Paitor nor Grig was likely to have let him get away without knowing how to balance a pod.  Granted, *Elthoria* could probably ship all *Market's* pods in one of hers, but the art of the thing ought to be constant.

Jethri cleared his throat.  "I have had some training in this area, Master Trader," he said, hoping he had the right mix of polite and assured.

"Ah, excellent!" she said, spreading jam over the second half of her roll.  "Then you will be more of a help than a hindrance to my good friend per'Etla."

Somehow, Jethri thought, that didn't sound as encouraging as it might have.  He glanced down at the roll in his hand, and reached for the jam pot.

"I have some news from the Guild which you may find of interest," Norn ven'Deelin murmured.

Jethri glanced up from spreading jam.  "Ma'am?"

"Another game of counterfeit cards has been exposed and closed, this at the port of Riindel."

He blinked, at a loss for a heartbeat, then memory caught up with him.  "They weren't using your card, ma'am, were they?"

"Our card, my son.  But no—you may put any fear of a taint to our melant'i aside.  Those at Riindel had chosen to honor Ziergord with their attention."

Whoever Ziergord was.  Jethri inclined his head.  "I'm glad the wrongdoers were caught," he said, which had the advantage of being both true and unlikely to be found an improper response.  "Surely any others who have been tempted will see that the…game…is dangerous and refuse to play."

There was a small silence.  "Indeed, perhaps they will," Master ven'Deelin said politely.

Too politely, to Jethri's ear. He looked up, questioning, only to be met with a smile and a small movement of her hand.

"Eat your breakfast, my son," she murmured. "It will not do to be late to trade."

BUSINESS WAS BRISK at the booth, with merchant folk and traders lined up to have a word of business with Master ven'Deelin. As near as Jethri could tell, every last one of them was invited to "dinner"—not that he had all that much time to eavesdrop, being busy with customers of his own.

Today, the textile was of interest. Over and over, he showed his samples, and gave his speech about hand looming and plant dyes. Occasionally he caught what was—he thought— a careful glance at his new pin, claiming him of Ixin. Yet it was not curiosity which drew these people, it was the trade, and he reveled in it. Often enough, the client left him with a counter and a trade-card, which he took great care to keep paired and ordered on the wire above his station.

He hung the last pair up and looked down, face arranged politely, to greet the next in line—and froze.

Before him stood Bar Jan chel'Gaibin, hands tucked into his sleeves and a gleam in his pale eyes that reminded Jethri forcibly of Mac Gold in a mood for a brawl.

Casually, the Liaden inclined his head. "Good day to you, *son* of ven'Deelin. I bring you tidings of your friend, Tan Sim pen'Akla, who has been sent to make his way along the tertiary trade lanes, for the best good of the clan." He inclined his head again, snarky-like, daring Jethri to hit him. "I thought you might find the news of interest."

Teeth grinding, face so bland his cheeks hurt, Jethri inclined his head—not far.

"One is always grateful for news of friends," he said, which was about as far as he could trust his voice with Tan Sim thrown off his ship in sacrifice of this man's spite…

chel'Gaibin lifted his eyebrows. "Just so," he said softly, and with no further courtesy turned his back and walked away.

In the momentary absence of customers, Jethri let his breath out in a short, pungent Terran phrase, and turned his attention to the samples, which were sorely in need of order.

"Young Jethri," Master ven'Deelin said some while later, during a lull in the business. "I wonder if you might enlighten me as to a certain Terran—I assume it is Terran—phrase that I have recently heard."

Ears warming, he turned to look at her. "I will do my best, ma'am."

"Certainly, when have you ever failed at that? I confess myself quite terrified of you—but, there, I will give over teasing you and only ask: This word *sobe*. What is its meaning?"

He blinked. "Sobe? I do not think…"

"Sobe," Master ven'Deelin interrupted. "I am certain that was the word. Perhaps it was directed at the departing back of a certain young trader. Yes, that is where I heard it! 'You sobe,' was the very phrase."

"Oh." His ears were hot now, and well on the way to spontaneous combustion. "That would, um, denote a person of—who has no manners, ma'am."

"Ah, is it so?" She tipped her head, as if considering the merit of his answer. "Yes, the particular young trader—it could perhaps be said that his manner wants polish. A useful word, my son; I thank you for making it known to me."

"Yes ma'am. Um." He cleared his throat. "I note that it is not…a courteous word."

"Understood. In the High Tongue, we say, 'thus-and-so has *no melant'i*.' It is not a statement made lightly."

"No, ma'am."

She reached out and patted him on the arm. "We shall speak of these matters at greater length. In the meanwhile, I have extinguished the light for an hour. Pray do me the kindness of seeking out the booth of Clan Etgora—it will be the glass and star on the flag—and say to my old friend del'Fordan that it would ease my heart greatly to behold his face, and that he must, of his kindness, dine with us this evening. Eh? After that, you may find yourself something to eat. If I am not here when you return, light the lamp and do your part. Any who have need of me will wait a few moments." She cocked her head. "Is that understood, young Jethri?"

He bowed. "Master Trader, it is."

"Hah." Once more, she patted his arm. "We must teach you, 'obedience to an elder.' Go now, and take my message to del'Fordan."

THE TRADE LAMP was still out when he returned to the booth, just under an hour later. Despite this, there were two lines of traders waiting patiently, a long line on the Master Trader's side; and a much shorter on his.

Jethri hurried forward, reached up and turned the key, waiting until the disk glowed blue before he ducked under the counter and pulled back the curtain. He ran a quick eye over his samples, then bowed to his first prospect.

"Good-day to you, sir. May I be honored to bring to your attention to these examples of the textile maker's art?"

He was deep into his third presentation when Master ven'Deelin arrived, took her place and began to trade. It seemed to him, even from his side of the booth, that her cadence and attention were off a bit, as if she were bothered by a bad stomach or headache or other ill.

It was some hours before there was a lull sufficient for him to ask her if something was wrong.

"Wrong?" She moved her shoulders. "Perhaps not— surely not." Her mouth tightened and she looked aside and he thought she would say no more, but after a moment she sighed and murmured.

"You surprise, Jethri my son. It is nothing so definite as *wrong*—but there, you have a proper trader's eye for detail, and a sense of the rhythm of trade...." She moved a hand, fingers flicking as if she cast that line of chat aside.

"It came to me," she said softly, reaching to the counter to straighten a display book that didn't need it, "that perhaps a certain practice—which is not, you understand, entirely against guild rule—had lately surfaced upon Tilene. So, I betook myself to the Trade Bar to learn if this was the case."

Jethri looked at her, feeling a little chilly, of a sudden.

Master ven'Deelin moved her shoulders. "Well, and it is not entirely against guild rule, as I said. Merely, it is a measure found...inefficient...and not clearly to the best interest of the trade." It seemed to Jethri that she sagged—and then straightened, shoulders thrown back with a will and a sparkle showing hard in her black eyes.

"Well, it is not ours, and never was. I had thought to meddle, but, there—the thing is done."

"But—" said Jethri, but just then a customer came up to his side of the booth, and he had no more chance to talk to Norn ven'Deelin for the rest of the long, busy day.

# Day 107
# Standard Year 1118

## *Elthoria* and Tilene

MASTER TEL'ONDOR BOWED, low and extravagant, Honor to a Lord Not One's Own, or so it read to Jethri, who was in no mood to be tweaked, tutor or no. His head ached from a long day on the floor, the spanking new shirt with its lacy cuffs foretold disasters involving sauces and jellies across its brilliant white field. And now he was here to learn the way to go on at an intimate dinner for two hundred of Master ven'Deelin's closest friends—all in the next twelve minutes.

Curtly, he answered the Protocol Officer's bow—nothing more than the sharpest and starkest of bows, straightening to glare straight into the man's eyes.

Master tel'Ondor outright *laughed.*

"Precisely!" he crowed, and held his hand out, fingers smoothing the air in the gesture that roughly meant "peace."

"Truly, young Jethri, I am all admiration. *Thus* shall impertinence be answered—and yes, I was impertinent. Some you may meet—at this gather this evening, or at other times— some may wish to dazzle you, some may wish to take advantage. You would do well to answer them all so—a ven'Deelin born would do no less."

Jethri considered him. "And what about those who merely wish to establish a proper mode?"

"Ah, excellent." Master tel'Ondor's eyes gleamed. "It will perhaps be done thus—" The bow between equals, that was.

"Or this—" Child of the House of an Ally. "Or even—" Senior Trader to Junior.

"Anything more…elaborate, we shall say, may be viewed with the sharpest suspicion. I leave to you to decide—as I see your intuition is sound—the scope of your answers there."

Jethri closed his eyes. "Master tel'Ondor…"

"Yes, yes! You are to learn the entire mode of a High House fosterling in the next eight heartbeats, eh? I will be plain with you, young Jethri—neither your skills nor mine are sufficient to meet this challenge. Demonstrate, if you please, your bow of introduction—yes. And of farewell?…adequate. Once more—yes. Now—of obedience?"

Jethri complied and heard the protocol officer sigh.

But: "It will suffice," Master tel'Ondor said, and moved his hands, shooing Jethri toward the door. "Go. Contrive not to shame me."

Jethri grinned and inclined his head. "Good evening, sir."

"Bah," said Master tel'Ondor.

HE NEEDN'T HAVE worried about ruining his pretty new shirt with sauce stains or soup spots. It soon became clear that, while Master ven'Deelin expected her guests to eat—and eat well—from the buffet spread along three of four walls of the so-called Little Hall, she herself—with him a shadow attached to her left elbow—prowled the room, with the apparent intent of speaking with everyone present.

She did supply herself with a glass of wine, and insisted that he do the same, with instructions to sip when she did, then slipped into the crowd, where her headway went down to a step or two at a time, in between bows and conversation.

Jethri found the conversation singularly frustrating; spoken wholly in modes other than the mercantile, and much more rapidly than his half-trained ear could accommodate.

The exception to this was the beginning of every exchange, in which he was brought a step forward by a soft hand on his arm. "One's foster child, Jethri," Master ven'Deelin would say, and he would make his plain bow of greeting. Then she would make him known to the person she was speaking with, who, almost without exception bowed as to the child of an ally.

He would then repeat their name, with a polite dip of the head, and the talk would jet over his head in a poetry of alien syllables.

A word or two here and there—he did catch those. Sometimes, a whole phrase unrolled inside his ears. Rarely enough to help him piece together the full sense of the conversation. He did find time to be glad that the default mode for facial expression was bland; at least he didn't have to pretend to be interested in what he couldn't understand. And he used his idle time to consider the scale and scope of the 'dinner party,' trying to figure what the point of it might be.

A gathering less like a common spacer's shivary would be hard to find, he thought. Where there'd be music and singing and boozing and smooching at a shivary, here there was the music of many different and low-key conversations. While everyone he could see had a wine glass in one hand, nobody seemed drunk, or even boisterous. And if there was any smooching going on…Well, frankly, he'd come to wonder how it was that any new Liadens got made.

"Good evening," a soft voice purred in his ear. Trade had never sounded so pretty, and Jethri jerked around and looked down, meeting a melting pair of gray eyes set at a slight angle in a heart-shaped golden face, framed by wispy gilt hair.

"Good…evening," he managed and bowed the bow of introduction. "Jethri Gobelyn. In what way may I serve you, ma'am?"

Her lips curved in a tightly controlled smile. "Parvet sig'Flava. I had in mind a way in which we might each serve the other, if you are of like mind. The evening grows tedious and I would welcome a…diversion…such as yourself." She swayed half a step forward, her melting gray gaze never leaving his face.

Jethri jumped back, ears burning. He'd just been propositioned for bed duty, or all Dyk's tales and teasing was for naught. That everything he knew on the subject was from tales and health tapes was due again to being juniormost. None of his cousins had wanted to bed the baby...

"Come," Parvet sig'Flava murmured—and he thought her voice was a little slurred, like maybe this wasn't her first, or even her third, glass of wine on the evening. "My ship departs within the two-day, and shall, regrettably, miss Tilene's Festival. So," she leaned toward him, her pretty face upturned to him like one of the flowers that Gaenor so missed from her home.

"So," she said again, "since we will be denied the opportunity to meet in the park, perhaps we may embrace Festival a few days early. Perhaps we might rent us an hour-room and have joy of each other before dawn calls us each to our duty."

"Ma'am, I—that is—"

"That is," Norn ven'Deelin's voice cut in over his stammer, and very firmly, too, "that this my son is needed at his station this evening, though he thanks you most sincerely for your offer."

"Indeed," Jethri grabbed at his lagging wits and inclined his head, very respectful. "I am flattered, ma'am, but duty calls."

She looked at him, gray eyes unreadable, then bowed, senior to junior, which was right enough, Jethri thought bitterly, though making him even more aware of the potential gifts she'd had on offer.

"I understand. Fair profit." She bowed then to Norn ven'Deelin, trader to master.

"Master Trader," she murmured and faded away into the crowd.

Ears on fire, and uneasily aware of the blood pounding in his veins. Jethri turned to face Norn ven'Deelin.

"Truly, young Jethri," she said softly, "you have a knack. No one less than the sig'Flava wishes to attach you. Indeed, you are a paragon." She moved her hand, inviting him to walk with her.

"Attend me, now. Later, we will speak of Festival and...those other...lessons which you may require."

"Yes, Master Trader," he murmured, feeling four kinds of fool, and not quite able to make up his mind whether he was more grateful to her for the rescue or aggravated with himself for needing one.

She patted his arm. "Softly, child," she said, and then used her chin to point out a certain black-haired gentleman in the crowd. "Look, there is del'Fordan's heir. We must make you known to him."

# Day 108
# Standard Year 1118

## Tilene Docks

SCHEDULED TO MEET Cargo Master per'Etla on the stroke of the shift-change, Pen Rel and Jethri arrived a dozen ticks or more before time—unusual, Pen Rel being a man who valued punctuality.

The unusual was explained soon enough, as, Jethri at his shoulder, Pen Rel inspected the dockside security cameras and checked the duty clerk's roster of scheduled deliveries. After that was done, there was still some time left over to wait.

Together, they leaned on the waist-high boundary wall, Jethri trying not to yawn.

Tilene's docks, like many world-side docks, were covered topside against the outside elements with sealable domes and great sliding panels. Unlike worlds where the ambient temperature or atmosphere was downright noxious, Tilene's docks were an integral part of the city, with portions of local roads and transit lines running through at odd heights.

As Pen Rel explained it, pointing here and there to make his points, the expanse of stained 'crete they stood on—currently crowded with modular bins destined for transshipment in *Elthoria's* pods—was just a wide spot in an industrial ribbon that extended across the continent in both directions, being part of a celebrated world-spanning planned city. The tremble beneath them was not from starship generators but from the flow of traffic tunneled beneath the floor they stood on; the overhead transit sets joined them to flow as an artery across mountain, farm, and plains.

The wonder of it all was somewhat lost on Jethri, who didn't much care how Grounders got from place to place, though he did try to pay attention. Knowing Pen Rel, there'd be a test—and when he least expected it, too.

A low groan came from overhead. Jethri glanced upward, and saw the dome in motion, beyond it an empty and horrifying blue-green sky. Stomach churning, he started to look away, but a sudden glitter in the high air caught his gaze.

"'ware!" he yelled, jerking right out of his lean. Grabbing Pen Rel's arm, he spun toward *Elthoria's* ramp.

"Hold!" His own arm was gripped, none too gently. "It is merely water!"

Perforce, he froze, heart pounding, and in a few moments there came a massive splash as the falling sheets met the 'crete a pod's length away, and settled into a fading mist. Pen Rel released his arm.

"It must have rained overnight," he said, shockingly calm. "The water would have collected in the guide channels." As if it explained everything. Clearly he was not concerned, and probably thought Jethri an idiot, though, as usual, he didn't say so.

From the edge of his eye, Jethri saw some winged creature pass over head, and next a silver jetship lifting for the stratosphere. He quickly averted his gaze, staring instead at the waiting bins.

"Yes, there is much to see in a city!" Pen Rel, said, apparently agreeing with something Jethri was supposed to have said.

He took a hard breath.

"You pardon," he said, glad to hear that his voice held steady. "I wonder why they opened the dome. There are no ships preparing to leave, nor any warning of an incoming..."

Pen Rel glanced fearlessly upward, and then back to Jethri.

"Ah, I see. Proper ship-board concerns." He swept an arm over his head, encompassing not only the dome, but the wide, empty sky beyond. "One likes to keep control of the ports, the atmosphere, and access—and how is that to be done if birds are free to fly where they might?"

Jethri almost shook his head, the neck muscles protesting as he caught the motion and produced instead a small bow of acknowledgment.

"Ah," Pen Rel said again, and inclined his head. "Mostly, it is a matter of temperature control. How much simpler, after all, to let the wandering air take the heat away than to condition the dock entire."

"My thanks," Jethri said, remembering to keep his voice soft, his gaze stringently at dock level.

A dusty vehicle trailing modular pallets was arriving hastily at their section of 'crete, various warning beeps and the noisy whine of high power hybrid electric motors an active discouragement to conversation. The victualer's sigil on the side of the vehicle was familiar enough—Jethri had seen a half-dozen or more of the same type of van running up and down the concourse as they'd waited.

The driver swung his rig in a final semi-circle, stopping amidst the puddled remains of the recent downpour. The clerk looked up from his record-keeping with a grimace.

"Well before shift-change we ask for, and what do we get? Excuses and a delivery at the hour."

"It is always thus," Pen Rel said, and then in a lighter voice, "Jethri, turn about please."

Behind him and at very nearly his own height, stood a Liaden of indeterminate age. What most distinguished him was not his height, nor even the fact that he was out-and-out grinning, but his dark, wide-brimmed hat, which he failed to doff in greeting, though he bowed a sort of all-purpose greeting in Pen Rel's general direction.

"So, my friend. You bring to me the sudden son, that we may instill in him my sixty Standards of experience in sixty hours?"

His bow to Jethri was much more complex—layered, even: retainer to son of the house, master to adult student—and a hint of something else. There was a careful  extravagance in his motion Jethri put down to dealing with an awkward situation in good humor.

"Jethri ven'Deelin Clan Ixin, I—Cargo Master Gar Sad per'Etla—I welcome you to my dirt-side office. I advise you that we must hurry, for your new mother would have you ready to take any position on the ship at short notice. And, given my age, I suspect she means you to replace me soonest."

Jethri returned the bow as honestly as he could, junior to senior, with an attempt—he hoped subtle—at member of the house to retainer.

"All very pretty," Pen Rel said briskly, "but allow me to take my leave of both of you else the tradespeople will run me down." A quick bow, encompassing perhaps the entirety of the dock, its length and height, the cars beneath and the stars above, and he was off.

"We are here, young sir," the cargo master said after a moment, "to insure that you understand how the cargo department on *Elthoria* operates—and how it may vary from other tradeships you may be expected to deal with as one soon to be trading on your own. You will note that, on *Elthoria*, my department is responsible for all items  coming on board, other than hand luggage.

"Now, let me ask you this: In all of your life, how many pods have you loaded?"

Later, it came to Jethri that perhaps the question had been intended rhetorically. Caught in the moment, however, he bent his brain to the count, frowning slightly at the victualers's van…

The cargo master laughed.  If he'd been a Terran, Jethri would have considered him just a little dotty.

"No need to be embarrassed that you have no experience, young sir," the old man said.

"But I do, Master," Jethri interrupted. "I have never loaded an entire pod by myself, but in the last ten Standards I have done initial load checks on at least seventeen pods, and was final load check assistant on about the same number. I did the initial strap-downs on ten or so, and did net-string on a bunch of odd lots. I…"

"Enough!" Cargo Master per'Etla waved a hand. "I am cheered immensely! Now instead of needing to cover sixty years of knowledge in sixty hours we'll need only cover the final fifty-five years in sixty hours! We are saved!"

Despite himself, Jethri laughed.

"Ah, so now," the man in the hat went on, with a smile and a wink, "will you share with me? How came you by all this experience when you are so new to a house of trade?"

They leaned together on the boundary wall, per'Etla honestly interested in his charge's background. Periodically, he inclined his head, so slightly as to appear a nod, as Jethri explained how a family ship was unlikely to have a full-time cargo master and how at certain ports and with certain cargo, the entire crew might be pressed into the loading and offloading.

As he spoke, Jethri absently watched the food truck's driver using a lift-cart to offload pallets, which he deposited on the 'crete regardless of the puddled water or the marked driving lanes. Finally, he stacked them into a pile, and Jethri could see water dripping from the top pallets onto those lower in the pile—which pile he aimed in the general direction of the ship's dock as his lift-cart gathered speed.

Stopping in mid-sentence, Jethri pointed toward the incoming tradesman, whose approach was yet unnoticed by the clerk.

"The modules, master, contaminated in the dock-water!"

Master per'Etla glanced to the clerk, who was concentrating on his computer.

The master gestured toward the clerk, and then looked Jethri hard in the face. "What would you do, apprentice? The dock is yours to direct."

Jethri bowed quickly and strode forward, stepping into the gate and holding his hands up, palms forward, to stop the cart.

The driver appeared oblivious, then attempted to wave Jethri aside.

"Halt!"

The driver turned his rig so sharply that it tilted, pallets shifting, and finally came to a stop. He came off the seat angry, yelling so hard and fast that Jethri couldn't get more than the basic idea of what the guy was saying, which was close enough to fighting words.

Jethri found himself turning sidewise to the man, reacting automatically to the volume and the threat...

The driver got closer, and now the clerk was at Jethri's side, adding his voice to the general clamor, but no matter—it was suddenly like the deliveryman had gotten a good, hard look at one of the scarier ghosts of space.

Again his words came so quickly that Jethri wasn't completely sure of what they were, but the depth of the bows, and the number of them, convinced him that the driver was seriously sorry.

"I would say that your clan-pin was noted," said per'Etla quietly from his left side, "I suggest you continue with your instructions."

Jethri took a breath, and centered himself like Pen Rel was always telling him to do.

"These items here—" He pointed to the dripping edges of the pallets, to the wet tire tracks— "did you plan to bring them into the ship's hold that way? This is not some storeroom where the wind blows as it might. A ship must control its environment and avoid contamination. As a youth I once spent two dozen hours sealed in a space suit while a hold was decontaminated from a careless spot of walked-in goo. What will you have brought us on these?"

"Sir, pardon, I had not considered. Normally, I deliver to warehouses and such is not a difficulty. I mean no—"

"These cannot come onto the ship. Our clerk will contact your office and have replacements brought. These—" Jethri waved a hand, trying for one of Master tel'Ondor's showier effects— "I care not what you do with them."

The clerk, whose name Jethri still didn't have, bowed and began to speak, sternly, to the driver.

Jethri turned his back on them both, feeling a little gone in the knees, and looked to the attentive cargo master.

"That is what I would do, were I directing the dock, Master."

The old man inclined his head.

"Indeed. I cannot argue with you entire; it is in fact the most efficient way to approach the problem, and the lesson was well given. But let me speak a moment."

Jethri took a deep breath, and inclined his head

The master motioned him toward the open port and began walking. Jethri, perforce, followed.

"Our ship is, I suspect, somewhat larger than that of your family. True it is that the sheer random nature of the dockside might permit some contaminant—oh, what a wonderful word you have taught me!—some *goo* as it were, to belabor our air system or corrode our floors.

"There are measures we can take which would likely require none of us to be suited for a Standard Day, or even a Standard Hour. Some of these measures will be taught you— *must* be taught you—that you know the capabilities of *Elthoria*. But, for the moment, you are correct. The clerk ought to have been more alert, and I believe your lesson has taught him as well as the driver; I shall not belabor him more on this.

"Yet still, sir," the master continued, as they crossed the threshold into the ship's cargo port itself, "I ask you to riddle me this: what shall the master trader and the captain feed to their guests at luncheon?"

Jethri froze between one step and the next, face heating. "Lunch?"

"Indeed." The cargo master laughed lightly. "I do believe that what you have turned back just now was the afternoon meal my friend Norn has ordered in for the local jeweler's shop association."

THE FLOW OF schedules was such that Jethri found himself in the hold, cargo deck, and pod-control offices more than in his regular haunts. When he saw someone he knew well— Pen Rel or Gaenor for example—they were usually going the opposite direction and in conversation with someone else. By day three he'd nearly forgotten the incident with the lunch-truck; indeed, for two nights he'd dreamed cargo density patterns for three different pod styles, lading codes, and the structural dynamics of orbital pod transfer.

On his way to the dockside galley for a quick lunch— he still had to finish a test balance on the bulk—he ducked unwittingly by someone ambling slowly down the 'crete.

"Ah," came Master tel'Ondor's familiar voice, "do you wish to avoid speaking with me as much as that?"

Ears a-fire, Jethri ducked back, bowing a hasty apology

"Your pardon, sir. My mind was on my numbers and my stomach on lunch."

"A compelling combination, I agree," the master allowed. "I rejoice to see you thus engaged upon the work of your house. You bring joy to your mother."

A test. Great. Jethri kept his sigh to himself and bowed, wincing only a little when his stomach audibly growled.

Master tel'Ondor moved a languid hand, motioning Jethri onward.

"Please, you have need. But first, let me congratulate you upon your defense of our ship at dockside."

Jethri stiffened. Not a lesson, then—a lecture.

"But no," said the master, apparently recognizing something in Jethri's face, despite his efforts to remain bland—"this is not a problem. The ship speaks well of you, as does the cargo master and the clerk. I am told that you had the mode perfectly in dealing with the incident. The cargo master insists that you were prepared to take a charge and repel boarders!"

He bowed, gently. "I wish merely that all the traders I have taught would have the sense you've shown. I believe you will be quite ready for the next part of your voyage!"

And with that, he swept his hand forward again, and Jethri went, thinking as much about inertial restraints as about lunch.

# Day 116
# Standard Year 1118

## *Elthoria*

THEY WERE FOUR Standard Days out of Tilene, bound for Modrid. There, they'd do a couple days of fill-in trading and set course for the inner worlds.

Inner *Liaden* worlds, where somebody as Terran as a Jethri Gobelyn would speedily become a three-day wonder. At best.

Say that he worried; it was true enough. Gaenor and Vil Tor, together and separately, assured him that he'd do better than fine, but he considered that they might be a thought biased, being friends. Pen Rel sig'Kethra, who wasn't necessarily a friend, had responded to the news of their amended route by intensifying the self-defense sessions 'til they weren't much shy of a shore-leave brawl. Master tel'Ondor had done the same with the protocol lessons, though at least those didn't leave bruises.

And Norn ven'Deelin, who should've been as terrified of the whole business as he was—if not more so, having, as he blackly suspected, a much sharper understanding of what exactly *would* happen if he made hash out of things—Norn ven'Deelin smiled, and patted his arm, and called him her son, and said that she was certain he would acquit himself with honor.

All that being so, it was no wonder, Jethri thought, throwing back the blanket and slapping on the light, that he couldn't sleep.

He pulled on the most comfortable of his Liaden-made clothes—a pair of tough tan trousers, with a multitude of pockets, and an equally tough brown shirt—which was close enough to the coveralls that'd been standard ship wear on the *Market* to be comforting—slipped on a pair of soft ship slippers, and sorted through his pile of pocket stuff until he had his fractin, the Combine key and the general ship key. He slipped them into a pocket, a wrench set and folding blade into another and left his quarters.

There wasn't any need to sneak overtime studies on *Elthoria*, where the rule 'mong the crew was that the trader knew best what the trader required. He'd come to have a fondness for that rule, no more so than now, as he swung down the wide corridor toward his personal bin.

He'd several times over the last ten ship-days thought of the B-crate from home. Finding time to do something about it was the challenge there, his schedule being as crammed as it was.

Which made his present state of nervous sleeplessness nothing less than a gift, looked at in a certain way. At least he'd be able to open the crate at his leisure, and take care over those things his mother had said he should have.

He passed one other person on the way to the cargo section—Kilara pin'Ebit, who inclined her head, murmuring a polite, "Sir."

"Technician," he replied, and that was that—no muss, no fuss, as Dyk used to say—and a few minutes later was standing in front of his bin.

He touched the lock pad in the proper sequence; the door slid open, the interior lights coming up as he stepped into the room.

Lashed against the far wall was one Terran-standard B-crate, looking like it'd taken the rocky route through an asteroid belt to reach him.

Releasing the netting, he knelt down, feeling in his pocket for the wrench set.

There was a dent the size of his head in the side of the crate. Frowning, Jethri ran his hand over it. B-crates were *tough*, and the most likely outcome of taking a whack at one with a heavy object was that the object would bounce—unless it broke. Something hard enough to stave in the side of one...

"Must've got hit by a flying rock," Jethri muttered, fitting his wrench around the first tog.

There were a couple bad seconds with the third and sixth togs, which had gotten jammed when the crate deformed, but he finally got them loose, pulled the panel out, and leaned it against the wall.

Inside, the crate was divided into four smaller magnetically sealed compartments over one larger compartment. Jethri reached for the seal of the upper right hand compartment, then sat back, his hand dropping to his knee, fingers suddenly cold.

"C'mon," he whispered. "It's just kid stuff."

'cept it was kid stuff his mother had seen fit to take into custody, hold for more'n ten years before sending it all after him. Say what you would about Iza Gobelyn's temper, and no question she was cold. Say it all—and when it was said, the fact remained that she was a canny and resourceful captain, who held the best good of the ship in her heart. That being so, she would've had a reason, beyond her own personal grief, for locking his things away. And a reason for finally letting them loose.

He felt the scarebumps rise up on his arms—and then he laughed, breathy and a little too light. "Get a grip! What? You think Iza set you up for a double-cross, like one of Khat's scare-stories? She sent your stuff because it's yours by right an' Paitor talked her into doing the decent."

Which Khat hadn't said, but, then, Khat wouldn't. The more he thought on it, though, the likelier it did seem that such a conversation had taken place; he could almost hear Uncle Paitor's voice rumbling around inside his ears, comforting and comfortable.

Jethri leaned forward and pulled open the top right door.

A plain black purse sat in the center of the small space, a piece of paper sticking out of the fold. Slowly, he reached in and pulled the paper free; unfolded it and blinked at Khat's messy scrawl, laboriously spelling out, "Stinks Money."

Jethri sat back, a breath he hadn't known he was holding escaping in a *whoosh!* He put the paper on his knee, flipped open the purse and counted out a ridiculous amount of Combine paper. All this, from Stinks? It was hard to believe. Harder, in the end, to believe that Khat could cheat the ship. A right stickler, Khat. In a lot of ways, he thought suddenly, she'd've made a good Liaden. He slipped the purse and the note into a pocket and looked back to the crate.

Feeling less spooky about the process, he opened the next door, withdrew a small metal box, and held it between his two hands. The metal was red-gold, burnished 'til it glowed. The sides were decorated—etchings of stars, comets and moons. Three fancy letters were etched into the flat lid, intertwined like some dirtside creepers—AJG. Arin Jethri Gobelyn.

The lock was a simple hook-and-eye; he slid it back with a thumb and raised the lid with care.

Inside, it was lined with deep blue velvet. Scattered 'round the velvet, like stars, were half-a-dozen expired Combine keys, a long flat piece of what might be carved and polished bone— and a ring.

He picked it up between thumb and forefinger. It was a massive thing—arrogant, if jewelry could be said to have attitude—the wide band engraved with stars, comets, moons— just like the side of the box. The top was oval, showing the stylized ship-and-planet of the official Combine seal.

Jethri frowned. His father hadn't been one to wear rings— plainly said, rings on a working ship were foolish, they had too much of a tendency to get caught in machinery and on rough edges. A commissioner, though—a commissioner might well wear a ring or a patch or somelike, to alert folks to the fact that here was somebody with connections.

The gold was cold and unfriendly against his skin. He put it back in the box and reached for the bit of bone.

As soon as his fingers touched it, he knew it wasn't bone. Cool and slick, the symbol repeating down one face eerily familiar, it felt just like his lucky fractin.

Frowning, he had that piece out of his pocket and put it side-by-side on his knee with the—whatever it was.

By eye and touch, the two of them were made of the same material. Not exactly scientific, but it would do for now. And the repeating symbol? The very same as the big doughnut-shape on the face of his fractin, set end-to-end down the whole length of the thing.

He picked it up and held it on his palm. Thing had some weight to it—heavier than you expected, like his fractin, which Grig had said enclosed alien workings. A sort of large economy size fractin, then, Jethri thought, smoothing his thumb over the soothing surface. That would have appealed to Arin, with his fascination with the regular sort of fractin. Jethri ran his thumb over it once more, then replaced it on its nest of old Combine keys, lowered the lid and put the box aside.

The next compartment gave up a pair of photocubes. He snatched one out, hands shaking, and flicked through the images quickly, breathless, then more slowly, as he registered that the pictures were of people he didn't know, had never seen. Spacers, most of them, but a few ground-based folk, too, the lot of them looking tired and wary. He put it down.

The second cube—that was the one he had expected, and missed, and wished for. Images of family—Arin, naturally, with the half-grin on his face and his hands tucked into the pockets of his coverall, broad in the shoulder and stubborn in the jaw, brown eyes sitting deep under thick black eyebrows. After that was Seeli, Cris; a picture of Dyk up to his elbows in some cooking project, and a manic grin on his round face; and another of a thin and serious young Khat, bent over a piloting simboard.

Another picture of Arin, with his arm around a woman that it took two blinks to recognize as Iza—the two of them laughing at some forever secret joke. Then a picture of a skinny kid, big eyes and his ears sticking out, coverall grubby, sitting on the floor of the galley at Arin's side, the two of them contemplating the mosaic they'd fitted together. Jethri grinned at the memory. They'd used three dozen fractins in that design, and held up dinner for primary shift, while Arin snapped close-ups from every angle, like he did with every design they'd built.

Still grinning, he clicked the button again, and came back to the first picture of Arin. He put the cube down and opened the last of the small compartments, discovering a notebook and a thick sheaf of hardcopy

Grinning wider, he pulled out the book, riffling the pages, seeing the meticulous lists that Jethri-the-kid had kept of imaginary cargo, imaginary sales, imaginary buys, all worked out with his father's help; each pretend deal discussed as seriously as if the merchandise and money were real. The pages fluttered toward the back, his eye snagged on a different script, and he flipped back...

Angular and as plain as printout, Arin's writing marched down the page in a simple list of ship names. Jethri ran a quick glance down the line, seeing names he was familiar with, names he wasn't—

*WildeToad.* He blinked, remembering the gritty yellow paper crackling in his hand, and the printout of a ship's dying.

*Breaking clay...*

And why had Arin been keeping a ship list in the back of a kid's pretend trade journal?

Jethri shook his head. A mystery for later—or never. Likely it had just been a doodle, on a shift when things were slow; or an illustration meant to go with a conversation long talked out and forgotten. Come to remember it, his father had often doodled in the margins of his book—he riffled the pages again, slower this time, catching glimpses of the odd shapes Arin had drawn to help his thinking along.

Jethri closed the book and reached for the hardcopy, already knowing they'd be the various rules for the games invented to put use to fractins.

Something was left behind, though—and Jethri let out a whoop, dropping the game rules unceremoniously to the floor. He'd almost forgotten—

A mirror no bigger than the palm of his father's hand, framed and backed in some light black metal. Except, the reflecting surface didn't reflect, not even the ghost a spacer might catch in the back of a work screen, which was his own face. As a kid, Jethri had amused himself periodically by trying to surprise the mirror into giving him a reflection, pressing his nose against the glassy surface, or leaving the device on a table top and sneaking up around the side, rushing forward at the last second, more often than not yelling "boo!" into the bargain.

But the mirror never reflected one thing.

What it did do, was predict the weather.

Not a gadget that'd be much use on a spaceship, some might say, and they'd be right. No telling that it was all that useful dirt-side, just at first. Between them, though, him and Arin had puzzled out the symbol system and by the time his father died and his mother locked the thing away with the fractins and his trade journal—by that time, if they was dirt-side, Jethri could tell with a glance whether rain was due, or snow; lightning or hail, and from which planetary direction it would come.

Grinning, he looked into the black, unreflective surface, for old time's sake, then slipped it away into his shirt pocket.

That left the big bin—no surprises, there.

Except it was a surprise—he hadn't remembered that there'd been so many. He opened the box and scooped up a handful of the cool squares, letting them run through his fingers, watching the shapes flicker, hearing the gentle clatter as the tiles tumbled against each other.

The second box was counterfeits and brokens—what his father had called the *ancillary* collection. Some of the fakes looked pretty good, until you'd held a couple genuine fractins, and saw how fine and precise they were, no rough edges, each notch in exactly the same place, no deviation. Once you had that experience, you were unlikely ever to mistake a fake for the real thing again.

He closed the box, looked back into the compartment…

A rectangular wire frame lay in the far back corner. He brought it out, surprised at how light it was. He didn't immediately place the metal, or the thing itself—a simple rectangle, sealed at the bottom, open at the top, the four walls gridlike. Not a big thing, in fact it looked to be about the size to—

He reached into the box holding the genuine fractins, fingered one out and dropped it into the top opening. It slid down the rack to the bottom.

Jethri smiled, eyeing the thing, figuring maybe fifty-sixty fractins would fit in the frame. Why anybody'd want to slot sixty fractins into a metal holder was another question— probably a new game variation.

Still smiling, he yawned, and looked down at his wrist, stifling a curse. He was scheduled to be in Master ven'Deelin's office, bright-eyed, intelligent and *awake* in something less than five hours.

Moving quickly, he packed the fractins, sealed the lids and slid them and the wire frame back into their compartment, along with the game rules, his old trade journal, Arin's box, and the photocube of the strange spacers and Grounders.

Then, he resealed the crate, and netted it snug against the wall.

Rising, he slipped the purse into a side pocket. The photocube was too big for any of his pockets, so he carried it with him, down the hall and back to his quarters.

# Day 123
# Standard Year 1118

## *Elthoria*
## Modrid Approach

THE ALARM BOUNCED Jethri out of sleep two subjective seconds after he hit the bunk.

He threw the blanket back and swung out immediately, having learned from his newly accelerated shifts that the best thing to do when the alarm sounded was get up and get the blood moving toward the brain.

His feet hit the floor and he rubbed his hands briskly over his face, trying to encourage the blood—or maybe his brain— and began to review his shift schedule. First thing was a breakfast meeting with Pen Rel, who wanted to talk about the theory of self-defense. Then, he needed to go over the list of Ixin's regular local trading partners, and a history of *Elthoria's* last six trading missions to Modrid, that Vil Tor had pulled for him. Gaenor's Terran lessons had gone on hold since the change of course, though they'd been managing impromptu sessions on the run; so, after his hour in the library, he was scheduled for a long session with Master tel'Ondor, and after *that*—

The door chimed, interrupting his thoughts. He snatched up his robe and pulled it on as he crossed the room and slapped the plate.

Gaenor stood in the hall, in full uniform. She bowed formally as the door slid open.

"The captain's compliments, Apprentice Trader," she said, speaking each word distinctly, so that he would have no trouble following her, though she spoke in a mode other than the mercantile. "You are invited to join the master trader at the trade bench as soon as convenient. The master trader bids you 'be sure to breakfast heartily'."

Jethri bowed his thanks and straightened to find her outright grinning. Her hand rose, making a sign he did not recognize. "At last we have you in the thick of things! I will see you soon!"

Invited to the bridge by the captain to watch the master trader at her work, up close and personal? Jethri grinned a grin of his own, though he did remember to bow again, in light agreement. When he came up from that, she was gone, leaving him blinking at an empty hall.

He closed the door and ran for the shower, talking to himself as he soaped and rinsed.

"'kay, kid—you're going live crew on a live deck, ain't that something special? Watch the master and learn your heart out…"

He skimped a little on the dry cycle and bounded, damp, to the closet, pulled out a blue shirt and darker blue trousers and hurriedly dressed, pausing in front of the mirror to affix Ixin's pin to his collar and run hasty palms over his spiky, growing-out hair.

Grabbing his pocket stuff, he rushed from the room, heading for the cafeteria at just under a run, and wishing, not for the first time, that *Elthoria* kept 'mite available to its crew.

HE CHOSE HIS breakfast not by what he wanted to eat, but by which lines were shortest at the serving tables. Fortunately, there were two lines for tea—tea being to Liadens what coffee was to Terrans; and his choice of the shorter one put him next to Pen Rel.

The arms master glanced to him, and bowed what looked to be the bow between comrades, which, Jethri thought, *had* to be him reading wrong. He made sure his answering bow was the perfectly safe and unexceptional junior to senior.

Pen Rel cocked his head to a side, and while it couldn't precisely be said that he *smiled*, there was a noticeable lightening of his usually stern face.

"I see that our schedule has been altered by the captain's order, young Jethri," he said, selecting a tea bottle from those on the table. "Never fear, we will pursue your studies as time—and the captain—allow us." He inclined his head. "Good shift to you."

"Good shift," Jethri answered, snagging a bottle for himself and moving off to an empty table to gulp down his meal.

HE MADE THE bridge in good time, his fractin dancing between his fingers, and found Technician Rantel ver'Borith, who he had met a couple times in the library, waiting for him at the door.

"Apprentice Trader." She bowed, and handed him a pocket locator clip and an ear-and-mouth com. He put the button in his ear and smoothed the wire against his cheek. When she saw he was situated, Rantel put her hand against the door, and led him across the threshold, past Captain yo'Lanna, who glanced up and acknowledged their presence with a seated bow strongly reminiscent of Iza Gobelyn's usual curt nod to outsiders on her bridge, and down-room.

It was an eerily quiet bridge, with none of the cheerful chatter that had been common 'mong his cousins as they brought the *Market* into approach. They went by Gaenor's station, she intent on her screens to the exclusion of all else. In fact, the bridge crew, to a man, sat in rapt concentration over their screens, monitors, and map displays.

Norn ven'Deelin sat at a station far removed from the captain, her nearest neighbor what looked to be an automatic weather scanner. She greeted him with a smile and tapped her finger on the arm of the empty chair beside her.

He slid in, finding the seat a bit tighter than he might have liked, and a thought too close to the floor, so that he needed to fold his legs around the base.

"Apprentice, you made excellent time," Master ven'Deelin said, very softly. "Your expertise will be required very soon. Now, if you please, we will familiarize you with the equipment. Please touch the blue switch—yes—now, press forward one click, and your console will come to observer status."

He followed her instructions carefully, feeling a tingle in the pit of his belly when the screen lit and the button purred static in his ear.

"Good," Master ven'Deelin said, her voice in his ear an odd, but definite, comfort.

"When you press again—which you will do, but not touch anything else—your board is now live and in tandem trade mode. That means you will be seeing what trades I see. The green boxes represent my offers. If you suggest an offer it will appear on my screen, and I will accept it or not." She paused.

"Now, if you go forward once more—which you will do now but not touch anything else—you are in the solo trade mode. In that mode you commit us as utterly as if I had signed my name on a contract or placed hard cantra on the counter." Another pause.

"Take a moment to study what the screen tells you, child."

Truth told, he needed a chance to study the screen. He bent forward eagerly, one hand fiddling with the fractin, the other curled into a fist on his knee.

The screen was beyond high-info—it was *dense* info. At the bottom left corner was a schematic of *Elthoria*, full cans and cargo holds limned in green; empties colored red. Bottom right was marked *Funds* and showed a balance of zero. The top half of the screen was divided into columns—Incoming, Outgoing, Bids Made, Bids Taken, Bids Refused. Right now, there wasn't much action, but he thought the columns would start to fill up quick as soon as they came into Modrid's approach space.

His fractin slipped out of his fingers. He caught it before it had fallen far, palmed it, slipped it into his pocket—and looked up to find that Norn ven'Deelin had noticed his movement.

He braced himself, waiting for her to ask what silly toy he had in his pocket; then she spoke and he realized that she had misunderstood his sudden movement.

"Forgive me. Please return your board to observer status with the reverse-ward clicks. Very good. Now on either side of your seat you will find several tabs and buttons. I suggest you take some time with them until your hands know what they do—they are adjustments for length and height, for spin and—but you must discover them and adjust what is necessary, for we may sit for some time today."

He put his hands down, fingers discovering the advertised buttons and tabs. He quickly found that one button adjusted the inflation of his seat, and another the angle compared to the console, another the height of the seat relative to the deck, which allowed him to straighten his legs. Only the pilot's chair had these kinds of extra adjustments on the *Market*, and if a lowly 'prentice trader's observation chair was so equipped what must the captain have available? Meditatively, he cycled the chair to the very back of its track, then slowly forward.

"...and when you are comfortable," Norn ven'Deelin murmured, "you will say something to me so that we know your com is working and at proper volume..."

Face burning, he locked the chair where it was and touched the button in his ear.

"Yes, Master Trader."

She smiled at him, gently. "Always the silver tongue, my child. Perhaps you will tell me what you think of the two offers at the top of the board, which came in as you were adjusting your chair."

Startled, he glanced at his screen and saw an offer to sell two MUs of cheese...he blinked, then laughed. Two MUs—that was two cargo pods!

"Ma'am, I'd tell the first one thanks but no thanks," he said, dropping into Trade. "At that price we'd need to be carting locally on a prepaid rush delivery—or we'd need to broker it on planet, and that's a time waster."

"Yes, thank you, we shall decline. And the second?"

That was harder, the offer being a half-can of specialty spices and herbs. Jethri frowned, mentally running through the manifests he had studied.

"Ma'am, in general I don't believe you have *Elthoria* carrying foodstuff," he said tentatively.

"Excellent," she murmured in his ear. "You see what they wish us to do—to broker this and that. Were we at leisure, perhaps I might allow myself—but this is not such a trip. Now, attend your controls once more."

He brought his attention to the console.

"You see the red tabs set on either side of the blue control wheel. For details of what is on offer, if needed, select the right, and again if need be—sometimes there are as many as a dozen detail levels. If these leave you uninformed, make a record—that is the left tab—and we will add it to our analysis list. Now, if you see something which you think I should note, click the yellow button above the wheel here—and I will have a highlight informing me."

Jethri began to nod, caught it and inclined his head. "I understand," he said, and looked at his screen, where two more offers had appeared in the Incoming column.

"Ah, good," the master trader said.

The run-in to orbit took several hours and for awhile he sat in observer mode, watching as she filed *Elthoria's* availables. As he'd suspected, the incoming offers picked up momentum as they moved further in. Teeth indenting lower lip, he bent forward, trying to move his eyes fast enough; caught an offer of a twelfth MU of compressed textiles—highlighted it, and heard her murmur, "Yes, that looks likely. However, there is history—we have not used that source for some time. There was a bad load. Watch and see if the price falls…"

The bridge behind them got busy—maneuvers as they entered planetary nearspace, or so he thought, and she said quietly in his ear—

"Please go to tandem. Note that we have emptied a pod entire; check on that textile and if it is still available highlight it for me...also, I have accepted a tranship of a half pod; that will show up as a block on your diagram about now..."

The original lot of textile was gone, but he found another near enough, and a better price, highlighted it, and continued down the list, as the incoming column filled, spawned an overflow column and did its utmost to overfill it. He highlighted an offer of raw lumber; another of frozen chicken embryos, billed as genuine Roque Eyeland Reds and a marvelous low price the seller was asking for them, if true.

"We have now the odd-spots to fill in three pods," Master ven'Deelin said. "You will finish Pod Seventeen—note your cubes and balance limits. Your credit draw is unlocked and our complete manifest is open to you. Do not purchase anything we already own without asking. Please click one forward now—yes. You are the buyer of record. If desirable items which will not fit into your space come to note, please highlight."

In moments, he was sweating, leaning over the screen, shoulders stiff with tension. The credit account showed a ridiculous number of *cantra* for him to draw on. He flicked down the lists, trying for density; found hand tools at a good price, reached to place his bid—and the lot was gone, snatched away by a quick-fingered trader on another incoming ship.

Frustrated, he went back to the list, found a case of Genuine Blusharie on offer, touched the tab for more information—and the item vanished from his screen, claimed by another.

He put his hand on the buy switch and hunched forward, breath maybe a little short—and suddenly there was Uncle Paitor, frowning at him from memory and delivering a lecture on "auction fever"—the urge to buy quickly in order to buy first, or to buy first in order to beat the market—and how a trader above all needed a cool head in a hot situation.

Carefully, Jethri sat back and eased his hand off the switch. He flipped back through the items that had been on offer for awhile—and smiled. Reasonable cost, good density, real wooden products that would likely sell in both Terran and Liaden markets. Yes. He reached out and pushed the 'buy' button.

The screen blinked at him; the offer accepted, the trade made. Jethri nodded and returned to the list, calmer for having committed some of his capital to solid stock.

The diagram at the bottom left showed Pod Seventeen ninety-two percent full. He could use something like that twelfth of textiles, or maybe some stasis wheat...

Concentrating, he barely noticed when *Elthoria* achieved orbit, though he did register Gaenor's voice, speaking over the intercom.

It seemed that the offerings were coming in slower now; he had time to access the deep infoscreens. He highlighted several, and heard the master trader murmur once, "Excellent," and, again, "I think this is too large a quantity to carry in, Apprentice."

Pod Seventeen glowed green in the diagram—full. He blinked, and sat back, felt a light touch on his sleeve and looked over to Norn ven'Deelin. She smiled.

"If you buy anything more, my son, you will be buying for yourself. We have done well, you and I. Now, I suggest a meal, if you will honor me."

Now that he thought about it, he was hungry, Jethri realized. Carefully, he shut down his console, slid the chair back on its track and looked around.

About a third of the bridge crew was gone, relieved while he sat over his console, their work done while his continued. Gaenor's station was empty; at the far end of the bridge, the captain sat his board.

Jethri rose, cleared the chair's settings in case someone followed him in it, and walked with Norn ven'Deelin toward the door. She reached out and put her palm against the plate—

"Master Trader." Captain yo'Lanna had spun his chair and was looking at them, his face empty of any emotion that Jethri could read. "A moment of your time, if you will."

Master ven'Deelin sighed, largely. "Bah. Details, always details." She patted his arm. "Go—eat. When you are through, present yourself to Pen Rel and learn about those things he considers it prudent for you to carry portside here."

"Yes, ma'am." He inclined his head and she hurried away.

He touched his ear, remembering the comm, and looked to the officer on deck.

"Keep it, of your kindness, Trader," he said. "Doubtless, you will have need of it again."

That warmed him, and he slipped the comm off and stowed it in a pocket.

From across the bridge came the master trader's voice, sounding outright irritated. Jethri paused, frowning. He was beginning to be able to follow her quicker conversations, and this one was fraught with words sounding like, "Vouch for every transaction?" "Recertification is absurd!" and "I will speak to the Guild, and I am a master!"

None of that sounded like business for a 'prentice, and, besides, he'd been given his orders and his course—lunch; then Pen Rel.

He strode out and away from the bridge, feeling something just this side of a headache and just that side of an earache trying to form. Despite which, he did note that he was in possession of a good deal more information about his ship and its business than he had before this shift.

It was off-schedule for lunch, but the second cook filled him a plate of goodies, which he ate by himself in the empty cafeteria, mulling over the cargo buys that had gotten away.

# Day 125
# Standard Year 1118

## Modrid

THE TRADING TOUR of Modrid went at lightspeed, with Jethri doing nothing more useful than standing at the master trader's elbow while she negotiated for luxury pieces and high-sell items—gemstones, wines, porcelains, and three packs of what were billed as "playing cards" that cost twice what the rest had, total.

"So, now, that is done," Master ven'Deelin said, turning away from the last table, and motioning him to walk with her. "What did you learn, young Jethri?"

"Well," he said, thinking over her approach, the deft assurance with which she had negotiated—it had been like watching a play-act, or a port bully shaking down a mark. "I learned that I have a fair distance to go before anyone mistakes me for a master trader."

"What's this?" She threw a bright black glance into his face. "Do you aspire to silver tongue after all?"

He blinked at her. "No, ma'am—at least, not unless it's something you think I should learn. I was merely trying to convey that I am all admiration of your style and skill."

"Worse and worse!" She put her hand on his sleeve. "As to whether it is something you should learn...You should know how to flatter, and you should cultivate a reputation as one who does not flatter. Do you understand me?"

He thought he did, as it seemed to echo something of Master tel'Ondor's philosophy of bows.

"A reputation as someone who does not flatter is a weapon. If I…am required to flatter someone in order to gain advantage, then they will know me to be sincere, and be disarmed."

Her eyebrows lifted, and her fingers tightened, exerting brief pressure before she withdrew her hand.

"You learn quickly, my child. Perhaps it will not be so long until you wear the amethyst." She waved her hand, perhaps by way of illustration, the big purple ring flashing its facets.

"We will now adjourn to Modrid trade hall to set you properly on the path to glory."

Which could, Jethri thought, mean just about anything.

"I would be interested," she said as they walked on, "in hearing your opinion of our last items of trade, if you would honor me, young Jethri."

He thought back to the decks—sealed with a pale blue ribbon and a blot of wax. The vendor had set the price at two kais per and Master ven'Deelin had barely dickered at all, taking him down to one kais six per more as a matter of keeping her hand in, as it seemed to Jethri, than because she had thought the original price over-high.

"I could not see the seal properly from where I stood, ma'am," he said slowly, "but I deduce that the decks may have been bought for certain collectors of your acquaintance, who set a high value on sealed decks from gaming houses." He paused, considering the price again, and added. "It may be that these particular decks are a rarity—perhaps from a gaming house which no longer operates."

"Hah." She inclined her head slightly. "Well reasoned, and on point. We have today purchased three decks of cards made for the Casino Deregar, which had been built in the depleted mining tunnels of an asteroid, and enjoyed much renown until it disintegrated some twenty-three Standards ago. We are very fortunate to have found three in their original condition, and at a price most commonly paid for broken decks."

Her praise warmed him, and he nearly smiled, which would never do, out here in public. He took a second to order his face before he asked, "How are the broken decks pedigreed?"

"An excellent question!" Master ven'Deelin said as they passed a food stall. The spicy smell woke Jethri's stomach, as they moved on, walking briskly. "Deregar cards are most distinctive. I have a broken deck aboard *Elthoria*. When we return, you must examine it. Ah, here we are! I ask your indulgence for a short time more, my son, and then we will provide us both with a well-deserved meal."

Jethri felt his ears warm. He hadn't thought his stomach's complaint had been that loud!

Master ven'Deelin paused before a large metal door, and swiped a card through the scan. The light clicked from yellow to orange, and the door opened. She strolled through, Jethri at her heels.

Inside, he paused, somewhat taken aback by the scope of the thing. The hall stretched out, the ceiling just this side of uncomfortably high, with long vents cut into it, allowing the outside light to fall through and down to brighten up the red stone floor. The walls were white and nubbly. A long wooden ledge had been built into the right-hand wall, a light red cushion laid along its length. The left wall was covered in a large tapestry of surpassing ugliness, which was undoubtedly, Jethri thought, catching the tell-tale signs, handmade—and probably historic, too.

Along the back wall was a wooden counter, and that was what Master ven'Deelin was on course for, her boots making little gritty skritches against the stone floor.

Jethri stretched his legs to catch up with her, passing through pockets of sunlight, and caught up just as she put her hand over a plate built into the counter.

Somewhere far back, a chime sounded. A heartbeat later, a young man in an orange jacket embroidered with the sign of the Liaden Trade Guild stepped to the other side of the counter and inclined his head respectfully.

"Master Trader. How may I serve you?"

"I wish to speak with the hall master. You may say that it is ven'Deelin who asks it."

The head-tip this time was a little deeper, Jethri saw, as if 'ven'Deelin' was worth an extra measure of respect even above 'master trader.'

"I will inform the hall master of your presence. A moment only, of your goodness."

He vanished back the way he'd come. Master ven'Deelin moved her shoulders and looked up at Jethri, though he hadn't said anything.

"Soon, my child. This should encompass but moments."

He was going to tell her that he wasn't *that* hungry when the door at the end of the counter opened and the man in the orange jacket bowed.

"Master Trader. Sir. The hall master is honored to speak with you. Please, attend me now."

"MASTER TRADER ven'DEELIN, well met." The man who stood up from behind the glossy black desk was white-haired; his face showing lines across his forehead, by his eyes, around his mouth. He stood tall and straight-backed as a younger, though, and his eyes were blue and clear.

"I am Del Orn dea'Lystra, master of Modrid Trade Hall. How may I be of service to you?"

"In a small matter of amending the record, Hall Master. I am embarrassed that I must need bring it to your attention. But, before we continue, allow me to introduce to you my apprentice, Jethri Gobelyn." She moved a hand, calling the hall master's attention to Jethri, who tried to stand tall without looking like a threat. He might have saved himself the trouble.

Hall Master dea'Lystra's clear blue eyes turned chilly, and he didn't bother to incline his head or take any other notice of Jethri other than, "I see," directed at Master ven'Deelin.

"Do you?" she asked. "I wonder. But! A hall master is not one who has many moments at leisure. Allow me, please, to proceed directly to my business."

The hall master inclined his head, granting her permission with, Jethri thought, a noticeable lack of enthusiasm.

"So," said Master ven'Deelin. "As it happens, *Elthoria* achieved orbit yesterday. We, of course, took advantage of the time incoming to place goods and make purchases." She moved her hand, once again showing Jethri to the hall master, who once again didn't bother to look.

"At my direction, and using his assigned sub-account, this my apprentice did make numerous purchases. And yet, when the trading was done and recorded, what do I have but a message from Modrid Trade Hall, demanding that I recertify all the purchases made by my apprentice, at my direction, using the proper codes." She inclined her head, slightly.

"Clearly, something has gone awry with the records. I would ask that you rectify this problem immediately."

The hall master moved his shoulders and showed his hands, palm up, in a gesture meaning, vaguely, 'alas'.

"Master Trader, I am desolate, but we may not allow a Terran guild status."

"May we not?" Master ven'Deelin asked, soft enough to send a chill running down Jethri's neck, if the hall master didn't have so much sense. "I wonder when that regulation was accepted by the masters."

Hall Master dea'Lystra bowed, lightly and with irony. "Some things are self-evident, I fear. No one disputes a master trader's right to take what apprentice she will. Guild status is another consideration all together." He spared Jethri a brief, scathing stare. "This person has no qualifications to recommend him."

Like being Norn ven'Deelin's 'prentice wasn't a qualification? Jethri thought, feeling his temper edge up—which was no good thing, the Gobelyns being known for their tempers. He took a breath, trying to swallow it, but then what did the fool do but incline his head and say, like Master ven'Deelin was no more account than a dock monkey, "I trust that concludes our business. Good-day."

"No," Jethri heard his own voice say, in the mode between traders, "it does not conclude our business. Your assertion that I have no qualifications pertinent to the guild is, alas, in error. I hold a ten-year key from the Terran Combine."

Out of the corner of his eye, he saw Master ven'Deelin throw him a stare. The hall master moved his shoulders, indifferent.

"Produce this ten-year key," he said, and his mode was superior to inferior, which was no way to cool a het-up Gobelyn.

Jethri reached inside his collar and pulled the chain up and over his head, holding it high, so the key could be plainly seen.

"If you will show me your Combine computer, I will verify that it is in fact a valid key, registered—"

"It is a matter of indifference to me and to this hall," Hall Master dea'Lystra interrupted, "who holds the registration for that key." He turned back to Master ven'Deelin.

"Master Trader, good-day," he said, trying to be rude, now, or so Jethri heard it.

Norn ven'Deelin didn't budge. She did cock her head to a side and look thoughtfully, and maybe a touch sorrowfully upon the hall master.

"You, the master of Modrid Trade Hall, give as your judgement that the possession of a Combine key is insufficient to demonstrate that the trader who holds the key is qualified to stand as an apprentice in the Guild. Is that correct?"

Hall Master dea'Lystra inclined his head.

"The master of Modrid Trade Hall gives as his judgement that possession of a Combine key is insufficient to demonstrate that the Terran who holds the key is qualified to stand as an apprentice in the Guild. *That* is correct."

Master ven'Deelin inclined her head. "That is most wonderfully plain. My thanks to you. Jethri, attend me, of your kindness."

Of course, he had to attend her—he was her 'prentice. Still, thought Jethri, following her out the door and down the hall, he would have welcomed the opportunity to put some of Pen Rel's lessons to the test, with Hall Master dea'Lystra as his subject.

"Peace, child," Master ven'Deelin murmured as they marched across the wide entrance hall. "A brawl is neither seemly nor warranted."

"Not seemly," Jethri said, keeping his voice low, "but surely warranted, ma'am."

The only answer was a soft, "Young things." Then they were at the door and through it, back on the noisy, odoriferous street.

"Come," she said. "There is a very pleasant restaurant just down this next street. Let us bespeak a booth and a nuncheon, so that we may be comfortable, and private, while you tell me the tale of that key."

THE 'BOOTH' WAS more like a well-appointed small room, with comfy seats, and soft music coming out of a grid in the wall, and a multi-use computer within reach at a corner of the table.

Master ven'Deelin called for wine, which came quickly, and gave the order for a "mixed tray," whereupon the server bowed and went away, closing the booth's door behind him.

"So," Master ven'Deelin poured wine into a glass and set it on the table by Jethri's hand, before pouring another glass for herself. "This Combine key, child. May I have the honor of seeing it?"

For the second time in an hour, Jethri slipped the chain over his head. He put the key into Master ven'Deelin's palm and watched as she considered the inscription on the face, then turned it over and read the obverse.

"A ten-year key, in truth. How came you to have it?"

Jethri fingered his wine glass—and that wouldn't do at all, he thought suddenly. Master tel'Ondor would pin his ears back good if he caught him fidgeting in public. Casually, he released the glass and folded his hands in bogus serenity on the table top, looking straight into Norn ven'Deelin's amused— he would swear it—black eyes.

"As an apprentice on *Gobelyn's Market*, I brought a favorable buy to the attention of the trader. A remaindered pod, it was, and more than a third of it *vya*, in stasis. I knew Ynsolt'i was on the schedule, and I thought it might do well there. Uncle Paitor said, if it did, he would sponsor a key." He glanced down at the table, then made himself look back to her eyes. "A ten-year key—that was unexpected, but the *vya* had done— very well for the ship."

"Hah." Master ven'Deelin put the key on the table between them and picked up her wine glass.

"What else was in the pod?"

He frowned, trying to remember. "A couple of crates of broken porcelain—plates and cups, we thought. Cris sold the pieces to an art co-op—that covered what we had in the pod. Some textile—that was a loss, because there had also been...a syrup of some kind, which had escaped its containers. The porcelain and the vya cans both were double-sealed, and the syrup was easily rinsed off the outer cases with water. The textile, though..." He sighed, still regretting the textile, and reached for his wine glass, taking a tiny cautious sip.

Dry, bitter with tannin, and—just as he was about to ask for water—a surprising and agreeable tang of lemon.

Across from him, Norn ven'Deelin smiled a small smile. "You approve of the wine?"

'Approve' didn't exactly seem to cover it, though he found himself anticipating his next sip. "It's—unexpected," he offered, tentatively.

"Indeed it is, which is why we drink it in your honor." She raised her glass in a tiny salute and sipped, eyes slitted.

"Yes, excellent." Another sip, and she set the wine aside, leaned forward and tapped the power switch on the multi-use. The screen snapped live; she ran her guild card through the slot, then typed a rapid string of letters into the keyboard. Jethri raised his wine glass.

The multi-use clicked, loudly, and a drawer popped out of its face, displaying an indentation that could only accommodate a Combine key.

Jethri lowered his glass.

Master ven'Deelin touched his key with a delicate forefinger. "You permit?"

Well sure, he permitted, if only to watch the multi-use in action. He'd never seen such a—he inclined his head.

"I believe I see a theme," he said, and moved his hand in the 'sure, go ahead' gesture. "By all means, ma'am."

Deftly, she had the key off its chain and pressed it into the indentation. The multi-use hesitated a moment, then emitted a second *click* as the drawer withdrew into the face of the machine.

There was a moment of inaction, then the screen flickered and displayed the key's registration code, registered to one Jethri Gobelyn, with 'free trade' checked instead of a ship name. A trade history was indicated. Master ven'Deelin touched the access key.

There, written out in a few terse sentences, was the *vya* deal, with himself listed as acquiring trader and Paitor Gobelyn assisting, which was, Jethri thought, eyes stinging, more than good of Uncle Paitor.

Master ven'Deelin touched the access key once more and there was the cellosilk sale, Cris Gobelyn acquiring, Jethri Gobelyn assisting. No more history was available.

"So." She typed another string of letters, the multi-use clicked one more time and the drawer extruded. When the key was removed, the drawer disappeared back into the console's face. Jethri remembered his wine and had another sip, anticipating the lemon note.

Master ven'Deelin threaded his key back onto the silver chain and held it out. He slipped it over his head and tucked the key into its usual position inside his shirt.

"Del Orn dea'Lystra is a fool," she said conversationally, picking up her glass.

Jethri paused with his hands at his collar. "You won't let him get away with—ma'am, he insulted you!" he blurted.

Her eyebrows lifted. She sipped her wine and put the glass down. "No more than he insulted you. But tell me, my son, why did you not show me this key ere now?"

His face heated. "Truthfully, ma'am, I didn't think to do so. The key—I had not understood Trader Gobelyn's —his melant'i in the matter. I saw the key as a—sop, or as a going-away present, and of no interest to yourself."

There was a small silence, followed by a non-committal, "Ah."

In his experience, Master ven'Deelin's 'ah' was chancy ground. Jethri sipped his wine, determined to wait her out.

"You raised the question of Balance," she said eventually. "It seems to me that the failure of *Elthoria* to any longer stop at a port which had realized some profit from her presence is not too strong an answer. A port that will not alter itself to accommodate the trade—that is not a port *Elthoria* cares to accommodate."

He gaped at her. "You're going to cut them off?"

She looked at him serenely. "You think the Balance too stringent? Please, speak what is in your heart."

He thought about it, frowning down at the composite table top. Consider a fool of a hall master, he thought, insulting a master trader, insulting a master trader's apprentice, thereby calling into question the master trader's judgement, if not her sanity—and then there had been the by-play about the masters not having accepted the no-Terrans rule...

Jethri looked up, to find her gazing thoughtfully upon him.

"On consideration," he said slowly, "I think it an appropriate Balance, Master."

She inclined her head, by all appearances with serious intent. "My thanks, young Jethri. It shall be done—on behalf of ourselves and the trade."

A chime sounded, discreetly, and the door opened to admit their server, bearing a tray laden with foodstuffs, most of which, Jethri's stomach announced, smelled *wonder*ful.

"Indeed," said Master ven'Deelin. "We have done work this day, my son. Now, let us relax for an hour and enjoy this delightful repast, and speak of pleasant things."

# Day 135
# Standard Year 1118

## *Elthoria*

THE PATTERN OF his studies changed again, with more
emphasis on the modes of High Liaden, which meant more
time with Master tel'Ondor and much more time with the
language tapes—even tapes that played while he slept!

Despite the frenzy, he and Gaenor and Vil Tor had managed to meet in the cafeteria to share a meal—late-shift dinner
for Jethri, on-shift lunch for Vil Tor and mid-sleep-shift snack
for Gaenor.

"So, you will be leaving us for a time," Vil Tor said. "I
am envious."

"Not I," Gaenor put in. "Tarnia frightens me to death."
She glanced up, catching the edge of Jethri's baffled stare.
"She frightens you, too, does she? I knew you for a man of
good sense!"

"Indeed," he stammered. "I have no idea who the gentle
may be. As for leaving you—why would I do such a thing?"

"Has the master trader's word no weight with you, then?"
Gaenor asked, while Vil Tor sent a speculative glance into
Jethri's face. "In that wise, you have no need to fear Tarnia.
ven'Deelin will have you first."

"Don't tease him, Gaenor," Vil Tor said suddenly. "He
hasn't been told."

She blinked at him. "Not been told? Surely, he has a need
to know, if only to have sufficient time to properly commend
himself to his gods."

"I was told," Jethri said, before his leg broke proper, "that we would be visiting an old friend of Master ven'Deelin's, who is delm of a house on Irikwae."

"Then you have been given the cipher, but not the key," Gaenor said, reaching for her tea. "Never fear, Vil Tor and I will unlock it for you."

Jethri looked to the librarian, who moved his shoulders. "Stafeli Maarilex has the honor to be Tarnia, which makes its seat upon Irikwae. She stands as the ven'Deelin's foster mother, even as the ven'Deelin stands foster mother to you."

*So now I have a foster-granmam?* Jethri thought, but decided that was taking silly too far into nonsense.

"Who better, then," Gaenor said, jumping in where Vil Tor had stopped, "to shine you?"

*Now I have a foster-granmam.* He sighed, and frowned down at his dinner plate.

"No, never put on such a long face!" Vil Tor chided. "Irikwae is a most pleasant world and Tarnia's gardens are legendary. You will enjoy yourself excessively, Jethri."

He bit his lip, reminding himself that Vil Tor meant well. It was just that—well, him and Gaenor and—all of *Elthoria's* crew, really—were Grounders. They all had homes on *planets,* and it was those homes, down 'midst the dust and the mud and the stinks, that they looked forward to going back to, when *Elthoria's* run was through.

Well, at least the visit wouldn't be long. He'd been over the route *Elthoria* would take through the Inner Worlds, Master ven'Deelin having made both route and manifest a special area of his studies since they'd quit Modrid, and knew they was scheduled for a three-day layover before moving on to Naord. What kind of polish the old lady could be expected to give him in such a short time wasn't clear, and Jethri took leave to privately doubt that he'd take much shine, anyway. Still, he guessed she was entitled to try.

The hour bell sounded and Vil Tor hurriedly swallowed the last of his tea as he pushed back from the table.

"Alas, duty," he murmured. "Gaenor—"

She waved a hand. "Yes, with delight. But, go now, dear friend. Stint not."

He smiled at that, and touched Jethri on the shoulder as he passed. "Until soon, Jethri. Be well."

Across the table, Gaenor yawned daintily. "I fear I must desert you, as well, my friend. Have the most enjoyable visit possible, eh? I look forward to hearing every detail, when you are returned to us."

She slipped out of her chair and gathered her empties together, and, like Vil Tor, touched him on the shoulder as she left him. "Until soon, Jethri."

"Until soon, Gaenor."

He sat there a little while longer, alone. His dinner wasn't quite eaten, but he wasn't quite hungry. Back at quarters, he had packing to do, and some bit of sleep to catch on his own, his regular shift having been adjusted in order to accommodate a morning arrival, dirt-side. Wouldn't do to show stupid in front of Master ven'Deelin's foster mother. Not when he was a son of the house and all.

Sighing, and not entirely easy in his stomach, he gathered up the considerable remains of his meal, fed the recycler and mooched off toward quarters, the fractin jigging between his fingers.

# Day 139
# Standard Year 1118

## Irikwae

IRIKWAE WAS HEAVY, hot and damp. The light it received from its primary was a merciless blare that stabbed straight through the eyes and into the skull, where the brain immediately took delivery of a headache.

Jethri closed his eyes, teeth clenched, despite being only inches away from a port street full of vehicles, all moving at insane velocity on trajectories that had clearly been plotted with suicide in mind.

"Tch!" said Master ven'Deelin. "Where have my wits gone? A moment, my child."

Through slitted eyes, he watched her bustle back into the office they had just quit. In the street, the traffic roared on. Jethri closed his eyes again, feeling the sun heating his scalp. The damp air carried a multitude of scents, none of them pleasant, and he began to hope they'd find that Master ven'Deelin's friend wasn't to home, so they could go back to *Elthoria* today.

"Here you are, my son. Place these over your eyes, if you will."

Jethri opened his eyes to slits, saw a tiny hand on which a big purple ring glittered holding a pair of black-lensed spectacles under his nose. He took them, hooked the curved earpieces over his ears, settled the nosepiece.

The street was just like it had been before he put the glasses on, except that the brutal sunlight had been cut by a factor of ten. He sighed and opened his eyes wider.

"Thank you, ma'am."

"You are welcome," she replied, and he saw that she wore a similar pair of glasses. "I only wish I had recalled beforetime. Have you a headache?"

It had faded considerably; still...

"A bit," he owned. "The glasses are a help."

"Good. Let us then locate our car—aha!—it arrives."

And a big green car was pulling up to the curb before them. It stopped, its driver oblivious to the horns of the vehicles in line behind—or maybe, Jethri thought, she was deaf. Whichever, the back door rose and Master ven'Deelin took his arm, urging him forward.

The inside of the car was cool, and dim enough that he dared to slip his glasses down his nose, then off entirely, smiling at the polarized windows, while keeping his eyes off the machinery hurtling by. Prudently, he slipped the glasses into the pocket of his jacket.

"Anecha," Master ven'Deelin called into the empty air, as the car pulled away from the walk and accelerated heedlessly into the rushing traffic, "is it you?"

"Would I allow anyone else to fetch you?" came the answer, from the grid set into the door. "It has been too many years, Lady. The delm is no younger, you know."

"Nor am I. Nor am I. And we must each to our duty, which leaves us too little time to pursue that for which our hearts care."

"So we are all fortunate," commented the voice from the grid, "that your heart cares so well for the trade."

Master ven'Deelin laughed.

"Look now, my son," she said, turning to him and directing his attention through the friendly windows. "There is the guildhall, and just beyond the Trade Bar. After you are settled at the house, you must tour the bazaar. I think you will find Irikwae to be something unique in the way of ports."

Jethri's stomach was beginning to register complaints about the motion and the speed. He breathed, slow and deep, concentrating on keeping breakfast where it belonged, and let her words flow by him.

Suddenly, the car braked, swung to the right—and the traffic outside the window was less, and more moderately paced. The view was suddenly something other than port—tile-fronted buildings heavily shaded by the trailing branches of tall, deeply green vegetation.

"Rubiata City," Master ven'Deelin murmured. He glanced at her and she smiled. "Soon, we shall be home."

"Awaken, my child, we are arrived." The soft voice was accompanied by a brisk tap on his knee.

Jethri blinked, straightened, and blinked again. He didn't remember falling asleep, but he must've, he thought—the view outside the windows was entirely changed.

There was no city. The land fell away on either side of the car and rose up again in jagged teeth of grayish blue rock; on and on it went, and there, through the right window and far below—a needle glint which must be—could it be?—the port tower.

Jethri gasped, his hand went out, automatically seeking a grab-bar—and found warm fingers instead.

"Peace," Norn ven'Deelin said, in her awful Terran. "No danger is there here, Jethri. We come up into the home of my heart."

Her fingers were unexpectedly strong, gripping him tightly. "All is well. The mountains are friendly. I promise you will find them so, eh? Eh?"

He swallowed and forced himself to look away from the wide spaces and dangerous walls—to look at her face.

The black eyes held his. "Good. No danger. Say to me."

"No danger," he repeated, obedient, if breathless.

She smiled slightly. "And soon will you believe it. Never have you seen mountains?"

He shook his head. "I—the port. There's no use us going out into—" He swallowed again, engaging in a brief battle of wills with his stomach. "I'm ship-born, ma'am. We learn not to look at the open sky. It makes us—some of us—uncomfortable."

"Ah." Her fingers tightened, then she released him, and smiled. "Many wonders await you, my son."

THEY HAD PASSED between high pillars of what looked to be the local blue rock, smoothed and regularized into rectangles. Afterward, the view out the window was of lawns, interrupted now and then by groups of middle tall plants. Gaenor's descriptions of the pleasant things she missed from her home led him to figure that the groups scratched an artistic itch. If this lawn had been done the way Gaenor thought was proper, then there'd be some vantage point overlooking the whole, where the pattern could be seen all at once.

The car took a long curve, more lawn sweeping by the windows, then came to a smooth halt, broadside to a long set of stairs cut from the blue rock.

The doors came up, admitting a blare of unpolarized sunlight and an unexpectedly cool breeze, bearing scents both mysterious and agreeable.

Master ven'Deelin patted him on the knee.

"Come along, young Jethri! We are arrived!"

She fairly leapt out of the vehicle. Jethri paused long enough to put the black glasses on, then followed rather more slowly.

Outside, Master ven'Deelin was in animated conversation with a gray-haired woman dressed in what looked to be formal uniform—their driver, maybe...*Anecha*, he reminded himself, mindful of Uncle Paitor's assertion that a successful trader worked at keeping name and face on file in the brainbox— which was, by coincidence, a point Master tel'Ondor also made.

So—Anecha the driver. He'd do better to find her last name, but for now he could get away with "Master Anecha" if he was called upon to do the polite. Not that that looked likely any time in the near present, the way her and Master ven'Deelin were jawing.

Deliberately keeping his eyes on objects nearby—no need to embarrass Master ven'Deelin or himself with another widespaces panic—he moved his gaze up the stony steps, one at a time, until all at once, there was house at the tiptop, posed like a fancy on the highest tier of one of Dyk's sillier cakes.

Up it went, three levels, four—rough blue rock, inset with jewel colored windows. There was greenery climbing the rock walls: vines heavy with white, waxy flowers, that swayed in the teasing breeze.

Nearer at hand, he heard his name and brought his eyes hurriedly down from the heights, to find Master ven'Deelin at his right hand.

"Anecha will see to our luggage," she said, with a sweep of her hand that encompassed both stair and house. "Let us ascend."

Ascend they did—thirty-six stone steps, one after the other, at a pace somewhat brisker than he would have chosen for himself, Master ven'Deelin bouncing along beside him like gravity had nothing to do with her.

They did pause at the top, Jethri sucking air deep into his lungs and wishing that Liadens didn't considered it impolite for a spacer to mop his face in public.

"You must see this," Master ven'Deelin said, putting her hand on his arm. "Turn about, my child."

Panting, Jethri turned about.

What he didn't do—he didn't throw himself face down on the deck and cover his head with his arms, nor even go down on his knees and set up a yell for Seeli.

He did go back a step, breath throttling in his throat, and had the native sense to bring his eyes *down*, away from the arcing empty pale sky and the unending march of rock and peak—*down* to the long stretch of green lawn, which outrageous open space was nothing less than homey by comparison with the horror of the sky.

So—the lawn, and the clumps of bushes, swimming before his tearing eyes, and suddenly, the random clumps weren't random, but the necessary parts of a larger picture showing a common cat, folded in and poised on the feet, ready to jump.

Jethri remembered to breathe. Remembered to look to Master ven'Deelin and incline his head, politely.

"You approve?" she murmured, her head tipped a little to a side.

"It is—quite a work," he managed, shamelessly swiping Master tel'Ondor's phrase. He cleared his throat. "Is the hunting cat the sign of the house?"

Her eyebrows lifted.

"An excellent guess," she said. "Alas, that I must disappoint you. The sign of the house is a grapevine, heavy with fruit. However, several of the revered Maarilex ancestors bred cats as an avocation. The breed is well-established now, and no more to do with Tarnia, save that there are usually cats in the house. And the sculpture, of course." She inclined her head, gravely. "Well done, Jethri. Now, let us announce ourselves."

She turned back to the door, and Jethri did, keeping his eyes low. He had the understanding that he'd just passed a test—or even two—and wished that he felt less uncertain on his legs. All that openness, and not a wall or a corridor or an avenue to confine it. He shuddered.

Facing the door was a relief, and it took an active application of will not to lean his head against the vermillion wood. As it happened, that was a smart move, because the door came open all at once, snatched back into the house by a boy no older than ten Standards, Jethri thought—and then revised that estimate down as the kid bowed, very careful, hand over heart, and lisped, "Who requests entry?"

Master ven'Deelin returned the bow with an equal measure of care. "Norn ven'Deelin Clan Ixin is come to make her bow to her foster mother, who has the honor to be Tarnia. I bring with me my apprentice and foster son."

The kid's eyes got round and he bowed even lower, a trifle ragged, to Jethri's eye, and stepped back, sweeping one arm wide.

"Be welcome in our house, Norn ven'Deelin Clan Ixin. Please follow. I will bring you to a parlor and inform the delm of your presence."

"We are grateful for the care of the House," Master ven'Deelin murmured, stepping forward.

They followed the kid across an entry chamber floored with the blue stone, polished to a high gloss, from which their boot heels woke stony echoes, then quieted, as they crossed into a carpeted hallway. A dozen steps down the carpet, their guide paused before an open door and bowed.

"The delm comes. Please, be at ease in our house."

The parlor was smallish—maybe the size of Master ven'Deelin's office on *Elthoria*—its walls covered in what Jethri took to be pale blue silk. The floor was the same vermillion wood as the front door, and an oval rug figured in pale blue and white lay in the center, around which were situated two upholstered chairs—pale blue—a couch—white—and a low table of white wood. Against the far wall stood a wine table of the same white wood, bottles racked in three rows of six. The top was a polished slab of the local stone, on which half-a-dozen glasses stood, ready to be filled.

"Clan Tarnia makes wine?" he asked Master ven'Deelin, who was standing beside one of the blue chairs, hands tucked into her belt, watching him like he was doing something interesting.

She tipped her head to one side. "You might say so. Just as you might say that Korval makes pilots or that Aragon makes porcelains."

*Whoever*, Jethri thought, irritable with unexpended adrenaline, *they are*.

"Peace," Master ven'Deelin said. "These things will be made known to you. Indeed, it is one of the reasons we are come here."

"Another being that even you would be hard put to explain this start to Ixin!" A sharp voice said from the doorway.

Jethri spun, his boot heels squeaking against the polished floor. Master ven'Deelin turned easier, and bowed lightly in a mode he didn't know.

"Mother, I greet you."

The old, old woman leaned on her cane, bright eyes darting to his face. Ears burning, he bowed, junior to senior.

"Good-day, ma'am."

"An optimist, I apprehend." She looked him up and looked him down, and Jethri wasn't exactly in receipt of the notion that she liked what she saw.

"Does no one on *Elthoria* know how to cut hair?"

As near as he could track it, the question was asked of the air, and that being so, he should've ignored it or let Master ven'Deelin deal. But it was *his* hair under derision, and the theory that it had to grow out some distance before he was presentable as a civilized being wasn't original with him.

"The barber says my hair needs to grow before he can do anything with it," he told her, a little more sharply than he had intended.

"And you find that a great impertinence on the side of the barber, do you?"

He inclined his head, just slightly. "I liked it the way it was."

"Hah!" She looked aside, and Jethri fair sagged in relief to be out from under her eye.

"Norn—I ask as one who stands as your mother: Have you run mad?"

Master ven'Deelin tipped her head, to Jethri's eye, amused.

"Now, how would I know?" she said, lightly, and moved a hand. "Was my message unclear? I had said I was bringing my foster son to you for—"

"Education and polish," the old lady interrupted. "Indeed, you did say so. What you did not say, my girl, is that your son is a mess of fashion and awkwardness, barely beyond halfling, and Terran besides!"

"Ah." Master ven'Deelin bowed—another mystery mode. "But it is precisely because he is Terran that I took him as apprentice. And precisely because of chel'Gaibin that he is my son."

"chel'Gaibin?" There was a small pause, then a wrinkled hand moved, smoothing the air irritably. "Never mind. That tale will keep, I think. What I would have from you now is what you think we might accomplish here. The boy is Terran, Norn—I say it with nothing but respect. What would you have me teach him?"

"Nothing above the ordinary: The clans and their occupations; the High modes; color and the proper wearing of jewels; the Code."

"In short, you wish me to sculpt this pure specimen of a Terran into a counterfeit Liaden."

"Certainly not. I wish you to produce me a gentleman of the galaxy, able to treat with Liaden and Terran equally."

There was another short pause, while the old lady gave him second inspection, head-top to boot-bottom.

"What is your name, boy?" she asked at last.

He bowed in the mode of introduction. "Jethri Gobelyn."

"So." She raised her left hand, showing him the big enameled ring she wore on the third finger. "I have the honor to be Tarnia. You may address me informally as Lady Maarilex. Is there a form of your personal name that you prefer?"

"I prefer Jethri, if you please, ma'am."

"I will then address you informally as Jethri. Now, I have no doubt that you are fatigued from your journey. Allow me to call one of my house to guide you to your rooms. This evening, prime meal will be served in the small dining room at local hour twenty. There are clocks in your quarters." She glanced to Master ven'Deelin.

"We have him in the north wing."

"Excellent," Master ven'Deelin said.

Jethri wasn't so sure, himself, but the thought of getting doors and walls between himself and this intense old lady; to have some quiet time to think—that appealed.

So he bowed his gratitude, and Lady Maarilex thumped the floor with her cane loud enough to scare a spacer out of his suit, and the kid who had let them in to the house was there, bowing low.

"Thawlana?"

"Pet Ric, pray conduct Jethri to his rooms in the north wing."

Another bow, this to Jethri. "If you please?"

He wanted those walls—he did. But there was another portion of him that didn't want to go off into the deep parts of a Grounder house on a planet no Terran ship had ever touched, leaving his last link with space behind. It wasn't exactly panic that sent him looking at Master ven'Deelin, lips parting, though he didn't have any words planned to say.

She forestalled him with a gentle bow. "Be at peace, my child. We will speak again at prime. For now, this my foster mother wishes to ring a terrifying scold down upon me, and she could not properly express herself in the presence of a tender lad." She moved her hand, fingers wriggling in a shooing gesture. "Go now."

And that, thought Jethri, was that. Stiffly, he turned back to the kid—Pet Ric—and bowed his thanks.

"Thank you," he said. "I would be glad of an escort."

THEY WERE HARDLY a dozen steps from the parlor when a shadow moved in one of the doorways and a girl flickered out into the hallway, one hand raised imperiously. His guide stopped, and so did Jethri, being unwilling to run him down. The girl was older than Pet Ric—maybe fourteen or fifteen Standards, Jethri guessed—with curly red-brown hair and big, dark blue eyes in a pointy little face. She was dressed in rumpled and stained tan trousers, boots and a shirt that had probably started the day as yellow. A ruby the size of a cargo can lug nut hung round her neck by a long silver chain.

"Is it him? The ven'Deelin's foster son?" She whispered, looking up and down the hall like she was afraid somebody might overhear her.

"Who else would he be?" Pet Ric answered, sounding pettish to Jethri's ears.

"Anybody!" she said dramatically. She lowered her hand, raised her chin and looked Jethri straight in the eye. "Are you Jethri ven'Deelin, then?"

"Jethri Gobelyn," he corrected. "I have the honor to be Master ven'Deelin's apprentice."

"Apprentice?" another voice exclaimed. A second girl stepped out of the doorway, this one an exact duplicate, even in dress, of the first. "Aunt Stafeli said *foster son.*"

"Well, he could be both, couldn't he?" asked the first girl, and looked back at Jethri. "Are you both apprentice and foster son?"

*No getting out of it now,* he thought and inclined his head. "Yes."

The first girl clapped her hands together and spun to face her sister. "See, Meicha? Both!"

"Both or neither," Meicha said, cryptically. "We will take over as guide, Pet Ric."

The boy pulled himself up. "My grandmother gave the duty to me."

"Aren't you on door?" asked the girl who wasn't Meicha.

This appeared to be a question of some substance. Pet Ric hesitated. "Ye-es."

"What room has the guest been given?" Meicha asked. "The Mountain Suite."

"All the way at the end of the north wing? How will you guard the door from there?" She asked, folding her arms over her chest. "It was well for you we happened by, cousin. We will escort the guest to his rooms. You will return to your post."

"Yes!" applauded her twin. "The house cares for the guest, and the door is held. All ends in honor."

It might have been that Pet Ric wasn't entirely convinced of that, Jethri thought, but—on the one hand, his granmam had given him the duty of escorting the guest, and on the second, it seemed clear she'd forgotten about the door.

Abruptly, the boy made up his mind, and bowed to Jethri's honor.

"I regret, Jethri Gobelyn—my duty lies elsewhere. I leave you in the care of my cousins Meicha and Miandra and look forward to seeing you again soon."

Jethri bowed. "I thank you for your care and honor your sense of duty. I look forward to renewing our acquaintance."

"Very pretty," Meicha said to Miandra. "I believe Aunt Stafeli will have him tutoring us in manner and mode."

Jethri took pause and considered the two of them, for that might well have been a barb, and he was in no mood for contention.

Miandra it was who raised her hand. "It was a jest, Jethri— may we call you Jethri? You may call us Meicha and Miandra— or *Meichamiandra*, as Ren Lar does!"

"You will find us frightfully light-minded," Meicha added. "Aunt Stafeli despairs, and says so often."

"Jethri wants to be alone in his room to rest his head before prime," Miandra stated, at an abrupt angle to the conversation.

"That's sensible," Meicha allowed, and turned about face, marching away down the hall. Between amused and irritated, Jethri followed her, Miandra walking companionably at his side.

"We'll take you by the public halls this time, though it is longer. Depend upon Aunt Stafeli to quiz you on every detail of the route at prime. Later, we'll show you the back halls."

"That is very kind of you," Jethri said, slowly. "But I do not think I will be guesting above a few days."

"Not above a few days?" Meicha looked at him over her shoulder. "Are you certain of that, I wonder, Jethri?"

"Certain, yes. *Elthoria* breaks orbit for Naord in three Standard Days."

Silence greeted this, which didn't do much for the comfort of his stomach, but before he could ask them what they knew that he didn't, Miandra redirected the flow of conversation.

"Is it very exciting, being at the ven'Deelin's side on the trade floor? We have not had the honor of meeting her, but we have read the tales."

"Tales?" Jethri blinked at her as they rounded a corner.

"Certainly. Norn ven'Deelin is the youngest trader to have attempted and achieved the amethyst. Alone, she re-opened trade with the Giletti System, which five ambassadors could not accomplish over the space of a dozen years! She was offered the guildmaster's duty and turned it aside, saying that she better served the Guild in trade."

"She has taken," Meicha put in here, "a Terran apprentice trader under her patronage and has sworn to bring him into the Guild."

The last, of course, he knew. The others, though—

"I am pleased to hear these stories, which I had not known," he said carefully. "But it must go without saying that Master ven'Deelin is legend."

They laughed, loudly and with obvious appreciation; identical notes of joy sounding off the wooden walls.

"He does well. In truth," gasped Meicha, "the ven'Deelin is legend. Yes, even so."

"We will show you the journals, in the library, if you would enjoy them," Miandra said. "Perhaps tomorrow?"

"That would be pleasant," he said, as they began to ascend a highly polished wooden staircase of distressing height. "However, I stand at Master ven'Deelin's word, and she has not yet discussed my duties here with—"

"Oh, certainly!" Meicha cut him off. "It is understood that the ven'Deelin's word must carry all before it!"

"Except Aunt Stafeli," said Miandra.

"Sometimes," concluded Meicha; and, "Do you find the steps difficult, Jethri?"

He bit his lip. "My home ship ran light gravity, and I am never easy in heavy grav."

"Light gravity," Miandra repeated, in caressing tones. "Sister, we must go to space!"

"Let Ren Lar catch us 'mong the vines again and we shall."

Miandra chuckled and put a light hand quickly on Jethri's sleeve.

"Be of good heart, friend. Six steps more to the top of the flight, and then a small walk to the end of a very short hallway, I promise you."

"Take good advice and first have yourself a nap," Meicha said. "Time enough to unpack when you are rested."

That seemed sensible advice, he allowed, though he was not wanting to sleep so much as to *think*.

"I thank you," he said, rather breathlessly, to Meicha's back.

She reached the top of the flight and turned, dancing a few steps to the right.

"Is your home light as well?" she asked, seriously, as he achieved the landing, and turned to look at her.

"My home..." He sighed, and reached up to rub his head where the growing-out hair itched. "I am ship-born. My home is—was—a tradeship named *Gobelyn's Market*."

The two of them exchanged a glance rich in disbelief.

"But—did you never come to ground?" Miandra asked.

"We did—for trade, repairs, that sort of thing. But we didn't *live* on the ground. We *lived* on the ship."

Another shared glance, then—

"He speaks the truth," said Meicha.

"But to always and *only* live on a ship?" wailed Miandra.

"Why not?" Jethri asked, irritated. "Lots of people live on ships. I'd rather that than live planet-side. Ships are clean, the temperature is consistent, the grav is light, there's no bad smells, or dust, or *weather*—" He heard his voice heating up and put the brake on it, bowing with a good measure of wariness.

"Forgive me," he murmured.

"Truth," Meicha said again, as if he hadn't spoken.

Miandra sighed. "Well, then, it is truth, and we must accept it. It seems an odd way to live, is all." She turned and put her hand on his sleeve.

"You must forgive us for our ignorance," she said. "I hope you will talk to us about your ship at length, so that we are no longer ignorant."

"And in trade," Meicha added, "we will teach you about gardens, and streams, and snow and other planet-side pleasures, so that you are no longer ignorant."

Jethri blinked, throat tightening with a sudden realization that he had been as rude as they had, and as such was a fitting object for Balance—

Except, he thought then, they had already declared Balance—him to teach them about ship-living, them to teach him about planet-life. He sighed, and Meicha grinned.

"You are going to be interesting, Jethri Gobelyn," she said.

"*Later*, he will be interesting," Miandra ordered, and waved a hand under her sister's nose. "At this present, we have given our word to guide him to his rooms in enough time that he might nap and recruit his strength before prime, none of which is accomplished by standing here."

"You sound like Aunt Stafeli." Meicha turned, crooking a finger behind her. "Come along then. Less than six dozen steps, Jethri, I promise you."

In fact, it was a couple dozen steps more than six, though Jethri wasn't inclined to quibble. Now that the room was near, he found himself wanting that nap, though he slept in the car—and a shower, too, while he was wanting comforts...

"We arrive!" Meicha announced, flourishing a bow in no mode Jethri could name.

The door was wood, dark brown in color. Set off-center was a white porcelain knob painted with what he thought might have been intended to be grapes.

"Turn the knob and push the door away from you," Miandra coached. "If you like, we will show you how to lock it from the inside."

"Thank you," he said. The porcelain was cool and smooth, vaguely reminiscent of his fractin.

The door moved easily under his push, and he came a little too quickly into the room, the knob still in his hand.

This time he shouted, and threw an arm up over his eyes, all the while his heart pounded in his ears, and his breath burned in his chest.

"The curtains!" a high voice shrilled, and there were hands on his shoulders, pushing him, *turning* him, he realized, in the midst of his panic and willingly allowed it, the knob slipping from his hand.

"Done!"

"Done," repeated an identical voice, very near at hand. "Jethri, the curtain is closed. You may open your eyes."

It wasn't as easy as that, of course, and there was the added knowledge, as he got his breathing under control, that he'd made a looby outta himself in front of the twins, besides showing them just as plain as he could where he stood vulnerable.

*Mud, dust and stink!* He raged at himself, standing there with his arm over his face and his eyes squeezed tight. His druthers, if it mattered, was to sink down deep into the flooring and never rise up again. Failing that, he figured dying on the spot would do. Of all the *stupid*—but, who expected bare sky and mountain peaks when they opened a sleeping room door? Certainly, not a born spacer.

"You are a guest of the house," one of the twins said from nearby, "and valued."

"Besides," said the other, "the ven'Deelin would skin us if harm came to you and then Aunt Stafeli would boil us."

That caught him in the funny bones, and he sputtered a laugh, which somehow made it easier to get the arm down and the eyes, cautiously, open.

One of the twins—now that they were out of formation, he couldn't tell one from her sister—was standing practically toe-to-toe with him, her pointed face quite plainly showing concern. To her right and little back, the other twin's face wore an identical expression of dismay.

"Not smart," he managed, still some breathless. "You stand back, in case I swing out."

She tipped her head. "You are not going to swing out," she stated, with absolute conviction. "You are quite calm, now."

And, truth told, he did feel calmer and neither in danger or dangerous. He took a breath, getting the air all the way down into his lungs, and sighed it out.

"What's amiss?" asked the twin who stood farthest from him. "Are you afraid of mountains?"

He shook his head. "Openness," he said, and, seeing their blank stares, expanded. "All that *emptiness*, with no walls or corridors—it's not natural. Not what a space-born would know as natural. You could fall, forever..."

They exchanged another one of their identical looks, and then the nearer twin stepped back, clearing his sight of the room, which was bigger than the *Market's* common room, and set up like a parlor, with a desk against one wall, uphol-stered chairs here and there, low tables, and several small cases holding books and bric-a-brac. The floor was carpeted in deep green. Across the room, a swath of matching deep green shrouded the window.

"The bedroom boasts a similar vista, in which the house takes pride, and takes care that all of our most honored guests are placed here," said the girl nearest him. She paused before asking, "Shall we close the curtains, or show you how to use them?"

*Good question*, Jethri thought, and took another breath, try-ing to center himself, like Pen Rel had taught him. He nodded.

"I think I should learn how to operate the curtains myself, thank you."

That pleased them, though he couldn't have said how he knew, and they guided him through a small galley, which, thank the ghosts of space, had no window, to his bedroom.

The bed alone was the size of his quarters on the *Market*, and so filled up with pillows that there wasn't any room left for him.  His duffle, and of all things, the battered B crate from his storage bin sat on a long bench under…the window.

He was warned, now, and knew to keep his eyes low, so it wasn't bad at all, just a quick spike in the heart rate and a little bit of buzz inside the ears.

"In order to operate the curtain," said the twin on his left, "you must approach the window.  There is a pulley mechanism at the right edge…"

He found it by touch, keeping his eyes pinned to the homey sight of his bag on the bench.  The pull was stiff, but he gave it steady pressure, and the curtain glided across the edge of his sight, casting the room into shade.

He sighed, and sat down on the bench.

Before him, Mcicha and Miandra bowed.

"So, you are safely delivered, and will be wanting your rest," the one on the left said.

"We will come again just ahead of twentieth hour to escort you to the small dining room," the one on the right said. "In the meanwhile, be easy in our house."

"And don't forget to set the clock to wake you in good time to dress," the twin on the left added.

He smiled, then recalled his manners, and got to his feet to bow his gratitude.

"Thank you for your care."

"We are pleased to be of assistance," said the twin on the right, as the two of them turned away.

"Aunt Stafeli will not allow you to fear mountains, or open space, or any being born," the girl on the left said over her shoulder.

"Then it is fortunate that I will only be with her for a few days," Jethri answered lightly, following them.

Silence from both as they passed through the galley and into the parlor.

"Recruit your strength," one said finally.  "In case."

He smiled.  Did they expect him to stay while *Elthoria* continued on the amended route?  He was 'prenticed to learn trade, not to learn mountains.

Still, it would be rude to ignore their concern, so he bowed and murmured, "I will. Thank you."

One twin opened the door and slipped out into the hall-way. The second paused a moment, and put her finger on a switch under the inner knob.

"Snap to the right is locked," she said. "To the left is unlocked. Until prime, Jethri."

"Until prime," he said, but she was already gone, the door ghosting shut behind her.

THE MIRROR SHOWED brown hair growing out in untidy patches, an earnest, scrubbed clean face, and a pair of wide brown eyes. Below the face, the body was neatly outfitted in a pale green Liaden-style shirt and dark blue trousers. Jethri nodded, and his reflection nodded, too, brown eyes going a little wider.

"You're shipshape and ready for space," he told himself encouragingly, reaching for the Ixin pin.

One eye on the clock, he got the pin fixed to his collar, and stood away from the mirror, pulling his shirt straight. It lacked six minutes to twentieth hour. He wondered how long he should wait for the twins before deciding that they had forgotten him and—

A chime rang through the apartment. Jethri blinked, then grinned, and went quick-step to the main room. He remem-bered to order his face into bland before he opened the door, which was well.

He had been expecting the same grubby brats who had guided him a few hours before, faces clean, maybe, in honor of dinner.

What he hadn't expected was two ladies of worth in match-ing white dresses, a flower nestled among the auburn curls of each, matching rubies hanging from matching silver chains. They bowed like they were one person, neither one faster or slower than the other—honor to the guest.

His answer—honor to a child of the house—was a bow that Master tel'Ondor had drilled him on until his back ached, so he was confident of his execution—until the cat.

He had seen cats before, of course—port cats.  Small
and fierce, they worked the docks tirelessly, keeping the rat
and mouse populations in check.  Their work took a toll, in
shredded ears, crooked tails, and rough, oily fur.

This cat—the one standing between the twins and looking
up into his face as if it was trying to memorize his features—
*this cat* had never done a lick of work in its life.

It was a tall animal; the tips of its sturdy ears easily on a
level with the twins' knees, with a pronounced and well-whis-
kered muzzle. Its fur was a plush gray; its tail a high, proud
sweep.  The eyes which considered him so seriously were
pale green—rather like two large oval-shaped peridot.

Timing ruined, Jethri straightened to find the twins
watching him with interest.

"What is that doing here?"

"Oh, don't mind Flinx—"

"He was waiting outside our rooms for us—"

"Very likely he heard there was a guest—"

"And came to do proper duty."

He frowned, and looked down at the animal.  "It's not
intelligent?"

"No, you mustn't say so!  Flinx is *very* intelligent!" cried
the twin on the right—Jethri thought she might be Miandra.

"Bend down and offer your forefinger," the other twin—
Meicha, if his theory was correct—said.  "We mustn't be late
for prime and duty must be satisfied."

Jethri threw her a sharp glance, but as far as he could
read her—which was to say, not at all—she appeared to
be serious.

Sighing to himself, he bent down and held his right forefinger out toward the cat's nose, hoping he wasn't about to get
bit.  Cat-bite was serious trouble, as he knew. 'way back, when
he was still a kid, Dyk had gotten bit by a dock cat. The bite
went septic before he got to the first aid kit and it had taken
two hits of super heavy duty antibiotics to bring him back
from the edge of too sick to care.

This cat, though—this Flinx. It moved forward a substantial step and touched its cool, brick colored nose to the very tip of his finger. It paused, then, and Jethri was about to pull back, duty done. But, before he did, Flinx took a couple more substantial steps and made sure it rubbed its body down the entire length of his fingers and arm.

"A singular honor!" one of the twins said, and Jethri jumped, having forgotten she was there.

The cat blinked, for all of space like he was laughing, then stropped himself along Jethri's knee and continued on into his rooms.

"Hey!" He turned, but before he could go after the interloper, his sleeve was grabbed by one of the twins and his hand by the other.

"Leave him—he won't hurt anything," said the girl holding his sleeve.

"Flinx is very wise," added the girl holding his hand, pulling the door shut, as they hustled him down the hall. "And we had best be wise and hurry so that we are not late for prime!"

THANKING ALL THE ghosts of space, the small dining room did not have a famous view on exhibit. What it did have, was a round table laid with such an amount of dinnerware, utensils and drinking vessels that Jethri would have suspected a shivary was planned, instead of a cozy and quiet family dinner.

They were the last arriving, on the stroke of twenty, according to the clock on the sideboard. The twins deserted him at the door and plotted a course for two chairs set together between Delm Tarnia and a black-haired man with a soft-featured face and dreamy blue eyes. At Tarnia's right sat Master ven'Deelin, observing him with that look of intent interest he seemed lately to inspire. Next to Master ven'Deelin was an empty chair.

Grateful that this once the clue was obvious, he slipped into the empty seat, and darted a quick look down table at the twins. They were sitting side by side, as modest as you please, hands folded on their laps, eyes downcast.

"Jethri," the old lady said, claiming his attention with a flutter of frail old fingers. "I see that you have had the felicity of meeting Miandra and Meicha. Allow me to present my son, Ren Lar, who is master of the vine here. Ren Lar, here is Norn's fosterling, Jethri Gobelyn."

"Sir." Jethri inclined his head deeply—as close to a seated bow as he could come without knocking his nose against the table.

"Young Jethri," Ren Lar inclined his head to a matching depth, which Jethri might have suspected for sarcasm, except there was Tarnia sitting right there. "I am pleased to meet you. We two must hold much in common, as sons of such illustrious mothers."

Oh-ho, that was it. The man's bow was a courtesy paid to Master ven'Deelin, through her foster son, and not necessarily to the son himself. The universe had not quite gone topsy-turvy.

"I am sure that we will have many stories to trade, sir," he said, which was what he could think of as near proper, though not completely of the form Master tel'Ondor had given him. On the other hand, Ren Lar's greeting hadn't been of the form Master tel'Ondor had given him, either.

"Trade stories at your leisure, and beyond my hearing," the old lady directed. "Normally, we are not quite so thin of company as you find us this evening, Jethri. Several of the House are abroad on business, and one has made the journey to Liad, in order to complete his education."

"And Pet Ric," said one of the twins, quietly, though maybe not quietly enough, "eats in the nursery, with the rest of the babies."

Lady Maarilex turned her head, and considered the offending twin with great blandness. "Indeed, he does," she said after a moment. "You may join him, if you wish."

The twin ducked her head. "Thank you, ma'am. I would prefer to remain here."

"Your preference has very little to do with the matter. From my age, young Meicha, there is not so much difference between you and Pet Ric, that he naturally be confined to the nursery, while you dine with the adults." A pause. "Note that I do not say, with the *other* adults."

Meicha bit her lip. "Yes, ma'am."

"So," the old lady turned away. "You must forgive them," she said to Master ven'Deelin. "They have no address."

"One would not expect it," Master ven'Deelin answered softly, "if they are new come from the nursery. Indeed, I am persuaded that they are progressing very well indeed."

"You are kind to say it."

"Not at all. I do wonder, though, Mother, to find dramliz in the house."

The old lady looked up sharply. "Hah. Well, and you do not find dramliz in the house, mistress. You find Meicha and Miandra, children of the clan. Healer Hall has taken an interest in them."

Master ven'Deelin inclined her head. "I am most pleased to see them."

"You say so now." She moved a hand imperiously. "House-children, make your bows to my foster daughter, Norn ven'Deelin Clan Ixin."

They inclined, deeply and identically, and with haste enough to threaten the mooring of the flowers they wore in their hair.

"Norn ven'Deelin," Meicha murmured.

"We are honored," Miandra finished.

"Meicha and Miandra, I am pleased to meet you." Master ven'Deelin inclined her head, not by much, but to judge by the way the twins' eyes got wide, maybe it was enough.

Somebody—Lady Maarilex or Ren Lar—must have made a sign that Jethri didn't catch, because right then, the door at the back of the room opened and here came an elder person dressed in a tight black tunic and tight black pants. He bowed, hands together.

"Shall I serve, Lady?"

"Yes, and then leave us, if you will."

THERE WAS TALK during the meal, family catch up stuff, which Jethri followed well enough, to his own surprise. Following it and making sense of it were two different orbits, though, and after a while he just let the words slide past his ear and concentrated on his dinner.

"Of course, I will be delighted to have Jethri's assistance in the vineyard—and in the cellars, too." Ren Lar's voice, bearing as it did his own name, jerked Jethri's attention away from dinner, which was mostly done anyway, and back to the conversation.

"That is well," Master ven'Deelin was answering calmly. "I intend to start him in wine after he has completed his studies here, and it would be beneficial if he had a basic understanding of the processes."

"Very wise," Ren Lar murmured. "I am honored to be able to assist, in even so small a way, with the young trader's education."

Carefully, Jethri looked to the twins. Miandra was studying her plate with an intensity it didn't deserve, being empty. Meicha met his eye square, and he got the distinct idea she'd've said *I told you so* right out if she hadn't already earned one black mark on the meal.

Jethri felt himself go cold, felt the breath shortening in his lungs. *Thrown off*, he thought, and didn't believe. Couldn't believe it, not of Master ven'Deelin, who, unlike his blood mother, had wanted him, at least as her apprentice. Who had plans for him, and who thought he might one day be useful to—

And there was the B crate sitting in the room upstairs, which he surely didn't need for a three-day visit...

"Ma'am," he heard his own voice, breathless and a thought too sharp. "You're not leaving me here?"

She tipped her head, black eyes very bright. "You object to the House of my foster mother?"

He took a breath, centering himself—trying to—like
Pen Rel kept insisting on.  It was important to be calm.
People who panicked made mistakes, and, by all the ghosts
of space, a mistake now could doom him to life in the mud...

Another breath, deliberately deep, noticing that the conversation had stopped and that Master ven'Deelin's question hung in the air, vibrating with an energy he wasn't near
to understanding.

"The house of your foster mother is a fine house, indeed," he said, slowly, carefully.  "Ignorant as I am, it is all
but certain that I will disgrace the honor of the House, or
of yourself, all unknowning.  I am space-born, ma'am.
Planet ways—"

Master ven'Deelin moved a hand in the Liaden version of
"stop."  Gulping, Jethri stopped.

"You see how it is with him," she said to Lady Maarilex.
"So much concern for my honor!"

"That is not an ill thing, I judge, in a foster child," the old
lady said gravely.  "Indeed, I am charmed and heartened by his
care of you, Norn.  For surely, his concern for you is but a pure
reflection of the care you have shown him.  I am pleased, but
in no wise surprised."

Trapped.  Jethri bit his lip, feeling panic clawing at his throat,
adrenaline arguing with his dinner.

Across the table, he saw Miandra swallow hard, and Meicha
close her eyes, throat working.

"So, then," Master ven'Deelin continued.  "Wine lore,
surely, and a decreasing of the sensibilities.  Modesty becomes
a lad of certain years, but a lad who hovers on the edge of
being a trader grown must have more to his repertoire than
modesty and a pleasant demeanor."

Lady Maarilex inclined her head.  "We shall do our possible," she murmured.  "A relumma may see some progress."

A *relumma*?  Ninety-six Standard Days?  He stayed in his
chair.  He didn't yell or give in to bawling.  Across from him,
though, Meicha sniffled.

"Mother," Ren Lar said softly. "It occurs to me that our guests, newly come from space, might welcome an early escape to their beds."

"Why, so they might," Lady Maarilex said, like the idea surprised her. "Thank you, my son." She inclined her head and sat poised until he had come 'round to her chair, eased it back and offered an arm for her to lean on as she rose.

"Good night, kin and guests. Repose yourselves in calmness, knowing that the house is vigilant on your behalf. Young Jethri, attend me tomorrow morning at eighth hour in my study. Miandra will show you the way."

She turned then, leaning hard on the arm of her son, and left the room at a slow walk. As soon as she cleared the door, the twins popped up, bowed their good-nights and were gone, leaving Jethri staring at Norn ven'Deelin and feeling about to cry.

"Well," she said, rising and looking down at him quizzically. "Allow me to escort you to your rooms, my son."

HE DID KEEP himself in hand until they reached the door of his quarters—he did. Master ven'Deelin chatted easily on about the house and how comfortable it was to be assigned to her very room—which, though nothing so exalted as the north wing, mind you!—suited her very well. Jethri returned monosyllables—maybe he did that. But he didn't start a fight until they he had opened the door and bowed her over into his parlor.

He pulled the door closed behind him—so gently, he could scarcely hear the lock *snick*, and stood for the space of a couple good, deep breaths, preparatory to laying the case out as calm and as forceful as he could.

"Master Flinx, how do you go on?" Master ven'Deelin said delightedly. Jethri turned and sure enough, there was the cat, curled up on one of the chairs, and there was Master ven'Deelin, bending down to offer a courteous finger.

"Come, do me the honor of renewing our acquaintance."

Surprisingly enough, the cat did just that, coming out of
his curl and sitting up tall, touching his nose to her fingertip.

"Always the gentleman!" She moved her hand, running
tickling fingers under the cat's chin. "I see that I leave my
son in good care!" Straightening, she sent Jethri a quick
black glance.

"Truly, young Jethri, you will do well here, with Flinx as
your sponsor."

He cleared his throat. "I'd like to talk to you about that, if
you please, ma'am." He said carefully.

She sighed, and folded her hands together, head to one
side. "Well, if you must, you must, and I will not forbid it.
But I will tell you that you are doomed to failure. Remain
here, you most assuredly shall, to sit at the feet of my foster
mother and learn whatever she wishes to teach you."

"Ma'am, will you not at least listen to me?" He heard the
desperation in his own voice and bit his lip.

"Did I not say that I would listen? Speak, my child. I
rejoice in the melodious sounds of your speech."

"Yes, ma'am. I don't wish to be tiresome and I know you
must be eager to seek your bed, so I will be brief. The case is
that I am space-based and I am apprenticed to learn trade.
The whys and whyevers of planet-based society—that falls
outside the scope of those things it is necessary for me to
learn in order to be an effective trader."

"A gentle set-down; appropriate between kin. And though
I might protest that I have done nothing to earn your anger, I
will refrain, for I well know that you consider yourself wronged.
So..." She moved a hand, showing him the chair unoccupied
by the cat.

"Sit, child, and give over *glowering* at me."

He sat, though he wasn't that certain in regard to the
glower.

"Good." She turned back to the second chair, scooped the
cat up deftly and sat, cat on knee. Flinx blinked, and stretched,
and curled round, obviously pleased with his position.

"The fact that you are able to argue with sincerity that knowledge of planet-based society has no bearing upon your abilities as a trader only demonstrates how deeply you are in need of such education."

"Master—"

She raised a hand. "Peace. You have made your throw. I now claim my turn with the dice."

He bit his lip. "Yes, ma'am."

"'Yes, mother' would be more appropriate to the case," she said, "but I do not insist. Instead, I will undertake to put your mind at ease. You are not abandoned. You are set down for the space of two relumma, that you might pursue independent study of value to the ship. These studies are two-fold." She held up a hand, and folded the index finger down.

"One, you will learn what my foster mother may teach you of the proper mode. Fear not that she will treasure you as I do—and insist that you extend yourself to your greatest of forts." She folded her second finger down.

"Two, you will also spend time in the trade hall at Irikwae Port. I have requested that the master of the hall see to your guild certification, which is a matter I have too long neglected." Points made, she dropped her hand to Flinx's flank.

"I have myself undertaken just such independent studies and certifications, to the benefit of the ship and the profit of the clan. It is what is done, and neither punishment, nor betrayal. Are you able to accept my word that this is so?"

His first inclination was to tell her *no,* but the plain truth was that he'd never known her to lie. Some things she said that he didn't understand—but that was his ignorance and not her deliberate misleading—

"*Two* relumma?" he blurted, his brain finally catching up with his ears. He bent forward in his chair. "Lady Maarilex said *one* relumma!"

"Tcha!" Master ven'Deelin looked up from scratching Flinx behind the ears. "She said that one relumma might begin to show progress. What profit do you bring to the ship half-trained?"

He closed his eyes, fists set hard against his knees. Two relumma on-planet, he thought, and shivered.

"Child..." There was a rustle, and a thump, and then arms put 'round his shoulders. He stiffened and then leaned into the hug, pushing his face against her shoulder like she was Seeli and him not much older than eight.

"Child, the worlds are not your enemy. Nor do ships enclose all that is good and proper in the universe. A trader must know his customers—and the greater number of your customers, when you are a trader grown, will be planet-based, not ship-born. Ignore their ways at your peril. Despise them..." There was a small pouf of sound over his head, and her arms tightened briefly.

"Despise them," she continued, "if you must, from knowledge, rather than ignorance."

"Yes, ma'am," he whispered, because there wasn't anything else to say. She was going to leave him here, right enough, whatever he said, or however he said it. His outlook now was to be sure she remembered to come back for him.

"You may think me heartless," she murmured. "You may perhaps think that I have never been bade to show a calm face to exile. Acquit me, I beg you. Well I remember the wildness in my heart, when my delm ordered that I be fostered to Tarnia, away from Solcintra and from Liad itself, which enclosed all that was good and proper in the universe." Again, that small pouf of sound, which might, Jethri thought, be a gentle laugh.

"A surly and aloof fosterling I was, too. I trust that you will be more seemly than I was—for my foster mother, I ask that you be gentle, and no more bitter than is strictly necessary."

He laughed—a surprising, hiccupy sort of sound—and heard her laugh, too. Her arms tightened once more before she stepped back, leaving him feeling comforted, and oddly comfortable.

"So then," she said briskly. "You have an early interview with our foster mother, and will doubtless wish to seek your bed soon. Be certain that I will return for you. I swear it, on Ixin itself."

Jethri blinked. To swear on the name of her clan—he had the sense that was something not lightly done, *could not* be lightly done. If her own name was more precious than rubies, how much more precious must be the name that sheltered all ven'Deelins, everywhere? He came to his feet, still chewing on the nuances, and bowed respect to an elder.

"I will look for you, in two relumma," he said, and straightened to see a smile on her face.

"Indeed, you will. And now, my son, I bid you deep sleep and sweet dreaming. Learn your lessons well—and mind Master Flinx whenever he cares to advise you."

He inclined his head, seriously. "I'll do that, ma'am."

Together, they walked to the door. He opened it for her; she stepped out—and turned back.

"You will wish to open that curtain, my child. The view of the nighttime sky is not to be missed."

"Yes, ma'am," he said, out of habit, and she smiled again and went away down the hall.

Jethri closed the door slowly, and turned to face the curtained window.

*You told her yes*, he said to himself.

It took a month or so to cross the room, and another week to pull the cord. The curtains came back, slow and stately. Lower lip gripped tightly between his teeth, Jethri looked up from the cords and the folds of cloth…

The sky was a deep blue, spangled with fist-sized shards of icy white light. A pale blue moon was rising, casting shadows on the shoulders of the mountains. Further out, and considerably down, there were clustered lights—a city, or so he thought. He remembered to breathe, and then to breathe again, looking out over the night.

The moon had cleared the mountain peak before he turned away and went into the bedroom, walking on his toes, as if the floor was tiled in glass.

# Day 140
# Standard Year 1118

## Tarnia's Clanhouse
## Irikwae

"SO, THEN, YOUNG Jethri," asked Stafeli Maarilex, "how do you find the view from the north wing?"

He paused with his teacup halfway to his lips and favored her with a straight look over the rim. She returned his gaze, her face so entirely empty of expression that the lack might have been said to be an expression of its own. Glancing aside, for Liadens counted a too-long stare at the face as rudeness, he sipped his tea and put the cup gently back in its saucer.

"I found the view astonishing, ma'am," he said, and was proud to hear his voice steady on.

"I am gratified to hear you say it. Honor me with your thoughts regarding our moons."

*Moons?* He tried not to look befuddled, and supposed he failed completely.

"I saw only one moon, ma'am—pale blue and rising behind the mountain."

"So?" She paused, one hand on her cup, then threw her free hand slightly up and to the side, fingers flicking out. "You must forgive an old woman's memory. Of course, we are in single phase anytime this six-day! Never mind, you will soon have the pleasure of beholding all three riding the skies. Indeed, I will ask Ren Lar to form an excursion for the House's children later in your stay, when the nights will be warmer. I am sure you will find it most amusing. Local legend is that good luck comes to those who sleep beneath the full moons."

He inclined his head, which was polite, and put away for later wondering—or asking of the twins—the notion of a special excursion to look at moons. It might be, he thought, that Tarnia owned a starhouse and an optical scope for—

"There are certain matters of a personal nature which we must discuss," Lady Maarilex said, interrupting his thought. "Pray forgive me if my questions seem impertinent. I assure you that I would not ask these things did necessity not exist."

"Yes, ma'am," he said, sitting up straighter in his chair. He was speaking in the mercantile mode, by special permission of the lady. She was speaking in a mode that was not mercantile, but perfectly intelligible, so long as he kept his ear on it.

"We will need to know certain things. Your family, for instance. Norn tells me that Terrans do not form into Houses and Clans, which I must say seems very peculiar to me. However, I suppose you must have some other method for tracking lineage." She inclined her head.

"Enlighten me, then, young Jethri. Who are you?"

He took a little time to think about it, lifting his cup and taking a leisurely sip while he did, so as not to seem rude.

"I am of the mainline Gobelyns," he said slowly. "Off of the tradeship *Gobelyn's Market*."

"I see." She lifted her cup, buying time herself, Jethri thought, and wasn't particularly encouraged by thinking it.

"May I know more, young Jethri?" she murmured, putting her cup down and apparently giving most of her attention to choosing a piece of fruit from the bowl in the center of the table. "Despite all Norn's efforts, I am woefully ignorant of shiplore."

"Yes, ma'am," he said, mortified to hear his voice break on the second word. "My mother is Iza, captain; my father was Arin, senior trader. My elder siblings are Cris, first mate, and Seeli, administrative mate. My mother's brother is now senior trader, brought on board when my father died." He took a deep breath, and met her eyes firmly, rudeness be spaced.

"The Gobelyns have been shipfolk since before space took ships. Arin Tomas, as he was before he married, his line was scholars and explorers; he served his turn as a Combine commissioner before he was senior trader."

He didn't expect her to value that—to know how to value it—and so he was surprised when she bent her head solemnly, and murmured, "A worthy lineage, Jethri Gobelyn. It could not, of course, be otherwise."

That might've just been the polite—she couldn't very well disapprove of Master ven'Deelin's choice of a foster son, after all—but he was warmed anyway.

"I wonder," she said gently, "if I might know your age."

"Seventeen Standard Years, ma'am."

"Hah. And your name day?"

He blinked, then remembered that Liadens celebrated the anniversary of a baby's being named, which might, as Vil Tor told it, be done within seconds of the birth, or as long as twelve days past. Near as he knew, he'd been named simultaneous with being born. He inclined his head slightly.

"Day two-thirteen, ma'am."

"Delightful! We shall have the felicity of ushering you into your eighteenth year. The House is honored."

He didn't exactly scan why that should be such an honor, 'specially when stood against the fact that his birthday was more often forgot than not. When he'd been a kid, Seeli'd made sure there was some special favorite eatable in his dinner, and Cris would give him a little something by way of a present—a booktape, maybe, or an odd-bit he'd found during the trade rounds. His fourteenth birthday, there wasn't any special tasty in his dinner, though the occasion of his birth had been marked by Cris, who had given him the grown-up wrench set he still wore on his belt. After that—well, he was too old for wanting after special tidbits and gee-gaws.

Carefully, he inclined his head. "I am grateful, but the House need not exert itself on my account."

Lady Maarilex raised an eyebrow. "Norn is correct. *Far* too much sensibility. Hear me, Jethri Gobelyn: The House exerts itself on your behalf because it is what the House demands of itself. Your part is to strive to be worthy of our care. Am I plain?"

He swallowed and looked down into his teacup. "Yes, ma'am."

"Good. Now, lift up your face like the bold young man I know you to be and tell me how you came to meet Norn."

Of the questions he might have expected from her, this one might have been dead last. Master ven'Deelin must have told her—

"Your pardon, young Jethri," the sharp old voice cut across his thoughts. "May I expect the felicity of an answer soon?"

It was near enough in tone to Master tel'Ondor to jerk him upright and meeting her eye before he took a deep breath and began his tale.

"We met in Ynsolt'i Port, which is located in what the Terrano call the Edge and Master ven'Deelin calls the far-outside. There was a...man...who had a deal with a four-on-one payout, guaranteed with a master trader's card..."

# Day 140
# Standard Year 1118

## Kinaveral

"SEELI GOBELYN?" THE man's voice was hurried and high—not familiar, just like his face, when she turned her head and gave him a stare, the while continuing to move. She was running close to late for the regular inspection visit and she knew from experience that the yard-boss wouldn't wait for her one tick past the hour. Not good timing on the part of the spacer who was doggedly keeping pace beside her, though his face was red and damp with sweat.

"Can we talk?" he panted, as Seeli stretched her legs a little more.

"If you can talk and walk at the same time, we can," she said, not feeling any particular pity for him. "I'm late for an appointment and can't stop."

"Maybe we can meet after your appointment," he said. "I'm authorized to offer a trade for fractins."

Authorized to offer a trade on fractins? Like fractins was something rare and expensive, instead of the over-abundant nuisance they happened to be. Seeli sighed, wondering if the guy was a headcase or a joker. Not that it mattered.

"Sorry," she said, moving on at her top ground speed. "No fractins."

"We'll make it worth your while," he insisted. "I'm authorized to trade generous."

"Does you no good if we got none to sell." The gate was in sight; damn if she wasn't going to be *right* on time.

"Wait—"

"No time to wait!" she snapped, more than a little out of breath. "And we ain't got any fractins."

She was under the canopy, then, her body breaking the beam of the spy-eye.

"Maybe I can call on your trader!" The man called behind her and Seeli sighed. Headcase.

"Sure," she yelled over her shoulder as the gate swung open. "Talk to our trader."

# Day 140
# Standard Year 1118

## Irikwae

UPSTAIRS, DOWNSTAIRS, UPSTAIRS, downstairs, front stairs, back stairs. Secret stairs, too. Not to mention the hallways, public, private and almost-forgot. By the time they made it back to ground level and toured the big kitchen and the little one, Jethri was ready for a solid couple hours of sleep.

After breakfast, Lady Maarilex had put him in the care of the twins, instructing them to provide him with a "thorough" tour of the house. It was in Jethri's mind that they had taken that "thorough" just a little too literal. What reason for him to know how to find the butler's closet, or Pan Dir's rooms—Pan Dir being the cousin who was gone to Liad for his studies, and Mr. pel'Saba the butler looking impartially sour at the three of them while the twins did the polite and he made his bow.

*And who would have expected that there could be so many stairs inside of one structure*, Jethri thought, panting in the wake of his guides. *Who would have thought there could be so many hallways giving on to so many rooms?*

Half-a-dozen steps ahead of him, the twins fair danced along, their soft-booted feet hardly seeming to touch the floor, talking in turns over their shoulders, and neither one having the common grace to show breathless.

"The tour is almost done, Jethri!" called Meicha, bouncing 'round to face him. "This hallway ends in a stair—a very *small* stair, I promise you! At the end of the stair, is a door, and on the other side of the door—"

"Is a garden!" Miandra sang out. "The cook has promised us a lovely cold nuncheon, so that you may recruit your strength before your afternoon in the winery."

Jethri's feet stopped moving so suddenly he almost fell on his face. One of the twins said something short and nasty half under her breath before the two of them turned and walked back to him.

"It is," said Miandra, who tended, in Jethri's limited experience, to be the more serious of the two, "a very nice garden."

"With a wall all around it," Meicha added.

"It's open?" He managed, and was obscurely proud to hear that his voice did not break on the question.

"Open?" She frowned, not certain of his meaning, but Miandra caught it right enough.

"To the sky? Of course it is open to the sky. Gardens are, you know."

"We had thought to offer you a pleasant respite before your afternoon's labors," Meicha said. "This is our own *favorite* garden."

Jethri took a breath—another one, centering himself. Pen Rel had sworn three solemn swears that centering and right breathing would all come natural to him, with practice. *If I keep the current course,* Jethri thought irritably, *I'll be in practice and back out again before the shift changes.*

"Much better," Miandra approved, as if he'd said something fortunate.

"Anger is a powerful tool," Meicha added, like that made everything clear and wonderful. She reached out and grabbed his hand, her fingers surprisingly strong.

"Come along, Jethri, do. I promise, only a short walk, then you may rest and refresh yourself and frown at us all you like—"

"While we entertain you with tales of Ren Lar and his beloved vines, and give you the benefit of our—"

"Vast—"

"*Sorrow*ful—"

"Experience."

He looked from one to the other, and thought he saw the glimmer of a joke around the edges of their eyes.

"Ren Lar pushes the crew hard, does he?" he asked lightly, thinking of the soft-spoken, dreamy eyed man he'd met last night at prime meal.

"Ren Lar lives for the vines," Meicha said solemnly. "Pan Dir swore to us that he was given in contract to the mother vine, with the child—that being Pet Ric—coming to the house, naturally enough, so that the vines should never want for aught."

She sounded so much like Khat on the approach to a story that he almost laughed out loud. He did smile and move one shoulder. "Pan Dir was having fun with you, I think."

"I think so, too," Miandra said briskly. "I also think that *I* am hungry, and that nuncheon awaits us."

"And that time marches," her sister agreed. She pulled on Jethri's hand. "Come, son of ven'Deelin. It is a churlish guest who starves the children of the house."

There really wasn't anything else to do. Vowing to keep his head down and his eyes on his plate, Jethri let himself be pulled along, freighter to Meicha's tug.

THE TREES MADE the thing tolerable, when all was counted and tallied. They were tall trees—old, said Miandra; older even than Aunt Stafeli—and their wide-reaching branches broke the sky into manageable pieces, if a spacer should happen to look up too quick, or too high.

The "lovely, cold nuncheon" was set out on a table at the garden's center. There was a wall, as he had been promised, well grown with flowering vines and other creepers.

"Summer is before us still," Miandra said, as they mounted the dias and pulled out their chairs. "Not all the flowers are in bloom, now. At the height of the season, you can see nothing but flowers, and the air is sweet with their scent."

The twins ate with a delicate intensity that made him feel clumsy and over-large  until he forgot about it in the amazements of the meal.

There was nothing that he ate that he would not have willingly eaten more of, though he found particular favor with a few tasties.  He asked the twins the name of each, to their clear approval.

"Learn the names of the things you favor, first," Meicha said.  "There is all the time you like, to learn the names of those things you care for less."

Finally, they each come to enough, and Miandra poured them all refills of grape juice, and settled back in her chair.

"So," Jethri said, trying to keep an eye pinned on each. "Ren Lar is unkind?"

"Never think so!"  That was Meicha.  "Ren Lar is capable of great kindness."

"The most of which," Miandra continued, "is reserved for his vines and his vintages, and then a bit for his heir."

"Aunt Stafeli figures there, too, I think.  But, yes, Ren Lar principally cares for the vines, which is to the good of the House, for wine is our wealth. Whereupon hangs our tragic tale."

"It was," Miandra said, sipping her juice, "our own fault."

"We didn't know our own strength," Meicha returned, which might have been excuse or explanation.

"Still, we knew that *some*thing might happen, and our choice of target was…"

"Infelicitous."

"Extremely."

Jethri considered them over the rim of his glass. "Are you going to tell me what happened," he asked, like he was their senior, which he had an uneasy feeling he wasn't, no matter how the Standards fell. "Or talk to yourselves all shift?"

They laughed.

"He wants a round tale, and no foolishness!" Meicha crowed.  "You tell it for us, sister."

"Well." Miandra moved her shoulders and sat up, putting her glass on the table.

"Understand, this happened at the start of last year—planetary year, that would be, not Standard."

Jethri inclined his head to show that he did indeed understand.

"So. It was a few weeks later in the season than it is now, and we—with the entire rest of the household who could wield shears—were in the vineyard, pruning the vines."

"Which is tedious, at best," Meicha put in, "and horrid, at worst."

Her sister turned to look at her, eyebrows well up.

"I thought this was mine to tell?"

The other girl blinked, then inclined her head. "Forgive me. Indeed, it is yours to tell."

Miandra inclined her head in turn, and took up her tale.

"As Meicha says, pruning is no task to love—unless one is Ren Lar, who loves everything to do with the vines. Alas, neither of us is Ren Lar, and while we may respect the vines, I believe it is fair to say that Flinx holds a higher place in our personal affections."

"*Far* higher," Meicha declared, irrepressible.

Miandra sipped juice, pointedly ignoring her, and put the cup down.

"We had been some days at the pruning, and some hours on this particular day, having risen early to the work, and it came to me—I cannot quite say how it should have done—that I loathed pruning the vines and that it would be much more convenient, and far less tedious, if I could simply will the work done." She sat up straight and looked Jethri right in the eye.

"I felt a certain, let us say, heat rise in my blood, my fingers, my toes, and my head fair tingled. My shears dropped to the ground, and I stood, quivering. Meicha asked me what I was about, but I was unable to do anything, but reach out and grasp her hand, and direct my thought at the rows of vines that Ren Lar had said we should prune that day."

It was a good place to pause for dramatic affect—and pause she did, much to Jethri's admiration. It was an interesting story, if different than Khat's usual, and he was enjoying himself. Two more heartbeats, and he realized that he was behind hand in his duty.

"What happened?" he asked.

Miandra inclined her head. "Nothing. Or so we thought then. Wearily, and now both afflicted with the headache, we picked up our shears and set back in to work." She paused, briefly.

"Three days later, we found that we had been wrong—we *had* wrought something, after all. Every one of the vines we had tended that day had died, and Ren Lar was as angry as I have ever seen him. Aunt Stafeli banned us from the vines until a Healer could be summoned to test us. Ren Lar..." She faltered.

After a moment, Meicha said, softly. "It is true that in the old days, when such things were possible, might well have mated with the mother vine. He mourned the fallen as if they were his own children." She shivered slightly. "Indeed, he mourns them still."

"And we," Miandra said, calm again, "are now in training to be Healers." She lifted the chain up from around her neck, so the ruby spun in the sunlight. "As you may see."

*Not too bad*, thought Jethri appreciatively, and inclined his head.

"I am instructed by your tale," he said, seriously. "But, as I have no such unusual talent, I think that the vines will be safe with me."

Meicha grinned. "The vines will be safe with you, friend Jethri. For be sure that Ren Lar will not allow you to leave his sight while you are in his vineyard."

"He knew your name?" Grig sounded worried, and Seeli sighed, mentally giving herself a quick kick for having mentioned the headcase at all.

"Not exactly a secret, is it?" she asked. "My name's on the clearances and the licenses, all on public file—'s'what Admin does, ain't it?"

"Still, him stopping you in the street and wanting to talk fractins…"

"Headcase," she said firmly. "Took the idea the *Market* was shipping fractins, and set out to do something about it. Said he was going to call on our trader. Luck to him, is what I hope, 'specially if he's hopin' to buy fractins from Paitor."

"No problem Paitor selling him fractins, if fractins is what he'll have," Grig said, taking a sip of his brew. "Simple broker deal. Must be three, four warehouses of 'em on port here."

"That's why he's a headcase," Seeli pointed out, glad that his thought was tending that way. Grig was a good man— none better—but he did like his theories and conspiracies. "He wants game pieces, port's prolly full of them, and no need to suppose that *Market's* carryin' the motherlode."

Grig looked at her, not saying anything.

"*What?*" she snapped, exasperated.

He moved his eyes. "Nothing. Likely nothing. Just—take a cab, Seeli, willya? Man being a headcase don't excuse him from being quick to grab."

Seeli smiled, and had a slow sip of brew. "Think I can't hold my own against some spacer, Grig Tomas?"

He smiled back, eyes warming in that way she especially liked. "Want to prove otherwise?"

# Day 145
# Standard Year 1118

## Kinaveral

THEY WERE HAVING themselves a quiet meal—Grig and Khat and Seeli—talking over the events of the day, of which there hadn't been that many, and figuring out the share-work for the next while.

"Port's got me scheduled for a long-fly, week after next," Khat said, putting her finger down on the grid they had on the table between them. "Liaden edge, near enough. Top rate. Bonus, too. Be good for the bank and I'd like to go, just for the jig of it. Getting tired of station shuttles and ferry-jobs."

Seeli craned her head to read the grid upside down. "Five days out?"

"If you need me down here, I'll tell 'em to find somebody else. No problem, Seeli."

"I don't see any reason to do that. Got the monthly comin' up, but Grig was wantin' to do the walk-through. Got that all straight with the yard-boss, so he can't squawk crew-change and lock us out."

"Man's a couple decimals short of an orbit," Khat muttered.

"Yard's top-rated, though," Grig said. "Which is enough to keep a body awake at night."

Seeli slanted him a look. "Is that what's keepin' you awake at night?"

He gave her the Full Dignified, nose tipped up, and slightly wrinkled, mouth rumpled like he'd tasted something slightly bad. "That, and certain importunate young persons."

She slapped her hand flat on the table. "*Importunate*, is it? I'll importunate you, Grig Tom—"

"Ho, the ship!" came the hail from the outer room.

"Paitor!" Khat yelled. "In the galley! Grab a brew and tell us the news!"

In he came, looking dusty and tired, gave a general nod of hi-there, threw his jacket over the back of an unclaimed chair and made a line for the cold-box.

"Handwich makin's there, too, Paitor, if you're peckish," Grig said, quiet and serious of a sudden.

"Brew's fine," the other man said, coming back to the table with one in his hand. He dropped into the chair, broke the seal on the bottle and had a long drink.

"That's good," he sighed, leaning back, eyes slitted, though if it was in pleasure or plain exhaustion Khat couldn't have said.

"What's the news, Uncle?" Seeli asked, quiet, like Grig had been. Feeling out trouble, Khat thought, considering the slump of Paitor's shoulders.

He sighed, and straightened, and got his eyes opened.

"Funny thing," he said, and it was Grig he was looking at. "You might find it so. Fella come by Terratrade today, asking for me by name. They sent him on up. Turns out he was in the market for fractins."

"The headcase," Seeli said, understanding, and reached for her brew. "I hope you sold him a warehouse full, and at a favorable price, too. Ship's General could use the cash."

He flicked a glance at her, then back to Grig. "I'd've done that, but it was special fractins he was after."

Grig shrugged, expressionless, and Khat felt something with lots of cold feet run down her spine.

"Seems what this fella was after, was Arin's fractins. Said he was willing to offer a handsome sum—he named it, and it was. Told him I couldn't oblige, that Arin's son had everything Arin had cared to leave behind, and the boy was 'prenticed to another ship."

There was a small pause, growing longer, as Paitor waited for Grig to say something.

Eventually, the lanky crewman shrugged again. "Should've been an end to it, then."

"Should've," Paitor agreed. "Wasn't. 'stead what he wants to know is if we got any other Befores on trade. Especially, he's interested in light-wands and duplicating units."

Grig laughed, sharp and ugly. "Man's a fool."

"Headcase," Seeli said again. "Told you."

"Close enough," Grig agreed, and reached for his brew.

"I'm asking," Paitor said, his hands folded 'round his own bottle and the knuckles showing, Khat saw, a shade or two pale.

Grig looked up and put the brew down. "Ask it, then."

"Was Arin dealing Old Tech?" The words came out kinda gritty and tight.

Grig lifted an eyebrow. "Dirt makin' you squeamish? Never took cash for a fractin, I guess."

Paitor took a hard breath, lifted his brew and had another long drink, thumping the bottle back to the table, empty. Khat got up and went to the cold-box, pulled four new bottles and brought them back to the table. She broke the seal on one and put it in front of Paitor, took another for herself and sat down. Across the table, Seeli was sitting tall, looking a frown between Paitor and Grig.

"Sure, I sold 'em—a piece of this, a part of that," Paitor said at last, his eyes pegged to Grig's. "Maybe a frame an' some fractins. Who knows what they were, or what they did?"

"I thought you wasn't a believer."

Paitor grinned, no humor in it at all.

"Don't need to be a believer when I got one across the table, asking for whole, working gadgets *by name*."

"Point." Grig lifted his brew and finished it off, put the bottle back soft on the table. "So you asked—yeah, Arin traded the underside in Old Tech. Far as I know, he was mostly buying—bought some few things, myself, now and then, like that

weather maker Jeth adopted. Most of the stuff, it went—
someplace else. And before you ask—no, I don't know where
it is or how it went. Arin's business, first and finish. He didn't
tell me everything." He reached to the middle of the table and
snagged another brew; glanced back to Paitor's face. "You
know how Arin was."

"This guy was buying," Paitor said, but Khat could see
that he was finding Grig's story believable and in some part
comforting.

Grig shrugged. "Man's running with old info," he suggested, breaking the seal on his brew. "Headcase, too." He
flicked a quick smile at Seeli, who didn't let go of her frown.
"You want me to talk to him?"

A pause, then a headshake. "No need. I told him we
didn't have no fractins; told him we're fresh outta Old Tech.
On planet for a refit, I told him. Got nothing worth trading at
all." He lifted his bottle, but didn't quite drink. "Seemed
satisfied with that. Though he left me a beam-code." Paitor's
lips thinned. "In case I should come across something."

"Which won't happen, 'cause we ain't looking," Seeli said,
firmly, reaching for the last bottle and breaking the seal with a
vengeance. "We're well out of it." She favored Grig with a
glare, and he dipped his head, agreeable-like.

"Sure, Seeli."

# Day 155
# Standard Year 1118

## Irikwae

"GOOD-DAY, JETHRI." Ren Lar looked up from his lab table, meter held delicately in one hand, blue eyes soft as ever. Somehow, he managed to look cool and elegant, though his apron was liberally painted with stains, and his sleeves rolled to his elbows.

Jethri, his own sleeves rolled up in anticipation of another long shift spent readying barrels to receive their next batch of wine, inclined his head, which he had found was considered respectful enough, in this circumstance.

"Good day, sir. I hope I'm not late." He wasn't, just, which was no fault of the tailor who had been summoned to produce what Lady Maarilex was pleased to call "appropriate" clothes for himself. Not satisfied with the first set of readings, the tailor—one Sun Eli pen'Jerad—had measured him again—and yet again, muttering over his readings, and at last jerked his chin at Jethri, giving him leave to cover himself decently.

"I will bring samples, in six days," Mr. pen'Jerad said, gathering up his measuring devices and his notes. "Tarnia informs me that you are a trader-under-study, eh? What you wear now tells the world that you are a cargohand-for-hire. We will amend this." He patted his pockets, making sure of his notes and bowed farewell. "Six days."

Six days or never—it made no nevermind to Jethri, who cut out the door as soon as he was dressed and ran down the back halls to the winery, prudently pausing on the outside of the door until his breathing had returned to something like normal before entering and presenting himself to Ren Lar.

That gentleman looked dreamily amused. "My mother had warned me that you were with the tailor this morning. The pen'Jerad is a marvel with his needle. Would that he were as sure with his measure-tapes." A device on the table chimed, and he glanced down with a slight frown, and then back to Jethri.

"In any case, I had not hoped to see you so soon. Now that you are here, however..."

Jethri sighed to himself, knowing what he was going to hear.

"Ah." His face must've let something slip, 'cause Ren Lar smiled his slight, dreamy smile. "The barrels grow tedious, do they? Then you will rejoice to hear that the end of the racking approaches. The last of the blends will be assembled by the end of the twelve-day. Soon, we shall take to the vineyard and the pruning."

He said it like pruning was a high treat. On the other hand, he had shown Jethri the barrels, and explained the necessity of having them scrubbed spotless as if it were the most important job in the winery, which, Jethri thought now, having had some days to consider the matter, it might well be. Bacteria would grow in dirty barrels, and bacteria could spoil a whole batch of wine, so clean barrels was important, right enough.

'Course, cleaning a barrel wasn't anything so simple as shoving it into an ultraviolet box, because the UV broke down the wood too fast. No, cleaning a wine barrel involved gallons of hot water, scrub brushes, sodium carbonate and of all of things a length of plain chain. After the barrel was scrubbed down on the outside, and the inside filled with water, sodium carbonate and chain, then it was sealed up tight and rolled over to the agitator, locked in and shook up but good, while the faithful barrel-scrubber rolled another dirty over to his work space and started the process over again.

It was tiresome and tiring work, make no mistake. Empty barrels were heavy; full barrels heavier. Jethri figured he was earning gravity muscles, but that hardly made up for the ache in his arms and his shoulders and his back.

Halfway into his first shift, he'd come up with the conviction that chemical disinfection would be the surer—and easier—way to go, but he hadn't made the mistake of saying that to Ren Lar. After a session with the house library, he was glad he'd kept his mouth shut on the point, for it transpired that disinfectants turned the taste of the wine, which meant "spoiled" just as sure as if the bacteria'd got in.

"There are only a few barrels today," Ren Lar was saying. "When you have done with them, make yourself available to Graem, in the aging cellar. She will be able to put another pair of hands to good use."

"Yes, sir." Jethri inclined his head again, and went to see how many barrels was only a few.

# Day 158
# Standard Year 1118

## Irikwae

"TELL US ABOUT living on your ship," Miandra said, shuffling the cards with bewildering speed between nimble fingers.

Jethri blinked, and shifted in his chair, trying for a position that would ease his back. The three of them were alone in a little parlor situated closer to the kitchen than the front door. In theory, the twins were teaching him to play *piket*, which unlikely pastime had the full approval of Lady Maarilex.

"Indeed, a gentleman should know his cards and be able to play a polite game." She fixed the twins in her eye, one after the other. "Mark me, token wagers only. And all may practice the art of graceful loss."

"Yes, Aunt Stafeli," said Meicha.

"Yes, Aunt Stafeli," said Miandra.

"Yes, ma'am," said Jethri, though he'd been taught not to show temper for losing by kin years his elder in the subtle art of poker.

"What do you want to know?" he said.

"Everything," said Meicha, comprehensively, while Miandra continued to shuffle, with a thoughtful look directed downward at the dancing cards.

"I would like to know how the kin groups sustain themselves," she said slowly.

"Sustain themselves? Well, there's ship life support, for air, temp and—"

Meicha laughed. Miandra didn't, though she did stop shuffling and raise her face to frown up at him.

"That was not at all funny," she said sternly.

"I—" he began, meaning to say he was sorry, though he didn't know, quite, what he should be sorry for, except that she was mad at him. His brain refused to pitch up the proper phrase, though, and after a moment's floundering he produced, "I am sad that you are angry with me."

"She's not so angry that you must be sad for it," Meicha said, matter-of-factly. "Only answer her question sensibly and she will be appeased."

"But you see, I don't understand why my previous answer was...annoying. We *do* sustain ourselves via ship's life support. If something else was meant by the question, then I don't know how to unravel it."

There was a small silence, then Meicha spoke again.

"He *is* a stranger to our tongue, sister. Recall Aunt Stafeli? We are only to speak to him in Liaden, and in proper mode and melant'i, to aid and speed his learning."

Miandra sighed and put the cards face down on the table. "Well enough. Then he must learn idiom." She raised her hand and pointed a finger at Jethri's nose, sharply enough that he pulled back.

"An inquiry into how the kin group sustains itself is an inquiry into genetics," she said, still tending toward the stern. "What I wish to know is how your kin group maintains its genetic health."

Maintains its... Oh. Jethri cleared his throat, thinking that his Liaden, improved as it was by constant use, might not be up to this. Good enough for Lady Maarilex to set rules on the twins for the betterment of his understanding, but nobody had drawn any lines for him about what was and wasn't considered proper topics of conversations between himself and two of the House's precious youngers.

"Is he shy?" Meicha inquired of her sister.

"Hush! Let him order his thoughts."

Right. Well, nothing for it but to tell the thing straight out and hope they took it for the strange custom of folk not their own—which, come to think, it would be.

"There are...arrangements between ships," he said slowly. "Sometimes, those. My older brother, Cris, came from an arrangement with *Perry's Promenade*. Seeli—my sister—she came out of a—a *shivary*, we call it. That's like a big party, when a lot of ships get together and there's dancing and—and—" He couldn't put his tongue to a phrase that meant the polite of "sleeping around," but it turned out he didn't have to—Miandra knew exactly what he was on course for.

"Ah. Then your sister Seeli is as we are—Festival get and children of the House entire." She smiled, as if the translation comforted her, and looked over to Meicha. "See you, sister? It is not so different from the usual way of things. One child of contract and one from Festival—the genes mix nicely, I think."

"It would seem so," her sister agreed, unusually serious. "And you, Jethri? Were you contracted—or joyous accident?"

Well, *there* was the question that had formed his life, now, wasn't it? He shrugged and looked down at the table—real wood, and smooth under his palm, showing stains here and there, and the marks of glasses, set down wet.

"Unhappy accident, call it," he said to the table. "My parents were married, but my mother wasn't looking for any more children. Which is how I happened to be the extra, and available to 'prentice with Master ven'Deelin."

"The third child is produced from a lifemating," Miandra summed up. "It is well. And your cousins?"

He looked up. "My cousins? Well, see, the Gobelyn's are a wide family. We've got cousins on—I don't know how many ships. A couple dozen, I'd say, some small, none bigger than the *Market*, though. We're the mainline. Anyhow, we share around between us to keep the ships full. The extras—they take berths on other ships, and eventually they're..." He frowned after the word. "...assimilated."

"So." Miandra smiled and put her hand over his. "We are not so brutal of our 'extras', but perhaps we have the luxury of room. Certainly, there are those who go off on the far-trade and return home once every dozen Standards—if so often. Your foster mother is one such, to hear Aunt Stafeli tell the tale. But, in all, it seems as if your customs match ours closely, and are not so strange at all." This was accompanied by a hard stare at Meicha, who moved her shoulders, to Jethri's eye, discomfited.

"But," he asked her, "what did you think?"

"Oh, she had some notion that the Terran ships used the Old Technology to keep their crews ever young," Miandra said. "Aunt Stafeli says she reads too many adventure stories."

"You read them, too!" Meicha cried, visibly stung.

"Well, but I'm not such a dolt as to *believe* them!"

Meicha pouted. "Terrans trade in Old Tech—Tutor Vandale said so."

"Yes, but the Old Tech mostly doesn't work," Jethri pointed out. "The curiosity trade gets it, and sometimes the scholars."

"Vandale said that, too," Miandra said.

"And Pan Dir said that there is still some Old Tech in the out beyond that *does work!*" her twin snapped, with a fair sitting-down approximation of stamping her foot.

"If you want to know what I think," Jethri said, feeling like he'd better do his possible to finish the subject before the matter came to blows. "I think that Pan Dir likes to tell stories. My cousin Khat's exactly the same way."

There was a pause as Meicha and Miandra traded glances.

"There's that," Meicha said at last, and, "True," agreed Miandra.

Jethri sighed and reached for the cards, sitting forgotten by her hand.

"I thought you two were going to win my fortune from me."

*That* made them both laugh, and Meicha snatched the deck from him and began to shuffle with a will.

"I hear a challenge, sister!"

"As I do! Deal the cards!"

# Day 161
# Standard Year 1118

## Irikwae

"OOF!"

The weight hit him right dead center, and Jethri jackknifed from sound asleep to sitting up, staring blearily down into a pair of pale green eyes.

"You!" He gasped. Flinx blinked his eyes in acknowledgment.

"Might let a man get his rest," Jethri complained, easing back down to the pillows. Flinx stayed where he was, two ton paws bearing Jethri's stomach right down onto his spine.

He yawned and turned his head to look at the clock. Not enough time to go back to sleep, even if the adrenaline would let him. Stupid cat had jumped on his stomach yesterday morning, at just this hour. And the morning before that. He was starting to wonder if the animal could tell time.

Down-body, Flinx began to purr, and shift his weight from one considerable front foot to the other—and repeat. He did *that* every morning, too. The twins swore that the purring and the foot-shifting—kneading, they called it— were signs of goodwill. Jethri just wondered why, if the cat liked him so much, he didn't let him sleep.

He sighed. The house crew tended to take Master ven'Deelin's view that he was fortunate to have fallen under Flinx' attention. What the cat got out of it, Jethri couldn't say, unless it was making notes for a paper on xenobiology.

Flinx had upped the volume on the purrs, and was pushing a little harder with his feet; the tips of his claws pierced skin and Jethri was off the pillows again with a yell.

"Hey!"

Startled, the cat kicked with his back feet, twisted and was gone, hitting the floor with a solid thump.

"Mud!" He flung to the edge of the bed, and peered over, half afraid he'd find the animal with a broken leg or—

Flinx was standing on four sturdy legs at the edge of the rug, his back to the bed. He looked over his shoulder—accusingly, to Jethri's eye.

"I'm sorry," he said, settling his head onto his crooked arm and letting the other arm dangle over the edge of the bed. "I don't like to be scratched, though."

There was a pause, as if Flinx was considering the merit of his apology. Then, he turned and ambled back to the bed, extending his head to stroke a whiskery cheek along Jethri's dangling fingers.

"Thanks." Carefully, he slipped his fingers under the cat's chin and moved them in the skritching pattern Meicha had shown him. Flinx immediately began to purr, loud and deep.

Jethri smiled and skritched some more. Flinx moved his head, obviously directing the finger action to his right cheek, and then to the top of his head, all the while purring.

*Well*, Jethri thought drowsily, fingers moving at a far distance, *what a relaxing sound.*

Across the room, the alarm chimed.

Flinx skittered out from under his hand a heartbeat before he snapped upright out of his doze.

Sighing, he rubbed his hand over his head, frowning at the lengthening strands, and swung out of bed.

Shower, breakfast, tailor—that was the first part of his day. Then an afternoon with Ren Lar. Pruning vines, it was today. After that, he was to join the twins with their dancing instructor, Lady Maarilex being of the opinion that a gentleman should show well on the floor, and then supper.

Supper done, he could retire to the library with the list of books the twins' tutor had produced for him—history books, mostly, and a bunch of marked-out sections of a three-volume set titled, *The Code of Proper Conduct.*

"Busy day," he said to the empty room, and headed for the shower.

COMPARE BANTH PORT to Kinaveral and Kinaveral came to look like the garden spot of the universe, Khat thought, throwing her duffle over one shoulder and heading across the wind-scoured tarmac. She had her goggles polarized, and her head down, much good it did. The constant hot wind was super-saturated with sand particles, stuff so fine it sifted through any join, clogged the nose, filled the mouth, and sank through the pores. Nose plugs helped some. So did keeping your mouth shut. Other than that, it was walk fast and hope the pilots' crash was climate controlled.

After a couple Standards of walking bent against the wind, she came to a service tunnel. Her body broke the sensor beam, the door irised open, and she ducked inside, barely ahead of the door closing.

Inside the tunnel, the light was dim and slightly pink. Khat pushed the goggles up onto her forehead, took a good, deep lungful of filtered air—and started to cough; deep, wracking spasms that left an acid taste in her mouth, overlaying the taste of the sand.

Eventually, she was coughed out and able to take some notice of her surroundings. A hatch closet built into the right wall of the tunnel said "drinking water" in Terran, which she could read fine, and, underneath, the written pidgin for the same—a stylized drawing of a jug—for them as couldn't read Terran.

The taste in her mouth wasn't getting much better. Khat stepped over and inserted her thumb into the latch. Inside the closet were a couple dozen sealed billy bottles carrying the same bilingual message. She snagged a bottle, slapped the door shut and popped the seal, taking a short, careful swallow, then another, and so on until the bottle was empty.

Feeling more or less human, she slid the billy into the wall recycler, and looked about her.

There were arrows painted in flourescent green on the floor, and the words, "Banth Port Admin," the Admin part repeated in pidgin, which was apparently her direction, whether she was going there or not. Though, as it happened, she was Admin bound.

She pulled the goggles off her forehead and snapped them onto her belt, taking another deliberately deep breath of filtered air. No coughing this time, which she took as a smile from the gods, even as she shook her head. She had some sympathy for the 'hands who would eventually be unloading her cargo, and shuddered with the memory of the constant dust storm, heat and battering white light of the world outside.

*Granted, most Grounders're glitched in the think-box*, she thought, setting her feet on the green arrow and walking on, *but a body'd think even a Grounder would know better than Banth.*

Khat sighed. Well, now she knew why Kinaveral Admin had put such a nice bonus on this job—and now she knew better than to take another flight to Banth.

"Live 'n learn," she said, and her voice sounded as gritty as her face felt, despite the water. "You live long enough, Khatelane, an' someday you might turn up smart."

"THERE! NOW WE see a son of a High House in his proper estate!" Sun Eli pen'Jerad was pleased with himself and his handiwork, and Jethri supposed he had a right. Himself, he'd thought the trading coat and silk shirts provided by *Elthoria* plenty fancy enough and hadn't aspired to anything in the way of collar ruffles so high they tickled the tips of his ears, or belled sleeves that reached all the way to his fingertips. Then there were the trousers—tighter than his own skin and not near as comfortable—and over them both a long, and pocketless, black vest.

"Very good," Lady Maarilex said, from her chair, Flinx asleep on her lap. "Do you not think so, young Jethri?"

He sighed. "Ma'am, I think the work is fine, but the sleeves are too long and the trousers too tight."

Mr. pen'Jerad made an outraged noise. Lady Maarilex raised a hand.

"These things you mention are the current fashion, and not open to negotiation. We all bow to fashion and rush to do her bidding. How else should we show ourselves to be a people of worth?"

Jethri looked at her. "Is that a joke, ma'am?"

"Hah. Progress. Some bits, yes. Discover which bits and we shall have progress, indeed. In the meanwhile, we are pleased with Master pen'Jerad's efforts on behalf of evening clothes. Of your kindness, young Jethri, model for me the calling clothes."

Calling clothes weren't quite so confining, though they still showed a serious deficiency in the pocket department. The trousers were looser, the cream colored jacket roomy, the shirt dark blue, with an open collar and no ruffles anywhere. They were close enough to trading clothes to be manageable, and Jethri stepped out into the main room and made his bow to the seated matriarch.

"These please you, eh? And well they should. The jacket hangs well, despite what would seem to be too much breadth of shoulder. Well done, Sun Eli."

The tailor bowed. "That you find my work adequate is all that I desire," he murmured. "However, I must object— the shoulders are not too wide, but balance the rest of the form admirably. It is a balanced shape, and pleasing, taken on its own. It is when we measure it against the accepted standard of beauty that we must find the shoulders too wide, the legs too long, the chest too deep."

"Do you say so?" She raised a hand and motioned Jethri to turn, slowly, which he did, liking the feel of the silk against his skin and the way the jacket hugged his shoulders, too wide or not.

"No, I believe you are correct, Sun Eli. Taken in the context of himself alone, there is a certain pleasant symmetry." Jethri's turn brought him 'round to face her again and he stopped, hands deliberately loose at his sides.

"So tell me, young Jethri, shall you be a beauty?"

And that *had* to be a joke, given the general Gobelyn face and form. He bowed, very slightly.

"I expect that I will look much as my father did, ma'am, and I never did hear that he was above plain."

Surprisingly, she inclined her head. "Well said, and honest, too." She looked into his eyes and smiled, very slightly. "We must teach you better. However, there are still the day clothes to inspect, if you would do me the honor?"

THE TUNNEL WIDENED, and widened some more, and by the third widening it was a large round room, crowded with desks and chairs and people and equipment—and that was Banth Admin.

Khat stopped her steady forward slog and blinked, something bemused by all the activity, and scouted the room by eye, looking for her contact point.

The desks were on platforms a little higher than floor level, and each one had a sign on the front of it, spelling out its official station name in Terran and pidgin. Some of the signs weren't so easy to spot, on account of the people wandering around, apparently in search of *their* contact points. Lot of long-spacers in the mix, which she'd expected. Good number of Liadens, too, which surprised her. This close to the Edge, there was bound to be a couple working, looking for advantage, but to see so many…

"Edge is widenin' out again," Khat muttered. "Pretty soon, won't be nothing to edge."

She considered the crowd, rising up on her toes to count the Liadens, and filing that number away for Paitor's interest, on the far side of the trip. Might she'd head down to the Trade Bar, after a shower and a change, and scope out the ship names.

Right now, though, she was after Intake Station. Sooner she had her papers stamped and her cargo in line for off-load, the sooner she could hit the pilots' crash and have that shower.

After a time, it occurred to her that the only thing cran-ing around the crowd was getting her was a cricked neck, and she settled the duffle and charted a course into the deeps of the room.

Up and down the rows she cruised, careful not to bump into anybody, Liaden or Terran, being not wishful of starting either a fistfight or a Balance. Admin crew was solidly Terran, sitting their stations calm enough, for all each one was busy.

Intake was on the third row, which made sense, Khat thought sarcastically. There were only two in line ahead of her—yellow-haired Liaden traders, looking enough alike to be mother and son. The boy was apparently determined on giv-ing the clerk a difficult life experience. As Khat came to rest behind them, he was leaning over the desk, waving a sheaf of papers too close to the woman's face and talking, loud and non-stop, in Liaden, which was just stupid. Anybody who came to the Edge to trade ought to at least speak the pidgin.

*And if the pidgin's too nasty for your mouth*, Khat thought at the boy's expensively jacketed back, *you'd have done better to stay home and tend your knitting*.

In the meantime, his voice had risen and he was leaning closer over the desk, the wild-waving sheaf of papers now an active danger. Khat took a step forward, meaning to haul him back to a respectful distance, but the clerk had her own ideas.

"Security!" She yelled, and simultaneously hit a yellow button embedded in the plastic desktop.

The boy paused in his harangue, like he was puzzled by her reaction, the papers wilting in his hand.

"Peliche," Khat said helpfully, that being the pidgin for 'cop.'

He sent her an active glare over his shoulder, in the space of which time his mother stepped forward, hands moving in a pretty rippling motion, apparently meant to be soothing.

"Your pardon," she said to the clerk in heavily accented, but perfectly understandable pidgin. "We have cargo to be off-loaded. There is urgency. We must proceed with quickness."

The clerk's mouth thinned, but she answered civil enough. "I will need to see the manifests. As I said to this trader," a nod of the head indicated the boy, "since the manifests are written in Liaden, the cargo must be inventoried before it is off-loaded. Admin provides inventory-takers. There is a fee for this service."

The Liaden woman inclined her head. "What is the price of this fee?"

"Fifteen Combines the quarter-clock," the clerk said.

*Now, that's steep*, thought Khat, touching the zip-pocket where her own manifest rode, snug, safe, and printed out in plain, good Terran. *No wonder the boy's in a snit.*

His mam, though, she just bowed her head again and said, cool as if it weren't no money at all, "That is acceptable. Please produce these inventory-takers at once."

*That cargo better be guaranteed profit*, thought Khat, darkly.

The clerk reached for her keypad, and then looked up, annoyed for all to see, as a big guy in standard blues came striding toward her station.

"You call Security?" he demanded, hand on his stun-gun.

The clerk shrugged, eyes on her schedule screen. "Took your time."

His face, broad in all directions and unshaven on the south side, reddened. "I'm coverin' the whole floor by myself."

She glanced up at him, then back to the screen. The two Liadens were frankly staring.

"Sorry to bother you," the clerk said, in clear dismissal.

The cop stood for a couple heartbeats, giving a fair impression of a man who'd welcome a chance to put his fist authoritatively against somebody else's chin. He glared at the Liadens, daring them to start something. The woman touched the boy's arm and the two of them turned back to the clerk, the boy rolling his sheaf of papers into a tube, which Khat thought might have been nerves.

Finally, the cop turned and strode off into the crowd. The clerk slid a piece of paper out of her printer and handed it to the Liaden woman.

"The inspectors will be waiting for you at the security station in Access Tunnel Three. Give them this paper and follow their instructions. The red arrows are your guide to Access Tunnel Three."

"Yes," the woman said, folding the paper into her sleeve. She turned, her boy with her, and Khat was briefly caught in the cold stare of two pair of blue eyes, before they separated to walk around her—boy to the right, mam to the left.

Khat let go a breath she hadn't known she'd been holding and stepped up to the desk, pulling her papers out of the zip-pocket.

"Disaster shift?" she asked the clerk, crew-to-crew.

The clerk took the manifest. "Be nice if it was that calm," she said, unfolding the papers. "Let's take a look at what you got here…"

ESCAPED AT LAST into his own clothes from *Elthoria*, he slipped into the kitchen and wheedled an off-hours lunch from Mrs. tor'Beli, the cook.

"For the vines today, are you?" She asked, handing him a plate so full of eatables that he had to hold it in both hands for fear of losing some of the contents.

"Yes ma'am," he said politely, guiding his plate over to the table and setting it down.

"Be sure you have a hat and a pair of heavy gloves out of the locker before you go out," she said, placing a glass of grape juice on the table next to his plate. "Summer is still before us, but the sun is high enough to burn, and the vines not as weak as they might appear."

"Yes, ma'am," he said again. She returned to the counter where she was enthusiastically reducing a square of dough into a long, flat sheet, with the help of a wooden roller. Jethri nibbled from his plate as he looked around the kitchen, with its multiple prep tables, and its profusion of pots, pans and exotic gadgets. *Dyk would love this*, he thought, and gulped as tears rose up in his eyes.

*C'mon, kid, what's up?* he said to himself sharply. *You crying over Dyk?*

Well, in point of fact, he thought, surreptitiously using his napkin to blot his eyes, he *was* crying over Dyk—or at least crying over the fact that Dyk would never see this place, that would have given him so much pleasure…

"You had best hurry, young ven'Deelin," the cook called over her shoulder. "Ren Lar Maarilex puts the vines before his *own* lunch, much less yours."

He grinned, and sniffled, and put serious attention on his plate, which was very soon empty, and drained his glass. Pushing back from the table, he looked around for the dishwasher…

"Leave them," Mrs. tor'Beli said, "and betake yourself to the wine room—at a run, if you are wise."

"Yes, ma'am," he said for a third time, pushing in the chair. "Thank you, ma'am."

"Hurry!" she responded, and to please her he left at a pace, stretching his legs.

Outside of the kitchen, he kept moving, taking a right into the hall the twins had shown him, and arrived handily at the door to the wine room. It opened to his palm, and he clattered down the stairs, through the vestibule and tapped the code into the keypad set in the wall next to the ancient wooden door.

The lock *snicked*, and he worked the old metal latch. The door was slow on its metal hinges, and he put some shoulder into hurrying it along, stepping into the wine room proper only a little out of breath and scarcely mussed at all.

Ren Lar was not at his accustomed place at the lab table. Instead, there was Graem, busy with the drops and the calibrator. She glanced up as he entered, and frowned.

"The master's gone to the vineyard; he said that you're to find him on the north side."

*Late*, Jethri thought, and sighed, before remembering to incline his head. "Thank you, I will. Before I go, can you tell me where I might draw a hat and a pair of gloves?"

She jerked her head to the left, her attention already back with her calibrations. "Locker over there. Take shears, too."

"Thank you," he said again and moved to the locker indicated.

A few minutes later, wide brimmed hat jammed onto his head, too-small leather gloves on his hands as best he could get them, and shears gripped firmly in his right hand, he left the wineroom by the side doors and entered the vineyard.

No one was waiting for him, in the yard, and there were no signs to tell him which way to go. He considered, briefly, returning to the cellar and asking Graem for directions, but—no, blast it. He was tired of depending on the directions and help-outs of the various members of the household, like he was a younger—and a particularly backward younger, at that.

There had to be a way to figure out which way to go. If he put his thought on it, he ought to be able to locate north. He remembered reading a story once, where someone lost on a planet discovered his direction by observing which way a stream ran—not that there were any streams in his sight.

"And not that it would work, anyway," he grumbled to himself. "Meicha isn't the only one who reads too many stories, I guess."

He shifted his shears from his right hand to his left, pushed his hat up off his forehead and frowned around him. You'd think there'd *be* signs, he thought. What if somebody got turned around and didn't have a navigation device?

*Navigation device.*

He slapped his pockets, found what he wanted in the right leg and pulled it out. The mirrored black face grayed, displaying swirls, like clouds, or kicked-up dust, then cleared, showing the old, almost-forgotten icons along the top and bottom of a quartered screen.

Jethri frowned down into it, trying to put sense to symbols he hadn't seen for ten Standards—and suddenly, he *did* remember, the memory seating itself so hard that the inside of his head fair vibrated with the snap.

The icons at the top—those were detail buttons; the ones at the bottom indicated direction, while the quartered screen was meant to be read left-right/down-up, with the first square representing planetary north.

He touched a direction icon, and touched the north square. The screen changed, and now he was looking at a vid of the yard he was standing in, with a blue line superimposed over the image, shooting off to the left.

Making sure of his grip on the shears, he moved left, one eye on the screen and one eye on the treacherous dirt underfoot.

The next thing he'd do, Jethri thought some while later, would be to puzzle out if the device had a *distance* indicator. He'd walked a goodly distance, by his reckoning, along a dirt path crossing long corridors of wire fencing, against which bare wooden sticks leaned, dead vines like tentacles sprouting from their heads. It was an eerie landscape, and the vines just tall enough that he couldn't see around them, and sufficiently complicated to the eye that there was no need to look up at the unfettered sky. He did look the length of each corridor as he crossed it, and saw not one living thing. The birds, which sang outside his window, and in Meicha and Miandra's favorite garden, were silent, here in the vineyard—or maybe they preferred other circumstances.

Jethri had worked up a fair sweat and was reassessing how good an idea striking out on his own actually was, when he finally heard voices up ahead. Relief fetched up a sigh from approximately the soles of his boots, and he slipped the device back into his pocket before moving forward, quicker now. He turned right—and braked.

Ren Lar, hat on head, gloves tucked into his belt and looking just as comfortable as if he were standing in the coolness of the wine cellar, was talking with two men Jethri didn't know.

"This section here, today. If you finish while there is still sun, then begin tomorrow's section. We race the weather now, friends."

"Yes, sir," one of the men murmured. The other moved a hand, and Ren Lar acknowledged him with a slight nod of the head.

"Shall I call in my cousins, sir? They're able and willing for a day or three, while the warehouse refits."

Ren Lar tipped his head. "How many cousins?"

"Four, master. They tend our house vines and understand the pruning. If I call tonight, they can be here at first sun."

A small pause, then a decisive wave of a hand. "Yes, bring them up, of your kindness. It is, after all, a wind year— bitter beyond bearing last relumma, and now it grows warm too early. I do not wish the sap to surprise us."

The man inclined his head. "I will call them."

"Good. Then I leave you to your labors." He looked up. "Young Jethri. I trust you left Master pen'Jerad well?"

"Your honored mother was present, sir," Jethri said carefully, "so there was no hope of anything else."

Ren Lar's eyebrows rose. One of the strangers laughed.

"A stride, in fact. Well said. Now, walk with me and we will find you a section in need of your shears."

He moved a hand, beckoning, and turned left. At his feet a shadow moved, flowed, and gained shape.

"Flinx," Jethri said. "What are you doing out here?"

Ren Lar glanced down, and moved his shoulders. "He often comes to help in the vineyard. For which assistance we are, of course, grateful. Come with me, now."

Down the row they went, turned right down a cross-path— which would be north again, Jethri thought with pride.

"You will be tending to the needs of some of our elders," Ren Lar said, moving briskly down the pathway. "I will show you how to go on before I take up my own duty. But have no fear! I will be but one section over, and easily accessible to you."

That might have been a joke, though on consideration, Jethri didn't think so. He very likely *would* need a senior nearby. The wonder of it was that Ran Lar was apparently not going to be in the same row with him and keeping a close eye on the precious "elders."

"Here we are," the man said, and dodged left down a corridor, Jethri on his heels and Flinx flowing along in the shadows beside them.

The vines here were thick-bodied; some leaned so heavily into their support that the wires were bowed outward.

"Now, what we will wish you to do," Ren Lar said, pausing by a particularly bent specimen, its head-tentacles ropy and numerous. "Is to cut the thick vines, like this, you see?" He pulled a branch forward, and Jethri nodded.

"Yes, sir. I see."

"That is good. I must tell you that there is a reason to take much care, for *these* " he carefully slipped his hand under a thin, smooth branchlet—"are what will give us this season's fruit, and next year's wine. So, a demonstration..."

He lifted his shears, positioned the blades on either side of the thick branch, and forced the handles together. The wood separated with a brittle snap, and before the severed twig had hit the ground, Ren Lar had snipped another, and a third, the shears darting and biting without hesitation.

The old wood tumbled down into an untidy pile at the base of the vine. Ren Lar stepped back, kicked a few stray sticks into the larger heap, and inclined his head.

"At first, you will not be so quick," he said. "It is not expected, and there is no need for haste. The elders are patient. The cuttings will be gathered and taken to burn, later." He moved a hand, indicating the next vine down.

"Now, let us see you."

Teeth indenting lower lip, Jethri looked over the problem, taking note of the location of the new growth inside the woody tangle. When he had those locations in his head, he carefully lifted his shears, positioned the blades and brought the handles together.

The wood resisted, briefly, then broke clean, the severed branch tumbling down to the ground. Jethri deliberately moved on to his next target, and his next.

Finally, there was only new wood to be seen, and he stepped back from the vine, being careful not to tangle his feet in the grounded branches, and pushed his hat back up from his face.

"A careful workman," Ren Lar said, and inclined his head. "The elders are in good hands. You will work your way down this row, doing precisely what you have done here. When you reach an end of it, you will go one row up—" he pointed north—"and bring your shears to bear. I will be six rows down—" another point, back toward the house and the wine cellar—"should you have need of me."

"Yes, sir," Jethri said, still feeling none too good about being left alone to do his possible with what were seemingly valuable plants.

Ren Lar smiled and put his hand on Jethri's shoulder. "No reason for such a long face! Flinx will doubtless stay by to supervise."

That said, he turned and walked off, leaving Jethri alone with the "revered elders," his shears hanging loose in his right hand. Ren Lar reached the top of the corridor and turned right, back down toward the house, just like he'd said, without even a backward glance over his shoulder.

Jethri sighed and looked down at the ground. Flinx the cat was sitting three steps away, smack in the center of the dirt corridor, casually cleaning his whiskers.

*Supervise. Sure.*

Well, there was nothing for it but to step up and do his best. Jethri approached the next plant in line, located the fragile new growth, and set to snipping away the old. Eventually, he moved on to the next vine, and a little while after that, to the next. It was oddly comforting work; soothing.

He didn't precisely *think*; it seemed like all his awareness was in his eyes and his arms, as he *snip, snip, snipped* the old wood, giving the new wood room to breathe.

It was the ache in his shoulders and his forearms that finally called him back to wider concerns. He lowered his shears and stepped away from his last vine. Standing in the middle of the dirt corridor, he looked back, and whistled appreciatively.

"Mud and stink," he said slowly, looking down the line of pruned vines, each with a snaggly pile of twigs at its base. He looked down at the base of his last victim, saw a twig 'way out in the corridor and swung his foot, meaning to kick it back into the general pile.

The twig—*moved*.

Jethri jerked back, overbalanced and fell, hard, on his ass, and the twig reared back, flame flicking from the rising end and a pattern of bronze and white scales on its underside, moving toward him and he was looking to see *how* it was moving, exactly, with neither feet nor legs, and suddenly there was Flinx the cat, with his feet on either side of the—the *snake*, it must be—and his muzzle dipped, teeth flashing.

The snake opened its mouth, displaying long white fangs, its twig-like body flailing in clear agony, and Flinx held on, teeth buried just behind the head.

"Hey!" Jethri yelled, but the cat never looked up, and he surely didn't let go.

"Hey!" he yelled again, and got his feet under him, surging upward. Flinx didn't flick an ear.

"Ren Lar!" He gave that yell everything he had and it worked, too. His panicked heart had only beat half-a-dozen times more before the master of the vine rounded the corner, running flat out.

But by the time, the snake was dead.

THE DOORMAN AT the pilots' crash scanned her Kinaveral Port willfly card, and gave her a key to a sleeping room with its own sonic cleaner, which device Khat made immediate, grateful use of. She then hit the hammock for two solid clocks, arising from her nap refreshed and ravenous. Pulling on clean slacks and shirt, she remembered her idea of checking the Trade Bar for the names and numbers of Liaden ships at dock, for Paitor's eventual interest, and thought she'd combine that interest with the pleasure of a brew and a handwich.

The doorman provided a map, which she studied as she walked.

It seemed that most of Banth, with the notable exceptions of the ship yards and the mines, was under roof and underground. Ground level, that was the Port proper. Down one level was living quarters, townie shops, grab-a-bites, and rec centers. Khat thought about that—living *under* the dirt—and decided, fair-mindedly, that it was a reasonable idea, given the state of the planet surface. Why somebody had taken the demented notion to colonize Banth at all remained a mystery that she finally shrugged away with a muttered, "Grounders."

The Port level, now, that was Admin, of course, and the pilots' crash, hostels for traders and crew, exhibit halls, Combine office, duty shops, eating places—and the Trade Bar.

Khat traced the tunnel route from her room to the bar, and checked the color of the floor arrows closely.

"Yellow arrow all the way," she said to herself, folding the map away into a pocket. Up ahead, her hall crossed another, and there was a tangle of color on the floor of the convergence. The yellow flowed to the right, and Khat did, too, lengthening her stride in response to her stomach's unsubtle urging.

Banth was close to Kinaveral-heavy, despite which Khat arrived at the Trade Bar barely winded.

*Look at you,* she thought smugly, swiping her card through the reader. There was a small hesitation, then the door swung open.

She'd expected a crowd, and she had one. Terrans outnumbered Liadens, Liadens outnumbered the expectable, just

like Admin, earlier. Noisy, like Trade Bars were always noisy—
no difference if they was small, which this one was, or large—
with everybody there trying to talk loud enough to be heard
over everybody else.

Khat waded in, heading for the bar itself, and found it
standing room only.

No problem. She got herself a place to stand, and swung
an arm over her head, catching the eye of a bartender with
spiked blue hair and a swirl of tattooed stars down one
cheek.

"What'll it be, Long Space?" she bellowed

"Handwich an' a brew!" Khat yelled back.

"It's processed protein," warned the barkeep.

Khat sighed. "What flavor?"

"Package says chicken."

At least it wasn't beef. "Do it," Khat yelled, and the other
woman gave her a thumbs-up and faded down-bar.

Khat fished a couple bills out of her public pocket, and
eased forward, careful not to step on any toes. The bartender
reappeared, and handed over a billy bottle of brew and a zip-
bag. Khat tucked them in the crook of her arm, and handed
over the bills in trade.

"Got change comin'," the woman said.

Khat waved a hand. "Keep it."

"You bet. Good flying, Long Space."

"Same," Khat said, which was only polite. The bartender
laughed, and turned away, already tracking another patron.

Provisions firmly in hand, Khat squinched out of the crowd
surrounding the bar, and looked around, hoping to find a ledge
to rest her brew on. The booths and tables were full, of
course, as was the available standing space—no, there was a
guy coming off of his stool, his recyclables held loose in one
hand. Khat moved, dancing between clusters of yelling, ges-
ticulating patrons, and hit the stool almost before he left it.

Cheered by this minor bit of good luck, she popped the
seal on the billy and had a long swallow of brew. *Warm, dammit.*

She had another swallow, then unzipped the food bag.

She'd expected to find her flavored protein between flat rectangles of ship cracker, and was pleasantly surprised to find it served up on two fine slices of fresh bake bread, which was almost enough to make up for the warm brew.

A bite confirmed that the protein was no better than usual, with the bread contributing interest and texture. Khat made short work of it, and settled back on the stool, nursing what was left of her brew.

Good manners was that she should pretty soon surrender the stool and the little table, so someone else could have their use. Still, she had a couple minutes left before she hit the line for rudeness, and she wanted to study the floor a little closer before she went back to being part of the problem.

The Liadens traveled in teams—no less than two, no more than four—and all of the teams she could see from her stool were in conversation with Terrans. That struck her as funny, being as Liadens were always so stand-offish. On the other hand, shy never made no trades.

It did make a body pause and consider what it was that Banth had, that Liadens wanted.

She chewed on that while she finished her brew. *The mines— what did they mine on this space-forsaken dustball?* She made a mental note to find out, and slid off the stool, on-course for a view of the ship-board.


"AND NO ONE thought to tell our guest, before he was left alone among the vines, that kylabra snakes are poisonous?" Lady Maarilex inquired gently. *Too gently,* Jethri thought, sitting stiff in the chair she had pointed him to, Flinx tall and interested beside his knee.

Her son was standing, and his face had regained its normal golden color. He hadn't known that it was possible for a Liaden to pale, but Ren Lar had definitely lost color in the instant that he took in the snake, and whirled back to Jethri, snapping, "Are you bit?"

"Mother," he said now, voice quiet and firm. "You know that the kylabra do not usually wake so early."

"And you know, *Master Vintner*, that the weather in this wind year has been unseasonably warm. Why should the snakes sleep on?"

"Why, indeed?" murmured her son, and despite his level shoulders and expressionless face, Jethri was in receipt of the distinct idea that Ren Lar would have welcomed the ability to sink into and through the floor.

He cleared his throat and shifted a little in his chair.

"If you please, ma'am," he said slowly and felt like he wanted to sink through the floor on his own account when she turned her face to him—and took a breath. *Dammit*, he thought; *you took whatever Cap'n Iza was serving, you can sure take this.* He cleared his throat again.

"The fact is," he said, keeping his voice settled and easy, just like Cris would do, when their mutual mother was needing some sense talked to her, "that I wasn't left unguarded. Ren Lar left Flinx with me, to supervise, he said. I thought it was a joke—I've been studying on what is and isn't a joke, ma'am, as you'll remember—but it comes about that he was serious. Snakes—I read about snakes, but I've never seen one. And Flinx was there to do what was needful."

"I see." She inclined her head, maybe a bit sarcastic— he thought so. "You would argue, then, that the House provided adequate care to one who is perhaps naive in some of the...less pleasant aspects of planet-bound life."

"Yes, ma'am, I do," he said stoutly, and thought to add, "All's well that ends well, ma'am."

"An interesting philosophy." She turned to face her son. "You have an eloquent champion in the one whose life you endangered. Pray do not rest upon your good fortune."

Ren Lar bowed. "Mother."

She sighed, and moved an impatient hand. "Attend me a moment longer, if the vines can spare you. Jethri, you have had adventures enough for a day. Go and make yourself seemly for the dancing master."

"Yes, ma'am." He rose, made his bow and headed for the door, Flinx prancing at his side, tail high and ears forward.

THE SHIP-BOARD WAS hung along the backmost wall, the Combine-net computers lined up just below.

The computers was all taken, of course, not that Khat had need of a beam or a quote. She did want a clear view of the 'board, though, and that took some fancy dancing around various clustered jaw-fests.

Finally, she got herself situated behind a rare group—half-a-dozen Liadens, talking low and intense 'mong themselves and not minding anything else. No problem seeing over *those* heads, and there was the ship-board, plain as you please, showing the names of five Terran ships, including her own—and four Liaden ships, their names a garble of Terran letters and pidgin hieroglyphic.

Khat frowned at the listings, trying to work out the names and having a little less luck than none. Four Liaden ships at Banthport was *some* news and no doubt Paitor'd be glad of it. Nameless, though, that wasn't much good, especially as there was a Combine key graphic next to two of the four indecipherables, and Paitor would *really* want to know those names, so he could run a match through Terratrade's main database.

Some Liaden traders held Combine keys—it was 'specially found 'mong those who worked the Edge. Banth being the Edge, it wasn't out of the question to find a Liaden-held key on-port. You might even stretch to two on a port the size of Banth, given the random nature of the universe. But *four* Liaden ships, two carrying keys?

Khat's coincidence bone was starting to ache.

She stared at the 'board, not really seeing it, trying to figure the odds of getting anything useful out of Admin and what plausible reason she might offer for her need-to-know. And how much it was likely to cost her.

"…long time!" an exuberant male voice bellowed into her off-ear.

She started and blinked, coming around a thought too fast for such cramped quarters—and lowered her hand with a half-laugh.

"Keeson Trager, you near scared me outta my skin!"

"No more than you did me, thinking that strike was gonna land!" he retorted, blue eyes dancing in a merry round face. "Least I'd've been able to tell my captain it was Khat Gobelyn who decked me."

She cocked an eyebrow. "Your captain figure brawl fines by who takes you down?"

He pushed his chest out, pretending to be a tough guy. As Khat knew for certain, there wasn't no need to pretend, except for the joke of it. Keeson Trager was plenty tough.

"My captain says, anybody takes me down in a brawl, she'll waive the fine and give double to the one who done the deed." He let his chest deflate a little, and cast her a bogus look of worried concern.

"Not short on cash this trip, are you, Khati?"

She laughed and shook her head. "Even if I was, there's easier ways."

His relief was obvious—and ridiculous. "Well, I'm pleased to hear you're doing OK." He glanced over to the 'board.

"*Market* not with you?"

"*Market's* at Kinaveral for refit. Right now, I'm a hired wing." She waved a hand at the 'board. "Brought *Lantic* down today. The unloading goes timely, I'll lift out tomorrow."

"My luck," said Keeson with a sigh. "*Wager's* lifting inside the hour—I'm sweep. Of course."

Of course. "Who's missing?" Khat asked.

"Coraline."

Of course. Keeson's youngest sister had a restless urge to explore every station and port *Wager* put in to, roof beam to secret cellars, and she'd more than once been the cause of the *Wager* refiling a scheduled lift.

"Funny to look for her here," Khat commented. "You try the residences, down below?"

"Tried that first. Then all the tunnels and the crawlways. Figure she might be here on account she's takin' her approach from your Jeth and givin' some study to the Liaden side of things."

"What's with all the Liadens, anyway?" Khat asked, since Keeson would know, if anyone did. "Port the size of Banth, with hardly no trade…"

He shrugged. "Maybe they're looking to buy it for a resort."

Khat wrinkled her nose at him. "Seriously."

"Seriously—I don't know, nor neither does the captain. All Banth's got is the mines. Now, they're bringing high-quality gold up outta the ground, but it's still only gold. Ain't ever seen Liadens much interested in raw gold—even processed, it's a ho-hum, though they'll buy some, every once in a while, just to be polite."

This was true. "Something else comin' out of the mines, then?"

Keeson shrugged again. "Bound to be, but I don't know what it is, and my guess is Admin don't, too, though right about now they're prolly scrambling to find out."

"What about the ship names?" Khat asked abruptly, with a jerk of the head toward the 'board.

He grinned. "Bothered you, too, huh? Farli worked 'em out—I'll drop a beam under your name to the crash when I get back to the ship. Assuming." He shook his head. "Oughta leave her once, so she'd learn."

Khat could see where it might be tempting, given Coraline's rare ability to vanish, mud-side, but still—"Remember the Stars," she said, which family had done just that—left their wanderaway youngest and lifted, to teach him. When they set back down, couple hours later, the boy was dead.

He'd been up on one of those observation decks Grounders favored—nothing more than a platform and a rail. The

Grounders who saw it, they said he panicked, but every spacer who heard the tale knew better'n that.

What more natural, after all, seeing your ship's running lights come up and knowing down to the heartbeat how much time you had to gain the hatch—what more natural than to calculate your angle and take off over that rail, all forgetful, until it was hideously too late, of planetside grav…

"I know," Keeson said. "But still."

Khat put her hand on his arm. "I'll help out. Let's take it to the back corners and sweep toward the door."

He looked around, firmed up his shoulders and nodded. "Good idea. Obliged."

"FLINX IS A hero!" Meicha cried, swooping down to snatch the big cat into her arms. He flicked his ears and lifted his head to rub a cheek against her chin. She laughed, and spun away, her feet describing patterns that Jethri thought might be Liaden dancing.

"Are you well, Jethri?" Miandra had come forward to stand next to him, her eyes serious.

He grinned and shrugged, Terran-style. "Too ignorant to know my own danger. I shouted for Ren Lar, true enough, but because I didn't think it was right for Flinx to kill that thing. It turns out that it was a good job he didn't get bit, since I learn that the…kylabra…bite will leave you ill."

"The kylabra bite," she corrected, her eyes even more serious. "Will leave you dead, more often than not. If you have been bitten by a young snake, or one newly wakened, perhaps you will merely become ill, but it is wisest to assume that any snake you encounter is both mature and operating at full capacity."

He considered that, remembering how small the snake had been. But, then, he thought, a mouthful of anhydrous cyanide will kill you, sure as stars, no matter how big you are. If the kylabra carried concentrated poison…

He frowned.

"Why allow them to remain in the vineyard, then? Wouldn't it be better to simply kill them all and be sure that the workers are safe?"

"You would think so," Miandra agreed, her eyes on Meicha, who was bending so that Flinx might jump from her arms to the upholstered window ledge. "And, indeed, the winery logs show that there had at one time been a war waged upon the kylabra. However, the vines then fell victim to root-eaters and other pests, which are the natural prey of the snakes. The damage these pests gave to the vines was much greater than the danger kylabra posed to the staff, and so an uneasy truce was struck. The snakes are shy by nature and attack only when they feel that they have been attacked. And it is true that they do not usually wake so early."

"The weather has been unseasonable, Ren Lar said."

She glanced up at his face, her own unreadable. "Indeed, it has been. We pray that it remains so, and we have no sudden frosts, to undo what the early warmth has given us."

Jethri frowned. Frost was condensed water vapor, but— "I am afraid I do not understand weather as it occurs on-planet," he said slowly. "Is there not an orderly progression—?"

She laughed and Meicha smiled as she rejoined them. "Is Jethri telling jokes?"

"Not quite," her sister said. "He merely inquires into the progression of weather and wonders if it is orderly."

Meicha's smile widened to a grin. "Well, if it were, Ren Lar would be a deal more pleased, and the price of certain years of wine would plummet."

He worked it out. "The vines are vulnerable to the...frost. So, if there is a frost after a certain point, there are less grapes and the wine that is made from those grapes becomes more valuable, because less available."

Together, they turned to look at him, and as one brought their palms together in several light claps.

"Well reasoned," said Meicha and he shrugged a second time. "Economic sense. Rare costs more."

"True," Miandra murmured. "But weather is random and there are some grapes of which we need to have no shortage. It is better, if rarity is desirable, to reserve the vintage to the house and sell it higher, later."

That made sense. The weather, though, you'd think something could be done.

"Do you watch the weather?"

"Certainly." That was Meicha. "Ren Lar has a portable station which he carries on his belt and listens to all his waking hours—and his sleeping hours, too, I'll wager! However and alas, the reports are not always—one might say, hardly ever—accurate, so that one must always expect that the weather will turn against you. Only think, Jethri! Before you is yet the experience of being awakened by the master in the still of night, in order that you might assist in tending the smudge pots, which will keep the frost from the buds."

*There had to be a better way*, he thought, vaguely thinking of domes, or the *Market's* hydroponics section, or—

"Good-day, good-day, Lady Meicha, Lady Miandra!" The voice was brisk and light and closely followed by an elderly gentlemen in evening clothes. He paused just inside the room, bright brown eyes on Jethri's face.

"And this—I find Jethri, the son of ven'Deelin?"

He made his bow, light and buoyant. "Jethri Gobelyn," he said in the mode of introduction. "Adopted of Norn ven'Deelin."

"Delightful!" The elderly gentleman rubbed his hands together in clear anticipation. "I am Zer Min pel'Oban. You may address me as Master pel'Oban. Now, tell me, young Jethri, have you been instructed in the basic forms and patterns?"

"I can dance a jig and a few line dances," he said, neither of which likely hit any of the basic forms and patterns, whatever they might be. Still, he was accounted spry on his feet, and at the shivary during which he came to sixteen, Jadey

Winchester—mainline, right off the *Bullet*—had danced with him to the positive exclusion of the olders who were trying to court her—or, rather, to court the *Bullet*, since Jadey was in line for captain, as he found out later. But not 'til him and Mac Gold had come to blows over who had a right to dance and who was just a kid.

"A jig," Master pel'Oban murmured. "I regret, I am unfamiliar. Might you, of your goodness, produce a few steps? Perhaps I may recognize it."

*Not likely*, thought Jethri, but since he'd brought the subject up, there really wasn't any way he could ease out of a demo.

So—"I will attempt it, sir," he said, politely, and closed his eyes, trying to hear the music inside his head—flutes, spoons, banjo, drums, some 'lectric keys, maybe—*that* was shivary music. Loud, fast and jolly for a jig. Jethri smiled to himself, feeling his feet twitch as the remembered twang of Wilm Guthry's banjo echoed through his head. He closed his eyes, and there was Jadey, smiling a challenge and tossing her head, kicking high, once, twice—and on the third kick he joined her, then both feet down and hands on hips, look to the left and look to the right, and your feet moving quick through the weaving steps...

"Thank you!" he heard, and opened his eyes to the dancing room with its wooden floor and blue-covered walls, and Master pel'Oban standing before him, his hands folded and a look on his face that Jethri thought might have been shock. The twins, at his right and left hands, were visibly trying not to smile.

He let his feet still, dropped his hands from his hips and inclined his head.

"A few steps only, sir. I hope it was—instructive."

Master pel'Oban eyed him. "Instructive. Indeed. You have grace, I see, and an athletic nature. Now, we will show you how the dance is done on Irikwae." He waggled his fingers at Miandra and Meicha.

"If the ladies will oblige me by producing a round dance?"

THE BAR WAS less frenzied now. In fact, the blue-haired bartender was leaning at her ease at the near end, in earnest conversation with a little girl wearing a ship's coverall, sitting cross-legged atop the bar.

"This one yours, Long Space?"

"Belongs to a friend," Khat said, sparing a hard frown for Coraline. "Her ship's going up in a quarter-clock and her brother's lookin' for her."

The 'keeper produced a frown of her own. "Bad business, worrying your brother," she said sternly.

Coraline bit her lip and stared down at the bar. "I'm sorry," she whispered.

"You tell him that," the barkeep recommended and tapped her on the knee. "Hey."

The girl looked up and the woman smiled. "It's been good talking to you. Next time you're here, stop by and give me the news, right, Cory?"

Coraline smiled. "Right."

"That's set, then. Go on now and find your brother."

"All right. Good flight." Coraline scooted to the edge of the bar and dropped to the floor, landing without a stagger.

Khat held out her hand. "Let's go." She said, and the two of them crossed the last bit of the bar and went out into the corridor.

"YOU!" KEESON'S BELLOW got the frowning attention of a cluster of Liadens near the door. He ignored them and swept his sister up in his arms.

"I oughta break you in half," he snarled, giving her a hug that looked close to doing the job.

Coraline put her head next to his. "I'm sorry, Kee."

"You're *always* sorry," he said. "What you gotta be, is *on time*. You keep up like this an' captain'll confine you to ship for sure." He set her on her feet, keeping a tight grip on her hand, and turned to give Khat a grin and an extravagant salute.

"Khat Gobelyn, you're my hero!"

She sputtered a laugh and shooed him down the tunnel. "Go on, or your captain'll leave both of you."

"And count herself ahead," Keeson agreed. He gave her another salute and tugged on Coraline's hand. "C'mon, Spark. Show me how fast you can run in grav."

"'bye, Khat," the little girl called and the two of them were gone, moving out with a will.

Khat shook her head and raised a hand to stifle a sudden yawn. *Time to get back to the crash*, she thought, and looked around for her guiding arrows.

"Gobelyn," a soft malicious voice said behind her. Khat spun, and met the cold blue eyes of the yellow-haired trader who'd been giving Intake so much grief.

"What about it?" she asked him in pidgin, not even trying to sound sociable.

He frowned. "Kin you are to *Jethri* Gobelyn?"

What was this? One of Jeth's new mates? "Yes," she allowed, slightly more sociable, trying to see Jethri having anything cordial to do with such a spoiled, pretty fellow, and having a tough go of it, even given that business was business...

"Your kin has damaged my kin," the Liaden was saying, and Khat felt her skin pebble with chill. "You owe Balance."

The Liadens standing all around were real quiet, watching them. A couple of Terrans slammed through the door, talking loudly, barged through the crowd without seeing it and disappeared down the tunnel.

"What did he do?" Khat asked the Liaden. "And who are you?"

"I am Bar Jan chel'Gaibin. Jethri Gobelyn by his actions has stolen from me a brother. He does not pay the lifeprice. You are his kin. Will I Balance the loss exactly? Or will you pay the lifeprice?"

What *was* this? Khat wondered wildly. Jethri had killed somebody—this man's brother? And now she was being threatened with—exact Balance—death? Or she could pay up? And

Master ven'Deelin was allowing Jeth to dodge a legitimate debt? That seemed unlikely at the least.

Khat drew a careful breath, not cold now that her brain was engaged.

"How much?"

His eyes changed, though the rest of his face remained bland. "For a gifted trader at the start of a profitable career—four hundred cantra."

She almost laughed—if he'd been Terran, she *would have* laughed. If he'd been Terran, they wouldn't be having this conversation.

She shrugged, indifferent. "Too much," she said and turned away, tracking the yellow arrows out of the side of her eye, moving firm but not so fast that he'd think she was running.

He *grabbed* her, the damned fool. Grabbed her arm, hard, and yanked her back around.

She came around, all right; she came around swinging, and caught him full across the face. The force of the blow lifted him off his feet and dropped him flat, backbone to deck, and there he laid, winded, at least, or maybe out cold.

A shout came out of the watching Liadens, and she figured it was time to show she was serious, so she kept on turning, until she was facing the lot of them, crouched low and the boot knife in her hand.

She let them see it, and when nobody seemed disposed to argue with it, eased out of the crouch.

"We can take it to Security, or we can leave it," she snarled. "We take it to Security, be sure I'll let them know that this man tried to rob me, and made threats against my cousin and myself—and that you stood by and watched."

There was a stir among the group of them, and another boy, not quite so pretty as the one on the floor, stepped forward.

"We leave it," he said. "No Security." He moved a hand so deliberately that the gesture must have meant something. "Safe passage."

*Well, now, wasn't that sweet?*

Khat bared her teeth at him, in no way a smile. "You bet," she said, and turned away, keeping the blade ready.

Nobody tried to stop her.

IT WAS EDGING onto the middle of the world-night, and he should have been well a-bed. Thoughts were buzzing loud inside his head, though, most notably thoughts regarding supply and demand and the unpredictability of weather.

So it was that Jethri was kneeling on the bench beneath the window in his bedroom, swearing at the latch, instead of sweetdreaming in his bunk.

The latch came down all at once and the window swung out on well-oiled hinges. He damn near swung out with it, in the second before he remembered to let go and lean back, and then he just knelt there, waiting for his heart to slow down, breathing deep breaths of the cool mid-night air.

The breeze was slightly damp, and carried a confusion of odors. Tree-smells, he guessed, and flowers; rocks, grapes and snakes. The sky showed a ribbon of stars and two of Irikwae's three moons, riding the shoulders of the mountains.

The cushion he was kneeling on moved and he looked down to find Flinx. The cat looked at him, eye to eye, and blinked his, in what Miandra insisted was a cat-smile.

"Guess I owe you Balance," Jethri said, reaching down and tickling the underneath of the chin. Flinx purred and his eyes melted into mere slits of peridot. "Your life ever needs saving, you don't hesitate, take me?" Flinx purred even louder, and Jethri grinned again, gave the chin another couple skritches for good measure, then sat carefully back on his knees and pulled the weather device out of his pocket.

Sometime during the endless repetitions of the basic pattern of a round dance, it had come to him that the little machine might be well-used on behalf of Ren Lar's grapes. He frowned down into the screen, touched the icon which him and his father had figured out accessed the predictive program and knelt tall once more, elbows on the window ledge, the device held firmly between his two hands, slightly extended, allowing it to taste the night.

The screen displayed its characteristic transitional swirls, then cleared, showing a mosaic of symbols. Jethri frowned at them, then at the starry and brilliant night.

*Rule of opposites,* he thought, which was nothing more than whimsy, and touched the icon for "rain".

The screen swirled and cleared, showing him a duplicate image of the sky outside his window—and nothing else.

*Well, that didn't exactly prove anything, did it?*

Jethri tapped the upper right corner of the screen, and the icons reappeared. He touched another, at exact random. Nothing at all happened this time; the screen continued to display its mosaic of exotic icons, unblinking, unchanging.

He sighed, loud and frustrated. Beside him, the cat sputtered one of his rustier purrs and banged his head deliberately against Jethri's elbow.

"You're right," he said, reaching down and rubbing a sturdy ear. "The brain's on overdrive. Best to get some sleep, and think better tomorrow." He gave Flinx's cat one more tug, slid off the window seat and headed for the bed, taking a small detour to leave the weather gadget on the table with the rest of his pocket things.

He snapped the light off and climbed into bed, hitting a solid lump with his knee. Flinx grunted, but otherwise didn't move.

"Leave some room for me, why don't you?" Jethri muttered, pushing slightly.

The cat sighed and let himself be displaced sufficiently for Jethri to curl on his side under the covers, head on his favorite pillow, eyes drooping shut. He yawned, once. Flinx purred, briefly.

"GOT A PRINTOUT for you," the doorman said. "Come down from *Trager's Wager*."

It took a second, her mind still being on the problem back at the Trade Bar and thinking maybe Security'd be waiting for her at the crash, wanting to discuss the open showing of knives in a Combine port. But, no—Keeson had promised to send Farli's list, when he got back to the ship.

"Thanks," she said taking the gritty yellow sheet. She unfolded it, read the names—*Winhale, Tornfall, Skeen, Brass Cannon*—and tried to remember why she'd cared.

Right. Paitor would've been interested in the names, especially the ones that carried the keys. She glanced back at the paper and half-smiled. Never let it be said that Farli Trager was anything less than thorough. Both *Skeen* and *Brass Cannon* carried a key behind their names.

Well, Paitor would be happy, anyway. Assuming Khat managed to get off Port in one piece, and without acquiring a Liaden knife in her back. Which brought her back to wondering if Jethri *had* killed the blond Liaden's brother and if in that case he was all right. Or if, as she considered more likely, the boy had been trying to earn a little—a lot—of extra money by playing the stupid Terran for an idiot.

"You OK?" the doorman sounded genuinely concerned.

Khat shook herself and looked up at him.

"Had a little trouble at the Trade Bar. Heard some bad news about kin. You got a fastbeam I can use?"

He shrugged. "We got one. It'll cost you, though."

Well, what else were bonuses for? Khat nodded.

"I can cover it."

DYK'S BEEN MESSING *with the climate control again,* Jethri thought muzzily, pulling his blanket up around his chin. *Khat's gonna take his ear this ti—*

He sat up, clumsily, because of the heavy, hot boulder resting against his hip, blinked stupidly at the huge space, looming away into darkness—*Tarnia's house,* he remembered then, and shivered in a sudden flow of cool air, from, from—

"Mud!" He flung out of bed and went over to the open window, climbed up on the window seat, leaned out, got a grip on the cold, wet latch and hauled the window closed, pushing down on the lock with considerable energy.

"Ship kid," he muttered. "Think you'd know enough to be sure the hatches was sealed." He shook his head, and slid off the ledge, which was slightly damp where the rain had come in, and, yawning, went back to bed, shoved the cat out of his spot and snuggled back under the covers.

# Day 165
# Standard Year 1118

## Irikwae

"WHAT IS THAT?" Miandra asked. Jethri started and looked up, fingers closing automatically around the gadget. "A mirror?" She settled onto the bench beside him, her arm pressing his as she craned to see.

"Not exactly." He held it out, displaying the screen in its transition phase. "It's a weather device."

She frowned down at it, extended a hand—and paused, sending a direct glance into his face. "May I?"

"Of course." He opened his fingers wide and she plucked the thing from his palm, eyes on the swirling screen, head cocked a little to one side. Jethri twisted around, so he could watch, too, without giving himself a crick in the neck.

Eventually, the swirls cleared and the icon dictionary appeared. Miandra's frown deepened.

"What does it do?"

"More than I know about," he said truthfully. "I'm trying to study it out, because one of the things it *does* do is show weather patterns. There should be a way to set it to watch for particular patterns in a specific area, and give a warning." He shrugged. "I haven't figured out quite how to do that, though."

"Perhaps if you consulted the instructions?" She murmured, her attention still on the screen.

"That would be a good idea," Jethri admitted, "if I had the instructions. There might be instructions on-board, but, if so, I've never found them—nor even my father."

"What a peculiar device." She extended a long forefinger and touched the screen, carefully between the rows of icons. "What do these symbols mean?"

"They represent kinds of weather." He put his finger under a sort of squiggle with dashes falling out of it. "That's rain. And this one—" a similar squiggle shape, but the stuff falling out of it was rounder and fuzzy looking—"that's snow. Snow is frozen rain."

Miandra looked up at him, still frowning. "I know what snow is. We have enough of it during the cold season."

He felt his ears heat and inclined his head. "Forgive me. Of course, you know more of these matters than a shipborn. Perhaps you might do me the favor of identifying those symbols that match weather you are familiar with."

She blinked, glanced down at the device and then back to his face.

"I think we do you no favor in teaching you to sharpen your words," she said. "What would you have said to me just then, if we had been speaking in your home-tongue."

"Eh?" He shrugged, feeling a brief sense of dislocation before the words slid into his mouth. "Figure it yourself, if you know so much."

Miandra blinked again. "I see—irritation sharpens your words, not our teaching."

"Well, see—" he began, and shook his head, hearing himself back in Terran. He raised a hand, signaling that he required a moment to himself, closed his eyes and took a deep breath, letting his mind just sort of go blank for a moment....

"Jethri, are you well?" Miandra's voice was worried, her words in Low Liaden. He felt something sort of twist inside his head, and opened his eyes.

"I am well," he said. "A momentary dislocation of language. To continue—my father wasn't able to break the puzzle of this device—nor was his cousin, and neither was a shy man with a puzzle. I've only been trying to work out how to operate it for last few days, but I am afraid my frustration—has the better of me. For something that seems so simple, it is remarkably difficult to understand!"

She laughed, and shifted closer to him, holding the device between them. "Well, let us see what we may deduce between us, then. Surely, *this*—" she ran her finger under a simple straight line, "is clear skies—no weather, as we say, though of course there is always weather…" Her voice trailed off, and she bent her head closer, reaching up absently to tuck a curl of reddish hair behind her ear. Jethri stared, then pulled his attention back to the problem at hand.

"This…" She tapped her finger on a crazy, swirly mess of lines. "Surely," she said, tapping again, "this is a wind-twist? No other weather pattern would be so—" She gasped to a stop, staring down at a screen gone smokey and opaque.

"What is happening?" She thrust the device at him, her eyes wide and panicked. "Jethri—what is it doing?"

Almost, he laughed at her. Almost. And then he remembered all the times neither she nor her sister had laughed at him, though he didn't doubt he was nothing less than comical.

So. Gently, he slid the little machine out of her hand. The transitional clouds were thinning on the screen, and he tipped it so she could see.

"It's only going to the next phase—see? Here is a picture of our day, here and now."

And so it was. Miandra gazed at it in silence, then looked back to him, her dark blue eyes showing unease.

"Now what does it do?"

"Nothing," he said, and smiled down at her. "We can go back to the icon screen—" he touched the go-back button; the screen swirled, then solidified. He held the device out to her. "Touch another icon. Any one."

She raised her hand, then slowly lowered it, her face troubled. "I—believe that I do not wish to do that."

"It's all right," he assured her. "Nothing else will happen at all. See?" He pressed the symbol for rain. The icons in place; the screen steady.

"I—see," she replied, but he got the idea she wasn't made easy by the demonstration.

"It's just an old weather predictor," he said, trying to jolly her, "and probably not very stable. I just thought it would be...convenient...if we had warning of—frost, or any other weather damaging to the vines."

"The weather net is in place," she pointed out.

"But you said it wasn't accurate," he countered.

She used her chin to point at the device in his hand. "That does not appear to be accurate, either."

He had to admit that she looked to be right there, and slipped the device into his sleeve.

"I suppose," he said, a trifle glumly.

Miandra laughed. "Come now, Jethri, do not be cast down! It is a most marvelous puzzle!"

Her laugh was infectious and he grinned in response. "I guess I like my puzzles to have answers."

"As who does not?" she said gaily, and bounced to her feet, the ruby pendant flashing in the brilliant day.

"It is nearly time for the gather-bell. Let us be at our places early and astonish Ren Lar!"

Since Ren Lar actually expected everyone to be in the yard the instant the shift-bell sounded, this was a remarkably sensible suggestion and Jethri got to his feet with alacrity, following her out of the small garden and toward the wine yard.

"What are wind-twists?" he asked as he came to her side. She glanced up at him, her face serious.

"Very destructive and unpredictable weather," she said. "A wind-twist might level a vineyard with a touch, or fling a house into the tops of the trees."

A breeze touched his face, moving off the side of the hill. "*Wind* can do that?" he asked, starting to believe that this was a joke.

"Oh, yes," she assured him. "Fortunately, they are very rare. And never in this season."

THE HYDRAULICS WAS up to spec for a wonder, and the yard boss wasn't available to talk. That was all right. Myra Goodin, his second, didn't talk much, but she did listen a treat, and tagged his specific concerns and problems in her clipboard, after which, she handed the 'board to him.

Grig read over what she'd input, nodded and thumbprinted it.

"Yard's doing good for us," he said, easy and companionable, as he handed the 'board back. "We appreciate the attention."

Myra looked him firm in the eye. Firm sort of woman, and not one to joke. Serious about her work in a way her boss didn't appear to emulate—or value. Which was too bad, so Grig thought, given that the reputation of the yard sat square on her shoulders.

She took the clipboard back, and counter-printed it, her eyes steady on his. "We got off to a rugged start," she said seriously. "I place the blame equal, there. Your captain shouldn't have popped off like she did and Roard shouldn't've egged her." She nodded. "We've been able to get back on a business-like footing since you and Seeli took over the inspections. I appreciate that you took the initiative, there. This is a joint project—we're all here to see that the refit's done right."

Which was true enough, but not something you'd hear comin' outta Boss Roard's mouth. Grig smiled at Myra.

"Joint project, right enough—and a pleasure to be working on it with you." He stood, and nodded at the 'board in her hand. "When d'you want me by to okay those?"

She frowned and touched the keypad, calling up her schedule.

"Three-day," she said after a moment. "I'll give you a pass."

Myra had been the one who had worked out the pass system that allowed them in the yard more often than Roard's so-called Official Inspection Schedule. It was best for all of them, if okays on inspection problems didn't have to wait 'til the next scheduled inspection, which you'd think a yard boss would understand. Well, Grig amended, a yard boss who wasn't thinking with his spite gland.

He reached out a long arm and snagged his jacket from where he'd thrown it across the back of a chair. Myra went across the room, pulled a green plastic pass from its hook, set it in the 'coder and tapped a quick sequence in. The machine beeped, she slid the card free and held it out.

"We will speak again in three days," she said, which was dismissal, and right enough, busy as she was.

Grig took the card with smile and put it away in an inner pocket of the jacket. "Three days, it is," he said, gave her a nod for good-day, and let himself out of the office.

He cleared the gate and was maybe eight, nine steps on his way back toward the lodgings when he was joined by a long, soft-walking shadow. He sighed, and didn't bother to look, knowing full well what he'd see.

"Grigory," her voice was familiar. Well, of course it was.

"Raisy," he answered, still not looking, which maybe wasn't right, when a man hadn't seen his sister in so long, but *damn* it...

"Uncle wants to see you," she said, which he'd known she was going to, so it wasn't exactly surprise that spun him around, boot heels stamping the road.

"Well, now, there's welcome news!" he snapped, and watched Raisy's eyebrows go up on her long forehead.

"Trouble?" she asked, quiet enough to make him ashamed of showing temper.

"Not 'til you showed up."

She grinned. "Same could be said for yourself."

"'cept I'm where I was, doin' what I've been, and didn't go lookin' for relatives to complicate my life," Grig said. "And you know for a space cold fact that Uncle is more trouble than any of the rest of us, living or dead."

She appeared to consider that, head tipped to one side. "Exceptin' Arin."

He laughed, short and still sharp with temper.

"True enough. We'd none of us be anywhere, if it wasn't for Arin." He sighed. "What's Uncle want?"

His sister shrugged. "Wants to talk to you. Catch up. It's been—what?—twenty years?"

"Long as that?" He closed his eyes, not wanting it. Not wanting it down deep in his bones. Seeli—Seeli'd be after takin' his head, and she'd have nothing but the right of it on her side.

"Time flows," Raisy was saying, "when life is good."

He opened his eyes and looked at her, long and hard. "Life's *been* good," he said, sternly. "Don't laugh at me, Raisy."

She shook her head, and put a long hand on his sleeve. "No mocking here, brother," she said, serious as only Raisy could be. Her fingers tightened briefly, then withdrew. "You know Uncle won't let it rest. Why not come along, get it over with? Be a shame to make him send an escort."

Uncle would, too, as Grig knew from bitter experience. Still—"What're you?" He asked Raisy.

She smiled. "Your older sister, here to show you the best course to not getting your arm broke. Or didja forget what happened the last time you turned stubborn?"

"I remember," he said and sighed, accepting it, because Uncle *wouldn't* let it go and there was some small advantage to showing meek and biddable in the first round.

"All right," he told Raisy. "You're persuadable; I'll come. They're expecting me back at the lodgings by a certain time. Lemme find a comm and file an amended course. Then Uncle can have me."

THE JOB TODAY was gathering up all the clippings they'd clipped over the last week and putting them in a cart parked at the end of each row. Filled carts were taken away, and an empty arrived to replace it.

Meicha was on cart duty, along with some youngers from the kitchen and maintenance staff. Jethri was on gather-up, and Miandra, too, him working the left hall off the main corridor, her working the right. Flinx was about, lazing under the vines, and amusing himself however cats did; Jethri'd see him out of the side of an eye when he'd bend down to pick up a bundle of sticks.

On one level, it was stupid, repetitive work—worse even than Stinks. But, where Stinks was a solitary aggravation that let a bad mood grow on you, the stick picking up was a group effort—and it was by large a merry group. The kitchen youngers sang when they pushed their carts, and laughter could be heard along the rows. The weather might have helped the spirit of the day, too—cool, with a light breeze to fan away the sweat of exertion, and some progressively denser clouds to cut the glare of the sun, as the day went on.

Jethri met Miandra at the cart. She threw her armful of sticks onto the growing pile, smiling. He placed his more carefully, because the cart was almost full and he didn't want to start a cascade of sticks to the ground.

"That's all for me!" the tender said cheerfully, reaching down to touch the power switch. She glanced up at the sky. "Hope it's not going to—Gods!"

Instinctively, Jethri looked along her line of sight, blinking up into a sky now almost entirely overcast with green-gray clouds, that seemed to be orbiting each other, picking up speed as he watched.

"Wind-twist!" the cart driver shouted, and shouted again, loud enough to hurt Jethri's ears. "Wind-twist! Everybody get to shelter!"

Apparently suiting her actions to her words, she snapped off the power switch, turned and ran down the hill, toward the house, and the cellar.

The green-gray clouds were moving faster, now, elongating, and there came a downward roar of ice-cold air, slapping the vines flat and abusing the ears, and he felt his arm grabbed and tore his attention away from the spectacle in the sky to Miandra's horrified face, her hair twisting and tangling in the wind.

"Jethri, quickly!" Close as she was, and shouting, too, he could barely hear her above the growing roar of the wind. "To the cellar!"

"You go!" He yelled back. "I'll get Flinx!"

"No!" She grabbed his arm. "Jethri, a wind-twist can pick you up and break you—"

"And you!" he yelled, and pushed her. "Run! I'm right behind you!" And he threw himself forward, away from the wagon, back down the row he'd been working. The vines were snapping like wild cable in the growing disturbance, and about halfway down the row, where he hadn't finished cleaning up yet, some loose twigs started to stir, and dance above the ground, following a spiral path up into the sky.

Just before that, crouched under a vine, all four feet under him, tail twice its normal size and ears laid back, was Flinx.

Jethri jumped, grabbed the cat by the loose fur at the back of his neck, hauled him up and got him against his chest, arms wrapped tight. Flinx bucked, and he might have yowled, but the wind was roaring too loud for Jethri to be certain. Cat crushed against him, head down, so that none of the airborne sticks would hit his face, he ran.

All around him, the wind roared, and there was the end of the corridor, and the abandoned cart, and a slender figure in wind-torn red hair, her ruby pendant flaring bright as a sun—

"Hurry!" she shouted, and he heard her, somewhere between the inside of his head and the outside of his ears. "Hurry! It's slipping!"

He hurried, stretching his legs and the cat wrapped close, and he was past the cart and Miandra was beside him and they were running faster, *faster*, down the hill, and—

Behind them came a boom like a ship giving up all its energy at once. Ahead of them, a meteor-shower of sticks and metal shred. Jethri faltered, felt Flinx's claws in his flesh—

"Run!" screamed Miandra.

And he ran.

THE FAMILY HAD lodgings in an up-port hotel, which shouldn't have surprised him any. Raisy's jumpsuit was a serviceable, sensible garment, but it weren't spacer togs, no more than his good jacket and respectful trading clothes could pass him as a credit-heavy Grounder.

He did see some of those they passed in the lobby notice him, then look back to Raisy and form certain opinions not particularly generous of either of them.

"Should've stopped and bought me some dirt duds," he muttered, and Raisy sent him a look before pulling a key out of her pocket and sliding it into a call box. Up on the lift board, a light glowed blue and a second or two later a door opened, showing carpet, mirrors, and soft lights.

"After you, brother," Raisy said, and he stepped in, boots sinking into the carpet.

Raisy settled herself beside him. The door slid closed, soundless, and the lift engaged with a subtle purr. Grig glanced to the side, catching their reflections in the mirror: Two long bottles of brew, craggy in the face and lean in the frame, both a little wilted with the heat. The man had his dark hair in a spacer's buzz; the woman kept hers long enough to cover her ears. Despite that, and given a change of clothes for either, they looked remarkably similar. Family resemblance, thought Grig, and laughed a little, under his breath.

"Something funny?" Raisy asked, but he shook his head and pointed at the numbers flicking by on the click-plate.

"Rent the rooftop?" He asked, not quite joking.

"Uncle likes the view," she answered, matching his tone precisely. "The equipment needs to be dry, though. So we compromise."

The numbers stopped flicking, settling on 30. The almost subliminal purr of the machinery stopped and the door slid open.

Raisy stepped out first, and turned to look back to where he stood, hesitating at the door, having fourth and fifth thoughts, and staring down a hall as deep in carpeting and showy with mirror as the lift.

"Come on, brother," she said, holding out a hand, like she was offering a tow. "Let's get you a brew, and a chance to clean up."

Grig shook his head and came into the hall under his own power, though he did give Raisy's hand a quick squeeze.

"Why not fast-forward?" he asked, with a lightness he didn't particularly feel. "I've always found Uncle went down better on an empty stomach."

Her smile flickered, and she shrugged, turning to lead the way. "Your call."

JETHRI SETTLED HIS shoulders against the cool wall and closed his eyes. His chest hurt, inside and out, and multicolored stars were spinning around inside the dark behind his eyelids. Miandra had been appropriated by Meicha the second they cleared the winery door. He'd dropped Flinx about that same time and gone to find himself a nice, secluded piece of wall to lean up against.

It came to him, in painful bursts of thought uncomfortably timed to his gasps for air, that the weather device in his pocket was far more powerful—and far more dangerous—than he, or his father, had ever guessed. Definitely not a toy for a child. Possibly not a toy for a trader grown and canny. Certainly, the occasions that he mistily remembered, when Arin had used the device to "predict" rain, might just as easily been cases of rain being somehow produced by an action of the device. His father and Grig used to argue about it, he remembered, his breathing less labored now, and his brain taking advantage of the extra oxygen. His father and Grig used to argue about it, right. Arin had insisted that the little device was a predictor, Grig had thought otherwise—or said he thought otherwise. Jethri remembered thinking that Grig was just saying it, to tease, but what if—

"There he is!" A voice cried, 'way too loud, sending his overbusy brain into a stutter. He opened his eyes.

Meicha was standing close, Miandra a little behind her shoulder. Both were staring at his chest.

"Unfortunate," Meicha commented.

"Flinx was frightened," Miandra said, her voice slow and limp sounding. The other girl's mouth twisted into a shape that was neither smile nor grin.

"Flinx was not alone." She extended a thin hand, and brushed her palm down the front of Jethri's shirt.

"Hey!" He flinched, the contact waking long slices of pain.

"Hush," she said, stepping closer. "There's blood all over your shirt." She brushed his chest again—a long, unhurried stroke—and again, just the same, except now it didn't hurt.

"Much improved, I think." She stepped back. "Ren Lar wishes to speak with you."

Now there was an unwelcome piece of news, though not exactly unexpected. Ren Lar would have a duty to find out in what shape the foster son of his mother's foster child had survived his first encounter with wild weather. A duty he was probably more than a little nervous about, considering he had just lately almost lost that same foster son to a wild animal attack. Wild reptile. Whatever.

Still, Jethri thought, pushing away from the wall, he wished he could put the meeting off until he had sorted out his personal thoughts and feelings regarding the weather...device.

"Ren Lar," Meicha murmured, "is very anxious to see you, Jethri."

He sighed and gave the two of them the best smile he could pull up, though it felt unsteady on his mouth.

"I supposed you had better take me to him, then."

REN LAR WAS perched on a stool behind the lab table, but the calibration equipment was dark. A screen over the table displayed an intricate and changing pattern of lines, swirls and colors that Jethri thought, uneasily, might be weather patterns, the depiction of which held Ren Lar's whole attention. Flinx the cat sat erect at his elbow, ears up and forward, tail wrapped neatly 'round his toes. He squinted his eyes in a cat smile as the three of them approached. Ren Lar didn't stir.

"Cousin?" Miandra said in her limp voice. "Here is Jethri, come to speak with you."

For a moment, nothing happened, then the man blinked, and turned, frowning into each of their faces in turn.

"Thank you," he said to the twins. "You may leave us."

They bowed, hastily, it seemed to Jethri, and melted away from his side. Flinx jumped down from the lab table and went after them. Jethri squared his shoulders and met Ren Lar's eyes, which weren't looking dreamy at all.

"Miandra tells me," the man said, with no polite inquiry into Jethri's health, or even an invitation to sit down on the stool opposite. "That you have in your possession a...device...which she believes has the ability to influence weather. I have never seen nor heard of such a device, and I have made weather a lifelong study. Therefore, son of ven'Deelin, I ask that you show me this wonder."

*Mud.* He'd been hoping for time to think, to—but he couldn't, in justice, blame Miandra for bringing the business straight to her senior. Nor blame the senior for wanting a looksee.

Reluctant, he slipped the little machine out of his pocket and put it on the table. Ren Lar extended a hand—and then snatched it back like he'd been burned, a phrase Jethri didn't catch coming off of his tongue like a curse.

Ren Lar drew a hard breath and treated Jethri to a full-grown glare. "So. Put it away." He turned his head, calling out into the depths of the workroom. "Graem?"

"Master?" Her voice came from somewhere deep within the shadow of the barrels.

"Call the Scouts."

"GRIGORY," THE MAN who stood up from behind the desk was long, craggy and lean. His hair was hullplate gray, short, but not buzzed; his eyes dark and deep. He smiled, which was worth sixth thoughts. Uncle in an affable mood was never good news.

Well, there wasn't nothing for it, now. He was here. Just get it over with, like Raisy said.

Thinking that, he nodded, respectful-like, and made himself smile.

"Uncle Yuri," he said, soft-voiced. "You're lookin' well, sir."

The older man nodded, pleased with him. "I'm doing well," he allowed, "for an old fellow." He moved a hand, showing Grig a deep, soft chair at the corner of the desk.

"Sit, be comfortable! Raisana, your brother wants a brew."

Grig sat, though he wouldn't have owned to comfortable, and raised a hand. "No brew for me, thanks. Can't stop long."

Uncle didn't frown, but he did let his smile dim a bit. "What's this? You haven't seen your family—your own sister!—for twenty Standards and you can't stop for a couple hours, have a brew, catch us up on your news?"

Raisy had settled on the arm of a chair somewhat back from the desk; Grig dared a quick look at her out of the corner of his eye, much good it did him. She had on her card-playing face, and if there was only one thing certain in the universe as it was configured, it was that Grig would never be his sister's equal at cards. Sighing to himself, he put his attention back on Uncle Yuri.

"Raisy said you wanted to talk to me, Uncle. Made it sound urgent, or I wouldn't have come today. Ship's down for refit and there's only me and Seeli to do the needful, with part-time help from young Khat."

Uncle's smile had dimmed even more. He sat, carefully, and folded his hands on the desk. "I didn't realize you were doing the refit yourself," he said, only a little sarcastic. "I'd've thought even Iza Gobelyn would be smart enough to bring her ship to a yard."

Grig sighed, letting it be heard. "She did, but there's issues and the yard wants close watching. They started out shorting us on the shielding and when Iza called it, the boss pushed her into a fistfight and had her banned from the yard, on risk of losing the *Market*."

Uncle's face was a study in disinterest. Tough. Grig settled his shoulders against the back of the chair and made himself smile again.

"So, we got Iza bailed out and off-planet with a nice, safe pilot's berth, and the rest of the crew'd already done the same, excepting Khat, who signed on as a willfly for the port—and Seeli, who's Admin and hasn't got no choice but to stay. And me, backing up, just like I was born to do."

That last, it maybe wasn't smart; a sideways glance at Raisy's face certainly left him with that impression, but Uncle was still holding course on affable, despite the provocation—and that was bad.

"I'm glad to hear you're such a rich resource for your ship," Uncle said. "You do your family proud."

Uh-huh. Grig ducked his head. "Thank you, sir."

There was a small pause, during which Uncle traded stares with Raisy, which didn't do much for Grig's stomach. Raisy was his sister, but she advised Uncle—and handled him—that too. Another thing she'd always been better at than Grig.

"In fact," Uncle said, having gotten whatever advice Raisy had to give him, "it was about your ship that I wanted to talk. Word is that Arin's youngest brother is missing—and that *Gobelyn's Market* no longer trades in fractins."

Grig shrugged. "There's a wobble in your info, sir. For instance, the boy ain't 'missing'—he's 'prenticed. The fractins—what there was left of 'em, after certain experiments and explorations—he's got them, too."

Uncle's smile was back, full-force, mixed with no little measure of relief.

"The work continues, then. Excellent. And you are to be commended for your part in securing the position with the

Liaden trader. Our studies indicate that there are many caches within Liaden-held space."

Old studies, those were. Extrapolations and wishful thinking. Gettin' wishfuller as the timonium ran down toward inertia.

"I didn't have no part in gettin' Jethri his 'prenticeship— he did that his own self," he said, into the teeth behind Uncle's smile. "And I don't exactly think he knows that there's any work he oughta be carrying on, for the good of the family, or otherwise."

Uncle *frowned.*

"Surely, you saw to his education, after Arin's death. Why else were you on that ship?"

Grig sat up straight, feeling his mouth forming a frown to match Uncle Yuri's. "I was there as Arin's back-up, and after he died, it fell on me to make sure the boy survived to adult. Which mostly came down to making sure Iza didn't shove him out an airlock or leave him grounded somewhere. It sure didn't have nothing to do with teaching him the family trade. If I'd tried, Iza'd've spaced *me.*"

Uncle stared, not saying nothing which was more natural. Out of the corner of his eye, he saw Raisy shake her head, just a mite, but the hell with that. Grig sat forward and gave Uncle his full attention.

"Arin shouldn't've played Iza Gobelyn for a fool. He knew it an' spent the rest of his life trying to amend it. If he'd lived, he might've reconciled her to the boy. If he'd lived, she might've been able to forget how she'd got him. Might've. So, anyhow, there's Iza, and she's got the cipher. Then *Toad* went down with the tilework overridin' ship's comps."

"*Toad* knew the risk." That was Raisy. Grig sent her a glance.

"They did. Some of us, though, we started asking if the risk was worth the prize."

"You're telling me that *Arin* thought of giving up on the project?" Grig could almost taste Uncle's disbelief.

Grig shook his head. "I'm tellin' you that the fractins are dying. They're dying, no matter what we do. It's inevitable. Irreversible. We need to give it up, Uncle."

"Give it up," Yuri repeated. "You're asking us to embrace death, Grigory."

"No, sir. I'm asking you to embrace life. We *know* what some of the Befores are capable of. We've made them the study of generations. Now—while the old ones still function and can serve as a baseline—now's the time for us to start trying to build our own, based in science that we understand."

"Grig," said Raisy, "some of that tech does stuff that is *no way* based in science we understand."

"That's right," he said, turning to face her. "That's right. And we been lucky—lucky that all we did was lose a ship every now an' then, or a couple arms and legs from somebody getting careless with a light-wand. Do you thank the ghosts of space that we never come across a planet-cracker? Do you, Raisy? I do."

"We don't know that they built planet-crackers."

"Do we know that they didn't?" he countered.

She said nothing.

"Grigory," Uncle said, talking soft, like maybe Grig needed calming down. "Where, exactly, is Arin's brother?"

"Arin's *son*," Grig snapped, and closed his eyes. "He's 'prenticed to Master Trader Norn ven'Deelin. Jethri's good at the trade—got a real flair for it. Wouldn't surprise me if Master Trader ven'Deelin sets him up as the first trader fully licensed by Terra and by Liad, both. It's sure how I'd work it, given what we're seeing at trade level."

"And where," Uncle continued, "are Arin's notes?"

Grig shrugged. "Jeth's got 'em, if anybody does. Understand, Iza went a little crazy when Arin died, spaced a lot stuff right off. Cris talked her into stowing the rest 'til she was cooler. That's what went after Jethri—the rest. His by right." He grinned. "Which you can't dispute."

"Of course not." Uncle put his hands flat on the desk and pushed down, though he didn't quite stand up.

"Grigory, it is time for you to return to the bosom of your family. We have need of your talents and your…particular… viewpoint."

"No."

Uncle blinked. "I beg your pardon?"

"I said," Grig explained, and not daring to look at Raisy. "No. I'm staying with the *Market.*"

"Grig…" Raisy began, but he shook his head without looking at her yet, and rose to his full, gangly height.

"Sorry to leave so soon, sir," he said to Uncle, real polite. "But, like I said, I've got business elsewhere." At last he looked at his sister.

"Favor, Raisy."

"You got it," she answered, which he'd known she would.

"Keep that headcase you got working for you away from Seeli. He wants to talk to Paitor, that's your business, I guess. But you oughta know he was asking for duplicating units."

She nodded. "I'll take care of it."

"Good," he said and smiled, warmed, and feeling a little gone in the guts. Uncle allowed deviance, but there was always a price.

"Grigory, if you leave this room, you no longer have any call on us." Uncle's voice was cool, spelling out exactly how much this was gonna cost. Grig nodded.

"I can afford that, sir," he said, his own voice just as cool. "Good-bye, now."

He walked out and neither one stopped him, down the long hall, to where the lift stood, door open, waiting.

"HEALER HALL IS sending one of the masters," Miandra said, her voice a little stronger, and her hair neatly combed behind her ears. "I wonder who will arrive first?"

They were sitting in the parlor where Jethri had first met Lady Maarilex, in company with Norn ven'Deelin—and wouldn't he give a can full of canaries to see her walk through the door right now! Jethri had changed his sliced shirt for a whole one, taking a moment to marvel at the pale pink lines down his chest, each of which matched a cut in the ruined shirt. There hadn't been much time to wonder about it, though, and he'd hurried into the fresh shirt, hauled a brush over his hair, which mostly stayed flat, for a wonder, and run downstairs, to this very parlor, to find Miandra ahead of him, seated in the precise center of the white couch, one hand a fist around her ruby, and her face outright gloomy.

"Maybe," Jethri offered, deliberately trying to lighten her gloom, "the Healer and the Scout will arrive together and will entertain each other, leaving us free for other endeavors."

She didn't smile. He thought she clenched the ruby tighter.

The silence grew. Jethri shifted in his chair, looked around the room, and back at Miandra. She was staring, with great intensity, at a spot he calculated to be some ten feet beneath the vermillion floorboards.

Jethri cleared his throat. "An…unusual…thing," he said. "When I took my shirt off, there were these pink stripes—like brand-new scars—down my chest. I had expected, because there was blood, you know, to have found fresh cuts."

Miandra looked up. "Flinx was frightened," she said, as she had in the winery. "He is a very strong cat, and I am afraid he clawed you rather badly. The adrenaline masked the pain, but you would have felt it soon enough, so Meicha Healed you."

Sitting in the chair, he heard the words, blinked, listened to them again in his mind's ear, and then repeated the phrase, with the inflection that signaled a query: "Meicha Healed me?"

Miandra's mouth tightened. "Indeed. It is what we train to be—Healers. Meicha is—more skilled than I."

"Oh." He considered that, running his hand absently down his chest. No pain. He looked, tucking his chin in order to stare down his own front. No blood on the fresh shirt. Beyond dispute, he was patched, but—

"She—you—can make fresh wounds into new scars? In moments? How?"

Miandra moved her shoulders. "It is a talent, much like a talent for music, perhaps—or trade. For those of us with the particular talent to Heal, the...physics...and the methods are obvious. Intuitive." She smiled, very faintly. "Control is what must be taught, and...efficient use of one's energy."

Right. He had the idea she was simplifying things in order to save his feelings and almost laughed, considering what he carried around in his pocket.

"What else do Healers do?" he asked, to keep her talking, mostly. Talking, she seemed less gloom-filled, more like her usual self.

"Heal afflictions of the spirit. That is why a Healer is most often called. Someone is—sick at heart, or frightened. Perhaps they see things which are not there, or refuse to see those things which are directly before them. Those sorts of things. Physical Healing—there are not many Healers who can do that." Her face lightened a little—with pride, he thought. "Meicha will be a Healer to behold."

Well, that wasn't too unlikely, he allowed, given Meicha. But, wait—

"So it was—you or Meicha—who calmed me down that first day, when the curtains were open and I had the widespaces panic?"

"Yes," she said. "I calmed you and Meicha closed the curtains. It was not very difficult—you project a very solid...pattern, we call it. You are extremely easy to work with."

He didn't know as he particularly liked the sound of that, but before he could pursue the matter the door to the parlor opened and Lady Maarilex entered, leaning heavily on her cane and followed by a ginger-haired man whose thinness was accentuated by his black leather clothing.

"Scout Lieutenant Fel Dyn yo'Shomin," said the old woman. "Here is Jethri Gobelyn, foster son of ven'Deelin. Jethri, if you please, make your bow to the Lieutenant."

Cautiously, Jethri rose, and Lieutenant yo'Shomin's ginger-colored eyes followed his progress. There was something in the man's stance that irritated Jethri straight off. A little bit of a thrust in the shoulder, maybe, or an attitude with respect to the hips—a subtle something that said Scout Lieutenant yo'Shomin was the better of most men alive, and infinitely superior to grimy Terran 'prentice traders, no matter whose foster son they claimed to be.

That being his reading of the man, in between the time it took to start to rise and reach his full height, he made short shrift of the bow—crisp and brief, it was, and it could be that it would have given Master tel'Ondor pleasure. Certainly, its recipient took the point, and his sharp face got even sharper, the narrow mouth thinning 'til the lips all but disappeared.

The return bow was hardly more than a heavyish tip of the head, which was arrogant, but, then, Jethri thought, wasn't that what he had expected?

"It has been reported that you have in your possession a piece of forbidden technology," the lieutenant said, not even trying to sound polite. "You will surrender it at once."

"No." It had been his intention to hand the device over to the Scout. It was possible, after all, that the thing *had* somehow called the big wind, and if that was so, then it was better off in the keeping of folks who knew its treacheries. Too bad for him, the Scout had shown him reason to doubt. He'd rather take his own chances with the device than meekly hand it over to this...incompetent.

Jethri crossed his arms over his chest like Uncle Paitor did to show there was no joking going on, and added an out-and-out frown, for good measure.

The ginger-haired Scout drew himself up as tall as he could and delivered a respectable glare.

"The Scouts have jurisdiction in this. You will relinquish the dangerous device to me immediately."

Jethri kept the frown in place. "Prove it," he said.

The ginger eyebrows pulled together. "What?"

"Prove that the device is dangerous," Jethri said.

The Scout stared.

"Well," Lady Maarilex said, still leaning on her cane next to the door. "I see that this may be amusing, after all. Miandra, child, help me to the chair, of your goodness. If you please, gentlemen—a moment."

"Yes, Aunt Stafeli." Miandra leapt up and moved to the old lady's side, solicitously guiding her the first of the blue chairs, and seeing her seated.

"Yes—ah. A pillow for my back, child—my thanks." Lady Maarilex leaned back in the chair and put her cane by. Miandra took a step toward the couch—"Bide," Lady Maarilex murmured, and Miandra drifted back to stand at the side of the chair, hands folded demurely, her pendant—Jethri blinked. There was something odd about her pendant, like it was—

"Now," said Lady Maarilex, "the play may continue. The line is yours, Lieutenant. You have been challenged to prove that the device is dangerous. How will you answer?"

For a heartbeat, the Scout said nothing, then he bowed, very slightly, to the old woman in the chair, and glared up into Jethri's face.

"The device described by Lord Ren Lar Maarilex as being in the possession of the Terran Jethri Gobelyn, is unquestionably of the forbidden technology. The form and appearance of such things are well known to the Scouts, and, indeed, to Lord Maarilex, who has attended several seminars offered by the Scouts on the subject of the Old War and its leavings."

"Adequate," commented Lady Maarilex, "but will it compel your opponent?"

Jethri shrugged. "I admit that the device is Old Technology," he told Lieutenant yo'Shomin. "You, sir, stated that it is *dangerous*, an assertion you have not yet proved."

The Scout smiled. "It called the wind-twist, did it not? I think we may all agree that wind-twists are dangerous."

"Undoubtedly, wind-twists are dangerous," Jethri said. "But you merely put yourself in the position of needing to prove

that the device created the wind-twist—and I do not believe
you can do that, sir."

"No?" The Scout's smiled widened. "The weather charts
describe a most unusual wind pattern, spontaneously forming
from conditions antithetical to those required to birth a wind-
twist—and yet a wind-twist visited the Maarilex vineyard, a
very short time after you were seen experimenting with the
forbidden technology."

"I was the one," Miandra said, quietly, from the side of the
chair, "who touched the icon for 'wind-twist'."

"And yet," Jethri countered, keeping his eyes on the Scout's
face, "wind-twists do sometimes arrive out of season. I wonder if the same weather pattern anomaly was present on those
past occasions, as well."

"Well played!" Lady Maarilex applauded from the blue
chair. "Bravo!"

The Scout glowered. "Certainly, they would be," he
snapped. "Out of season wind-twists must obey the same
rule that forms all wind-twists."

"Then you agree," Jethri pursued, "that, unless it was
proven in the case of all out-of-season wind-twists that they
were every one created by grubby Terrans playing with Old
Technology, it is at least just as likely—if not more likely—
that the device which I own, and which was given me by a
kinsman, is a *predictor*, rather than an agent to form weather."

Not bad, he congratulated himself, though, truth told, he
didn't quite buy in to his own argument...

"This is a waste of my time," the Scout snarled. "You may
well have possession of a device that cures blindness, restores
lost youth, and everything else that is wholly beneficial—and
*still* it would be forfeit! Forbidden technology is *forbidden*, in all
its manifestations."

*So much for that*, Jethri thought. *You didn't really think this
was gonna work, did you kid?*

Truth told, he hadn't. On the other hand, it was a poor
trader who admitted defeat so easily. What was it Uncle Paitor

had said? About keeping your opposite in a trade uncertain on his feet, to your best profit?

Jethri inclined his head and changed trajectory.

"I am a Terran citizen," he said.

"Ah," Lady Maarilex murmured.

"As anyone can see," the Scout replied, nastily. "However, the point is unimportant. You are currently in Liaden space and are subject to Liaden law and regulations."

"Hah!" said Lady Maarilex.

Jethri raised a hand. "I am a Terran citizen and the device you wish to confiscate is a gift from a kinsman. Thus far, I have only your assertion that the confiscation of Old Technology falls into the duty of the Scouts. I will see the regulation in question before I relinquish what is mine." He lowered his hand. "Nor will I relinquish it to you, sir."

"You…" the lieutenant breathed and Jethri could see him tally up the insult and store it away for later Balancing. Much luck to him.

"I will relinquish the device—if it is proved that I must relinquish it at all—to Scout Captain Jan Rek ter'Astin."

There was a long moment of silence, strongly tinged with disbelief.

"Scout Captain ter'Astin is a field Scout," the lieutenant said, with a slight edge of distaste on the word *field*. "It will take some time to locate him, during which time the device will remain a danger to us all."

"Scout Captain ter'Astin was seen as recently as Day sixty-six at Kailipso Station, and I am persuaded that you will find him there still, for he had just recently been transferred," Jethri countered.

"Send for him," Miandra said, sharp and unexpected. "Jethri will swear not to use the device until the captain comes to claim it. And it will be better to give it over into the hands of a field Scout than a man who prefers the comforts of the regulations and his own bed—and who cares not to associate with *beastly Terrans*."

The Scout gaped at her.

"Do I have that correctly?" she asked, and there was a wild note to her voice that lifted the hairs up straight on Jethri's nape.

The Scout bowed, with precision, and straightened, his ginger-colored eyes like stone. "You have that most precisely," he said. "Dramliza."

Jethri shivered. Miandra had just made an enemy. A powerful enemy, with her stuck to the same ball of mud and not able to lift ship out of trouble...

"There are no dramliz in this house," Lady Maarilex snapped. "Merely two young Healers who are fond of parlor tricks."

"Of course," the Scout said cordially, and bowed once more.

"I will have the oath the *Healer* has promised for you," he said to Jethri. "And then I will go."

Jethri hesitated, wondering what this fellow might accept as a valid oath—and nearly laughed, despite the worry and upset in the air.

"I swear on my name—Jethri Gobelyn—that I will not use the Old Technological device and that I will hold it safe and harmless until such time as it is claimed by Scout Captain ter'Astin, bearing the regulation giving him the right."

"Witnessed," murmured Lady Maarilex.

Scout Lieutenant Fel Dyn yo'Shomin bowed. "On behalf of the Scouts, I accept your oath. Captain ter'Astin shall be summoned."

"Good," said Jethri. "I look forward to seeing him."

THE SCOUT WAS gone, intercepted by a pale-faced Meicha at the hall door. Jethri let out a long, quiet sigh, and very carefully didn't think about what he had just done.

"Miandra," Lady Maarilex said, very quietly.

"Yes, aunt?"

"May I ask at what date and time you lost your wits?"

Silence.

Slowly, Jethri turned. Miandra was standing, rigid, eyes straight ahead, hands fisted at her sides. The ruby pendant swung in an arc at the end of its long silver chain.

"Your ruby," he said, seeing it now. "It's melted."

Miandra shot him a look from eloquent sapphire eyes, though what they were eloquent of he couldn't exactly have said. A bid for allies—it might be that, though what she thought he might do to divert one of Lady Maarilex's high octane scolds, he didn't know.

"Melted?" the old lady repeated, frowning up at Miandra. "Nonsense. Do you have idea how much heat is required to melt a—" Her voice died. Miandra closed her eyes, her mouth a white line of pinched-together lips.

"Give it to me," Lady Maarilex said, absolutely neutral.

Eyes closed, fists at her sides, Miandra stood like a life-size doll.

"Now," said Lady Maarilex.

Miandra wet her lips with her tongue. "If not this error, another," she said, speaking rapidly, raggedly, her eyes screwed tight. "I cannot—Aunt Stafeli. It is—too big. I drown in it. Let it be known, and done."

"Done it surely will be, witless child!" Lady Maarilex held out an imperious hand. "Give me the pendant!"

The last was said with enough force that Jethri felt his own muscles jerk in response, but still Miandra stood there, rigid, willfully disobedient, with tears starting to leak from beneath her long dark lashes.

It came to Jethri in that moment, that, for all she sat there stern and awful, Lady Maarilex was frightened.

"Miandra," she said, very softly. "Child."

Miandra turned her face away.

He had no business interfering in what he didn't understand—and no possible right to short circuit whatever decision Miandra had made for herself. But Lady Maarilex was afraid—and he thought that whatever could scare her was something no lesser mortals ever needed to meet.

Jethri took three steps forward, caught the chain in one hand and the misshapen ruby in the other and lifted them over the girl's head.

Miandra made a soft sound, and brought her hands up to hide her face, shoulders shaking. Jethri stepped back, feeling awkward and more than a little scared himself, and dropped the pendant into the old woman's waiting palm.

"My thanks, young Jethri," she said. He looked down into her eyes, but all he saw was bland politeness.

"What's amiss, ma'am?" he asked, knowing she wouldn't answer him, nor did she surprise him.

"Nothing more than an unseemly display by a willful child," she said, and the pendant was gone, vanished into pocket or sleeve. "I ask that you not regard it."

*Right.* He looked at Miandra, her face still hidden in her hands. No question, Stafeli Maarilex was fearless—Miandra was no hide-me-quick, neither. Despite which, both her and her sister managed to mostly keep within the law laid down by their seniors, and answer up clear and sharp when they were asked a question. In his experience, willful disobedience wasn't their style—though he didn't put covert operations out of their range—no more than just standing by, crying.

"Hey," he said, and reached out to touch her sleeve. "Miandra, are you well?"

She sniffed, shoulders tensing, then very slowly lowered her hands, her chin coming up as they went down.

"Thank you," she said, with the dignity of a ship's captain. "Your concern warms me."

"Yes," he replied. "But are you well?"

Her lips moved—he thought it might have been a smile. "As well as may be," she answered, and seemed about to say something more, but the door came open just then and there was Meicha making her bow and announcing—

"Healer Tilba sig'Harat."

Jethri turned and dropped back a couple steps as the Healer strode into the room: Long in the leg—relatively speaking— and gaunt, her hair done in a single pale braid, falling over her shoulder to her belt. She was dressed in regulation calling clothes, and looked a little rumpled, like she had started her shift early and was looking to end it late.

"Healer," Lady Maarilex said, and inclined her head in welcome. "You honor us."

Tilba sig'Harat paused just before the chair, her head to one side. "The message did say that the matter was urgent."

"One's son certainly believed it to be so," Lady Maarilex replied, evenly.

So, Jethri thought, Ren Lar had called the Healers off his own board and his mother thought he'd overreacted. That could explain the particular sharpness of her tongue so far.

But it didn't explain the fear.

"Just so," the Healer was saying, and looked beyond Lady Maarilex to Miandra, who was standing tall now, chin up and face defiantly bland. "Miandra, your cousin has said that you told him you had held the wind-twist back from the vine-yard for a period of time before its strength overcame you. Is this correct?"

Miandra inclined her head. "It is."

"Ah. Would you care to explain this process of holding the wind back?"

Silence. Jethri, ignored, cast a quick glance aside and saw the girl lick her lips, her defiant chin losing a little altitude.

"Well?" asked the Healer, somewhat sharply. "Or is it that you cannot explain this process?"

Miandra's chin came back up.

"It is very simple," she said coolly. "I merely placed my will against the wind and—pushed."

"I—see." The Healer held up a hand. "Open for me, please."

The chin wavered; kept its position. Miandra closed her eyes and the Healer did the same. For the space of a dozen heartbeats, there was complete silence in the parlor, then Miandra sighed and the Healer opened her eyes and bowed to Lady Maarilex.

"I see that she believes what she has said, and that she has undergone a profound disturbance of the nerves. This is entirely commonplace; wind-twists unsettle many people. The hallucination—that she held back the winds until her friends reached her side—that is less common, but not unknown. In the immediacy of peril, knowing oneself helpless to aid those whom one holds dear, the mind creates a fantasy of power in which the wind is held back, the sea is parted, the avalanche turned aside. Sometimes, the mind remains convinced even after the peril has been survived. In its way, it is a kindly affliction, which is easily dispelled by a display of the facts—in this case, a recording of the path and pattern of the wind-twist."

Lady Maarilex inclined her head. "The child shall be shown the weather logs, Healer, I thank you." She moved a hand.

"Yes?" the Healer asked.

"You will see that Miandra has lost her apprentice's pendant in the wind. I would ask that the Hall send another."

A glance at Miandra showed her fingers curling into fists at her side, but no one was looking at Miandra except Jethri.

"Certainly," the Healer was saying to Lady Maarilex and Jethri cleared his throat.

"Well?" snapped Lady Maarilex, which Jethri chose, deliberately, to interpret as permission to speak.

He inclined his head. "If Healer sig'Harat pleases," he murmured, as polite as polite could be. "Isn't it possible that Miandra held the winds back? She and her sister do other things that seem just as impossible to myself, an ignorant Terran."

The Healer sent him a sharp glance.

"Jethri," Lady Maarilex murmured, "fostered of ven'Deelin."

"Ah." The Healer inclined her head.

"Certainly, Healers may work many marvels, young sir. But to do that which Miandra…believes herself to have done—that would require power and discipline as far from the abilities of a half-trained and erratic Healer as—as Liad is from Terra."

Well, and there was an answer that meant nothing at all, Jethri thought, though a quick glance at Miandra's rigid face suggested that maybe it meant something to her.

"Thank you, Healer," he said, politely. "I am grateful for the information."

"It is my pleasure to inform," she said, and bowed again to Lady Maarilex.

"My duty done, I depart," she said formally.

"Healer," the old lady replied. "We thank you for your care."

And so the Healer was hustled away by a pale-faced Meicha, the door closing behind both with a solid thump.

In the blue chair, Stafeli Maarilex stirred and reached for her cane.

"So, we survive this round," she said, using her cane as a lever, and struggling to get her feet under her. Jethri stepped forward and caught her arm to help her rise. Miandra held her position, face frozen.

"My thanks," Lady Maarilex gasped, straightening to her full height. She looked from one to the other and used her chin to point at the door.

"Both of you, go to your apartments. You will be served dinner there. Study, rest and recruit yourselves. It has been a long and tiring day—for all of us."

"Yes, Aunt Stafeli," Miandra said tonelessly. She bowed, stiffly, and was on her way toward the door before Jethri could do more than gape and make his own hurried bow.

By the time he reached the hallway, she was gone.

"WHERE'VE YOU BEEN?" Seeli asked, sharper maybe than she needed to.

*Balance of Trade*

On the other hand, Grig thought, taking a deep breath, a talk with Uncle had a way of making the whole universe seem edgy, if not outright dangerous.

"I left a message," he said, trying to trump sharp with mild.

"He left a message, the man says." Seeli flung her hands out in a gesture of wide frustration, by which he knew she wouldn't be bought by a smile and a cuddle. He closed his eyes, briefly. Dammit, he didn't *need* a fight with Seeli. Regardless of which, it looked like he was going to get one.

"*Yes*, you left a message," she snapped. "You left a message *six hours* ago saying you'd met an old mate and was going to share a brew. Six hours later, you manage to get your sorry self back to your ship—and you ain't even drunk!"

Trust Seeli to grab the whole screen in a glance. He was in for it bad, now—Seeli had a temper to match her mam's, except it was worse when she'd been worried.

Grig took another breath, looking for center. Despite that his whole life had been one form of lie or another, he'd never been near as casual with the truth as Arin. Well, and he was light on most all the family talents, wasn't he?

"Grig?"

He met her eye—nothing otherwise with Seeli—and cleared his throat. He'd worked this out, in the hours between leaving Uncle and arriving back at the lodgings. His choice was his choice, and he'd made it, for good or for bad. Despite which, there was family considerations. He owed Raisy and the rest of his sibs and cousins—and Uncle, too, damn him— the right to their own free lives. Parsing out his truth from their safety—that was what kept him hours on the Port, walking 'til his legs shook. He'd found what he believed to be a course that would pass close enough to the truth to satisfy Seeli, without baring the others to danger. Assuming he could find the brass to fly it.

"I gotta ask you again?" she said, real quiet.

He spread his hands. "Sorry, Seeli. Truth is, I wasn't straight in that message, and I'm not feelin' good about that.

What it was—you remember that headcase? Wantin' to buy fractins and Befores?"

He saw exasperation leach some of the mad out of her face, and took heart. Maybe he could pull this off, after all.

"Thought we agreed to leave that to Paitor."

"We did," he said. "We did—and I should've. No question, it was stupid. I figured, if I talked to the big man, I could show him there wasn't no sense promisin' to buy what we had none of, and tell him—" This was the approach to tricky. Grig kept his eyes straight on Seeli's. "Tell him that Arin's dead and the *Market* ain't in the business of sellin' Befores."

"Great," Seeli said, and shook her head. "So, what? The big man not at home?"

"He was home," Grig said, "and pleased to see me. Turns out, him, I knew—from the old days, when Arin was still Combine and we was dealing in the stuff pretty regular. Anyhow, He spent some considerable amount of persuasion, trying to get me to buy back in." He broke her gaze, then—it was that or die. "I'm not gonna hide it, Seeli—it was a mistake going to see this man."

She sighed. "If you'd called back, I'd've saved you the brain work. How much trouble you in?"

"Now, Seeli." He held up a hand and met her eyes, kinda half-shy. "I ain't in trouble. The man made me an offer—couple offers, as it happens. Didn't want to take 'no' for his final course, and it took some while to persuade him."

She frowned. "He likely to stay persuaded?" she asked, and trust Seeli to think of it. "Or might he want to talk to you again?"

"I—" Grig began.

The door to the hallway snapped open, spinning both of them around to stare as Paitor flung in, face flushed, and jacket rumpled.

Seeli started forward, hands out. "Uncle? What's gone wrong?"

He stopped and just stared down at her. Grig light-footed around him and pushed the door closed, resetting the lock.

"Got a beam from Khat," Paitor said as Grig made it back to Seeli's side. He put a hand inside his jacket and pulled out a piece of hardcopy—blue, with an orange stripe down the side. Grig felt his stomach clench. Priority beam—expensive, reserved for life and death or deals that paid out in fortunes…

"We got trouble," Paitor said, pushing the paper at Seeli. "Take a look."

HE SHOWERED, STANDING a long time under the pulsing rays of hot water, oblivious, for once, to the waste. By the time the water turned cool and he stepped out into the mirrored drying room, his fingertips were as wrinkled up as dried grapes, and he was feeling a little breathless from the steam.

Absently, he pulled the towel off its heated bar and applied it vigorously, first to his head and working methodically downward, where he noted that his toes were as wrinkled as his fingers.

*Probably your face is wrinkled up, too*, he thought, trying to josh himself out of a growing mood. *Bet your whole head's nothing but one big wrinkle.*

*Nothing more than I traded for*, he thought back at himself, in no state to be joshed, though he did, by habit, look into the mirror to see how bad his hair looked this time.

The hair was about as bad as he expected, but what made him frown was the smudge over his lip.

"Mud," he muttered. "All that time under water and your face isn't even clean?"

He used a corner of the towel to rub the smudge and looked again.

The smudge was still there, looking even darker against the pink rub mark.

"What the—" He leaned toward the mirror, frowning— and then lifted his hand, fingertips stroking the first hopeful hairs of a mustache.

"Well." He smiled at his reflection, and stroked the soft smudge again, then turned to the supply cabinet, in search of depilatory cream.

Several minutes later, he was frowning again. The supply cabinet was more comprehensive than most ship's medical lockers, and included several ointments that were meant to be rubbed into the skin—but nothing like a depilatory.

Sighing, Jethri closed the cabinet, and went to the bench where he had piled his fresh clothes. Tomorrow, he'd ask Mr. pel'Saba to provide the needed item. In the meantime, he had other rations to chew on.

Barefoot, shirt untucked, he walked into his sleeping room, and knelt next to the bench. Deliberately, he unsealed the B-crate and pulled open the big bottom hatch.

Deliberately, he removed the boxes of fractins, good and bad, the wire frame, and his old pretend trade journal and put them, one by one, on the rug by his knee.

Closing the crate, he settled down cross-legged and reached for the tattered little book, flipping through the laborious pages of lists—income, outgo, exchange rates and Combine discounts—

The door-chime sounded. Biting down on a curse, Jethri grabbed the box of true fractins—and then shook his head. No doubt fractins were Old Tech—and if Lady Maarilex or Ren Lar or the Scouts entire had decided that they was within their rights to search his room and belongings for Old Tech, then they'd find the fractins, whether they were on the rug or in the B-crate.

The door-chime sounded again.

On the other hand, it was probably one of the kitchen crew, come to collect his untouched dinner tray.

Sighing, Jethri came to his feet and went to answer the door.

The twins tumbled over the threshold and skittered 'round to the far side of the door.

"Close it!"

"Quickly, close it!"

So much for wilful disobedience. Still, he did close the door, and locked it for good measure.

The twins stood in a tangle beside the wall, their reddish hair damp and curling wildly. As usual, they were dressed identically, this time in plain black jerseys and slacks, soft black boots on their feet. One wore a silver chain 'round her neck, supporting a big ruby.

"I thought the pair of you were confined to quarters," he said, hands on hips, trying for the stern-but-friendly look Cris had employed on similar past occasions, with Jethri on the wrong side of the captain's word.

"And so we are in quarters," snapped the twin with the ruby 'round her neck. "Your quarters."

"Come, Jethri," said the other, stepping away from her sister's side and looking gravely up into his face. "We are in need of companionship—and counsel."

*Good line,* Jethri thought. He'd never been smart enough to come up with something half so clever for Cris.

And, besides, he was glad to see them.

He let his hands fall from his hips and waved them into the parlor. "Come in, then, and welcome."

"Thank you," they murmured in unison and drifted deeper into the room, silent on their soft boots. Meicha wandered over to the table, where his untasted dinner sat under covers. Miandra went further, to the window, and stood gazing out at the sunset clouds crowding the shoulders of the mountains. High up, where the sky was already darkening, stars could be seen, shimmering in the atmosphere.

"The wide spaces do not frighten you now?" She asked, and Jethri moved across the room to join her, bare feet soundless on the carpet.

"I am—becoming accustomed," he said, pausing just behind her shoulder, and looking out. There were purple shadows down deep in the folds of the rockface. 'way out, he could just see the Tower at the port, gleaming bright in the last of the sunlight.

"Mrs. tor'Beli sent delicacies," Meicha said from behind them. "Are you not hungry, Jethri?"

"Not much," he said, turning around to offer her a half-smile. "If you are hungry, have what you like."

She frowned, and put the lid back over the plate. "Perhaps later," she said, and sent an openly worried glance at Miandra's back.

"Sister?"

There was a pause, and a sigh. Miandra turned around and faced her twin.

"They are still arguing," she said.

"They are," Meicha replied. "And will be, I think, for some time. Aunt Stafeli will not yield the point. Nor yet will Ren Lar."

"Though surely it is his portion to yield to the word of the delm," said Miandra, "nadelm or no."

Meicha laughed. "Allow Ren Lar to tend the vines and he is complacent and calm. Invoke his melant'i as nadelm and remind him of his larger duty to the clan, and he is implacable." She paused, shrugged. "Aunt Stafeli trained him, after all."

Miandra actually smiled, though faintly. "True enough."

"What," asked Jethri, "are they arguing about? The Old Technology?"

Meicha and Miandra exchanged a glance.

"The Old Technology—that was the beginning," Meicha said, moving over to perch on the edge of one of his chairs, her ruby winking in the light. Miandra went forward and dropped to the rug at her twin's feet, legs crossed, face serious.

After a second, Jethri took the chair across, and leaned back, pretending he was comfortable.

"So," he said, "the argument started with the Old Technology."

"Just so," said Miandra. "Ren Lar, of course, wished the weather device to be away, *now*—the potential of harm to the vines distresses him, and rightly so. He *is* master of the vine, and it is his duty to protect and nourish them.

"Aunt Stafeli, however, felt that you had reckoned your melant'i correctly, that the Scout Lieutenant was well answered, and your oath rightly given. Ren Lar could scarcely argue with *that*."

Silence fell, stretched. Meicha was uncharacteristically quiet, sitting tense on the edge of the chair. Miandra—Miandra sat easily, her wrists resting on her knees, her fingers hanging loose, blue eyes considering a point just over his left shoulder.

Jethri cleared his throat; her eyes focused on his face.

"Yet, they are still arguing—your aunt and your cousin. About the two of you?"

"About *me*," Miandra said, with a depth of bitterness that startled him. Meicha reached down and put her hand on her sister's shoulder, but said nothing.

"It is well enough, to be a Healer," Miandra continued after a moment, her voice less bitter, though her eyes sparked anger. "But to be of the dramliz, here on Irikwae—that..." Her voice faded.

"Is untenable," Meicha finished quietly. "Irikwae was colonized by those clans who felt that the dramliz should be...should be..."

"Eradicated," Miandra said, and the bitterness was back in her voice. "It was believed that a mutation which allowed one such...abilities—that such a mutation endangered the entire gene pool. A purge was called for. The matter went to the Council of Clans, in very Solcintra, and debate raged for days, for who is truly easy in the presence of one who might hear your thoughts, or travel from port to center city in the blink of an eye? Korval Herself led the opposition, so the history texts tell us, and at last prevailed. The existing dramliz were allowed to live, unsterilized. The clans of the dramliz retained their rights of contract marriage, mixing their genes with the larger pool as they saw fit. And a guild was formed, much like the pilots guild, or traders guild, which gave the dramliz protection as a valuable commercial enterprise."

"The dissenting clans," Meicha said after a moment, "left the homeworld, and colonized Irikwae. At first, there was a ban on Healers, too. That was eventually lifted, as it became apparent that Healers worked for...social stability..."

Mentally breathless, Jethri held up a hand.

"Give me a little time," he said, and his voice sounded breathless, too. "Terrans do not commonly run to these mutations. You are the first Healer—and dramliza—I have encountered, and I am still not certain that I understand why one person who does things which are impossible is favored, while another, who does things which are just as impossible, is—feared."

Miandra actually grinned. "Prejudice is not necessarily responsive to cold reason—as you surely know."

He gaped at her, and Meicha laughed.

"Are all Grounders stupid? Why else would they live among the mud and the smells and the weather?"

"Ouch," he said, but mildly, because they were right—or had been right. "I am—growing accustomed—on that front, as well. Learning takes time."

"So it—" Meicha began—and froze, head turning toward the door.

It came again, a scratching noise, as if a file were being applied, lightly, to the hall side face of the door.

Jethri rose and crossed the room. Hand on the latch, he sent a glance to the twins, sitting alert in their places. Miandra moved her hand, motioning him to open the door.

All right, then. He snapped the lock off and turned the latch, opening the door wide enough to look out into—

An empty hall.

Frowning, he looked down. Eyes the color of peridot gleamed up at him; and something else as well.

Jethri stepped back. Flinx pranced across the threshold, head high, silver chain held in his mouth, ruby dragging on the floor beneath his belly. As soon as he was inside, Jethri closed and locked the door. By the time he turned back to the room, Flinx had reached Miandra.

She sat perfectly still as the big cat put his front feet on her knee. Slowly, she extended a hand and Flinx bent his head, dropping the chain on her palm.

"My thanks," she said, softly, and held it high. The melted ruby spun slowly in the light, glittering.

"Flinx is proud of himself," Meicha said. "Aunt Stafeli had thrown it in the bin for the incinerator."

Jethri came forward and knelt on the carpet next to Miandra and the cat. Flinx left the girl's knee and danced over to butt him in the thigh. Miandra looked up at him, blue eyes curious.

"May I see it?" he asked, and she put the chain in his hand without hesitation.

He sat back on his haunches and gave the thing some study. The fine silver links were neither deformed nor blackened. The ruby was—distorted, asymmetrical, the bottom bloated, as if it were an overfull water bulb, the force of the liquid within it distending the bulb nearly to the bursting point.

"So," he said, handing it back. "How did you do that?"

She moved her shoulders. "I—am not precisely certain. It—it may be that the gem, the facets, served as a focus for the power I expended but—I do not know!" she cried, sudden and shocking. "I need to be trained, before I—before…And all Aunt Stafeli will say is that I must be a Healer and a Healer only." She bent her head. "She does not know what it is like," she whispered. "I am—I am a danger."

He considered her. "Even if you cannot be trained on Irikwae, there are other places, isn't that so? Places where the guild of dramliz is recognized?"

"There are those a-plenty," Meicha said after Miandra had said nothing for half-a-dozen heartbeats. "The challenge lies in persuading Aunt Stafeli—and there we have been unsuccessful."

"What about Ren Lar?"

Meicha grimaced. "Worse and worse."

"Ren Lar," whispered Miandra, "sees the dramliz as no more nor less dangerous than the Old Technology." She laughed suddenly, and looked Jethri in the eye.

"Well, he is not so far in the wrong as that."

Despite himself, he grinned, then let it fade as he rocked off his knees and sat down on the carpet, crossing his legs in an awkward imitation of her pose.

"What about Master ven'Deelin?" he asked.

Two pair of sapphire blue eyes stared at him, blankly.

"What about her, I wonder?" asked Meicha.

"Well, she hails from Solcintra, on Liad, where the dramliz are allowed to go about their business unimpeded. She's your aunt's fosterling—who better to escort you?"

"Hear the lad," Miandra murmured, on a note of awe. "Sister—"

"We are still impeded," said Meicha. "Well to say that the ven'Deelin will escort you, yet it is empty hope unless Aunt Stafeli may be persuaded to let you go."

"Norn ven'Deelin is a master trader," Jethri commented, stroking Flinx's head while the big cat stood on his knee and purred.

"And master traders are all that is persuadable," Meicha concluded and inclined her head. "I take your point and raise another."

He moved his free hand in the gesture that meant "go on."

She took a deep breath. "It comes to me that Norn ven'Deelin—all honor to her!—may not love dramliz. Recall your first meal with us? And the ven'Deelin all a-wonder that there were dramliz in the house."

He had a particularly sharp memory of that meal, and he thought back on it now, looking for nuance he had been ill-able to detect, then...

"I think, perhaps," he said slowly, "that she was...joking. Earlier in the day—just before we met in the hall—I had understood that Lady Maarilex was about to read her a ringing scold for—for fostering a Terran and breaking with tradition. Seeing dramliz at the table, it might be that she merely remarked that she was not the only one who had broken with tradition."

"Hah," said Meicha, and bent her head to look at Miandra, who sat silent, running her chain through her fingers, eyes absent.

Jethri skritched Flinx under the chin.

"I judge that Jethri has the right of it," Miandra said abruptly. "Norn ven'Deelin has Aunt Stafeli's mark upon her. It is too much to hope that she would forgo her point, when the cards were delivered to her hand."

"True." Meicha slid back into her chair, looking relaxed for the first time since they had tumbled into his room. "The ven'Deelin is due back with us at the end of next relumma."

Jethri sent a glance to Miandra. "Can you hold so long?"

She moved her shoulders. "I will do what I might, though I must point out the possibility that the Scout Lieutenant will seek Balance."

"He would not dare!" Meicha declared stoutly. "Come against Aunt Stafeli in Balance? He is a fool if he attempts it."

"Jethri had already established him as a fool," Miandra pointed out. "And it was not Balance against the House that concerns me."

Meicha stared at her.

"He may try me, if he likes," Jethri said, the better part of his attention on Flinx.

"You are not concerned," Miandra murmured, and it was not a question. He looked up and met her eyes.

"Not overly, no. Though—I regret. He threatened you, and I did not understand that at the time. You need not be concerned, either."

Silence. Then Meicha spoke, teasing.

"You have a champion, sister."

"It was kindly meant," Miandra said placidly, and, deliberately, as if she had reached a firm decision, put the silver chain over her head. The deformed ruby swung once against her jersey, then stilled.

"I would like to hear more of this Scout captain you invoked over the head of the so-kind lieutenant," she said.

"I met him when I jumped off the edge of Kailipso Station," he began, and tipped his head, recalled of a sudden to his manners. "Would you like some tea?"

"Masterful!" Meicha crowed. "You have missed your trade, Jethri! You should 'prentice to a teller of tales."

He made his face serious, like he was considering it. "I don't think I'd care for that, really," he said, which earned him another crow of laughter.

"Wretch! Yes, tea, by all means—and hurry!"

Grinning, he put Flinx on the carpet and unwound, moving toward the galley. There, he filled the tea-maker, pulled the tray from its hanger and put cups on it. He added the tin of cookies Mrs. tor'Beli had given him a few days ago—it had been full, then; now it was about half-full. The tea-maker chimed at him; he put the pot on the tray and carried it out to the main room, being very careful of where he set his feet, in case Flinx should suddenly arrive to do his dance around Jethri's ankles.

He needn't have worried about that. The cat was sitting tall on the floor next to Miandra, tail wrapped tightly around his toes, intently observing the plates of goodies set out on the cloth from his table. The twins had set his neglected dinner out like party food. He grinned and went forward.

Meicha leapt to her feet and handed the cups, pot and tin down to Miandra, who placed them on the cloth. Jethri put the tray on the table and sat on the carpet between the two of them, accepting a cup of tea from Miandra with a grave inclination of his head.

"My thanks."

Meicha passed him a goody plate and he pinched one of the cheese roll-ups he was partial to and passed the plate around to Miandra. When they were all provided with food and tea, and each of them had taken a sip and a bite, Miandra looked up with a definite gleam in her eye.

"And, now, sir, you *will* tell us about your Scout captain and how it was you came to jump off the edge of a spacestation!"

He hid the grin behind another sip of tea. "Certainly," he murmured, as dignified as could be. "It happened this way..."

# Day 166
# Standard Year 1118

## *Elthoria*

"MASTER TRADER, THE captain bids me deliver this message to you." The first mate's voice was somber, and it was that which drew Norn ven'Deelin's attention away from the file she had under study. Gaenor tel'Dorbit was not a somber woman, and while she enjoyed a contract of pleasure with the librarian Norn had specifically instructed to deny her to all seekers, it could hardly be supposed that his melant'i was so lacking that he had let his paramour by on a mere whim.

Norn sighed. Somber first mates and disobedient, dutiful librarians. Surely, the universe grew too complex. She looked up.

Gaenor tel'Dorbit bowed and produced from her sleeve a folded piece of green priority paper.

The paper crackled as Norn received it and glanced at the routing line.

"Hah," she said, extending it. "Pray have communications forward this to my son at Irikwae."

The first mate bit her lip. "Master Trader," she said, more somberly, if possible, than previously, "the captain bids me deliver this message to you."

Oh, and indeed? Norn looked again at the routing: from Khatelane Gobelyn. The pilot cousin, was it not? And the same who had written before. That she sent now a priority message—that was notable. It was also notable that it had been some days in transit, for Khatelane had sent it to Avrix, where *Elthoria* would have been, had the schedule not been amended.

She glanced up at Gaenor tel'Dorbit, who was watching her with no small amount of anticipation. It came to her that Gaenor read Terran well and would certainly have been asked by the communications officer to vet a message written in Terran. She had also taken a liking to Jethri himself, saying that he reminded her pleasantly of the young brothers she left at home. Which handily explained, Norn thought, Kor Ith yo'Lanna's involvement in the proper disposition of a letter meant for a mere apprentice of trade.

"I expect," she said gently to Gaenor's tense face, "to read that Jethri's honored mother, Captain Iza Gobelyn, has passed from this to a more gentle plane, and that Jethri is called back to his kin, to mourn."

"Master Trader," the first mate inclined her head slightly. "To my knowledge, the health of Jethri's honored mother remains robust."

Well. Obviously, she was not going to be quit of Gaenor until she had read and made some disposition of Jethri's letter.

Leaning back in her chair, she flicked the page open and began, laboriously, to read.

> *Dear Jethri,*
> *Never thought I'd be sending you a Priority, but I think I made a bad situation worse for you, so I'm sending a heads-up quick.*
> *I'm here on Banthport at the Trade Bar and run into Keeson Trager and Coraline.*
> *Bunch of Liadens on the place, which don't figure, because you know as well as me, Jeth, Banth doesn't have nothing but the gold mines. But, anyhow, lots of Liadens, and one of them hears Kee name me. Pretty boy, in a skinny, sulky sort of way. Name of Barjohn Shelgaybin, near as I can make out. Said he knows you, that you lost him a brother, and you didn't settle up like you should've.*

*Said, that being so, and me standing right there, he could take exact balance, or I could pay him four hundred cantra in compensation, which, if I could've done I wouldn't've been at Banth on Kinaveralport business, because I'd be captain-owner of a brand-new Cezna with nothing less than twelve pod-mounts.*

*So, it was stupid, and I figure it's best for all to leave, except he up and grabs me and—I decked him. Conked his head on the floor and went out cold. Another boy tells me I got safe passage—though he didn't tell me his name— so I left it and come back to the crash. I'm sending this to Elthoria, and a copy to Paitor.*

*For what it's worth, Farli Trager worked out the names of the Liaden ships on Banth:* Winhale, Tornfall, Skeen, Brass Cannon. *Don't know which your friend is off of, but you might, if he hasn't made the whole thing up out of spare parts.* Skeen *and* Brass Cannon *hold Combine keys.*

*I'm real sorry, Jeth, and I hope you're OK. If this is some kind of Liaden blood feud, let us know, will you? If that pretty boy's a headcase, let us know that, too—and tell us how you're getting on.*

*I'm gone by the time you get this—follow-ups to Paitor at Terratrade, Kinaveral.*

*Love,*
*Khat*

Norn ven'Deelin folded the sheet and put it, carefully, atop the reader. She sat for a few heartbeats, eyes on the green paper, then looked up to Gaenor tel'Dorbit, standing patiently, her hands tucked into her belt, her face tense—worried. And she was right to worry, Norn thought. Indeed she was.

"So," she said softly. "I am informed. Of your goodness, First Mate, ask Arms Master sig'Kethra to join in my office for prime in—" she glanced at the clock—"one hour."

"Master Trader." Gaenor bowed, relief palpable, as if the problem—the problems—were now solved, with Jethri and his kin rendered impervious to chel'Gaibin spite. If only it were so.

The first mate removed herself from the study room. Norn ven'Deelin sat quietly for half-a-dozen heartbeats more, then slipped the green letter away into her sleeve, marked her place in the file, and went over to the wall unit to call the kitchen and alert the cook to her need for a working dinner for two to arrive in her office in an hour.

"So," PEN REL said, putting the green paper down and reaching for his wine. "The chel'Gaibin heir aspires to the melant'i of a port tough. Are you surprised?"

"Alas, I am not—and we will not discuss what that might say about ven'Deelin's melant'i." She sipped her own wine, staring sightlessly at the meal neither had addressed with vigor.

"What I believe we have, old friend," she murmured, "is a play in two acts. I hope that you will lend me the benefit of your wisdom in crafting an appropriate answer to each."

"Now, I know a matter to be dire when ven'Deelin comes to me with sweet words of flattery in her mouth," he commented, irreverently. "All I have is yours to command. Has it ever been otherwise?"

"Surely, it must have been, at one time—but, stay! I will not insult you with more flattery. As I said, a play in two acts, their separate action linked by the chel'Gaibin heir. Indeed, if what I believe is true, I can only suppose Infreya chel'Gaibin to be in a goodly rage regarding the heir's impromptu freelancing—for I believe the approach upon young Khatelane to be nothing more nor less than a moment seized to determine what profit might be wrung from it. And why, you may wonder, would Infreya chel'Gaibin be quite so angry at her heir's attempt to terrorize a mere Terran?"

"The ships," Pen Rel murmured. "The transliterations are…challenging. However, if the name the pilot renders as

*Brass Cannon* is, indeed, our own beloved *Bra'ezkinion*, then it's certain there's piracy afoot."

"And if *Tornfall* may be discovered to be *Therinfel*, we may add mayhem to the brew," Norn said, and fell silent for a long moment, her wineglass forgotten in her hand.

Pen Rel reached out and captured the letter, frowning at the Terran words.

"The pilot is right to wonder," he said eventually, "what interest Banth holds for such a mixed flight of ships—" He looked up and made a rueful face. "Only hear me assume that *Wynhael* stands in association with *Bra'ezkinion* and *Therinfel*."

"Not invalid, I think," Norn said, absently. "Not invalid. I allow the pilot to be a clever child and her questions on-point. For, indeed, there *is* nothing to want at Banth that cannot be had elsewhere, with less cost and more convenience. And yet four Liaden ships—two of them known to us as rogues, in addition to the most excellent *Wynhael*, and the as-yet-undiscovered *Skeen*—simultaneously converge upon this port. Credulity strains to the breaking point, my friend."

"Past the breaking point, I would say. So, Master Trader, what is there to want at Banth, after all?"

She glanced at him, eyes gleaming. "How many times must I explain that the skills of a master trader are not those of the dramliz?"

"Until I lay down my last duty, I expect," he retorted. "I have seen you too often work magic."

"Pah! Now who flatters whom, sir? However, your question has merit, despite your deplorable manners. What, indeed, does Banth have which is desirable and has been overlooked, thus far, by all?" She moved her hand, discovered the wine glass and sipped.

"I do not know. And perhaps I may never know. However, the convergence of those four ships—two rejoicing in substantial Guild misdemeanor files—allows me to call upon the masters of trade to interview the traders involved, immediately, to determine if there has been any breach of Guild rule."

"Thereby infuriating Infreya chel'Gaibin and the so-honorable heir."

"Very possibly," Norn agreed, tranquilly. "But Infreya will not resist a Guild investigation—she is, when all is counted, too canny a trader to bargain for her own downfall. It must be in her best interest to cooperate with the Guild—and that is where we gain the small hope that we will, after all, learn what it is that Banth has of value."

"You will need to know for certain the names of those ships," Pen Rel said. "I will undertake that proof."

"I thank you," she smiled, briefly, and sipped her wine. "So, that act. The second, I own, may be knottier, for it involves dramliz skills. One or both of us must look into the future and see whether chel'Gaibin will pursue its false Balance against Gobelyns, all and sundry, and, if they will, what measures we must take—in protection, I would say, preferring not to wait upon the necessity of retribution."

"I understand." He considered the matter for some time, frowning abstractedly at the table top. Norn sipped her wine and waited for him to return to himself.

"I believe that the larger population of Gobelyns need have no fear that the chel'Gaibin heir will attempt to pursue his Balance," he said after a considerable time had passed. "Like you, I consider that the attack upon Pilot Gobelyn was an opportunistic act, which it is unlikely he will repeat."

"Unlikely? Tell me why you say so."

He rattled the green paper. "The pilot states that she knocked him down for his impertinence in laying a hand upon her—and rightly so, may I say. You, yourself, know well that chel'Gaibins have no taste for being knocked down. I would consider that the encounter with the pilot will have provided a laudatory lesson to the heir." He raised his glass.

"And, too, when does *Wynhael* run so far out? Further opportunity to meet Gobelyns must be limited by the usual routes pursued by both."

"Fair enough," Norn murmured, "though I submit that *Wynhael* was at Banth as nearly as a few days ago."

"An isolated incidence, I believe," Pen Rel said stoutly. "I think we may assume that Gobelyns as a set reside at a safe distance from chel'Gaibins of any sort." He sipped his wine. "No, where we must focus our concern, I believe, is upon Jethri, who is at this moment well within Liaden space and, while more tutored regarding the rules of Balance than his most excellent kinswoman, is perhaps not as conversant with nuance as one might like."

"He has been living this while in the house of my foster mother," Norn said dryly. "Be assured that he will by this time be breathing and dreaming nuance. However, your point is taken. One does not leave an inexperienced player unshielded to danger. We know that Bar Jon chel'Gaibin has publicly proposed a grievance against Jethri Gobelyn—" she fluttered her fingers at the paper in his hand. "He must pursue satisfaction, or his melant'i suffers."

Pen Rel snorted. "As if it had not already. Shall we to Irikwae, then?"

She moved a shoulder. "Alas, we cannot. The cargo we have guaranteed for Lylan—"

"Ah," he murmured. "I had forgotten."

Norn sipped her wine. "Immediately, let us beam to Tarnia, with full particulars and a request to be vigilant. We have a little time, I calculate, purchased by the Guild investigation. We will fulfill our contract, and transship what we may." She sighed. "Gar Sad will pin my ears to my head."

"Of course he will." Pen Rel put his glass and the letter on the table and came to his feet, not quite as lightly as was his wont. "You will have clear proof of the ships involved by the end of next shift."

She smiled at him. "Old friend. My thanks to you, on behalf of my student and son."

"My student, also, remember," he said bowing lightly. "By your leave, Norn."

She flicked a hand in bogus impatience. "Go then, if you are so eager for work."

He smiled, placed his hand briefly over his heart, and left her.

# Day 166
# Standard Year 1118

## Irikwae

THE ALARM CHIMED, insistent. Jethri groaned and resisted the temptation to push his head under the bank of pillows to shut out the noise.

The chime grew louder. Manfully, Jethri flung the sheets back, got his feet on the floor. A few steps brought him to the alarm, which he disarmed, and then simply stood there, savoring the silence.

The clock displayed a time a few minutes later than his usual waking hour, which meant he was going to have to engage jets to get to breakfast on time. He yawned, the idea of engaging jets infinitely less attractive than collapsing back onto the bed and taking another half-shift of sleep.

Instead, he moved, at something less than his usual speed, on course for the 'fresher.

The twins had stayed late, trading stories of their own for his of Kailipso Station and Scout Captain ter'Astin, until Miandra looked out the window.

"The third moon has set," she said, whereupon Meicha pronounced the word Jethri considered to be the Liaden rendering of "mud!" and they both jumped up and took their leave, with smiles and wishes for his sweet dreaming, flitting like the ghosts of space down the dim-lit hall, Flinx the ghost of a cat, weaving 'round their silent feet.

Trouble was, he hadn't been at all sleepy and had spent some time more huddled over his old "trade journal," until he realized he had read the same entry three times, without making sense of it once, closed the old book and gone to bed.

Two hours ago.

He stepped into the shower and punched the button for *cold*, gasping when the blast hit him. Quickly, he soaped and rinsed, then jumped out, reaching for the towel. Drying briskly, he glanced in the mirror—and glanced again, moving closer and touching his upper lip, where last evening a hopeful mustache sprouted.

Gone now, stroked into oblivion by Meicha's magic fingers.

"I don't know how long that will last," she had said, half-scolding. "But you really *can*not, Jethri, go among polite people with hair on your face."

"I was going to ask Mr. pel'Saba for depilatory, tomorrow," he'd said, and Miandra had laughed, reaching over her twin's shoulder to put her palm against his cheek.

"He would not have had the least idea what you asked for," she said. "Leave it to Meicha until you may purchase some of this substance for yourself, perhaps at the port?"

"*Miandra...*" Meicha hissed, and her sister laughed again and withdrew her hand, leaving Jethri wishing that she hadn't.

In the bedroom, the alarm began again, signaling five minutes until breakfast.

Jethri swore and jumped for his closet.

THE BREAKFAST ROOM was empty, for all the food was laid out just like always on the long sideboard and the places were at the table set in the tall windowed alcove overlooking the flower garden. Someone had thought it a mellow enough day to prop open the middle pane, and the smells of flowers and growing things danced into the room on the back of a dainty little breeze.

Jethri paused at the window, looking out over the banks of sweet smelling, prickle stemmed flowers that Lady Maarilex favored.

The garden appeared as always: pink and white blossoms crowding the stone pathways; the sunlight dappled with shade from the tall tree at the garden's center. Nothing seemed disturbed by yesterday's rogue wind.

"Good morning, Master Jethri," murmured a voice grown very familiar to him. Jethri turned and inclined his head.

"Mr. pel'Saba." He looked into the butler's bland, give-nothing face. "I fear I have overslept."

"If you did, it was not by many minutes," the old man said. "However, Master Ren Lar went early to the vines—and Mrs. tor'Beli has instructions to send a tray up to their ladyships." That would be Meicha and Miandra, Jethri thought with a start.

"For yourself…" Mr. pel'Saba continued, reaching into his sleeve and producing a creamy, square envelope, "there is a letter."

A letter. Jethri took the envelope with a small bow, finger-tips tingling against the kiss of high-rag paper. "My thanks."

"It is my pleasure to serve," Mr. el'Saba assured him. "Please enjoy your breakfast. If anything is required, you have but to ring." He bowed and was gone, vanishing through the door at the back of the room.

Jethri turned his attention to the envelope. An irregular blob of purple wax glued the flap shut; pressed into the wax was a design. He brought the blob closer to the end of his nose, squinting—and recognized the sign of the traders guild.

Reverently, he flipped the creamy square over and stood staring at the name, written in purple ink the exact shade of the lump of sealing wax, the Liaden letters a thought too ornate: Jeth Ree ven'Deelin.

*Now*, he thought, *here's a message.* If only he knew how to read it.

Sighing, the envelope heavier in his hand than its weight accounted for, Jethri went to the sideboard, poured himself a cup of tea, and carried both to his usual place at the breakfast table. Only when he had seated himself and taken a sip of tea, did he slip his finger under the purple wax and break the seal.

Inside the envelope was a single sheet of paper, folded once in the middle. It crackled crisply when he unfolded it to find five precise lines, written in that over-ornate hand:

> *Jeth Ree ven'Deelin, apprentice to Master Trader Norn ven'Deelin, will present himself at Irikwae Guildhall on Standard Day 168 at sixth hour, local in order to undertake testing for certification. The course will encompass one-half relumma. The candidate will be housed at the guildhall for the duration of the certification program.*

That was it, the last line being a signature so over-written as to be nearly unreadable. Jethri sipped his tea, frowning at the thing until he finally puzzled out: *Therin yos'Arimyst, Hall Master, Irikwae Port.*

"Such a studious demeanor so early in the day!" Lady Maarilex remarked a few moments later, stumping to a halt on the threshold of the breakfast room. "Truly, Jethri, you are an example to us all."

He put the letter down next to his teacup and rose, crossing the room to offer her his arm.

"After yesterday, I wonder that you can say so, ma'am," he murmured, as he guided her to her usual place, and pulled back her chair.

She laughed. "Certainly, the portions of your yesterday which I was privileged to observe seemed to go very well, indeed. Your demeanor before the Scout Lieutenant—I live in the liveliest anticipation of sharing the tale with your foster mother."

*Oh, really?* "Do you think she will enjoy it, ma'am?" he asked.

She looked up at him, old eyes sparkling.

"Immensely, young Jethri. Immensely."

"Well, then," he said, with a lightness he didn't particularly feel, "I will judge that I have acquitted myself well, in the matter of the Scout." He paused. "May I bring you something, ma'am?" he asked, since neither Meicha nor Miandra was there to perform the service.

"Tea, if you will, child, and a bit of the custard."

He moved off to fulfill this modest commission, and returned to the table with tea and custard, and a sweet roll for himself.

"Ma'am, I wonder," he said, glancing at the letter as he took his place. "Does Hall Master Therin yos'Arimyst hold Master ven'Deelin in despite?"

She paused with her teacup halfway to her lips and shot him a sharp glance over the rim.

"Now, here's a bold start. What prompts it?"

Wordlessly, he passed her the letter and the envelope.

"Hah." She put her cup down, read the letter in a glance, considered the envelope briefly, and put both on the table between them.

"He gives you little enough time to arrive," she commented, reaching for her custard. "Today, you will pack—take what books you will from the library, too. I recall Norn telling us that there was precious little to read at the hall, saving manifests and regulations."

"Thank you, ma'am," he murmured, genuinely warmed.

A flick of her fingers dispensed with his thanks. "As to the other... Despite—perhaps not, though I would be surprised to learn that Therin yos'Arimyst counted Norn ven'Deelin among his favored companions." She spooned custard, contemplatively. Jethri broke his roll open and did his best to cultivate patience.

"It is, you understand," Lady Maarilex said eventually, "a difference in mode that separates Norn and the yos'Arimyst. In him, you will find a trader, oh, *most* conservative! Ring a rumor of change and be certain that Therin yos'Arimyst will be with the portmaster within the hour, speaking eloquently in defense of the proven ways. Norn, as I am certain you have yourself observed, is one to dance with risk and court change."

"I can see that the two of them might not have much to talk about," Jethri said, when a few moments had passed and she had said nothing else.

"Certainly, they would seem to be unlikely to agree on any topic of importance to either," she murmured, her eyes, and apparently her thoughts, on her custard.

Jethri sipped his tea, found it less than tepid and rose to warm his cup. When he returned, Lady Maarilex had finished her custard and was holding her cup between her two hands, eyes closed.

He slipped into his seat as quietly as he could, not wanting to disturb her if she was indulging in a nap. She opened her eyes before he was rightly settled, and extended a hand to tap the letter where it was between them on the table.

"I believe what you have here is politics, child. Mind you, I do not have the key to the yos'Arimyst's mind, but it comes to me that he *must* see you as a challenge to his beloved changelessness—indeed, you *are* just such a challenge—and never mind that change will come, no matter how he may abhor it, or speak against it, or forbid it within his hall. Norn ven'Deelin, who loves the trade more than any being alive, has taken a Terran apprentice. Surely, the foundations of the homeworld ring with the blow! And, yet, if not Norn, if not now—then another, later. Terrans exist. Not only do they exist, but they insist upon trading—and on expanding the field upon which they *can* trade. We ignore them—we deny them—at our very great peril."

Jethri leaned forward, watching her face. "You think that she was right, then, ma'am?"

"Oh, I believe she is correct," the old lady murmured. "Which is not to say—diverting and delightful as I find you!—that I would not have preferred another, and later. It is not comfortable, to be an agent of change." She shot him an especially sharp glance. "Nor is it comfortable, I imagine, to be change embodied."

He swallowed. "I—am not accustomed to thinking of myself so. An apprentice trader, set to learn from a…most astonishing master—that is how I think of myself."

She smiled. "That is very sensible of you, Jethri Gobelyn, fostered of ven'Deelin. Consider yourself so, and comport yourself so." She tapped the letter again, three times, and withdrew her hand.

"And do not forget that there are others abroad who find your existence threatens them, and who will do their all to see you fail."

*Nothing new there,* Jethri thought, retrieving his letter. *Just a description of trade-as-usual.* He folded the paper and slipped it into the pocket of his jacket.

"Anecha will drive you to the port and see you safe inside the hall," Lady Maarilex said. "If you require funds, pray speak to Mr. pel'Saba—he will be able to rectify the matter for you."

He inclined his head. "I thank you, ma'am, but I believe I am well-funded."

"That is well, then," she said and pushed back from the table. He leapt to his feet—and was waved back to his chair.

"Please. I am not so frail as that—and you have eaten nothing. A custard may tide an old woman until nuncheon, but a lad of your years wants more than a shredded roll for his breakfast."

He looked down at his plate, feeling his ears warm. "Yes, ma'am," he murmured, and then looked back to her face. "Thank you for your care."

She smiled. "You are courteous child." She bowed, very slightly. "Until soon, young Jethri."

"Until soon, ma'am," he answered, and watched her stump down the room, leaning heavy on her cane, until she reached the hall and turned right, toward her office.

# Day 168
# Standard Year 1118

# Irikwae Port

"I DON'T KNOW why he needs you here so early," Anecha muttered as she opened the big car's cargo compartment.

Jethri reached in, got hold of the strap and pulled his duffle out, slinging it over one shoulder.

"The port never closes," he said, softly. "Master yos'Arimyst has likely done me the courtesy of being sure that I arrive during his on-shift."

Anecha sent him one of her sharp, unreadable glances. "So, you interpret it as courtesy, do you? You've a more giving melant'i than some of us, then, Jethri Gobelyn." She swung the second bag out of the boot and got it up on a shoulder.

"I can carry that," he said mildly. She snorted and used her chin to point at the bag he already wore.

"Can isn't should," she said. "I'll have that one, too. Or do you think I will allow Norn ven'Deelin's son to walk into the guildhall dragging his own luggage, like a Low House roustabout?"

He blinked at her. "It can't be improper for an apprentice to carry his own bags—and his master's, too."

"Nothing more proper, if the master is present. However, when the apprentice is the representative of the master—"

Right. Then the honors that would properly go to the master were bestowed upon her 'prentice. Jethri sighed, quietly. Eventually—say, a couple years after he saw his eightieth birthday, he'd have *melant'i* thoroughly understood.

"So," said Anecha, with a great deal of restraint, really, "if the good apprentice will deign to give me his bag?"

The other option being a long stop in the street while they argued the point—which would earn neither his *melant'i* nor Master ven'Deelin's any profit. Jethri stifled a second sigh and handed over the duffle, settled his jacket over his shoulders and crossed the walk to the door of the Irikwae Port traders guildhall.

The door was locked, which didn't surprise him. He swiped his crew card from *Elthoria* through the lock-scanner, and then set his palm against the plate.

The status light blared red, accompanied by a particularly raucous buzzer—and the door remained locked.

"I see you are expected," Anecha commented drily from behind him, "and that every courtesy has been observed."

Thinking something closely along those lines himself, Jethri slipped his crew card into a pocket and put his hand against the plate, as might any general visitor to the hall.

The status light this time flared yellow, and there was an absence of rude noise, circumstances that Jethri tentatively considered hopeful. He dropped back two steps, head cocked attentively, waiting for the doorkeeper to open the door.

"*Every* courtesy observed," Anecha repeated some minutes later, voice edged.

Jethri moved forward to ring the bell again. His hand had scarcely touched the plate when it and the rest of the door was snatched away, and he found himself looking, bemusedly, down into the stern face of a man in full trade dress.

"What is the meaning of this?" The man snapped. "This is the traders' hall. The zoo is in the city."

Behind him, Jethri heard Anecha draw a sharp, outraged breath, which pretty much summarized his own feelings. Still, as Master tel'Ondor had taught him, it was best to answer rudeness with courtesy—and to remember the name of the offender.

Jethri bowed, gently, and not nearly so low as apprentice ought to a full trader. He straightened, taking his time about it, and met the man's hard gray eyes.

"I arrive at the hall at this day and hour in obedience to the word of Hall Master yos'Arimyst." He slipped the letter out of his pocket and offered it, gracefully, all the while meeting that hull-steel stare, daring him to compound his rudeness.

The man's fingers flicked—and stilled. He inclined his head, which was proper enough from trader to 'prentice, and stepped back from the door, motioning Jethri within.

The vestibule was small and stark, putting Jethri forcibly in mind of an airlock. Two halls branched out of it   one left, one right.

"'prentice!" the trader shouted. "'prentice, to the door!"

Jethri winced and heard Anecha mutter behind him, though not what she said. Which was probably just as well.

From the deeps of the hall came the sound of boots hitting the floor with a will, and shortly came from the left-most corridor a girl about, Jethri thought, the same age as the twins, her hair pale yellow and her pale blue eyes heavy with sleep.

"Yes, Trader?"

He flicked nearly dismissive fingers in Jethri's direction. "A candidate arrives. See him to quarters."

She bowed, much too low, Jethri thought, catching the frown before it got to his face. "Yes, Trader. It shall be done."

"Good," he said, and turned toward the right hall, his hard glance scraping across Jethri's face with indifference.

Behind him, Anecha stated, dispassionately, "*Every* courtesy."

Jethri turned his head to give her a Look. She returned it with an expression of wide innocence Khat would have paid hard credit to possess.

"Your pardon, gentles," the girl who had been summoned to deal with them stammered. "It is—understand, it is very early in the day for candidates to arrive. Though of course!— the hall stands ready to receive…at any hour…"

Jethri raised a hand, stopping her before she tied her sentence into an irredeemable knot.

"I regret the inconvenience to the hall," he said, as gently as he could, and showed her the folded paper. "Master yos'Arimyst's own word was that I arrive at the hall no later than sixth hour today."

The 'prentice blinked. "But Master yos'Arimyst is scarcely ever at the hall so early in the day. Though, of course," she amended rapidly, her cheeks turning a darker gold with her blush, "I am only an apprentice, and cannot hope to understand the necessities of the hall master."

"Certainly not," Jethri said smoothly. "I wonder if Master yos'Arimyst is in the hall this morning?"

Her eyes widened. "Why, no, sir. Master yos'Arimyst left planet yesterday on Guild business. He will return at the end of the relumma."

He heard Anecha draw a breath, and moved one shoulder, sharply. The crude signal got through; Anecha held her tongue.

"Certainly, Guild business has precedent," he said to the waiting girl. "My name is Jethri Gobelyn. I may be in your lists as Jeth Ree ven'Deelin."

"Oh!" The girl bowed, not as deeply as she had for the irritable trader who had opened the door, but too deep, nonetheless. Briefly, Jethri wondered about the hall's protocol master.

"Parin tel'Ossa, at your word, sir." She said, eyes wide. "Please, if you will follow me, I will show you to your quarters."

"Certainly," Jethri said, and followed her down the left hall, pausing a moment to send a glance to Anecha, who managed not to meet his eyes.

The quarters were unexpectedly spacious, on the top level, with windows overlooking an enclosed garden. Having thanked and rid himself of both Parin and Anecha, Jethri worked the latch and pushed one of the windows wide, admitting the early breeze and the muffled sounds of the morning port.

It certainly seemed that Master yos'Arimyst intended deliberate insult to Norn ven'Deelin, through her apprentice and foster son. Or, thought Jethri, leaning his hands on the window sill and sticking his nose out into the chilly air, did he?

After all, he, Jethri, was here for a certification—a test. What if this deliberate rudeness had a point *other than* insult? Suppose, for instance, that the masters and traders of the hall wanted a reading on just how well a beastly Terran understood civilized behavior?

He closed his eyes. Tough call. If the measuring stick for civilized was Liaden, then he ought to be making plans for a vendetta right about now—or ought he? A true Liaden would have the sense to know if he was being offered an insult or a test.

Jethri exhaled, with vigor, and turned from the window to inspect the rest of his quarters.

A work table sat against the wall to the right of the window. A screen and keyboard sat ready before a too-short chair. Jethri leaned over to touch a key, and was gratified to see the screen come up, displaying an options menu.

He chose *map*, and was in moments engaged in a close study of the interior layout of the hall. Not nearly as complex as Tarnia's house, with its back stairs, back rooms and half-floors, but a nice mix of public, private and service rooms.

The quarters were in what appeared to be an older wing—perhaps the original hall—the public and meeting rooms were off the right-hand hall from the vestibule—and could also be accessed from the Trade Bar, which opened into the main port street.

Map committed to memory, Jethri recalled the menu—yes. There was an option called *check-in*. He chose it.

A box appeared on the screen, with instructions to enter his name. Fingers extended over the keypad, he paused, staring down at the Liaden characters. Slowly, he typed in the name under which he had been summoned for certification; the name that Parin had recognized.

*Jeth Ree ven'Deelin.*

The computer accepted his entry; another screen promised that his mentor would be informed of his arrival. Great.

He returned to the options menu, lifting a hand to cover a sudden yawn. Despite the fact that he'd been able to nap in the car coming down from Tarnia's house, he was feeling short on sleep, which was not a good way to start a test. He glanced at his watch. If he was still at Tarnia's house, he'd have just under six seconds to get to breakfast.

He blinked, eyes suddenly teary and throat tight. He *wanted* to be in Tarnia's house, running as hard as he could down the "secret" back stairs and sweating lest he be late for breakfast. He missed Miandra and Meicha, Mrs. tel'Bonti, Lady Maarilex, Mr. pel'Saba, Flinx and Ren Lar. And while he was listing those he missed, there was Norn ven'Deelin and Gaenor and Vil Tor, Pen Rel, Master tel'Ondor; Khat and Cris and Grig and Seeli...

He sniffed, and reached into his pocket for a handkerchief.

*Put it in a can,* he told himself, which is what Seeli'd tell him when he'd been a kid and got to blubbering over nothing. He unfolded the handkerchief and wiped his face with the square of silk, swallowing a couple times to loosen his throat.

*Might as well unpack,* he thought, putting the handkerchief away. *Get everything all shipshape and comfortable, and you'll feel more like the place belongs to you.*

Anecha had left his bags on the bare wooden floor against the opposite wall, under the control panel for the bed. That item of furniture at the moment formed part of the wall. When he wanted it down, according to Parin, all he had to do was slide the blue knob from left to right. To raise the bed, slide the knob from right to left, and up she went, freeing a considerable area of floor space.

Jethri opened the first bag—bright blue, with the Tarnia crest embroidered on it—and commenced unpacking, carrying his clothes over to the built-in dresser. He took his time, making sure everything went away neat; that his shirts were hung straight and his socks were matched up, but at last he was shaking his second-best trading coat—the one Master ven'Deelin'd had made for him—out of the bottom of the bag, and hanging it with his shirts on the rod.

That done, he sealed the bag up, folded it and stowed it on the shelf over the rod.

The second duffle was dull green, *Gobelyn's Market* spelled out in stark white stenciling down one side. He unsealed it and pulled out the books he had borrowed from Tarnia's library. He'd taken mostly novels—some titles that he remembered from Gaenor's talks, and others at random—as well as a history of Irikwae, and another, of the Scouts, and a battered volume that appeared to be an account of the Old War.

He lined the books up on the worktable, and stood for a long moment, admiring them, before diving back into his duffle and emerging with the photocube showing his father, and Arin's metal box, with its etched stars, moons and comets.

He supposed he could've left his stuff in his room at Tarnia's house, but he'd got to thinking that maybe that wasn't a good idea, considering the fractins and the prevailing feeling against Old Tech—and he surely hadn't wanted to leave the weather gadget anywhere but secure in the inside pocket of his jacket, which was where it was right now. So, in the end, he'd tossed everything into his old duffle and left the empty B-crate behind.

The photocube he placed with great care in the center of a low black wooden table in the corner by the windows. Arin's box, he put on top of the dresser. He stepped back to consider the room and found it…better, though still too much trader's hall and too little Jethri Gobelyn.

He returned to the duffle and pulled out the other photocube, with its record of strangers, and carried it over to the black table. The family cube, he placed near the keyboard on the table, where he could see it while he worked.

The remainder of the duffle's contents were best not displayed, he thought, those contents being fractins, true and false, the wire frame, and his pretend trade journal— though on second thought, there wasn't any reason that the old notebook couldn't be in with the rest of the books. Nobody who might visit him here was going to be interested in old kid stuff—even assuming that they could read Terran.

He resealed the duffle and put it on the shelf in the wardrobe next to the blue bag, closed the door and went back to the work table. He settled as well as he was able into the short chair and reached for the keyboard, meaning to explore the remainder of the options available to him.

A single line of tall red letters marched across the center of the computer screen. It seemed that his mentor, Trader Ena Tyl sig'Lorta would see him at the top of the hour, at meeting booth three, in the Irikwae Trade Bar.

Jethri looked at his watch. Not much time, but no need for a full-tilt run, either, if his understanding of the scale of the house was correct.

He tapped the 'received' key, slid out of the chair, brushed his hands down the front of his coat and went off to meet his mentor.

"GOT SOME NEWS," Seeli said, serious-like.

Grig looked up from his calcs. The yard had filed an amended, which they were required by contract to do, whenever section costs overran estimate by more than five percent. It was lookin' to be damn near seven percent on the new galley module and Myra wanted to talk downgrade on some of the back up systems so as to make up the difference. He was doing the first pass over the numbers because Seeli'd been feeling not at the top of her form, and he'd finally this morning gotten her talked into going to the port clinic.

So, he looked up and got on a smile that the calcs made a little lopsided.

"Good news, I hope," he said, and even as he did felt his gut clench with the possibility of the news being bad.

"You might say." She sat down next to him, her arm companionably touching his. "Fact is, I hope you will say." She touched his hand. "I'm on the increase."

For a second he just sat there, heart in acceleration, mind blank—then all at once his brain caught up with his heart. He gave a shout of laughter and got his arms around her, and she was laughing, too, hugging him hard around the ribs, and for a while it was a mixup of kisses and hugs and more laughing, but finally they made it back to adult and sat there quiet, her head on his shoulder, their arms 'round each other still.

"How far along?" he asked, that being the first sensible sentence he'd made in the last half-hour.

"Couple Standard Months, the nurse said."

He felt his mouth pulling into another idiot grin. "The yard gets its promises in order, she'll be born in space, first newcrew on the refit."

Seeli snuggled a little closer against him. "We don't know what Mel might have cookin'. Come to it, Iza ain't beyond."

That took a little of the glow.

"Iza's done, beyond or not," he said, too seriously. "But I take your point about Mel. Girl's got the morals of a mink."

"What's a mink?" Seeli wanted to know, and it might've taken him the rest of the day to explain it to her, but the door come open and it was Paitor and Khat, each one looking as grim as Grig felt happy.

Seeli stirred, pushing against his chest to get upright. He let her go, and sighed gustily at the printout showing in the trader's hand.

"Paitor, I've been meaning to talk to you about this growing habit with the Priorities."

He shook his head. "Believe that I'd pay good cash never to get another." He tossed it on the table atop the printouts from the yard and headed into the galley.

"Who else wants a brew?" he called over his shoulder.

"I do," Khat said sitting in the chair across from Seeli, and rubbing a sleeve across her face. "Hot on the port."

"Brew'd be fine," Grig said, and looked over to Seeli, eyebrows up, asking.

"Juice for me," she called. "Thanks, Uncle."

Paitor could be heard clanking about in the cold box. Grig picked up the Priority, flicking a glance to Khat.

She shrugged. "I read it."

"All right, then," he said, unfolding the paper, with Seeli leaning close to read over his shoulder:

> *Honored Gobelyns:*
>
> *Felicitations and fair profit to you and to your ship.*
>
> *The priority message sent to the attention of Jethri from the esteemed Pilot Khatelane arrives at Elthoria. Your forbearance is requested, that I read this message, intended for the eyes of true kin only.*
>
> *I commend Pilot Khatelane for the information she sends regarding certain Liaden vessels at dock on Port Banth. Several of these vessels are known to us adversely. A Guild inquiry has been called and you may repose faith that intentions of mischief or mayhem will quickly be learned.*
>
> *Of the matter concerning the chel'Gaibin, I give you assurance that there lies no debt between himself and Jethri. The brother deprived was hale when we beheld him last, though deeply in the anger of his mother.*
>
> *In the event, Jethri has been set down at Irikwae, at the house of Tarnia in the mountains of the moons. There, he is tutored in the ways of custom and of wine. Be assured that Tarnia values him high, as I do, and will stand as his shield and his dagger, should a false debt be called.*
>
> *I am hopeful that these tidings will find you in good health, and I remain*
>
> *Norn ven'Deelin Clan Ixin*
> *Master at Trade*

"Set *down*?" Seeli said, sounding every bit as horrified as Grig felt. "She left Jethri *alone*, on a Liaden world?"

"With a Liaden headcase after him for evenin' up a debt," Khat added, wearily, accepting a brew from Paitor. "Thanks."

"Welcome." He handed Seeli her drink, thumped Grig's down and folded into the chair next to Khat.

"Thing is," Grig said, glancing up from his second read. "She don't say the brother is alive now. She says he was OK the last time she saw him."

"Right." Khat nodded. "And the headcase, if you parse it right, never did say the boy *was* dead—though that's what I thought he must've meant. Thinking cold, though, it comes to me that there's more ways to 'deprive' somebody of a brother than by killing him. If Jeth had—what? Called the proctors and got the boy put in the clink for a couple years—that'd deprive his family of him, wouldn't it? Or if Jeth had somehow gotten the brother's license pulled—"

"The point is," Seeli interrupted, sharp, but, there—she'd been Jethri's mother more'n Iza'd ever tried to be. "The *point* is that this master trader has gone off and left Jethri on a mudball, with no ship to call on, *and* there's a headcase lookin' for him, and she hasn't even told him!"

They blinked at her, in unison. Seeli snatched the Priority out of Grig's hand and snapped it at Paitor's face. He pulled back, impassive.

"Where does it say on this piece of paper that she's sending Khat's letter on to Jethri? Where does it say she's going back for him? Or that she's called—anybody at all!—to have the headcase taken under advisement, or, or whatever it is you do when somebody tries to collect on a 'false debt?'"

"We could send again," Khat said, making a long arm and tweaking the paper away.

"No beam code for Tarnia," Grig said quietly. "And no guarantees that this chel'Gaibin won't pursue his debt 'gainst the rest of us, like he tried with Khat." He looked at Seeli and his breath came short.

"One of us could go for him," Paitor said. "Not knowing the headcase's trajectory, that's tricky. For all we know, he's based outta Irikwae, wherever it is, and is on the route for home."

Grig took a breath, forcing it all the way down past tight chest muscles, to the very bottom of his lungs.

"I'll go," he said. "I owe."

Paitor frowned. "Owe? What can you possibly owe the boy?"

Grig looked him in the eye. "I'm still settlin' with Arin," he said evenly.

The other man studied him a long moment, then nodded, slow. "Can't argue with that."

"Grig." Seeli wasn't liking this. He turned to face her. "How're you goin'? Got a fastship in your back pocket?"

"Know a pilot-owner," he said, which was true enough. "Might be they're still settlin' with Arin, too."

"Back-up," Khat said, nodding. "Seeli, you know we all got back-up. Grig's got it here, then he's the one to go. 'less you can think of any other way to get Jethri the news, and an offer of his ship?"

Seeli hesitated; shook her head. "I can't. But we *offer him* ship, and if he wants it, we *give him* a ship—and Iza can deal with me! You hear it?" She rounded on Grig.

"I hear it, Seeli." He reached out and touched her cheek with his fingertip. "Khat."

"Sir?"

"My Seeli here's on the increase. I'd take it favorable, if you went off roster and devoted yourself to not letting any headcases inside her phase space."

"You got it," Khat said, sending a grin to Seeli, and pushing back from the table. "I'll file that change right now."

"Good." Khat had the right of it, Grig thought. No use putting it off.

Seeli reached out and grabbed his hand, pulling him with her as she stood up. She looked down at Paitor, ignoring his grin, and nodded her head, formal as a Liaden.

"Excuse us, Uncle. Grig and me got some business before he flies out."

IRIKWAE TRADE BAR was modest, and modestly busy—three of the six working public terminals were engaged, and four of the twelve meeting booths. A seventh terminal had been pushed into a corner—probably awaiting a repairman.

At the bar, a mixed cluster of traders, cargo masters and general crew sipped tea, or wine, or ate a quick-meal, while the status board over their heads showed a good dozen ships at port.

Goods on offer, portside, were heavily weighted toward agristuff—soybeans, rice, yams—with a smattering of handicrafts, textiles, and wine. The ships were offering metals—refined and unrefined—patterns, textiles, furniture, gemstones, books—a weird mix, Jethri thought, and then thought again. Irikwae was what Norn ven'Deelin was pleased to call an "outworld," far away from Liad's orbit. Ships bearing luxuries, small necessities, and information from the homeworld itself ought to do pretty well here.

"Are you lost, sir?" a voice asked at his elbow. He turned and looked down into the amused, wrinkled face of a woman. Her hair was gray, though still showing some faded strands of its original yellow color, and she had the trade guild's sign embroidered on the sleeve of her bright orange shirt.

"Only distractable, I fear," he answered, turning his palms up mock despair. "I am here for a meeting with a trader, but of course, the board caught my eye, and my interest..."

"Information is advantage," she said sagely. "Of course the board caught you—how not? At which booth were you to meet your trader?"

"Three."

"Ah. Just over here, then, sir, if you will follow me."

No choices there, Jethri thought wryly, and followed her to the back wall, where meeting booth three showed a bold blue numeral. The door was closed and the privacy light was lit.

His guide looked up at him. "Your name, sir?"

"Jethri—" he began, and caught himself. "Jeth Ree ven'Deelin."

Her eyebrows lifted, but she said nothing, only turned to put her hand on the door, which slid open, despite the privacy light, to reveal two traders, obviously interrupted in earnest conversation, and of two different minds of how to take it.

The woman seemed inclined toward amused resignation, the man—and wouldn't it just be the same stern-faced trader who'd been on door-duty?—was tending toward anger.

The staffer, unperturbed by either, bowed gently to the table, and murmured. "Jeth Ree ven'Deelin has a meeting with a trader in booth three."

The female trader sent a sharp glance to his face, and inclined her head slightly. Jethri received the impression that she was more amused and less resigned. The male trader frowned ferociously.

"Yes, Jeth Ree ven'Deelin is expected shortly, however—" he stopped, and favored Jethri with a hard stare.

In this moment of frozen disbelief, the staffer bowed once more to the table and went, soft-footed, away.

"*You* are Jeth Ree ven'Deelin?" the man demanded.

*Not exactly encouraging*, Jethri thought, and bowed—not low.

"In fact, I am Jethri Gobelyn, apprentice and foster son of Master Trader Norn ven'Deelin. The communication from the hall named me Jeth Ree ven'Deelin, and I felt it wise to continue under that construction until I was able to ask that the database be amended."

"ven'Deelin's Terran," the female trader murmured, and inclined her head when he looked at her. "Forgive me, sir. I am Alisa kor'Entec. Your fame precedes you, to the wonderment of us all."

"I had heard the ven'Deelin signed a Terran apprentice," the stern-faced trader said, looking to his mate. "I thought then that she had run mad. But—foster son?"

"Even so," she assured him, with relish. "Precisely so. Is it not diverting?"

"Dangerously demented, say rather," the other snapped, and Jethri felt himself warm to the man. Still, no matter his own doubts and feelings on the subject of his adoption, he couldn't—really couldn't—son or 'prentice, just stand by while Master ven'Deelin was made mock of.

He drew himself up stiffly where he stood and stared down his nose at the stern-faced trade, and then at the other.

"The melant'i of Master Trader Norn ven'Deelin is above reproach," he said, with all the dignity he could bring to it and hoping the phrase was on-point.

Alisa kor'Entec *smiled* at him. "It is, indeed. Which makes the matter infinitely more diverting."

"Perhaps for you," the man said irritably. He looked up at Jethri and moved a hand. "Of your goodness, Apprentice....Gobelyn. Trader kor'Entec and I must finish a small matter of business. Please, have a cup of tea and rest somewhat from your labors. I will be with you in a very short time."

A cup of tea would actually be welcome, Jethri thought, abruptly aware that the gone feeling in his middle wasn't all due to his upcoming testing, whatever it was. *And maybe a snack, too.* He inclined his head.

"Thank you, sir. I will await you at the bar." He looked to the lady. "Ma'am. Fair trading."

She gave him a slight, conspiratorial nod. "Good profit, Jethri Gobelyn."

"Sorry to be late," Raisy said, slipping onto the bench across.

"'preciate you comin' at all," Grig answered, pushing the second brew across to her.

She cocked him an eyebrow. "Thought that's Uncle you was peeved with."

"I'm not *peeved* with anybody." Grig snapped open the seal on his brew. "It's just—time's done, Raisy. We gotta move to something else. Thing's—aren't stable, and you know that for truth. You want to talk birth defects, for starters?"

Raisy opened her brew, took a long draught, leaned back, and sighed. "You bring me out on an Urgent for this?"

He glanced sideways, out over the rest of the bar—slow night, slim on customers—and back to his sister.

"No," he said, quiet. "Sorry." He had some brew, put the bottle back on the table and frowned at it.

"News, Raisy," he said, raising his eyes. "Seeli's increasing. I'm bound for dad duty."

She grinned, broad and honest, and leaned across the table to smack him upside the shoulder.

"News, he says! That's *great* news, brother! You give your Seeli my congrats, hear it? Tell her I said she couldn't have no finer man—nor her kid no finer dad."

He smiled, warmed. "I'll tell her that, Raisy. You ought to come by, meet her."

"Maybe I will," she said, but they both knew she wouldn't.

"So, that was the Urgent?" she said, after a small pause.

He shook his head, pulled the two Priorities out his pocket and passed them over.

"These're the Urgent."

She sent him a sharp look, took the papers and unfolded them with a snap.

Grig drank brew and watched her read.

She went through both twice, folded them together and passed them back. Grig slipped them away and sat waiting.

"So, we got a renegade Liaden, do we? Who depends on us not being able to check up on the rules?"

"Like that," Grig said.

"Right. And then we got this side issue of what's to have on Banth, which I'll second Khat on and say—nothing."

"How side an issue is that? If we got a buncha pirates lookin' to set up a base there?"

She stared at him. "Dammit—you think like Uncle."

Grig laughed.

"OK, let's look at where Banth is, ease-of-route speakin'." Raisy closed her eyes, accessing her pilot brain. Grig, who had pulled up star maps to study on Banth's location when Khat's letter had first arrived, sat back and waited.

She sighed. "I'd have to check the maps to be sure, but—first look, it's in a nice spot for someone wanting to do a little slip-trading from one Edge to the other." She reached for her brew. "Now, Banth's got tight admin."

"But what if they get used to these Liaden ships comin' in an' there always seems to be a problem, but it always turns out not to be, so the inspectors start thinkin' they got the pattern of it—"

"And then the Liadens change the pattern, and start ops for real, right under the clipboards of the inspectors?" Raisy shrugged. "Way I'd do it."

"OK," she said, briskly, counting off on her fingers. "Renegade Liaden. Smugglin' ring maybe settin' up on Banth. What else? Oh—Arin's boy on the ground in Liaden space with no warning going his way. You think the master trader is in with the renegade?"

No surprise that Raisy's thoughts went there—he'd considered the same thing himself. Still—he shook his head.

"I think she's square. This business about Jethri being safe with Tarnia on Irikwae? Strikes me she might've been giving us the Liaden for 'the kid has a ship to call on.' I'm leaning toward that."

"But you got something that's still bothering you."

"I do." He leaned his elbows on the table, reached out and put his hands loosely around the brew bottle.

"I'm thinking we need to let Jeth know that he's got trouble. Could be, he's got trouble enough for all of us, if you take me."

"You're thinking this chel'Gaibin boy might make a hobby out of hunting Gobelyns?"

"And Tomases," Grig said. "Yeah, I do."

Raisy finished off her brew and put the bottle down with a thump.

"What do you want, Grig?"

"Lend of a fastship," he said. "Last I knew, you owned one."

"If you think I'm gonna let you fly my ship, *you're* a headcase!" Raisy said and Grig felt his stomach sink as she slid out of the booth and stood there, looking down at him.

"I'm coming with you," she said.

"I HAVE REVIEWED your file and I confess myself bewildered on several levels," Trader Ena Tyl sig'Lorta said, waving his hand at the screen on the table between them. "First, I find that there is no database error; you are correctly recorded as Jethri Gobelyn. A secondary entry was created for Jeth Ree ven'Deelin by the hall master's override. When it is accessed, however, the record it calls is precisely your own."

Jethri felt his stomach clench.

"Perhaps it was a test?" he offered, with as much delicacy as he could muster while cussing himself for plain and fancy mud-headedness.

Trader sig'Lorta stared at him, hard gray eyes wide with something near to shock. "You mean to suggest that the hall master had an interest in knowing how you would present yourself—as apprentice or as foster son?" His sharp face grew thoughtful. "That is possible. Indeed, now that I consider it—very possible. I see my task is not so simple as I had considered. Here…" He reached for the keypad, flicked open a log page and began, quickly, to type.

"I record in my mentor's notes—which will, you understand, be reviewed by a master at the end of your certification period—that your first request upon meeting your mentor was that the database be made to reflect your precise name." Another few lines, then a flick at the 'record' tab.

"So. That is well. We move on to lesser bewilderments." He touched a key, frowning down at the screen.

"I read here that the hall master at Modrid disallowed the trades you had completed at the word of your master trader—

for which you utilized monies drawn on her accredited and known apprentice sub-account—and that he required the master trader to re-authorize each transaction recorded under that sub-account. Is this summation correct?"

Just a bit giddy with having escaped the name fiasco with his *melant'i* intact, Jethri inclined his head.

"Trader, it is."

"Hah." He touched another key, and sat frowning down at the screen.

"I also find that you are the holder of a ten-year Combine key, and have two trades of some small level of complexity attached to your name."

Jethri inclined his head once more. "Trader, that is so."

"Good. We have a Combine terminal here. When we have finished, you will use it to record your location, so that any trades you may make during the course of your certification will be appropriately recorded to your key, as well as entering your Guild file."

Despite himself, Jethri blinked, which lapse went unnoticed by Trader sig'Lorta, who was still staring down at the screen.

Silence stretched, then Jethri cleared his throat.

"The hall master at Modrid said that no Terrans would be allowed into the Guild."

His mentor shot him a hard, gray glance. "That is a matter for the masters, who—in all truth—could not have met and decided on any such question, as you are the first Terran who has sought entry into the Guild. The rule as it is written—the rule which binds both the Guild and yourself is: *Any candidate who has demonstrated mastery over the requirements put forth in the previous section may enter the Guild as a trader. Those who once fail that demonstration may reapply after one Standard Year. Those who twice fail are banned from a third attempt.*

He tapped his finger sharply against the table top— *click,click,click*—and touched the 'forward' key again.

"In your case, we have something of a conundrum. In the first wise, Modrid Hall had no authority to disallow a master trader's apprentice for any reason. That, however, is another matter for the masters, and I make no doubt that Norn ven'Deelin will see it discussed and decided ere long.

"In the second wise, a hopeful trader with two trades comparable to those recorded upon your key in his Guild file would certainly rejoice in the melant'i of a junior trader, did he have no trader or master to whom he stood apprenticed." He gave the screen one more frowning glance and flicked the 'off' key.

"You and your master presented two claims to the hall master at Modrid—contracted association with a master trader, and the trades recorded on the key. Either should have assured you a place in the Guild—as an apprentice, or as a junior trader. Since Modrid Hall allowed neither claim to be sufficient, you now are come to Irikwae Hall with a request from your master trader that you be independently certified, and given a formal ranking within the Guild." He looked up, face serious.

"Understand, this is an unusual step. It has been done rarely in the past, most often when a dispute arose between traders regarding the talents or qualifications of a particular apprentice. In this instance, I would say that your master trader is wise to request independent certification—and doubly wise to ask it of Irikwae, where the hall master is known to be both conservative and stringent."

So, he was going to have to work his butt off, Jethri thought, and was surprised to find himself on his mettle, but not concerned. He was Norn ven'Deelin's apprentice, wasn't he? Hadn't he learned his basics from Arin and Paitor Gobelyn, neither one a slacker, if not precisely a master trader? Come to that, Trader sig'Lorta was shaping up to be the sort of mentor somebody might want for the upcoming tests—hard, and not exactly happy about Jethri *personally*, but a trader of virtue for all that, and upholding of the regs. He'd have to prove himself, right enough, but he didn't get the sense that his mentor would be changing the rules, if it got to looking like Jethri was about to win the game.

"May I know," he asked, "what the certification entails?"

"Surely, surely." Trader sig'Lorta flicked impatient fingers at the dark screen. "You will, I think, find it not at all unlike your apprenticeship. The hall will make an account available to you and you will be given various assignments of trade on the port. Those transactions will be recorded to your file, and at the end of the testing period, the file will be reviewed by a master trader, who will rule upon your precise level of skill. You will then be issued a card reflecting your standing within the Guild. Of course, as you successfully complete more, and more complex, trades, your standing will increase, and your Guild card will reflect that, as well."

Jethri took a couple minutes to think about that.

"The purpose of this exercise," he said, slowly, "is to gain a Guild card, so that I may not be denied the benefits and assistance of the Guild,"

"Say, so that it will be *less likely* that you will be denied those benefits," Trader sig'Lorta said, practically. "Certainly, there will be some who will risk the wrath of the masters over such niceties as whether Terrans may belong to the Guild— but less, I think, than might, had you no certified standing."

"I see," Jethri said. He shot a straight look at his mentor's face and decided to risk it: "I wonder, Trader, if you might tell me where you personally stand on the issue of Terrans in the Guild."

The hard gray eyes narrowed, with amusement or annoyance, Jethri couldn't have said.

"I believe that traders trade, Jethri Gobelyn. Show me that you are a trader, and I will accord you the respect due a Guild brother."

Well enough. Jethri inclined his head. "Thank you, Trader. I will certainly endeavor to show you that I am a trader."

# Day 177
# Standard Year 1118

## Irikwae Port

DURING HIS FIRST week at the hall, Jethri shadowed Trader sig'Lorta, learning the general lay of the port. In the evening, he set himself to solving the trade problems that had been uploaded to his screen. All of which was better than bowing lessons, but wasn't exactly what he was craving.

Waking on the morning of the day that he had decided he would ask his mentor straight out when he could expect to start his own trading, his first assignment was on his work screen. The timing led Jethri to suspect that maybe the week-long set-up had been a test of his own, and he'd shaken his head a little as he shrugged into his good trading coat.

First day, it had been soybeans. Next, it had been ore. Today, it was something a little odd—toys.

Jethri's assignment was to assess the items on offer from the trader of the good ship *Nathlyr*, and, if he found the items to have value, to make an offer on no more than a dozen lots and no less than six. If he found the items wanting, he was to write up a report detailing their defects.

It was an interesting assignment on the face of it, and Jethri left the hall with a whistle on his lips, which gained him a frown from passersby, and recalled him to a sense of where he was and what was proper behavior for a trader on the street.

So far, he was liking his certification just fine. Soybeans were deadly dull—nothing more or less than trading the day-price off the board. Not quite enough to put a body right to sleep, but scarce enough to keep him full awake, either. Still, he'd moved his lot with precision, and added the extra tor to his drawing account.

The ore had been a bit more interesting. He'd needed to put some of his capital into trade goods. Soybeans, of course—that was sure—and an odd lot of blended wine from the Maarilex cellars—which wasn't so sure, but not a bad risk, either, especially not after he'd talked the co-op seller into taking another twelve percent off the lot on account it *was* odd and would have to be hand-sold, most likely one barrel at a time. Since that had been the precise problem the co-op had been having, the twelve percent came off pretty easy.

So, he'd had one barrel sent to the Irikwae Trade Hall to be placed in his trade space, and betook himself and his soybean ticket down to the tables, where he found a trader willing to talk ore.

The soybeans got some interest, which they had to, but the "short lot" of wine sweetened the deal to the tune of a side measure of rough cut turaline, which Jethri thought he might place with a port jeweler, to his profit.

He received the tickets with a bow and took himself off to the Street of Gems, where he was fortunate enough to locate a jeweler who was willing to take the turaline ticket off him for roughly double what he had paid for the short lot of wine.

He closed the deal, feeling some sharp—and found later that night, as he went over his comparisons, that he had let the gems go too cheap. Still, he consoled himself, he'd had a quick turnover, and doubled his money, too, which wasn't bad, even if not as good as could have been.

So, now, the toys, and he was looking forward to them, as he strode down the street to the exhibit halls.

He was early to the day hall, but not so early that there weren't traders there before him. The toy exhibit, in a choice center hall location, had not drawn a large crowd, which seemed strange—and then didn't as he got a closer look at what was on offer.

Exhibit hall protocol required a trader to show no less than three and no more than twelve pieces representative of that which he wished to sell. If *Nathlyr's* trader had followed the protocol, he stood in clear and present danger of going away with his hold still full of the things.

The examples set out were seemingly made of porcelain, badly shaped, with unexpected angles and rough-looking finish. Nothing about them invited the hand, or delighted the eye or engaged the mind, in the way that something billed as a *toy* ought.

Jethri picked up one of the pieces—in outline, it looked something like an old fin ship. It felt as gritty as it looked, and was slightly heavier than he had anticipated. Uncle Paitor had taught him that it sometimes helped to get a sense for a thing by holding it in the palm and getting comfortable with the shape and the weight of—

The thing in his hand was buzzing, slightly reminiscent of Flinx, setting up a nice fuzzy feeling between his ears. The buzzing grew louder and it was almost as if he could hear words inside of it—words in a language not quite Terran and not quite Liaden, but close—so close. He screwed his eyes shut, straining to hear—and gasped awake as pain flared, disrupting the trance.

Quickly, he replaced the toy among its fellows, and glanced down at his hand. There was a brand of red across the palm, already starting to blister. The...toy...had malfunctioned.

Or not.

He bit his lip, fingers curled over his burned palm. That the so-called toys were Befores of a type he had personally never seen was obvious. Befores being specifically disallowed on Irikwae at least, it seemed that his duty was to alert the Master of Exhibits to the problem.

And then, he thought, grimacing as he slipped his wounded hand into his pocket, he would go down to one of the philter shops on the main way and get a dressing for his burn.

As it happened, somebody else had been dutiful sooner. He hadn't got half-way to the offices in the back of the big hall when he met a crowd heading in the opposite  direction.

Two grim-faced port proctors, a woman in the leather clothing of a Scout, and the Master of Exhibits himself, walking arm in arm with a slightly wide-eyed trader not much older, Jethri thought, than he was. *Nathlyr* was fancy-stitched across the right breast of the trader's ship jacket.

Respectfully, Jethri stepped aside to let them pass, though he doubted any of the bunch saw him, except the Scout, then changed course for the exit. His hand was hurting bad.

"CERTAINLY! CERTAINLY!" THE philterman took one look at the angry wound across Jethri's palm and ran to the back of the shop. By the time Jethri had arranged himself on the short stool and put his hand on the counter, the man was back, clutching a kit to his chest.

"First, we cleanse," he murmured, breaking the seal on an envelope bearing the symbol for "medical supply," and shaking out an antiseptic wipe.

Jethri braced himself, and it was well he did; the pressure of the wipe across his skin was painful, and the cleaning solution added another level of burn to his discomfort.

"Ow!" He clamped his mouth tight on the rest of it, ears hot with embarrassment. The philterman looked up, briefly.

"It is uncomfortable, I know, but with such a wound we must be certain that the area is clean. Now..." He pulled out a second envelope and snapped the seal, shaking out another wipe.

"This, I think, you will find a bit more pleasant."

The pressure still hurt—and then it didn't, as his skin cooled and the pain eased back to something merely annoying.

Jethri sighed, his relief so great that he forgot to be embarrassed.

"Yes, that is better, eh?" The philterman murmured, reaching again into his kit. "Now, we will dress it and you may continue your day, Trader. Remember to have the hall physician re-examine you this evening. Burns have a difficult nature and require close observation."

The dressing was an expandable fingerless glove that had a layer of all-purpose antibiotic against the skin. The largest in stock stretched to fit Jethri's hand.

"Else," the philterman said, "we should have had to wrap it in treated gauze, with an overwrap of sterile tape. So." He gathered up the spent wipes and broken envelopes and fed them into the countertop recycler.

"If I might suggest a portable kit, Trader?" he murmured. "It fits easily into a pocket, and includes three each of cleansing and pain alleviation wipes, and a small roll of antibiotic-treated gauze and wrapping tape. Two dex, only."

And cheap insurance at that, Jethri thought, glancing down at his gloved hand. Who expected toys to bite, anyway?

"An excellent suggestion," he said to the philterman. "I will have one of your kits. Also—" he said, suddenly remembering another item that might be found in such a shop. "I wonder if you have a sort of cream which is commonly sold to Terrans, which dissolves facial hair and keeps the face pleasing."

"Ah!" The man looked up at him interestedly. "Is there such a thing? I had no notion. We do not, you understand, much deal with Terrans at Irikwae. But hold..."

He bustled to the back and returned with a flat plastic pack prominently marked with the symbol for medical supplies. Slipping a finger under the seal, he unfolded the pack to display its contents—three each, cleaning wipes and painkiller wipes; one small roll of antibiotic gauze, one small roll of tape. Check.

"I thank you," Jethri murmured, slipping two dex from his public pocket and putting them on the counter.

"It is my pleasure to serve," the man said, folding the kit and resealing it. Jethri picked it up; it fit into one of the smaller of his jacket's numerous inner pockets, with room to spare.

"Of this other product," the philterman murmured. "There is a shop at the bottom of the street which does from time to time have specialty items on offer. It may be that you will find what you are seeking there. The shop is the last on the left side of the street. It has a green-striped awning."

"I thank you," Jethri said again and got himself disentangled from the stool and on his feet, heading for the door.

"DISSOLVES HAIR?" THE woman behind the counter at the philtershop at the bottom of the street stared at him as if he'd taken leave of his senses. "Nothing like that here, young trader—nor likely to be! We offer oddities from time to time, but nothing—well. Perhaps you want the Ruby Club? The director has been known to keep…exotic items on hand."

"Perhaps I do," Jethri said, by no means certain. "My thanks to you." He departed the shop of the green awning, feeling the woman's eyes on his back as he paused, looking up and down the street for a public map.

The Ruby Club was somewhat behind and at a angle to the warehouse district, not quite adjacent to the salvage yards. Well. The toys having fallen through, he figured he had an hour or two at liberty and, while Meicha's handi work had so far stood up, he didn't know how long that would be so, or if his first warning of its failure would be on the morning he woke up to find he'd overnight grown a beard down to his knees.

Prepared is better'n scared, he thought, which was something his father used to say, and Grig, too—and pushed the button on the bottom of the map to summon a taxi to him.

"YOU ARE CERTAIN that this is the location to which you were directed?" The taxi driver actually sounded worried, and Jethri didn't know as how he particularly blamed her.

The Ruby Club itself was kept up and lighted; with a red carpet extending from its carved red door right across the walkway to the curb. The surrounding buildings, though, were dark, not in repair, and in some cases overgrown with plants that Jethri's time in the vineyards had taught him were weeds.

"Is there another Ruby Club on the port?" he asked, half-hoping to hear that there was, and that it stood next to the Irikwae Trade Bar.

To his surprise, the driver leaned forward and tapped a command into her on-board map. After a moment, he heard her sigh, lightly.

"There is only this one."

"Then this is my location," Jethri said, with more certainty than he felt. He wasn't liking the looks of this street, at all. On the other hand, he thought, given the general feeling that Terrans were pretty good zoo material, maybe it wasn't surprising that a place known for carrying exotic Terran items was situated well away from the main port. He pushed open the door.

"Wait for me," he said to the cabbie. She looked over the seat at him.

"How long?"

Good question. "I shouldn't be above twelve minutes," he said, hoping for less.

She inclined her head. "I will wait twelve minutes."

"My thanks."

He left the cab and walked briskly down the red carpeting. Seen close, the red door was carved; the carving showing a lot of naked people having sex with each other, and maybe some things that weren't exactly sex—or if so, not the kind that had been covered in either his hygiene courses or the bits of the Code the twins' tutor had marked out for him to read.

It did come to him that he was not prepared to deal with the consequences of that door, and he began to turn away, to go back to the cab and uptown and his quarters at the trade hall—

The door opened.

He glanced back, and down, into a pair of jade green eyes, slightly tip-tilted in a soft, oval face. Jade-colored flowers were painted along the ridge of...the person's...cheekbones, and their lips were also painted jade. They were dressed in a deep red tunic and matching trousers, beneath which red boots gleamed.

"Service, Trader," the doorkeeper said huskily, and the voice gave no clue to gender.

Jethri bowed, slightly. "I was sent here by a merchant uptown," he said, keeping his voice stringently in the mercantile mode. "It was thought that there might be depilatory for sale here."

"Why, perhaps there is," the doorkeeper said, standing back, and opening the door wide. "Please, honor our house by entering. I will summon the master to your aid."

It was either go in or cut and run. He didn't especially want to go in, but found his pride wouldn't support cut and run. Inclining his head, he stepped into the house.

THE DOORKEEPER INSTALLED him in a parlor just off the main entryway and left him. Jethri looked about him, eyes slightly narrowed in protest of the decorating. A deep napped crimson carpet covered the floor from crimson wall to crimson wall. A couch in crimson brocade and two crimson brocade chairs were grouped 'round a low table covered with a crimson cloth. A black wooden bookshelf along one short wall held volumes uniformly bound in red leather, titles outlined in gilt.

Jethri was starting to feel a little uneasy in the stomach by the time the hall door opened and the master of the house joined him.

This was an older man, entirely bald, dressed in a lounging robe of simple white linen. His face was finely lined and unpainted, though a row of tiny golden hoops pierced the skin and followed the curve of his right cheekbone from the inner corner of his eye out to the ear.

Two paces into the room, he paused to bow, low, and to Jethri's eye, with irony.

"Trader. How may our humble house be of service?"

"House Master." Jethri inclined his head. "Pray forgive this unseemly disturbance of your peace. I had been told at a shop in the main port that perhaps I might find a certain cream here—it is often used by Terrans such as myself to remove hair and to condition the face."

"Ah." The man raised a hand and touched his shining bald head. "Yes, we sometimes have such a commodity in the house."

Jethri blinked. The amount of cream necessary to unhair a whole head would be considerable. Once the head in question was bald, it would take less cream to keep it that way, but the supply would need to be steady. The woman at the second philtershop had not sent him astray.

"I wonder," he said to the house master, "if I might purchase a small quantity of this cream from you. Perhaps, a vial—no more than two."

"Purchase? Let me consider…." The man ran his forefinger, slowly, along the line of tiny hoops, his eyes narrowed, as if it were pleasant to feel the gold slide against his cheek.

"No," he said softly. "I really do not think we can sell you any of our supply, Trader."

*Well, there was a disappointment*, Jethri thought. He took a breath, preparatory to thanking the man for his time….

"But we will trade for it," the house master said.

"Trade for it?" Jethri repeated, blankly.

"Indeed." Again, the slow slide of the forefinger along the row of piercings and the long look of narrow-eyed pleasure. "You are a trader, are you not?"

*When I'm not busy being what Lady Maarilex calls a moonling, well yes,* Jethri thought, *I am.* He inclined his head.

"I am a trader, sir, and willing to undertake a trade for the item under discussion. However, it is so small a transaction that I am somewhat at a loss to know what might be fair value."

"There, I can provide guidance," the man said, turning his hand palm up in the gesture that meant, roughly, 'service'. "I understand, as you do, that the item under discussion is a rarity upon this port, as much as it might be commonplace upon other ports. We receive, as I am sure you have surmised, a small but steady supply, from a source that I am really not at liberty to share with you. This source also provides other...specialties...to the house. However, we have not been able to procure formal masks. In trade for two tubes of the cream, I will accept four half-face masks made from crimson leather, or two whole-face masks."

Red leather masks?

"Forgive me, sir, but the trade is uneven," Jethri said, which was sheer reflex, rather than any real knowledge of how costly red leather masks were likely to be. "Two half-masks for two tubes achieves symmetry."

The house master *blinked*—and bowed.

"Of course," he said smoothly, "you are correct, Trader. Two half-masks in red leather for two tubes of Terran depilatory cream. It is done." Straightening, he motioned to the door.

"When you acquire the masks, return, and we will make the exchange."

"Certainly, sir."

Jethri inclined his head, and took the hint. At the outside door, the person with the flower-painted face bowed him out.

"Fair profit, Trader. Come again."

"Joy to the house," he answered and went down the red carpet to the taxicab, waiting at the curb.

He settled into the back seat with an audible sigh.

"I thank you for waiting above the twelve minutes," he said to the cabbie.

She slammed the car into gear and pulled away from the curb more sharply than she should have.

"Are all Terrans fools?" she asked, sounding merely interested in his answer.

"Only the ones that apprentice to master traders and take certification at the Irikwae Trade Hall," he answered, feeling like she'd earned honesty from him—and a good sized tip, too.

"Hah," she said, and nothing more. Jethri leaned back as well as he could in the short seat and looked out the window at the unkempt streets.

The cab glided through an intersection, Jethri glanced down the cross-street—and jerked forward, hand on the door release.

"Stop the cab!" he shouted.

The driver braked and he was out, running back toward the scene he had glimpsed: four people, one on his knees, and all four showing fists.

Jethri had size and surprise, if not speed or sense. He grabbed a handful of jacket and yanked one of the attackers back from the victim, putting him down hard on his ass. The other two shouted, confused by the arrival of reinforcements, while the lone defender seized the opportunity and the room to leap to his feet and land a nice, solid punch on the jaw of the man nearest. In the meantime, Jethri faced off with the third attacker, his body curling into the crouch Pen Rel had drilled him on, knees bent, hands ready.

The man yelled and swung, putting himself off-balance. Jethri ducked, grabbed the man's wrist and elbow, twisted— and shouted with joy as the attacker flew over his shoulder to land hard and flat on his back on the street.

His victory was short-lived. The first man was back on his feet, and moving in fast. This one had a cooler head—and maybe some training in Pen Rel's preferred style of brawl. Jethri dropped back, turning, caught sight of the yellow-haired victim, face cut and jacket torn, having heavy going with his man.

The guy stalking Jethri kicked. He sank back—but not quick enough. The edge of the man's boot caught his knee.

This time, the shout was pain, but he kept his feet, and there was a roaring in the street, growing louder, and then the blare of a klaxon, and it was the taxicab accelerating toward them, the cabbie's face implacable behind the windscreen.

The three attackers yelled and scrambled for the safety of the rotting sidewalk.

The taxi slammed to a halt, back door snapping open.

"In!" Jethri pushed the other man, and the two of them tumbled into the back seat, legs and arms tangled as the cab roared off, back door swinging. It slammed itself into place a few seconds later, when the cabbie took the next corner on two screaming wheels.

Fighting inertia, Jethri and the erstwhile victim slowly sorted out which legs and arms belonged to who and got themselves upright in the seats.

The yellow-haired man sank back on his seat with an audible sigh, and sat for a second, eyes closed. Jethri, blowing hard, leaned his head back, considering his rescue. It came to him that the man looked familiar, and he frowned, trying to bring the memory closer.

Across from him, the other opened his eyes a slit—and then considerably wider as he snapped straight upright.

"You! Jeth Ree Gobelyn, is it not?"

The voice rang the memory right up to the top of the brain. Jethri stared.

"Tan Sim?" he heard himself say, in a mode insultingly close to the one he used when talking with the twins. "What are you doing here?"

Tan Sim grinned, widely, then winced. "I could ask the same of you! Never tell me that the ven'Deelin sends you to the low port unguarded."

"That one," the taxi driver said over her shoulder, "should not be let to roam the high port alone. Where shall I have the extreme pleasure of dropping the two of you off?"

PATCHED AND WELL-SCOLDED by the hall physician, it occurred to them in a simultaneous way that they were hungry. Accordingly, they adjourned to the Trade Bar, where they were fortunate to find a booth open.

"Bread," Jethri said to the waiter. "And two of whatever the day meal is. Fresh fruit."

"Wine," Tan Sim added, and the waiter bowed.

"At once, traders."

Tan Sim sank into deep upholstery with a gusty sigh. "There's a day's work done and the afternoon still before us!"

Jethri grinned. "Now, tell me why you were walking alone on such streets."

"The short answer is—returning from inspecting a pod offered at salvage," Tan Sim retorted. "The longer answer is—longer."

"I have the time, if you have the tale," Jethri murmured, moving his hand in an expression of interest.

Tan Sim smiled. "Gods look upon the lad. Jeth Ree, you are more Liaden than I!"

"Surely not," he began, but a discreet knock upon the door heralded the arrival of the requested wine—a bottle of the house red, a comfortable blend, as Jethri knew—and two glasses.

"The meals are promised quickly, traders," the waiter said and left them, pulling the door closed behind him.

"Well." Tan Sim took charge of the bottle and poured for both of them. "If you will join me first in a sip to seal our friendship—"

Jethri put his glass down. Tan Sim paused, eyebrows up. "What's amiss?"

Jethri tipped his head, considering the other. The physician had cleaned and taped the cut on Tan Sim's face, muttering that bruises would rise by nightfall, and suggesting, with a fair load of irony, that perhaps the trader might wish to cancel any engagements for the next few days.

Truth told, bruises were starting to rise already, but it wasn't that which took Jethri's notice. It was the face beneath the cut—thinner than he had remembered, the mouth tighter. The torn jacket hung loose, which bore out Jethri's impression that maybe Tan Sim had been eating short rations lately.

"I believe," he said delicately, wishing neither to offend nor expose a weakness, "that there is a matter of Balance unresolved between us."

"Which would—naturally!—constrain you from drinking with me. Very nice. If such an unresolved Balance sat between us, I would commend you for the precision of your melant'i."

Meaning that Tan Sim didn't think there was a debt, and that didn't jibe.

"I had considered you my most grievous error," Jethri said, making another pass at getting it out in the open where they both could look at it. "It has troubled me that, all unknowing, and wishing only to honor one who had shown me the greatest kindness, I brought to that one only grief, and separation from clan and kin."

"If you believe for one moment that separation from my honored mother or my so-beloved brother is a matter of *grief*, then I must allow you to be in your cups," Tan Sim retorted and paused, face arrested. "No, that cannot be. We've not yet had to drink." He leaned forward slightly, to look earnestly into Jethri's face.

"My sweet fool—does it occur to you that you have just now preserved my life for me? Even supposing that I held you to book for my mother's temper and my brother's spite—that small matter would put paid to all." He raised his glass.

"Come, do not be churlish! At least drink to the gallantry of a taxi driver." /

Well, Jethri thought, 'round a mental grin, he could hardly refuse that. He raised his glass.

"To the gallant driver, who preserved both our lives—"

"And refused any tip, save a scold!" Tan Sim finished with a flourish of his glass.

They sipped, and again, the wine tasting more than usually pleasant.

"So, tell me then," Jethri said, putting his glass aside and relaxing into the cushions.

Tan Sim laughed lightly. "Demanding youth. Very well." He put his glass down and folded his elbows onto the table, leaning forward.

"Now, it happens that my mother was very angry indeed over the incident with the bow. She swore that I was a disgrace to her blood and that she would have no more of me. For some significant time, it did appear that she would simply cancel my contract and send me out to earn my own way. A not entirely unpleasing prospect, as you might imagine."

He extended a hand and picked up his glass, twirling it idly by the stem, his eyes on the wine swirling inside the bowl.

"Alas, it was then that my brother entered the negotiations, with a plea for leniency, which my mother was disposed to hear." He lifted the glass.

"Rather than cancel my contract, she sold it. I am now the trader of record aboard the good ship *Genchi*, which Captain sea'Kira allows me to know has never carried such a thing. Nor needs one."

A quick knock, and the door was opened by their waiter, bearing a tray well-loaded with eatables. He set it all out with noiseless efficiency, bowed and was gone, the door snicking shut behind him.

There was a pause in the tale, then, while the two of them took the day meal under consideration, Tan Sim eating with an elegant ferocity that confirmed Jethri's fears regarding short rations.

"Well," Tan Sim said at last, selecting a fruit from the basket between them. "Where did I leave the tale?"

"Your mother sold your contract to *Genchi*, though it had no need of a trader," Jethri said, around his last bit of bread.

"Ah. *Genchi*. Indeed. It happened that the ship owner had a desire to improve *Genchi's* fortunes and thought that a trader aboard might produce a rise in profit. Unfortunately, the owner is a person who has…limited funding available to him—and, very possibly, limited understanding as well. For I put it to you, friend Jethri: How does a ship on a fixed route raise profit?"

Jethri paused in the act of reaching for a fruit and looked over to him.

"By shipping more."

*Sharon Lee & Steve Miller*     403

Tan Sim raised his fruit in an exuberant toast. "Precisely!"

"And *Genchi* is podded out," Jethri guessed, in case there were bonuses involved.

Tan Sim smiled upon him tenderly. "It's a dear, clever lad. But, no—there you are slightly out. It happens that *Genchi* can accept two additional pods. Which the trader is to purchase from the elevated profits his very presence upon the ship will produce."

Jethri stared at him. "Your mother signed that contract?" he demanded.

Tan Sim dipped his head modestly. "She was most wonderfully angry."

"How long?"

"Until I am in default? Or until the contract is done?"

"Both."

"Pah! You have a mind like a trader, Jeth Ree Gobelyn!" He bit into his fruit and chewed, meditatively.

"I will default at the end of the relumma. The contract has six years to run."

Jethri blinked. "She's trying to kill you."

Tan Sim moved a shoulder. "Break me only. Or so I believe. And, in truth, I am not without some blame. Were I less like my mother, I might send a beam, begging her grace, and asking for terms to come home."

Jethri snorted.

"Yes," Tan Sim said gently. "Exactly so."

Glumly, Jethri finished his fruit, wiped his fingers and reached for his glass.

"But you aren't going to default," he said. "You went down to the salvage yard this morning to look at a pod."

"Indeed I did. I found it to be a most excellent pod, of an older construction. Older, even, than *Genchi*. It is in extraordinarily good shape—sealed and unbreached—and the yardman's final price is…not beyond reach. However, it's all for naught, for it must have new clamps if it is to marry *Genchi*, and while I may afford those—I cannot afford those and the pod."

Jethri sipped wine, frowning slightly. "Still sealed, you say. What does it hold?"

"Now, that, I do not know. As old as the pod is, its contents are unlikely to have much value. Were matters otherwise, I might take the gamble, but—I do not scruple to tell you, cash is at present too dear."

Jethri finished his wine and set the glass aside. There was an idea, buzzing around in the back of his brain, slowly gaining clarity and insistence. He let it grow, while across the table Tan Sim wrestled silently with whatever thoughts engaged him.

"How much?" he asked softly, so as not to joggle the idea before it was set.

"The yard wants to see a cantra for the pod, entire. Clamps are four kais."

The idea had set firm, and he was liking it from all the angles he could see. He had a knack for salvage, Uncle Paitor'd always said so...

"I wonder," he said, looking up into Tan Sim's bruised and weary face, "if you might have time tomorrow to introduce me to the salvage yard?"

"Oh," said Tan Sim wisely, "do you think you might manage it? I wish you shall. Certainly. Meet me here at the opening of day port and I will show you where."

"And this time," Jethri said with a smile. "We will take a taxi."

IT LOOKED LIKE red leather masks were going to be a problem, Jethri thought, leaning back in his chair and rubbing his eyes. He had written his report on the toys, and seen that his tomorrow's schedule had been amended to reflect the hall physician's orders that he "rest"—by which it was apparently meant that he not go on the port to trade, a concept that struck him as wrongheaded, at best. Still, it did give him a good piece of time to go to the salvage yards with Tan Sim and inspect the pod he had found.

But the masks, now. Never mind red leather—masks at all was a missing item along any of the lists open to the guild computer. He sighed and leaned way back in the chair, stretching—and grimacing, when the stretch woke muscles that had been pulled in the day's fisticuffs.

Nothing for it but to go back to the Trade Bar and use his key to find masks on the Combine net. Come to think of it, he might forget masks altogether and go for a pallet of depilatory, since there seemed to be a market.

He stood and reached for his second best jacket, his first being down at the laundry—and started badly when the door chime sounded.

Probably Trader sig'Lorta, come to read him Ship's General. Shrugging into his jacket, he walked over to the door and keyed it open.

"Why, look how the boy has grown!" Scout Captain ter'Astin said in cheery Terran. Miandra stood at his elbow, her face serious.

"Well met, Jethri," she said. "The captain came to the house and Aunt Stafeli said that I should bring him to you."

Captain ter'Astin bowed, lightly, hand over heart. "Summoned, I rush to obey."

Jethri felt his cheeks warm with the blush. "I have overstepped my melant'i, I fear," he admitted.

"Not a bit of it! The Scouts tend a wide business; it is our nature to answer summonses." He cocked his head. "Some, I do allow, with more alacrity than others."

Jethri smiled and stepped back, sweeping a bow. "Please, both, enter and be welcome."

The Scout entered first, Miandra trailing after, looking like a limp copy of herself.

Frowning, Jethri closed and locked the door, then turned to deal with his guests.

Miandra was already at the window, looking down into the garden. The Scout had paused to give the short row of books his consideration, and looked up as Jethri approached.

"I was asked to bring something besides myself to your side," he said, pulling a well-folded piece of paper from an inner jacket pocket. "Please, satisfy yourself. I have no other engagements to fulfill today."

"Thank you," Jethri said, receiving the paper with a bow. "May I call for tea? Wine?"

The Scout laughed. "You take polish well, Jethri Gobelyn. But, no, I thank you—I am not in need."

Jethri glanced over to the window, where his other guest still stared down into the garden.

"Miandra?" He asked, softly. "Would you like tea? Cookies?"

She flicked a distracted glance over her shoulder, tight lips moving in what she might have meant to be a smile.

"Thank you, but I am not—in need."

Which was as big a clunker as he'd ever heard, including the time Grig told Cap'n Iza that the odd lot of sweets he'd bought was a broker deal, and then shared them all out 'mong crew.

"What's amiss?" He asked, moving closer, the Scout's paper held close in his hand.

She turned her face away, and that—hurt. Weren't they friends, after all? He touched her sleeve.

"Hey," he said. "Miandra. Are you well?"

Her shoulders jerked, and a half-smothered sound escaped, sounding half laugh and half sob.

"You asked that—before," she said, and turned to face him squarely, chin up and looking more like herself, despite her wet cheeks. "Have we not taught you that strangers must keep a proper reserve?"

"Certainly, Lady Maarilex would not be behind in so basic a lesson," he allowed, inclining his head and putting on the gentleman. "However, such rules do not maintain between us, because we are kin."

Her eyes widened and the corner of her mouth twitched slightly upward. "Kin? How so?"

"What else would we be?" He held his hand up, fingers spread, and folded his thumb against the palm, counting. "I am Norn ven'Deelin's foster son." Forefinger down. "Stafeli Maarilex is Norn ven'Deelin's foster mother, my foster grandmother." Second finger joined thumb and forefinger. "You are a niece of Stafeli Maarilex." Third finger. "Therefore, we are foster cousins."

She laughed. "Well done! And the degree of consanguinity appropriate, too, I see!"

He grinned and reached again to touch her sleeve.

"So, cousin, if a cousin may ask it—are you well?"

She moved her shoulders and flicked a glance aside. He looked, as well, but the Scout was perched on the edge of the work table, to all appearances immersed in one of the novels brought from Tarnia's library.

"I am...unwell in spirit," she said, lowering her voice. "Ren Lar—he treats me as if *I* were a piece of Old Technology. He forbids me the vines, the cellar, and the yards. I am scarcely allowed to come to the dining table at prime. At his insistence, Meicha and I must undergo—separately—intensive evaluation, by the Healers. Meicha completed hers last night; Anecha drove down to pick her up this morning. In the meanwhile, a car was made ready to take me to Healer Hall—so that we should not be able to speak together before I am evaluated, you know—but your Scout happened by and offered to save the house the trouble, as he was going back down to the port to find you."

He had no idea what an "intensive evaluation" might mean, but allowed as it sounded bad enough.

"Do you need to report in?" he asked.

"Testing does not begin until tomorrow morning," she said. "It was arranged that I should overnight at the hall." Her mouth got tight again. "I....would...that other arrangements had been made."

"If they don't need you until tomorrow morning," he said, moving his hand, to show her his quarters, "you're welcome to spend the night here. I am at liberty tomorrow and can escort you to Healer Hall."

"Perhaps it might be—less stressful of the relations of kin and foster kin," the Scout said, so suddenly that both of them spun to stare at him, sitting on the edge of the table, with the book opened over his knee, "if the lady would instead accept my invitation to guest with the Scouts this evening."

"You were listening," Jethri said, sounding like a younger, even to himself.

Captain ter'Astin inclined his head. "Scouts have very sharp ears. It is required."

Miandra took a step forward, frowning slightly. "And in addition to sharp ears, you are a Healer."

He moved a hand, deprecating. "A receiver only, I fear. Though I'm told I build a most impressive wall. Honor me with your opinion, do."

To Jethri's senses, nothing happened, except that the Scout's expression maybe took on an extra degree of bland, while Miandra stared intently at the thin air above his head.

She blinked. Captain ter'Astin tipped his head to one side.

"It is," Miandra said, slowly, "a very impressive wall. But you must not think it proof against attack."

"Ah, must I not? Tell me why."

She moved her hands in a gesture of—untangling, Jethri thought. Untangling her perception into words the two of them could understand.

"You have a—need. A very powerful need to be—acutely aware of surrounding conditions, at all times. Data is survival. So, you have left a—chink, very small—in your wall, that you may continue to be aware. It is through that chink that you are vulnerable. If I can see it, others may, as well."

The Scout slid to his feet, catching the book up neatly, and bowed. Acknowledging a debt, Jethri read, and looked at Miandra in close wonder. She bit her lip and half-raised a hand.

Captain ter'Astin raised the book. "Peace. The gratitude of a Scout is worth holding, and is not given lightly. Your observation may well have saved my life. Who can say? Certainly, I shall not leave Irikwae without consulting a Healer and learning the manner of sealing this—chink."

"And now," he said, lowering the book. "I believe Jethri has a paper to read, after which he and I have business. Shall we proceed?"

Miandra moved to the table and picked up one of the novels, carrying it back to the window with her. The Scout resettled himself on the edge of the table. Jethri went to the black corner table, pushed the photocube of strangers back, unfolded the paper and smoothed it flat with his palm.

Despite that by now he read Liaden as well or better than he'd ever read Terran, it was dense going. Stoically, he kept with it and finally arrived at the last word with the understanding that the Liaden Scouts were, indeed, specifically charged with the confiscation, evaluation and appropriate disposal of "Old War technology," such technology having been designated, by an action of the Council of Clans, meeting at Solcintra City, Liad, "perilous in manufacture and intent."

Sighing, he straightened, and turned.

Miandra was sitting in his desk chair, seriously involved with her novel. The Scout was reading Jethri's old pretend journal.

"I shouldn't think that would hold much interest for you, sir," he said, moving forward, and slipping a hand into his most secret pocket.

Captain ter'Astin glanced up, bounced to his feet, turning to put the book back in its place.

"The workings of mind and custom are always of interest to me," he said. "It is the reason I am a Scout—and a field Scout, at that."

Jethri looked at him sharply. The Scout inclined his head.

"So tell me, Jethri Gobelyn, are you satisfied that the disposal of Old War technology falls within the honor of the Scouts, and that such disposal is mandated by whole law?"

"Unfortunately, I am." He placed the weather machine, lingeringly, on the table, and stood there, feeling kind of dry and gone in the throat of a sudden, staring down into the unreflective black surface.

"Ah." Captain ter'Astin put a hand on Jethri's sleeve. "I regret your loss. I believe you had told Scout yo'Shomin that this device was given you by a kinsman?"

Jethri licked his lips.

"It was a gift from my father," he told the Scout. "After his death, I was without it for many years. It was only recently returned to me, with—" He waved a hand, enclosing the photocubes, Arin's box and the silly old journal—"other things of value."

"Accept my condolences," the Scout said softly. The pressure of his fingers increased briefly, then he withdrew his hand and picked up the weather machine, slipping it away somewhere inside his jacket.

Jethri cleared his throat. "I wonder if you might tell me if you will yourself be involved in the—evaluation—of this device. Whether it will be—will simply be destroyed, or if the work that my father did will be preserved."

The Scout's eyebrows rose. "Yes. I would say that you take polish very well, indeed." He paused, possibly gathering his thoughts, then inclined his head.

"I may possibly be asked for a preliminary evaluation; I do have some small expertise in the area. However, you must understand that there is a corps of Scout Experts, who have studied, built databases and cross-referenced their findings through the many dozens of Standards that this policy has been in force. If it is found that your machine, here, is unique, then it will undergo the most intense scrutiny possible by those who are entirely knowledgeable. Many of the Old Technology pieces that we have recovered are uniquities—that is, we have recovered only one."

Jethri bowed his gratitude. "I thank you, sir."

"Unnecessary, I assure you. A word in your ear, however, child."

"Yes?"

"It might be wisest not to state in public that such devices were part of your father's work."

Jethri frowned. "Old technology is not illegal, in Terran space," he said, evenly.

"Very true," the Scout said and it seemed to Jethri that he was about to say more.

"Is this your father?" Miandra asked from behind them.

Jethri turned, and saw her holding up the photocube, Arin's picture on the screen.

"Yes—that's him."

She turned it 'round to face her. "You resemble him extremely, Jethri. I had supposed him to be your elder brother."

"May I see?" The Scout extended a hand, and Miandra gave him the cube.

"Ah, yes, that is how I saw him, on the day of his dying. Strong, doubt free and worthy. A remarkable likeness, indeed." Bowing slightly, he handed the cube back.

"Now, children, I suggest that we adjourn to Scout Hall, where Jethri may sign the necessary paperwork and we may place this item—" He touched the breast of his jacket—"into safekeeping. We will also contact the Healers, to advise them of Lady Miandra's guesting arrangements, and to confirm the time of her arrival tomorrow. *After* which, I ask you both to lend me the pleasure of your companionship over prime. There is a restaurant on Irikwaeport which has long been a favorite of mine. I would be honored to share it with friends."

Jethri glanced to Miandra, saw her eyes shining and her face looking less pinched, and bowed to the Scout.

"We are more than pleased to bear you company, sir. Lead on."

# Day 178
# Standard Year 1118

## Irikwae

IT WAS AN old pod, though he'd seen older; the seals were sound, the skin whole and undented. It rested on a cradle meant for a pod decades newer and massing twice as much; though its fittings could be said to be standard they were of an older and unfavored style. At some time in the past—perhaps not all that long ago—it had been underwater and a colony of hard-shells, now empty, still adhered to the hull. On the nose was a Liaden registry number, faint, but readable.

Jethri finished his circuit and paused, considering the thing as a whole.

"Well?" asked Tan Sim, who had been watching, one hip up on the wide windowsill, one booted foot braced against the rough crete floor. "Shall you take it for your own?"

Jethri turned. "You know what is in this pod," he said, not asking.

Tan Sim blinked, and then bowed slightly from his lean. "I know what was on the manifest," he said, "and the devil's own time I had finding it, too."

"So?" Jethri walked toward him. "What were they shipping? Flegetets, dead and rotted, these sixty years? Cheeses, moldy and poisonous? Wine, now vinegar?"

Tan Sim moved a shoulder, grimacing. The bruises had risen with a will overnight, leaving his face a patchwork of yellow and purple.

"Mind you," he said, raising a hand. "I could only trace the registry number, which is in series with those ceded Clan Dartom, some sixty Standards gone. Indeed, Clan Dartom is itself fifty Standards gone, and nothing to say but that this pod was sold and sold again on the unregistered market."

"Clan Dartom is—gone?" Jethri asked, thinking epic scales of revenge, like in one of Khat's stories—or Gaenor's novels.

"Peace," Tan Sim said, as if he had read Jethri's thoughts—or was perhaps himself a reader of novels. "Dartom was based upon a young outworld; a plague destroyed them and the rest of the population, very speedily. Not even a kitten left alive. Medical analysis failed to produce anyone who might even be named a cousin." He waved a languid hand in the direction of the pod.

"So, Dartom's remaining uncontaminated assets fell to the Council of Clans, which took what it wanted, and distributed the remainder by lot. They then wrote Dartom out of the Book of Clans, and put paid to the matter."

"Anyone could have bought this pod at auction, then," Jethri said. "Or, as you say, on the unregistered market. And those who buy such things sometimes have unregistered business."

"In pursuit of which they would be foolish in the extreme to file a manifest," Tan Sim agreed.

Jethri turned back to the pod, and once again subjected the seals to the most minute scrutiny possible. Unbreached. Impossible to tell how long they had been sealed.

"You found a manifest," he said, turning back to Tan Sim. "How long ago?"

"Fifty-three years, which does put it in a...problematic time frame."

"The pod spent some time in the sea," Jethri pointed out.

"True, but we have no date there, either." Tan Sim turned his palms up, showing them empty. "Indeed, we have but one firm date: The salvage rig's log shows that it was brought into port two Standards back, when it was purchased by this yard, in lot with another dozen newer. This—" Tan Sim wiggled his fingers in the pod's general direction. "This was on the list for break-up, but the scrap market is over-subscribed and there is for the scrappers the considerable risk involved in taking possession of unknown goods."

"So they would just as soon sell it and shift the risk to other shoulders." Jethri sighed. "The manifest is public record?" he asked.

"My friend, public record?" Tan Sim bent upon him a look of gentle reproof. "The manifest had been sealed, then deep archived after the seal expired. Your average salvager, with his mind properly on scrap, is hardly busy mucking about in municipal archives, much less completing the rather daunting forms required by the Guild before one who is not a trader may request permission to pull and cross-reference ancient databases."

Jethri bowed acknowledgment, offering honor for a difficult task well-performed.

Tan Sim's bow of acceptance was nearly lost against the wall of Jethri's thought.

Jethri looked back to the pod. He *liked* it. He couldn't have put it otherwise, except that he had a good feeling about whatever might prove to be inside.

"What was on the manifest?"

"Ore, raw gem, artisan's metals."

Nonperishables. High profit nonperishables, at that. If it was the right manifest. If it was the right pod, for that matter, it not being unknown for someone to borrow the legitimate registration number of a legitimate pod for illegitimate business.

"Buy the pod, sell the contents and realize more than enough profit to have the clamps refitted," he said. Again Tan Sim lifted a shoulder.

"A manifest, which may or may not be legitimate, for a pod which may or may not be this one? If I were plumper in the purse—perhaps. My present purse instructs me to assume that what is in that pod are dead flegetets, moldy cheese, and spoiled wine."

Jethri had done the math last night, worrying over his liquid. It were the Stinks money that made the difference—not quite enough to fund a ship, like Khat had joked, but close enough to fund this deal, after reserving an amount against the future. 'Course, there was more than enough money in his certification drawing account to cover the pod—and the clamps, too—but he didn't think the hall exactly wanted him to be using those funds for private deals.

"I will put four kais against the pod," he said to Tan Sim, "if we agree that the contents, whatever they are found to be, are mine, while the pod itself is yours."

Tan Sim raised his eyebrows, face thoughtful. Doing his own math, Jethri thought, and settled himself to wait.

"Four-six," Tan Sim said, eventually, which was about half the jump Jethri had been prepared to meet.

He inclined his head. "Done. Now, we shall need the pod moved to a less precarious position. What do you suggest?"

"As to that—nothing easier. The refit shop will send a hauler. They assured me that they have the means to unseal the pod without damaging the mechanisms, so the day after tomorrow should see an answer to your gamble. After which," he said, coming creakily out of his lean, "you may have free with whatever it is, and the shop will get on with the business of the clamps."

Jethri looked at him, and Tan Sim had the grace to look, just a little, discomfited.

"I thought you might do something like you have done," he said, softly. "So I made inquiries yesterday after we had parted." He sighed.

"I hope you will realize great profit, Jeth Ree."

"As to that," Jethri retorted. "I hope for a decent return."

Tan Sim grinned and offered his arm. "Spoken like a trader! Come, let us give the yardman his deposit and return to the hall to write the partnership papers."

THE PARTNERSHIP CONTRACT having been duly written, accepted and recorded by the hall scrivener, Jethri bounded up the stairs to his quarters, Tan Sim on his heels.

"Come and call the refit shop, so they may schedule an early pickup," he said as they moved down the hall. "For the salvage price—my part is in coin, which I will give to you, and you may transfer the balance to the yard."

Tan Sim smiled. "Such trusting ways. How if we both put our coin into the revolving account and authorize the hall to make the transfer in our names?"

Jethri paused in the act of unlocking the door to stare at him. "I had no idea such a thing was possible."

"Innocent. When we have sent the transfer, I will quiz you on the services a trader might expect a third tier hall to provide."

The lock twittered and Jethri pushed the door open. "Is Irikwae in the third—" he began—and stopped, staring into his room.

All was neat and orderly, precisely as he had left it, with one addition.

Miandra sat cross-legged on his work table, reading a book.

Behind him, Tan Sim made a small noise, very much like a sneeze.

Miandra raised her head, showing them a face that was eerily serene.

"Cousin Jethri," she said clearly. "We need to talk."

*Uh-oh.*

"Certainly," Tan Sim said briskly, "the necessities of kin carry all before it. Jeth Ree, I will make that call from the Trade Bar and meet you there, when you have done here. Lady."

Jethri turned, but the door was already closing, with Tan Sim on the other side. He engaged the lock, then walked over to where Miandra sat, and stood looking down into her face.

She met his gaze without flinching, chin well up, an I-dare-you look in her eyes.

He sighed.

"How much trouble are you in?"

The chin might've quivered; the eyes never faltered.

"None, until they find me."

Well, that was the way it usually was, wasn't it? Jethri frowned.

"I thought you wanted my help."

She bit her lip. "I—indeed, Jethri, I am not certain what is that you might do. But I *will not* remain with the Healers, and I—fear—that I *cannot* go home…"

Jethri sighed again and made a long arm, hooking the desk chair to him. He sat down and looked up at her, showing her his hands, palm up, fingers spread, empty.

"I think you had better lay it out for me, one step at a time."

"Yes, I suppose I had better." She closed the book and put it on the table beside her, then leaned forward, elbow propped against a knee, chin nestled on her palm.

"As you know, I was to be evaluated by the Healers. Indeed, by the master healer himself. The evaluation—" she shot him a sharp glance. "You understand, Jethri, that when I say in this context that I was pushed, or prodded or that thus-and-so hurt me, I am not speaking of physical things, but rather use those words as an approximation of the exact…sensation…because there are no words precisely for those sensations."

He inclined his head. "But I may still understand that you found those things so described to be distressing and not at all what you could like, is that so?"

She smiled. "That is so, yes."

"Very well, then," Jethri said, starting to feel grim. "The master healer himself was assigned to your evaluation. What came next?"

"I was asked to—to take my shields down and to submit my will to the will of the master," she began, after a moment—and sent him another sharp glance. "This is not at all unusual and I did as I was bid. The master then began his examination, pushing here, prodding there—nothing terribly painful, but nothing pleasant either."

It sounded, Jethri owned, tiresome enough, something like a clinic check-up, with the medic pushing hard fingers here and there, trying to determine what was in line and what was out.

"Unpleasant, but hardly worth running away," he commented.

Miandra inclined her head. "I agree. After a time, the master began to concentrate on—say, a section of my will— and to—assault it. The first strike was so painful that I threw my shields up before I had even thought to do so. The master, of course, was very angry and had me lower them, whereupon he once again brought all of his scrutiny to bear on—on this anomaly in my—in my pattern." She sighed sharply. "By which I mean to convey that there are certain…constructions of intertwining ego, will, and intellect, which are intelligible to those who have Healer talent. While each pattern is unique, there are those which tend to be formed in a certain way—and which, more often than not, are indicative of Healer ability."

"So, the master healer was saying he thought your pattern was—shaped oddly," Jethri said, to show he was following this.

Miandra inclined her head. "Indeed, he went so far as to state that he felt it was this anomaly which was responsible for limiting my growth as a Healer, and he proposed to— restructure that portion, in order to allow my talent to flow more freely."

Jethri frowned. "He can do that?"

"That, easily," she assured him. "It is what Healers do."

Right. Jethri closed his eyes. Opened them.

"All right. So the master decided he would reshape you so you would look more like he thinks a Healer ought to. Then?"

She bit her lip.

"It—I told him that the process was…causing me pain. He assured me that it was not, and—pushed—harder." She glanced aside, took a hard breath and looked back to him, blue eyes swimming with tears.

"The pain was—immense. Truly, Jethri, I felt that I was afire, my flesh crisping off my bones as I stood there. I *pushed*, and threw my shields up."

"I see." He considered that, staring down at his hands where they rested on his knee, the one sporting a slightly grubby bandage. He looked up to find her watching him worriedly.

"Which moon did he fall onto?" he asked, mildly.

Miandra smiled, shakily. "You overestimate my poor abilities, cousin. I merely put him onto the top shelf of the bookcase." She took a breath. "Then I walked out, through the main reception hall. I willed that no one would see me, and no one did. And then I came here, and—overrode the lock and sat down to wait for you."

"Are they looking for you?"

"I suppose they must be, eventually." Another shaky smile appeared. "But as long as I keep my shields in place, they will not find me."

For however long that might be. He forbore from asking what happened to her shields when she slept. First order of business was to tell her what she'd done right. So—

"The rule on the ship I was born to was that one is allowed to defend oneself. Defense should be delivered as quickly and as decisively as possible, in order to prevent a second attack." He inclined his head, solemnly. "You have fulfilled ship rule admirably and I have no complaint to make regarding your actions to this point."

Relief washed her face.

"Our challenge now," Jethri continued, "is to be certain that our actions from this point on continue to be honorable and in the best interest of the ship." He tipped his head.

"That means you can't just hide on the port for the rest of your life."

Miandra outright laughed. "My shields aren't that good."

Jethri grinned, and let it fade into as serious a look as he could muster.

"You will need to let the House know where you are. Sooner or later the Healers will have to call and admit that you've gone missing. That information is certain to distress your sister, your cousins and your delm, unless they know you are safe."

Miandra's look had turned stubborn.

"If I go home, Ren Lar will send me back. If I call, Aunt Stafeli will order me to return to Healer Hall."

Both probably true. But—

"If you explained to them what you have explained to me, that the examination was painful in the extreme and that you fear for your health if it continues?"

She considered it, chewing her lip. "That might bear weight with Aunt Stafeli, but Ren Lar—I do not believe that Ren Lar would be swayed, if I told him that the evaluation would, without doubt, murder me." She sighed. "Ren Lar is a badly frightened man. Old Technology and wizard's get, *both* in his household! It is too much to bear."

"What if the evaluation proves that you are a dramliza?" Jethri asked.

She moved her shoulders. "I don't know."

This, Jethri thought, was 'way too snarly for a junior's simple brain. Clearly, Miandra needed help—and not just in this present mess. She needed schooling, whether or not Ren Lar or Stafeli Maarilex chose to believe in wizards. Jethri was pretty sure he didn't believe in wizards, himself. Still, there was no doubt Miandra had some very strange talents and that she needed to be trained in their proper use before she up and hurt somebody. If she hadn't already.

"Is the master healer harmed?" he asked.

She sighed. "No."

Jethri suppressed a grin.

"This is what I propose: That you come with me to the Trade Bar and be my guest for lunch. My friend and I have some business to discuss, which I hope you won't find too tedious. After, you and I will go together to the Scouts and ask Captain ter'Astin to advise us. For you know I'm a block, Miandra, and we are well past anything I can think of to assist you."

"Well, I don't know that you're a block," she retorted, and sat for a moment, contemplating the floor. Jethri sighed and stretched in his chair, careful of protesting muscles.

"I think that asking the captain's advice at this juncture is the wisest thing that I—that we—may do," she said, unfolding her legs and sliding to the floor. "It was very clever of you to have thought of it."

TAN SIM HAD ordered a cold platter of finger-nibbles, cheese, crackers, and tea—more than enough to feed two, Jethri thought—and possibly enough to cover three, if Miandra wasn't feeling particularly peckish.

He inclined his head. "I thank you. My cousin and I are needed elsewhere later in the day, and she has graciously said that she will allow us to conclude our business before hers."

"On condition," Miandra said, and Jethri could almost hear the glint in her eye, "that you feed me."

Jethri moved his hand. "You can see that Tan Sim has already thought of that."

"Indeed." She bowed, hand over heart. "Miandra Maarilex Clan Tarnia."

Seated, Tan Sim returned her bow. "Tan Sim pen'Akla Clan Rinork." He moved a hand, showing them both the laden table. "Please, join me."

Join him they did and there was a small pause in the proceedings while they each took the edge off.

"Well." Tan Sim sat back, teacup in hand. "While you and your cousin dealt kin to kin, Jeth Ree, I have performed wonders."

Jethri eyed him. "What, not marvels?"

Tan Sim waved an airy hand. "Tomorrow is soon enough for marvels. Behold my labors of today! Moon Mountain Refit Shop has been called. By the luck, the hauler was enroute to deliver scrap and other oddments at the very salvage yard where our pod awaited. They simply off-loaded their scrap, onloaded our pod and very soon now it should be in a bay at the shop. They say they will immediately perform a magnetic resonance scan. They do this to locate any hidden flaws or structural damage, so that they may adjust their entry protocol as necessary." He raised his cup and sipped, slowly, teasing, Jethri thought—and then thought of something else.

"How was it the salvager let the pod go before the transfer was made?" He asked.

Tan Sim lowered his cup, looking sheepish. "As it happens, I made the full transfer out of my account, knowing that you will place the coin for your portion in my hand."

"Such trusting ways," Jethri said, and Tan Sim sighed, holding up a hand.

"I knew you were going to say so, and I cannot but agree, that, in the normal way of things, it was an extremely foolhardy thing to do. However, I am adamant. My partner in this endeavor is a man of honor, who pays his just debts promptly."

"And so he is," Jethri said quietly, reaching into the depths of his jacket and extracting the purse containing four kais, six tor. He placed it on the table by Tan Sim's plate.

"My thanks," Tan Sim said softly, and lifted an eyebrow. "Now, may I tell you that the shop desires a call back in—" he glanced at the watch wrapped around his left wrist— "only a few minutes now. A side profit of the scanning is that it will give a rough image of the contents of the pod. When we call back, you will be able to know, with fair certainty, whether you have in fact taken an option on that reasonable return. Indeed, you may well be able to increase that reasonable return, with some judicious and well-placed announcements."

"You may tell me so," Jethri said. "But now you must tell me what you mean by it."

"I expect he means that you might upload the image to the tradenet, and invite advance bids," Miandra said, surprisingly.

Tan Sim raised his cup to her. "Precisely." He glanced at Jethri. "I can show you the way of it, if you like."

"I would very much like," Jethri assured him.

"Good." He put his teacup down and reached for the multipurpose screen. "Finish your meals, children. I will find if the shop has uploaded that image yet."

There wasn't that much to finish by then, but he and Miandra made quick work of what there was and by the time Jethri had drunk the last of his tea, Tan Sim said, "Ah!" and spun the screen around.

The image was a muddle of shape, shadow, hard edges, and glare, reminding Jethri of the relative densities screen on a piloting board. He looked up.

"Traders will bid on the strength of this image?"

"Traders," Tan Sim said, "will very often *buy* on the strength of such an image." He spun the screen so they all could see it, though Miandra had to scrunch against Jethri's side, and sort of lean her head against his chest, which was comforting and distracting at the same time.

"Attend me, now," Tan Sim said severely and Jethri obediently put his eyes on the screen, trying not to notice that Miandra's hair smelled like Lady Maarilex's favorite flowers.

"You see these, here, here, here— " He touched the screen over three of the glare spots. "Those are stasis boxes that have failed. These—" Quick finger touches on half-a-dozen bland blobs, "are stasis boxes that are still functioning as they should." He flicked a glance at Jethri.

"Already, your gains outnumber your losses."

"Depending on the contents of the boxes," Jethri pointed out. "The manifest listed ores, gems and metals. Not the sort of cargo that normally ships in stasis."

Tan Sim tipped his head. "I thought we had agreed that manifests do not always reflect cargo?"

Jethri smiled. "So we had. Please, continue."

"Very well, what else have we?" He turned his attention back to the screen, subjecting the image to frowning study.

"Ah." A finger tap on a particularly muddy blur. "This, I believe, may be your ore. Were I interested in ore, I might well wish to be at hand when the pod is opened. For the rest...." He moved his hand, showing palm in a quick flip. "Who can tell? But there is enough possibility in the stasis boxes alone to warrant putting the image to the tradenet."

Jethri inclined his head. "I bow to the wisdom of an elder trader in this. May I impose further and ask that you teach me the way of putting an image to the tradenet?"

"Truly," Tan Sim said, round-eyed, "is this the lad I found practicing his bows in a back hallway, half-ill for fear of giving offense?"

"Who very shortly thereafter proceeded to give offense most spectacularly?" Jethri retorted.

The other trader grinned. "From which act springs both our fortunes."

"So you say." Jethri used his chin, Liaden style, to point at the screen. "How do I upload this image and invite bids?"

"Nothing simpler. First, feed your Guild card to the unit."

"Already, we find difficulty. I have no Guild card."

"*What?*" Tan Sim frankly stared. "Would the Guild not grant you a card, after all?"

"I am at the hall in order to be certified, as apprentice, or junior trader—"

"Or master trader," Miandra put in, her head against his chest.

"Certified?" Tan Sim repeated. "But—"

"I was registered as Master ven'Deelin's apprentice," Jethri explained. "Despite that, the hall at Modrid declined to accept any of the purchases I had made on her account, because the hall master did not believe that Terrans belonged in the Guild."

"Hah. The master of Modrid hall oversteps. As I am certain the ven'Deelin will demonstrate, in the fullness of time. So you tell me that you are on a hall account at the moment?"

"I have some liquid."

"Which you put into your speculation cargo, here. I see. However, matters become awkward if you lack a valid—"

"Will a Combine key do?" Jethri interrupted.

Tan Sim blinked at him. "Certainly," he said, adding delicately. "Have you a Combine key?"

"Yes." He reached inside his collar for the chain. Miandra ducked under his elbow and sat up, watching him pull the key up and then lift the chain over his head.

Tan Sim caught the key and held it in his palm, frowning at the inscription.

"A ten-year key?"

"With two trades on it—an acquisition and an assisting."

"And you are at the hall for certification?" Tan Sim raised a hasty palm. "No, do *not* tell me. I am merely a trader. The ways of the masters are too subtle for me. So." He released the key, and it swung gently at the end of the chain. "Well, then. If the young trader will do me the honor of using his key to access the Combine computer in the main bar, I will be pleased to guide him through the procedure for uploading an invitation to bid to the tradenet."

SCOUT CAPTAIN TER'ASTIN received them in Scout Hall's book-cluttered common room. After tea had been called for and tasted, he inquired as to the purpose of their visit, and listened in attentive silence while Miandra recounted her tale.

"And I *cannot* go home, sir, though I know you will think me beyond the pale for saying it—and I *will not* go back to the Healers," she finished, heatedly, her hands folded tightly on her lap.

"A knotty situation," the Scout said seriously. "I am honored that you thought me worthy of advising you. Let me consider."

He picked up his teacup and sipped, Jethri and Miandra following suit, and sat for some few minutes, eyes not quite focused on the overladen bookshelf just behind Miandra's shoulder.

"I wonder," he said eventually, bringing his gaze to her face, "if you might consider going on with the evaluation, should a different master healer be found to conduct it."

Miandra frowned, not liking the idea much—and the Scout held up a hand.

"I have in mind a particular master healer—in fact, a master healer attached to the Scouts. I am able to vouch for her personally, having several times made use of her skill. I think you will find her a deft touch, with a proper respect for the perceptions of others. I have never known her to cause inadvertent suffering. As a Healer-in-training, I am sure you understand that it is not always possible to spare the patient all pain."

"I do understand that, yes," Miandra said, somewhat stiffly, to Jethri's ear. "The master healer at the hall believes that pain strengthens."

"Ah," said Captain ter'Astin. He put his hands flat on the arms of his chair and made a show of pushing himself to his feet.

"If you like," he said, extending a hand to Miandra, "I will introduce you to the lady I have in mind and the two of you may consult. Should you both agree to go forward, then Healer Hall will be notified of your whereabouts, and you may complete your evaluation while remaining here as a guest of the Scouts. Will that answer, do you think?"

Miandra hesitated and surprised Jethri by throwing him a look. He inclined his head.

"Truly, Miandra, it sounds as though the captain's solution answers all difficulties," he said, and of course right then what happened but that another possible problem jumped to the front of his brain. He looked to the Scout, who inclined his head, black eyes amused.

"Healer Hall may take offense."

"No fear," Captain ter'Astin said. "I believe that my powers of diplomacy are equal to the task of explaining the matter to Healer Hall in such a way that they cannot possibly take offense."

# Day 180
## Standard Year 1118

## Irikwae

IT WAS A good thing Raisy'd insisted on coming along, Grig thought, drinking off the last of his 'mite. A fastship was one thing, but pilots needed to sleep.

They'd done the run from Kinaveral to Irikwae straight through, manning the boards in shifts, six hours on, six hours off; 'mite and crackers at the station. He'd done many a run just that way, back when him and Arin was active on Uncle's business. 'Course, he'd been a couple hundred Standards younger then.

"Hull's cool," Raisy said. Grig sighed, spun the chair and came to his feet, pitching the cup at the wall recycler.

"Let's go, then." Raisy handed him his jacket, and he shrugged into it as he followed her down the cramped hallway. She unsealed the hatch and swung out down the ladder; Grig followed, feeling the solid *thunk* of the hatch resealing as a vibration in the rungs.

On the tarmac, Raisy was surveying things, hands on hips, eyes squinted.

"Nice little port," she said as Grig came up beside her. "You got an approach planned, brother?"

"Figured to check the exhibit halls and Trade Bar—boy's 'prenticed, after all. Guild oughta have a record of him and his location." He shrugged, pulling his jacket straight. "How's your Liaden, Raisy?"

"Better'n yours," she answered, which wasn't strictly true.

"Good." He paused, giving the port his own stare, and pointed. "Exhibition hall."

"Right," said Raisy. "Let's go."

HE'D FINALLY FOUND masks.

Red leather half-masks, with gilding around the eye, nose and mouth holes. Jethri accessed the detail screens and found an image. The red-and-gold reminded him of the books in the Ruby Club's public parlor, and he thought the house master might find them to be exactly what he wanted.

Trouble was, he'd have to buy at least a gross of the things, and they were dear at that level.

Grumbling to himself, he filed the information to his personal account, so he could access it from the computer in his quarters.

He'd also found depilatory, which was a far cheaper proposition at the gross level, but still more than he either wanted or needed. In fact, Meicha's work showed no signs of failing yet, so it could be that he was fixed good and proper and would never sprout another whisker. He made a mental note to ask Miandra if she could figure out what her sister'd done, the next time he saw her. Since she'd opted to have the Scout's master healer do the evaluation and report, that meant three days. They'd promised to share a meal with Captain ter'Astin on the evening of her last day of evaluation, and he was looking forward to it, anxious to hear what the tests showed—

He brought his mind ruthlessly back to the matter at hand.

It might be, he thought, pulling up the secondary detail screen, that the master of the Ruby Club *would* be willing to buy a skid, less two tubes, of depilatory. He had been interested in the masks, though, and now Jethri was interested in the masks, too, as an unexpected, and unexpectedly complex, exercise in trade.

He filed the depilatory info to his personal account, ended his session with the Combine computer and waited for his key to be returned to him.

"Ah, here is the earnest trader, in the midst of his labors," a distinctive voice said behind his shoulder. Jethri inclined his head without turning around.

"Trader sig'Lorta. How may I serve you?" The machine whirred and his key was extruded. He stood, slipping it into an inner pocket.

His mentor looked up at him. "Have you time to join me in a cup of tea, Jethri Gobelyn? I wish to discuss your progress with you."

Not that there had *been* much progress, Jethri thought, grumpily, with him on rest leave for two days. Still, when a man's mentor wanted tea and a chat, it was a good idea to have time for him.

So, he inclined his head again, murmured, "Certainly, sir," and followed the trader to a booth, where a pot and cups were already set out on the table.

"If you would do me the honor of pouring?" Trader sig'Lorta murmured, pulling the multi use screen toward him.

Teapots were tricksy, the handles being just a bit too small to comfortably accept his hand. That aside, nobody could say that Lady Maarilex had neglected the niceties in her efforts to give him polish, no matter how many teapots it cost her.

He poured, with efficiency if not style, setting the first cup by his mentor's hand, taking the second for himself. Carefully, he replaced the pot on its warmer and composed himself to wait, cup simmering gently before him.

"Yes, here we are," murmured Trader sig'Lorta. He looked up from the screen, took his cup in hand and raised it to taste, Jethri doing the same.

Manners taken care of, the trader put his cup aside and folded his hands on the table.

"I hope," he said courteously, "that your injury no longer pains you."

"No, sir. The hall doctor renewed the dressing this morning and is very pleased with the progress of healing."

"That is well, then." He moved a hand, showing Jethri the multi-screen. "I find that you have been at trade on the days granted you to recover from your wound."

*Uh-oh.*

Jethri inclined his head. "Yes, sir."

"Ah." Trader sig'Lorta smiled. "You begin to demonstrate to me that you are, indeed, a trader, Jethri Gobelyn. I am further compelled by the…ambitiousness…of your offering on the tradenet. However, I am puzzled by something with regard to that, and I hope you may help me understand why I find no credit to your account, covering what I must believe to be a rather substantial cost."

"Sir, the merchandise under discussion was bought as a private speculation. Therefore, I used my own resources."

There was a small pause, then Trader sig'Lorta inclined his head.

"I see that I did not explain the process as well as I might have done," he said slowly. "In essence, any business that you conduct on port should be recorded to your file, so that the certification will reflect your actual skill level as nearly as possible. This includes private deals, side trades, and day-brokering. Have you any questions?"

So, he could have used the guild account to buy the speculation cargo, could he? Jethri sighed. Being as he had formed the intention to buy the pod's cargo to help Tan Sim out of defaulting on his contract in a way that wouldn't raise prideful Liaden hackles—maybe not.

"Thank you, sir. I had not understood that all my actions as a trader on port would be taken into balance by the master who will evaluate my file. The matter is now made plain."

"Good." Trader sig'Lorta sipped his tea, appreciatively. Setting the cup down, he reached again for the multi-use screen.

"I see that you have used your Combine key to record your offer—very good. I also see that the pod is scheduled to be opened this afternoon, so you should leave me very soon in order to be in good time. When you are returned this evening, I ask that you write a trade report of this particular transaction, and forward it to me. I will review it and enter it into your file."

Jethri inclined his head. "I will do so, sir." He hesitated. "Is there anything else I might do for you?"

"For today, I believe that will suffice." He raised his cup. "Drink your tea, Jethri Gobelyn, and may your speculation bring profit."

THE EXHIBIT HALL had a decent number of goods on display. Raisy, who'd never had any interest in that side of the business, strode right on past all the tables spread with tantalizing merchandise. Despite being wishful of locating Jethri, Grig's step slowed, his gaze darting from side to side, until Raisy retraced her steps, wrapped strong fingers around his wrist and pulled him along with her.

"I thought you wanted Jethri."

"Well, I do. But where's harm in seeing what's here and whether any of it could be had for a profit?"

She sighed gustily and dropped his arm. "Grigory, you are incorrigible."

"Maybe so—" He stopped, his eye drawn to one of the dozens of ceiling-suspended info screens. This one was only ten paces away, clearly visible over Raisy's left shoulder, and the phrase that had caught his eye—

*Jethri Gobelyn.*

"Raisy, turn around."

She caught the tone, and turned, cautious, checking for threats first, then put her attention on the screen, which had a resonance scan on display.

"Are you seeing what I'm seeing, brother?" Raisy breathed.

The screen changed to detail, all written out in plain Liaden, including the name of the trader-at-offer.

"*Just* like Arin!" Raisy shook her head, threw him a look over her shoulder. "I thought you said the boy didn't get his training."

"He didn't," Grig murmured, memorizing the address where the pod was due to be opened within the hour. "This has gotta be a fluke, Raisy. Boy likes salvage lots. Got a real touch with 'em. He's got a problem there, too, looks like to me."

"I saw it." She jerked her head at a sign bearing the Liaden for *Information*. "Get us a taxi?"

He nodded. "I've got the address."

WELL, THERE HADN'T been any advance bidders, but there was a fair crowd waiting outside Bay Fourteen of the Moon Mountain Refit Shop—at least, according to Tan Sim it was a fair crowd. Jethri counted nine traders as they followed the shop technician to the bay door.

"An additional few moments, traders," the tech said to those gathered, as he unlocked the access hatch. "We treasure the gift of your patience."

Tan Sim ducked through the hatch, Jethri on his heels, the tech on *his* heels. Inside it was dim and a little too warm, as if the noisy air-moving unit wasn't up to the job. The pod took up most of the available floor space; half-a-dozen porta-spots took what was left. Tan Sim went against the wall to the left of the hatch, Jethri, wondering where nine more traders were going to fit in this space, to the right.

The tech kept straight on to the pod, and wrapped both hands around the emergency stick by the hatch.

"The mechanism operated correctly, if slowly, during initial testing, but it is always best to be certain in such cases that functionality has not failed." He hauled on the stick, putting his back into it.

For a heartbeat, nothing happened, then the door began, slowly, and with a long mechanical groan, to lift.

"So." The tech notched the lever down and the door sealed. "In case the internal lights are not currently operational, we have the portable spotlights available." He stood back, wiping his palms down the side of his coveralls, his eyes on the pod.

"If one of you gentlemen would admit the others, I believe we are ready."

Tan Sim waved Jethri toward the pod and pushed the access hatch wide.

"Please, traders! Enter and be welcome!"

Jethri scooped up one of the portables and stepped to the side of the hatch opposite the tech.

The bay was rapidly filling, with traders and the voices of traders—rather more traders, Jethri thought, than the nine he had counted only a few moments before. A pair of taller shadows at the back of the crowd drew his eye—

"Business of the Scouts!" the unmistakable voice of Scout Captain Jan Rek ter'Astin rang out—and there was the captain himself, flanked by two women in the uniform of the Irikwae Port Proctors, striding briskly forward. The attending traders scrunched close to the walls, giving them a clear course to Jethri. He caught a glimpse of Tan Sim, gridlocked by the now silent crowd.

The Scout and his proctors settled into position to the left of Jethri, between the hatch and the attending traders. Jethri inclined his head.

"Have you come to arrest me, sir?" He asked, for the Scout's ears alone, not certain himself if he was joking.

Black eyes met his firmly. "That will depend on a number of things, young Jethri. And the sooner the hatch is opened, the sooner we will both know what duty demands."

Right. Jethri looked to the tech, who stood motionless, his hands around the emergency lever. He took a breath, held it, breathed, slowly, out.

"Technician," he said, loud enough to be heard to the back of the bay, "please open the hatch."

"Trader," the man murmured, and hauled down on the stick.

The hatch hesitated, and rose, moaning all the way to the top. Inside, lights flickered, and failed. Jethri pressed the switch on the porta-spot.

The beam flared, illuminating the inside of the pod with harsh blue light. Shapes leapt into being, sharply outlined.

A busted stasis box, canted on its side, a large shape that reminded Jethri of the weather machine, built a hundred times bigger, another—

"Technician, close the hatch!" Captain ter'Astin ordered. "Proctors, clear the room."

The proctors turned as one and moved toward the crowd, hands making long, sweeping motions. Jethri pressed the switch on the porta-spot, killing the glare.

"Of your goodness," said the proctor on the right, "please leave the room. Business of the Scouts."

"Move along," said the one on the left, "there is nothing here for you to see. Business of the Scouts."

Inexorably, the traders were swept back toward the door. Tan Sim held his ground, creating an eddy in the flow of departing traders. The proctor on the right paused, and moved her hands sharply.

"Please, sir. We are clearing the area. There is no business here for you."

"There is business," Tan Sim said, sounding a bit breathless, but calm. "Yon trader is my partner in this matter—and that is my pod."

"That trader may remain, proctors," Captain ter'Astin said over his shoulder. He inclined his head to the technician. "Sir, you are required elsewhere."

The tech bowed, hastily—"Scout"—and was gone, not quite running, pushing past Tan Sim, who was striding forward. The tech darted between the proctors and vanished out the hatch. The proctors continued their sweep. Jethri bent to put the porta-spot down.

"Jethri!"

He snapped upright and spun, staring down the dim hall to find the proctors confronting two tall people and one of them was—

"Grig!" He spun back to the Scout.

"That man is my kin!"

The Scout's eyebrows rose. "Indeed. So we will be playing with the Liaden deck? You do trade bold, young Jethri."

He raised his voice. "Proctors, those traders may remain, as well. Secure the door."

"Not a Liaden deck," Jethri said. "A human deck. In Terran, he's my shipmate."

The Scout tipped his head to one side. "I believe I begin to understand the scope of Norn's project. So—" He flicked his gaze to Tan Sim.

"Trader pen'Akla, I am Scout Captain Jan Rek ter'Astin."

"Sir," Tan Sim said stiffly. "I will be interested to learn what business Scouts have in interrupting the trading day."

Captain ter'Astin smoothed the air between them with a gentle palm. "Peace. Every matter in its time."

The confusion near the access hatch had sorted itself out and Grig was taking long strides forward, followed by a woman who looked familiar, though Jethri was sure he'd never seen her before.

"You OK, Jeth?" Grig reached out and grabbed his shoulder, squeezing, hard and comforting.

"I'm fine," Jethri said, though it took him a stupidly long time to get the Terran to his mouth. He glanced over Grig's shoulder at the woman. She smiled at him and nodded, agreeable-like. Grig turned, letting go of Jethri's shoulder.

"Don't tell me you're shy, now," he said to her. "Come up here and tell Jethri 'hey'."

She took a couple steps and came even with Grig. "Hey, Jethri," she said, her voice deep and pleasant. "I'm Grig's sister, Raisana." She held out a hand. "Call me Raisy."

He took her hand and squeezed her fingers lightly. "Raisy. I'm glad to meet you," he said, thinking that he'd never heard Grig mention a sister, but for all of that, they sure did—

"That's it," he said, the Terran coming a little *too* quick, now. "Couldn't place why you seemed familiar. You look like Grig, is why."

"Indeed," Scout Captain ter'Astin said, in his mud-based Terran. "It is a remarkable likeness, even for fraternal twins." He paused, head tipped to a side. "You *are* twins, are you not?"

Grig shrugged. "Raisy's older'n me," he said, eyeing the Scout's leathers. "Field Scout, are you?"

Captain ter'Astin bowed, hand over heart.

"Grig," Jethri said, quick, before his cousin thought of another way to provoke sarcasm out of the Scout. "What're you doin' here? Where's Seeli? How's Khat? Uncle Paitor—"

Grig held up a hand, showing palm. "Easy. Easy. Everybody's fine. You'll want to know that Seeli's increasing. She sends her love. Khat sends hers, too. Paitor tells me to tell you stay outta trouble, but I got a feeling he's too late with that one."

"I think he might be," Jethri said, suddenly and grimly recalled to the looming loss of four kais-six tor. He turned to glare at Captain ter'Astin, who raised an eyebrow and made a show of displaying empty palms.

"Tell me you did not know that this pod was filled with Old Technology, Jethri Gobelyn."

"He did not," said Tan Sim, speaking Terran as if it were Liaden, only much slower. He used his chin to point at the pod. "I find pod. I find manifest. Ore. Art metal. Jewels." He paused, bruised face showing grim. "I buy pod. Jeth Ree buys contents. Partners, we are."

"I see," said the Scout. "And neither one of you had the skill to read the image and deduce the presence of Old Technology?"

"Prolly neither one did," Grig said, matter-of-factly. "If the paper said ore, they'd've naturally thought the spot that caught my attention—and Raisy's—was ore. 'Course, I expect us three," he continued to the Scout's speculative eyes, "seen a lot more Old Tech than either of the youngers, there. You gonna get a blanket over that, by the way? 'Cause, if you're not, I'll beg your pardon, but me, my sister, our cousin and our cousin's partner have an urgent need to lift ship."

"As unstable as that?" Captain ter'Astin pulled a comm from his belt and thumbed it on. "ter'Astin. Dispatch a team and a containment field to Moon Mountain Refit Shop. Level three." He thumbed the device off and slipped it away.

"'preciate it," Grig said, giving him a nod. He looked to Jethri. "You seen them distortions in the scan you uploaded—kinda cloudy and diffuse?"

"Yes," Jethri and Tan Sim said in unison.

"Right. That's fractin sign. Non-industrial quantities of timonium being released as the tech degrades. Now, that blob—it does look convincing for ore, and the ghosts of space know I'd've been tempted to read it that way myself, if I was holding a paper that said ore. But what it is—it's one of the bigger pieces going unstable, releasing more timonium—and then more. That's why we gotta get a blanket over it right now. If it goes without being contained, it could leave a sizeable hole in this planet."

"Is that fact or fancy?" asked the Scout.

Grig looked at him. "Well, now, I'd say fact. My sister, there, she'd argue the point. You want to open the hatch, and we'll take a look at what else you got in there?"

"An interesting proposition," said Captain ter'Astin. "I wonder why I should."

"Grig an' me're the closest you're gonna find to experts on the Old Tech," Raisy said, surprisingly. "There's better, mind you, but I don't think Uncle'd be much interested in talking with you—no offense intended.

"Now, me, I'd ask day rate, if we was gonna do the thing right and clear the stuff for you. But a quick looksee—" She shrugged. "I'm curious. Grig's curious. The boys here are curious—and you're curious. Where's the harm?"

"A compelling argument, I allow." The Scout stepped forward, grabbed the emergency stick with one hand and hauled it down.

The hatch rose, screaming in agony. Tan Sim swept forward and came up with Jethri's portable, blue-white beam aimed inside.

"All right." The five of them stepped close, staring into the depths of the pod.

"That big one over against the far wall," Raisy said. "That'll be your unstable. Look at all the busted stasis boxes around it." She shook her head.

"Now, *that* one," Grig said, pointing to a device that looked peculiarly coffin-like. "That one I'd recommend you hold for study. I don't say it ain't treacherous. All Befores are treacherous. But that particular one can heal terrible wounds."

The Scout looked at him. "How do you know that?"

"Well, now, that's a story. Happens our point man had made a lucky guess or he really *could* read some of them pages from 'way back, like he claimed. No matter the how of it, we had the location of a significant cache. Biggest any of us, 'cept Arin an' maybe Uncle, had ever seen. Trouble is, we was about a half-Jump ahead of a couple field Scouts who'd taken it into their heads that this particular world I'm talking about was interdicted an' so we needed to work fast." He shook his head.

"That meant we had to use every pair of hands we could get, whether they was attached to a trained brain or not. Which is how we happened to have the kid doing his own packing. Now, he'd been told over and over not to just turn the Befores on, or ask them to do things, or think about them doing things, or listen to them, if they started to talk in the space between his ears where his brain ought've been. He'd *been* told, but he was a kid, and a slow learner, besides."

"So he picked up a piece of the Old Tech and it killed him," the Scout said, softly.

"Good guess," Raisy said. "But it didn't kill him—though no question he'd've died of the damage. Chewed his left hand to bits, fingertips to elbow. Happened so fast, he didn't have time to scream, did so much damage, he dropped into shock. It was Arin who shoved him in the—we call 'em duplicating units. Don't know what gave him the idea it'd do a bit of good, but as it turned out, it was the best thing he could've done.

"By the time we'd gotten everything else loaded, the machine chimed, lid popped and there was the kid, a little groggy, with two good hands on him and not a drop of blood on his coveralls."

Scout Captain ter'Astin frankly stared. "It regenerated the hand and arm?"

"Good as new," Grig said. "Never given me a day's worth o'trouble. Though here's a funny thing." He held his hands up, palms out toward the Scout. "The fingerprints on the left hand're the same as the fingerprints on the right, just reversed." He flexed his fingers and let both hands drop to his side. "Works fine, though."

"So I see. A most fortunate circumstance."

"Nothing fortunate about it. Arin told us later he'd read that the duplicating machines could do more than what we'd been using them for. He really could read them old pages— you ever seen any? Metal, but soft and flexible, like paper, with the characters etched in, permanent."

"There are one or two specimens at Headquarters," the Scout said. "Though I admit that deciphering them has thus far proven beyond our ability. Arin Gobelyn was an exceptional man."

"Well, he'd been at it a long time," Grig said, with the air of one being fair. "He'd had a key, but I'm thinking that got spaced early, right after Iza come back from identifying the body."

"Or he may have left an abbreviated form of it in the book he had made for his heir."

"What!" Jethri squawked, shaken out of a state of blank amazement. "My journal?"

Scout Captain ter'Astin turned stern black eyes upon him. "Indeed. Your journal. You say you did not know it?"

"There were some odd—" He stopped, seeing the pages in memory; his kid notes and next to them, the various weird squiggles of his father's doodling....

"Not until this minute did I realize, sir," he said, unconsciously dropping into Liaden. "Truly, as I had told you, I had been without the book and other remembrances of my father for many years, having only recently been reunited with them."

"Boy didn't get his training," Grig said softly. "Arin died too soon."

"You didn't train him?" the Scout asked. Grig shook his head.

"If Iza—his mam, you understand—had even thought I was, the boy was forfeit—me, too, more than sure, though Raisy'll tell you that's no loss."

"No such thing," she said, stoutly.

"Ah," said the Scout. "I wonder, this planet where you were a half-Jump ahead of a pair of field Scouts intent upon enforcing the interdiction—would that have been in the Nafrey Sector?"

Grig and Raisy exchanged a glance.

"Stuff's long gone," Grig said.

"True," Raisy answered. She nodded to the Scout. "You got a good mind for detail."

"I thank you. And you, if I may say so, are a great deal older than you look."

"That's because we got hold of some duplicating machines early," Raisy said, "and kept on reproducing the pure stock. We breed, like Grig here gone and done, the very next generation goes back to default."

"That's what was driving Arin to find out how to manufacture good fractins," Grig said. "The machines are going unstable, and he wanted his boy to be able to continue the line."

The Scout inclined his head. "I understand. However, the Old Technology is forbidden."

Jethri cleared his throat. Four pair of eyes turned to him, Tan Sim's looking more bewildered than anything else.

"I'm a—clone?" he asked, very calmly. He used his chin to point at the machine Grig had recommended for study. "I was born from one of those?"

"Almost," said Grig. "I'm sorry to tell you that Arin wasn't entirely straight with Iza, Jeth. I'll give you the details when we're private." He looked at the Scout. "Family business."

The Scout bowed.

"Captain ter'Astin?" A voice inquired. They all turned.

Four Scouts stood in the cramped bay behind them, equipment packs on their backs. The lead Scout saluted. "Containment Unit reporting, sir."

"Good." The Scout waved his hand at the big piece Raisy had identified as unstable. "There is your target. We will remove ourselves until the containment is complete. After...." He considered Grig and Raisy thoughtfully.

"After, I believe I would like to pay the pair of you dayrate, and sit at your feet while you *clear* the Old Technology in this pod."

Raisy shrugged. "All right by me." She sent a look and a grin to Jethri, who couldn't help but grin back. "We're fast, cousin. Couple days from now, the only thing you'll have to worry you is how to profitably place what's left."

# Day 185
# Standard Year 1118

## Irikwae

AFTER THE BEFORES were cleared and cleared out, and the broken stasis boxes sold for scrap, there'd been enough in the contents of the good boxes to return the initial investment, and one kais, three for profit.

"Not a large profit," Trader sig'Lorta commented, appending the information to Jethri's file.

"True," he'd replied. "However, if the coin had stayed in my pocket, I would have realized no profit at all."

His mentor glanced up, gray eyes amused. "The trade is in your bones, Jethri Gobelyn."

In between his assignments for the hall, and their work with the Scout, he spent time with Grig, sometimes with Raisy, though most often not. Family business, family secrets—he was clear he wasn't gettin' it all. Not even close to it all. No need, really.

As Grig said, "You ain't Arin. No need for an Arin now, if there ever was, with the machines going into unstable—but you're worried about the other. And you *ain't* Arin, Jeth, no more'n I'm Raisy. We're each our own self, give or take a shared gene-set. Like identical twins, if you know any.

"I will say Arin'd be proud of the way you're going about setting yourself up, building your credentials and associations. He *would* be proud if he was here for it—just like I'm proud. But—here's another secret for you—he'd've never gone at it like you done. Arin was smart about lots of things, but human hearts wasn't among 'em. I'm thinkin' it'll prove that your way's the better one."

"What was he trying to do with the fractins?" Jethri'd asked. "Remember how we built the patterns, an'—"

"Right." Grig nodded. "Remember what I told you? How all the fractins was dying at once? Duplicating units are powered by fractins, same as your weather maker, and that tutoring stick went bad on you in the exhibit hall. Arin, he had this theory, that if you put fractins together in certain ways—certain patterns—they'd know—and could do— some interesting things. So, he—"

"*WildeToad*," Jethri whispered, and Grig shot him a Look.

"What do you think you know about *Toad*, Jeth?"

"Nothing more than what's on the sheet of printout my father used to shim my nameplate," he said. "*Breaking clay*, it said. *Arming* and *going down*. If the clay was fractins, arranged in a certain pattern..."

"Then you got most of it," Grig interrupted. "Arin'd worked out what he figured to be an auxiliary piloting computer. *Toad's* captain agreed to give it a test run. Looked good, at first, the fractin-brain merged in with ship's comp. What they didn't figure on was ship's comp getting overridden by the fractins. Suddenly *Toad* was out of the control of her crew. Captain's key was worse than useless. The fractin brain, it locked in a set of coordinates nobody'd ever seen, and started the sequence to arm the cannons..."

"They broke the fractins, but they still didn't get the ship back," Jethri said, guessing. "So, they crashed it, rather than risk whatever had their comp getting loose."

Grig sighed. "Near enough." He paused, then said, real quiet:

"It was a bad business. So bad Arin stopped trying to figure out the thinking patterns—for awhile. But he had to go back to it, Jeth. See, he was trying to find the pattern that would produce the fractin-brain that would tell him how to make more fractins."

He leaned forward to put his hand on Jethri's arm.

"You listen to me, Jethri, if you forget everything else I ever told you. Befores, Old Tech, whatever you want to call it—*you can't trust it.* Nobody knows what they'll do—and sometimes it's worth your life to find out." He sat back with a tired grin. "And that was *before* they started to go unstable."

Jethri glanced down at his palm, the burn nothing more now than a broad red scar.

"I'll remember," he promised.

Eventually, they come around to the reason Grig and Raisy were on Irikwae at all.

"He said *what?*" Jethri demanded. "The trader who bought the pod—my partner?"

They nodded.

"That trader," Jethri said, "is the brother chel'Gaibin claims to be *deprived of.* He's pushing a false claim against people who aren't tied by the, the Code." He took a hard breath, and inclined his head. "Thank you," he said, dropping into Liaden for the proper phrasing. "Please be assured that this matter will be brought into proper Balance."

"All right. Now, I gotta ask you, for Seeli: You sure you're OK? 'Cause if you need a ship, Seeli says you got the *Market* to call on—and she'll deal with Iza."

Jethri felt tears rise up and blinked them away. "Tell her—the offer means a lot to me, but I've got a ship, and a crew, and a—course that I'm wanting to see the end of."

Grig smiled, and sent a glance to his sister. "Boy's got it under control, Raisy. We can lift on that news."

And by the next morning, they had.

"WHAT ARE THOSE?" Miandra asked, as he placed the wire frame and the boxes of fractins, true and false, before Scout Captain ter'Astin. They were once again in the common room of the Scout hall, sharing a pre-dinner glass of wine to celebrate Miandra's completion of her evaluation.

"Fractins," Jethri said, and, when she gave him a perfectly blank stare. "Old Technology. Put enough fractins together in the right order and you have—a computer. Only different."

"And dangerous," she added.

"Sometimes," he said, thinking of the healing unit. He met Captain ter'Astin's eyes, and moved his shoulders. "Usually." He reached into one of his inner pockets, his fingers touched the familiar, comforting shape. His lucky fractin. With a sigh, he brought it out and placed it on the table.

"Ah," the Scout said. "I do thank you for these, young Jethri, and appreciate your display of goodwill. I wonder, however, about the journal."

Jethri bowed, slightly. "The journal is not Old Technology, sir. The contents of the journal are of no use to the Scouts and of much sentimental value to me."

"I see." The Scout glanced down at the table and its burden. "I suggest a compromise. You will place the book in my custody. I will cause it to be copied, whereupon the original will be returned to you. I give you my word that all will be accomplished within the space of one day." He looked up, black eyes bright. "Is this acceptable?"

"Sir, it is."

"Spoken like a true son of a High House! Come now, let us put business and duty both behind us and drink to Lady Miandra's very good health!"

The wine being poured, they did that, and Jethri turned to Miandra.

"What was the outcome?" he asked. "Are you dramliza, or Healer?"

She sipped her wine. "Dramliza, though untrained in the extreme. I am offered a teacher upon Liad itself. If Aunt Stafeli agrees, the thing is done."

"Oh." Jethri lowered his glass.

"What's amiss?"

He moved his shoulders. "Truly—it is all that you hoped for—and I share your joy. It is just that—I will miss you."

Miandra stared—and then her laugh pealed.

"I have missed the joke, I fear," he said, a little hurt. She leaned forward to put her hand on his sleeve.

"Jethri—cousin. You are to leave very soon, yourself. Do you recall it? Norn ven'Deelin? *Elthoria*? The wide star trade?"

He blinked, and blushed, and laughed a little himself. "I had forgotten," he admitted. "But I will still miss you."

Miandra had recourse to her wine, eyes dancing.

"Never fear! I will certainly remain long enough to dance at your age-coming ball!"

"When does Norn come to port?" the Scout asked, sipping his own wine.

It took a moment to remember the date. "Day three-three-one."

"Ah," the Scout moved his shoulders. "A pity. I will have gone by then."

"Back to Kailipso, sir?"

"No, thank the gods. I have been given a new assignment, which may prove...interesting." He put his glass next to Jethri's lucky fractin.

"I have reserved our table for the top of the hour. We will stop at the desk to ask that someone from the proper unit come to collect those. Then, if you will accompany me, we may proceed to the restaurant. I believe it is a lovely evening for a stroll."

# Day 189
# Standard Year 1118

## Irikwae

THE ALARM RANG 'way too early. Jethri pitched out of bed and headed for the shower before his eyes were properly open, emerging some few minutes later, eyes open, hair damp. He pulled on trousers, boots and shirt and, still sealing that last garment, walked over to the computer to discover the instructions that would shape his day.

He was to meet Tam Sin for luncheon—a last agreeable meal before aged *Genchi*, now embracing a third pod, lifted. Besides that, there was a certain odd lot he wanted to have a look at, over—

Red letters blinked urgently on his screen, alerting him to a serious scheduling change. He touched a key and the day-sheet snapped into being, the new item limned in red.

Jethri swallowed a curse. He was to meet with the master trader in charge of evaluating his file in the hall master's office in—he threw a glance at the clock—now.

"Blast!"

He snatched his best trading coat off the hook and ran.

OUTSIDE THE HALL master's office, he did take a moment to catch his breath, pull his jacket straight, and run quick, combing fingers through his hair. One more deep breath, and he leaned to the annunciator.

"Jethri Gobelyn," he said, clearly.

The door chimed. He put his hand on the latch and let himself in.

The office had the too-tidy look of a place that had been out of use for a time. The desk top was bare, and slightly dusty; the books lined up, all orderly, in their shelves. Two chairs and a low table made a pleasant grouping by the window. A portable comp and a tray holding two glasses and a bottle of wine bearing the Maarilex Reserve label sat at the center of the table.

But for himself, the room was empty, though the wine and the comp indicated that he could expect the master trader soon.

Taking a deep breath to center himself, Jethri moved to the bookshelves, and brought his attention to the titles.

He had just discovered that Hall Master yos'Arimyst had an interesting half-a-dozen novels shelved among his volumes of Guild rule and trade regs, when the door chimed and opened.

Turning, he began his bow—and checked.

"Master ven'Deelin?"

She raised her eyebrows, black eyes amused. "Such astonishment. Do I not wear the amethyst?"

"Indeed you do, ma'am," he said, bowing the bow of affectionate esteem. "It is only that one's mentor has been at pains to let me know that my file will be evaluated by an impartial master."

"As if there were ever such a thing—or could be." She paused and looked him up and down, her hands tucked into her belt. "You look well, my son. Irikwae suits you, I think."

"I have learned much here, mother."

"Hah." Her eyes gleamed. "So it seems." She moved a hand, inviting him to walk with her to the pleasant grouping of chairs and table. "Come, let us sit and be comfortable. Open and pour for us, if you will, while I consult the notes left by the evaluating master."

He opened and poured, and settled into the chair across from her. She sat for a moment or two longer, perusing her screen, then sat back with a sigh.

"Yes, precisely did he say, when I met him just now in the Trade Bar," she murmured, and reached for her glass, lifting it in a toast, Jethri following.

"To Jethri Gobelyn, junior trader."

He sipped—a small sip, since his stomach suddenly felt like it didn't know how to behave.

"Truly, ma'am?"

"What question is this?" She slipped a card out of her sleeve. "Honor me with your opinion of this."

He received it, fingers tracing the Guild sigil on the obverse. On the front, there was his name, and *junior trader,* right enough, and the silver gleam of the datastrip that held the records of his transactions thus far.

"I find it a handsome card, ma'am."

"Then there is no more to be said—it is yours."

One more long look and then he slipped it away, into the same inner pocket that held his Combine key.

"You do well, my child. I am pleased. We will need to talk, you and I, to discover whether you wish to continue an association with *Elthoria,* now that you are a trader in your own name. First, however, I must bring you news of chel'Gaibin, which I fear and trust will not delight you."

He held up a hand. "If this has to do with Trader chel'Gaibin's attack upon my kinswoman on Banthport, ma'am, I have had that tale already."

"Have you indeed? May one ask?"

"My cousins Grig and Raisy found the incident so alarming that they came to me here on Irikwae, to inform me of my need for vigilance."

"All honor to them." Master ven'Deelin sipped her wine. "I have invoked a Guild inquiry, which will hold chel'Gaibin this next while. That he claims false Balance—that is a matter for the Council, and is not a matter that you must or may take under your own melant'i. Am I understood in this?"

"Ma'am, you are." He inclined his head. "Grig asked me to tell you, ma'am, that you should consider, not what Banth has, but where it is."

She paused with her glass half-way to her lips. "So. You have remarkable kin, young Jethri. I know nothing but admiration for them. I will consider, as he has suggested."

She flicked her fingers toward the comp. "I learn here that you partnered with young pen'Akla in the pod deal. How did you find that?"

"Well enough," Jethri said carefully. He put his glass down and sat forward, elbows on knees. "Ma'am, might you buy his contract?"

"Ixin, buy the contract of one of Rinork? chel'Gaibin will cry Balance in truth!"

*Right.*

"I had not considered," he confessed. "Then I—wonder if you will advise me."

She considered him. "Now, this has the promise of a diversion. Of course I will advise you, my son. Only tell me what troubles you."

"I find myself plumper in purse than I had anticipated," he said, slowly. "And it came to me that a good use of my resources might be to invest in—a trader."

Master ven'Deelin tipped her head to one side. "Invest in a trader, young Jethri?"

"Indeed, ma'am. Suppose I were to buy the contract of a full trader. Not only would I, a junior, have the opportunity to learn from him, my elder in trade, but as owner of his contract, a percentage of each trade he made would be credited to—"

"Your Guild card." She raised her hand. "Enough."

Jethri sat back, watching her as she sipped her wine, eyes closed.

"It only amazes me," she said eventually, "that no one has thought of this before. Truly, young Jethri, you have a gift." She opened her eyes.

"You will now tell me if this notion of yours was serious, or merely brought forward to plague me."

"Ma'am, you know I would never deliberately plague you—"

"Pah!"

"But, I *had* considered buying Trader pen'Akla's contract, so that he might find a ship and a route that will value him, to their mutual profit." He opened his hands, palm up, showing empty.

"I do quite see that such an arrangement would be—questionable, at best. But, if *Elthoria* bought his contract—" He leaned forward again, hands cupped, as if he held a rare treasure.

"Ma'am, allow me to present Tan Sim pen'Akla to you as a young trader of heart, imagination and energy. His melant'i is unimpeachable. He speaks Terran, he honors Guild rule, and—" He swallowed, keeping his eyes on hers. "And if he continues on that route, ma'am, it will break his heart and suck his spirit dry."

Silence. Jethri forced himself to sit back, to pick up his wine glass—

"You make a compelling case," Master ven'Deelin said softly. "I will speak to young pen'Akla."

Seated, he bowed, as deeply as he was able. "Thank you, ma'am."

"Such drama. So, while we are making dispositions of traders and contracts—what is your wish, Junior Trader Gobelyn? Shall you write contract with *Elthoria*, or has another ship caught your eye?"

Another ship? Jethri inclined his head.

"Ma'am, of course I wish to stay with *Elthoria*, and sit at the feet of her master trader. I have—much yet to learn."

"Yes," said Master ven'Deelin, smiling. "And so have I."

# The Authors

Sharon Lee and Steve Miller live in the rolling hills of Central Maine. Born and raised in Baltimore, Maryland, they met several times before taking the hint and formalizing the team in 1979. They removed to Maine with cats, books, and music following the completion of *Carpe Diem*, their third novel.

Their short fiction, written both jointly and singly, has appeared or will appear in numerous anthologies and magazines, including *Such a Pretty Face*, *Stars*, *Murder by Magick*, *Absolute Magnitude*, *3SF*, and several incarnations of *Amazing*.

Meisha Merlin Publishing has or will be publishing ten novels cleverly disguised as seven books in Steve and Sharon's Liaden Universe® *Partners in Necessity*, *Plan B*, *Pilots Choice*, *I Dare*, *Balance of Trade* and two as yet untitled—*The Tomorrow Log*, first of the Gem ser Edreth adventures, and the anthology *Low Port*, edited by Sharon and Steve. Sharon has also seen a mystery novel, *Barnburner*, published by Embiid in electronic and SRM Publisher, Ltd in paper.

*I Dare* and *The Tomorrow Log* have been Amazon.com and Locus magazine bestsellers. *Pilots Choice* (including novels *Local Custom* and *Scout's Progress*) was a finalist for the Pearl Award. *Local Custom* took second place in the 2002 Prism Awards for best futuristic romance, while *Scout's Progress* took first place. *Scout's Progress* has also won the *Romantic Times Bookclub* Reviewer's Choice Award for the best science fiction novel of 2002.

Both Sharon and Steve have seen their non-fiction work and reviews published in a variety of newspapers and magazines. Steve was the founding curator of the University of Maryland's Kuhn Library Science Fiction Research Collection, and former Nebula Award juror. Sharon served the Science

Fiction and Fantasy Writers of America, Inc. for five years, as executive director, vice president and president.

Sharon's interests include music, pine cone collecting, and seashores. Steve also enjoys music, plays chess, and collects cat whiskers. Both spend 'way too much time playing on the internet and have a web site at: www.korval.com.

# The Artist

Donato Giancola balances modern abstract concepts with realism in his paintings to bridge the worlds of fine and illustrative arts. He recognizes the significant cultural role played by visual art, and makes personal efforts to contribute to the expansion and appreciation of the science fiction and fantasy genre that extend beyond the commercial commissions of his clients. Since beginning his professional career in 1993 Donato's list of clients has continued to grow. From the major book publishers in New York to design firms on the West Coast, his commissions include companies such as LucasArts, National Geographic, DC Comics, The Free Masons of Philadelphia, Microsoft, Amazing Stories, Bantam Books, Ballantine Books, HarperCollins Publishers, Penguin, Playboy Magazine, Scholastic, Sony, Tor Books, Warner, Random House, Danbury Mint, Discover Magazine, The Franklin Mint, Milton-Bradley, Hasbro, and Wizards of the Coast.

Donato was born and raised in Colchester, Vermont. He moved to New York City shortly after graduating Summa Cum Laude with a BFA in Painting from Syracuse University in 1992 to begin his stellar art career.

Success as a science fiction illustrator has taken Donato around the world as a guest of honor at numerous events such as Magic: The Gathering tournaments in Santiago, Chile, to the Lucca Comic Book Convention in Italy, the Essen Toy Fair in Germany, and the Lisboa Comic Book Convention in Portugal. Donato is a frequent exhibitor at the Society of Illustrators and shows at many conventions around the states, including World Science Fiction Convention. He was given a Jack Gaughan Award for Best Emerging Artist in 1998, seven Chesley Awards including one for Artistic Acheivement

2002, and has been nominated five times for the Artist Hugo Award. Donato's work can also be seen in Spectrum: The Best of Contemporary Fantastic Art, who's juries have awarded him multiple medals from the recent Silver in Advertising Illustration in 2003 to a 2001 Gold in Editorial Art. He was also included in Infinite Worlds, a compendium of notable science fiction illustrators of the 20th century authored by Vincent DiFate.

In addition to a lucrative freelance career he has also taught at the School of Visual Arts, and in 1999 was an instructor at the Fashion Institute of Technology. He has served as Guest Lecturer at Syracuse University, Pratt Institute, Virginia Commonwealth University, and Pennsylvania School of Art and Design, and was a co-chair of the 1997 Student Scholarship Committee at the Society of Illustrators in New York.

Donato appears at various colleges, institutions, Magic tournaments and science fiction conventions, where he interacts with fans, performs demonstrations in oil paint, and displays original paintings. A comprehensive listing of his work, technique, and in depth biographical information is available on his website at www.donatoart.com.

Donato lives in New York City with his wife and two daughters. Any time away from his studio is spent in the museums, with his family, playing soccer, or attending various cultural events around the city.

On the following pages is a special treat for our readers. Meisha Merlin Publishing, Inc. would like to give special thanks to Donato Giancola for supplying us with some of his preliminary scketches for the cover of this book, *Balance of Trade.* We hope you enjoy them!

—Meisha Merlin Publishing, Inc.